REVENGE of The
Part '

CW01500970

by Mark Cunnington

To David Peach

Tight lines

Mark Cunnington

Trio Publishing

Also by Trio Publishing

The Syndicate
The Syndicate 2nd Edition
The Syndicate (R.I.P.) Part II
Return of The Syndicate Part III
Running The Syndicate Part IV

First published 2006

Published by Trio Publishing
50 Gillsman's Park
St. Leonards on Sea
East Sussex
TN38 0SW

ISBN 0 9537951 4 4

Printed and bound by Chandlers Printers Ltd
Bexhill-on-Sea, East Sussex

INTRODUCTION

The desire to get your own back is a basic and instinctive human emotion. As young children it may be a simple matter of retribution, but as adults we are confined and obstructed by the rules of society, its laws and its authorities. What is required is a vehicle of some kind to facilitate a burning revenge, preferably one that is clandestine, ordered, planned and focused. If this isn't forthcoming, there's always hope!

Our story starts from where we left it.

Chapter 1

I looked out of the opening of my bivvy and saw the sun rising above the horizon. To the foreground of the life-creating and sustaining, shining orb was the body of water known as Hamworthy Fisheries. A light breeze agitated its surface. Below this surface its main inhabitants, the large head of very large carp, were quietly going about their business of not picking up my baits. The bastards. Now the orb's rays were becoming stronger, due to the Earth's tilted axis, that business would soon turn to focus on the natural cycle of reproduction – of spawning and the subsequent making of new life. Once the carp's internal biological sensors were satisfied the water was warm enough, the wind and light were right, the spawning areas were suitable then the male fish would create their milt and the female fish their eggs. Only after all these criteria were in place would it begin. It was early May. Another fortnight, I reckoned, and the carp equivalent of carnal connectivity could commence.

Sex. It had a lot to answer for and I'm not necessarily talking of the piscine water-based variety.

The arrival of late spring, when all this underwater breeding was due to commence, was, personally speaking, a welcome one. Now whether the carp thought as much, or if such an anthropomorphic attribute could even be rationally applied to a fish, however large and allegedly cunning, I wasn't sure. But the late spring and associated fishing potential – albeit yet to be realised, note the mute Delkims and painfully static indicators – was a time of year to be greeted warmly, in both a literal and figurative sense. The autumn after my seventeen bullet, Glock-inspired gunning down of Rambo's would-be assassin after notification via the last leg of my psychic hat trick, (to remind you; 1) Mind-meld mirror, 2) Contact with the ghost, 3) Premonition of Rambo's assassination scenario) had been awesomely awful – but the winter had been way worse. I was glad to see the back of the pair of them. Not in respect that my dire situation had improved, it hadn't, but it meant with the imminent arrival of summer the strategy *might* soon commence. I still wasn't exactly sure what this strategy would comprise but it did give me a scintilla of comfort to know whatever it might turn out to be, it could be starting in the not too distant future. They say the desperate cling to matchsticks to keep them afloat.

"I'll go find a shovel," Rambo had said soon after I had expended the Glock's full payload into the asylum seeker who wasn't an asylum seeker, but who *was* an assassin trying to kill Rambo in revenge for Rambo killing one of his kin. "If we get our fingers out, I can have my baits back in the water by next feeding time. Then," he had said, his lips thinning, "we can discuss our *strategy*."

1

Rambo had said this after I had told him of Hollywood's successful run of revenge on myself. To reiterate, him shagging my Sophie to get back at me for being given Hamworthy Fisheries, lock, stock and barrel in Michael's will. Michael had left me the fishery because I, along with Rambo, had uncovered Michael's murder of the woman whose spirit had manifested itself as the ghost *and* Hollywood, Rocky and Darren's fish-stealing cartel. In my humble opinion Hollywood had fucked up big time and really had no grounds for complaint at having been expelled from the syndicate by the balding executor of Michael's will, Justin Furlington. After all, Hollywood had been Michael's right-hand man but for some reason had wickedly betrayed him by stealing fish from the pit and presumably selling them back to the fish farmer who had originally supplied them to Michael at the time of stocking. Only they were a lot bigger now, and, rather importantly, a *lot* more valuable. The reasons for him being expelled, along with his two other cronies, was of his making and his alone, but, and this was the big but, from his narrow-minded, hopelessly blinkered viewpoint it was *our* fault! I suppose he based this on the assumption that if it hadn't been for the pair of us he would have got away with it. Any sane person would have seen the big hole in his logic but raving mad Hollywood certainly hadn't and had acted accordingly.

So, Hollywood *didn't* get away with it and the whole episode festered in his brain and he devised his Machiavellian plan to shaft Sophie (in the sexual context) and shaft me (in the black-hearted deed context) along with it. When Hollywood unfurled his plan, as Sod's Law would have it, our relationship had deteriorated due to my involvement in the inaugural Hamworthy charity fish-in and my barely disguised infatuation with The Witches of Eastwick, Melina, Melissa and Melloney. As well as this she had also had the seeds of deceit sewn in her mind by my stupid denial of having ever met Rebecca at Pup's wedding reception. When Rambo had unwittingly gainsaid my denial via the sorority grapevine of Melina and Melloney, and in doing so fuelled her notions of deceit, things had degenerated further. Not unsurprisingly she had then smelt the hint of the rat called infidelity and her normal high principles had wavered. This had created a window of opportunity for the handsome Hollywood and he had successfully seduced a morally weakened Sophie like I knew he had seduced many, many other women. He hadn't seduced her out of desire in the usual sense of the word – although Sophie is an attractive woman – he had seduced her out of the desire to be wicked, hateful and hurtful. To *me* that is! Sophie had merely been a means to an end. I shudder to think how enjoyable an end she had turned out to be.

Hollywood's run of revenge had been designed to fuck up my life, to paraphrase his doorstep revelation quote, and sitting in my bivvy in early spring three-quarters of a year or so after it, I had to admit he had succeeded. Although Rambo and myself had moved ever closer (in more ways than one, but more of that later) in terms of our unique bond created originally when he had asked me to come in on bait with him all those years ago in the old SS syndicate, my bond with Sophie had unravelled like a snagged, home-knitted jumper.

Although I was twice the adulterer, once with Rebecca and once with Melina – who at the time, just to add a little more intrigue, had been Rambo's girlfriend – I hadn't been able to get my head around Sophie's one-off with Hollywood. (I'll pause now for catcalls of 'hypocrite' and 'male chauvinist pig'.) Every time I looked at her I didn't see the woman I had loved for many years. I didn't see the woman who had stuck by me during my TWTT madness and subsequent detention at Her Majesty's pleasure. I didn't see the woman whose mother had won the lottery and given us a shed load of cash. I didn't see the woman who had carried and gave birth to my only daughter. I didn't see the woman who had been my rock through all my strange and unbelievable escapades and I didn't see the woman who had been the one non-variable amongst all my weird, fluctuating escapades. No. What I saw, or at least saw in my mind's eye, was the woman who had sucked Hollywood's cock – after being shagged by it – and who had swallowed his payload. I mean, what was the more deadly? The Glock's or Hollywood's? What would you rather take in the head, seventeen 9mm bullets or an undisclosed volume of Hollywood's spunk? Bitterly I knew Sophie had taken the latter.

I was still alive, unlike the asylum seeker who had taken the 9mm bullets, but inside I felt dead. You see, when I had asked her if it was true, if in fact she really had done what Hollywood had said, she had never denied it. When I had asked why she had never done it to me she had never been able to give me an answer. Her eyes had simply dropped away from mine and silence had gripped the pair of us. Oh, twist the knife! Oh, rub salt in the gaping wound! I had speculated in my wilder moments of not being able to sleep as to whether or not Hollywood had thought to himself, 'Now what sexual act can I get her to perform on me that will *really* piss him off when I tell him?'

Although I had told Sophie I would forgive her before I had rushed off to save Rambo from certain death, in the ensuing months I found I couldn't. The pair of us had ground to a sickening halt over this time, both emotionally and physically. She had been unable to come to terms with what she had done, especially now the true motivation for Hollywood's action had come to light, and equally I had been unable to come to terms with what she had done. Then, in a moment of weakness – or was it madness, or perhaps guilt inspired lunacy, or double perhaps guilt inspired decency – I had told her the truth about Rebecca and then Melina. I had hoped our collective weaknesses would somehow help us through and it would help re-bond us. I had been hopelessly wrong. From that very moment, in a hideously gruesome symmetrical catastrophe, she had then been unable to come to terms with what I had done and when I had seen how my actions had hurt her, as if they had been newly revealed by a glowing light emanating from her hurt, I had then been unable to come to terms with what I had done. In short we were both well and truly fucked up a treat.

In retrospect – I tried to convince myself – at least I had told the truth and had wiped the slate clean, only the problem was the slate *wasn't* clean. In fact it was about as clean as a faeces-encrusted cell – one holding an Al Qaeda suicide bomber elephant, who, since its bomb had failed to detonate and consequent incarceration, had developed irritable bowel syndrome and a protest fixation. Hollywood's revenge had worked better than he could ever have dared hoped.

Of course, before all this had happened, within minutes of Rambo mentioning our *strategy*, there was the rather more immediate and inconvenient matter of a body to get shot of because I had shot it. You see, running nicely alongside all the other crap I have going on in my private life, there is the small detail of me being a murderer. The small detail of gunning down Rambo's adversary and whether or not I was going to get away with it. To get away with it not only in terms of the authorities never finding out, but also in terms of associates of the dead assassin never finding out. What if they did? Would they send out another assassin to assassinate the bloke who had assassinated the original assassin? I would have to assassinate *him* to survive! Then they might send out an assassin to assassinate the bloke who had assassinated the second assassin who had been sent to assassinate the bloke who had also assassinated the first assassin… and so on ad infinitum. More assassins than a Mainline warehouse in fact. All in all it was the sort of thing that could hang over you like a dark cloud, a very dark cloud, a cloud so dark it made your average hearse appear a pleasant shade of pastel. Even my imagery is morbid.

The dark cloud of whether either of the aforementioned parties would get wind of what had happened had been realised within minutes after the shooting. I had also wondered if I would ever be able to shut my eyes without seeing the monstrous exit wound in the back of the assassin's head. My dreadful deed, however needy – Rambo had to be saved – and its vile consequences were undoubtedly the stuff of video-in-the-head-replay-horror. Although obviously this was before Sophie's act of cum-gobbling fellatio with Hollywood had had time to redress the horror-in-my-head top billing and I had started seeing *that* going on every time I had shut my eyes!

Back to the shot dead body that needed getting shot of. Oddly enough, in those mad few moments after my gunplay, we had been in exactly the same predicament Michael had been in many years earlier. Like him, we too had a freshly murdered corpse lying on Hamworthy's banks to dispose of, but unlike Michael the choice of the island was a complete non-starter. We couldn't bury our body on the island like he had – I'm afraid it gets even weirder from now on – because we had found Michael's victim's remains there one night during our first season in the syndicate. Unfortunately some members had been alerted to our island escapade that night and to even think of repeating Michael's burial plans would have been madness. We couldn't take a chance on a curious member deciding to take a look for himself and discovering a hidden grave. Of course, once I had been left the syndicate one of my first jobs had been to dispose of *those* bones – not the ones of my own making but of Michael's – for the very same reason. Subsequently another trip to the island – when absolutely *no one* was around – to exhume the skeleton and get rid of it had taken place earlier. And now history was repeating itself. I surmised the only plausible explanation for the dastardly duplication was the desire of unfathomable forces to rot my brain even further – if that was possible and to be honest I doubted it. Rambo, though, had been rather pragmatic, matter of fact and unfazed by the strange ironic linking of deeds across the mists of time.

"We'll burn the fucker, then bury him," he had said, once I had finished throwing up due to the shock of committing murder. "On second thoughts *you* go find a shovel, a bow saw, a hammer and all the petrol we use for the mowers out of the lean-to. I'll get things ready here."

I had been thankful to walk away from the scene. My mind had been seriously jarred by what had happened in the past hour. It had been more jarred than a Robinson's jam factory. In fact it had felt as if someone had wielded the moon on the end of a gigantic golf club shaft and had played a three hundred yard drive with my head as the ball. As I had trudged back towards the clubhouse via the grass track running around the perimeter of the pit, I had realised my world and my head had been shattered. Forget winning the charity fish-in and edging out Horst and Helmut, the M & Ms (mullet and moustaches), the faithful, heterosexual lederhosen-clad lads. Forget catching an English sixty to do it. Forget the lust-filled supercharged bivvy-bang, doggy style with Melina. Forget Rambo not getting upset about it. Forget my psychic hat-trick and the saving of his life. Forget the short-lived feel-good factor of handing in the winning cheque worth ten grand to the local hospice. Forget them all. I had known then, as I had walked back for a shovel, a bow saw, a hammer and all the petrol we used for the mowers out of the lean-to, what lay ahead for me. Torment. Agonising torment… and a large dollop of purgatory. This was what lay ahead for me. Endless re-runs of a series of massive lifestyle threatening events and visions of snot, gore and spunk. And a relationship washed up on the rocks. And a dark cloud of murderous worry. Oh, and one more thing, what I was going to do about them all.

Sitting in my bivvy, nine or so months later, it gives me no satisfaction to report I had been completely right. But at least, now this time of the year had come, I was hoping to start doing something about some of the issues very soon. I didn't know exactly what as yet, didn't even have a vague notion, but I did know I was going to start it soon. Possibly. Any port in a storm, eh?

When I had returned with the bow saw, hammer, shovel and all the petrol, this time having driven back in my van, the body had gone. Rambo had moved it deep into the woods and I had followed Rambo, who had been waiting for me by the edge of the track, to the spot where he had moved it. Once there, Rambo had feverishly set to work by cutting down a mass of branches with the effortless pace and power only he seemed capable of and with the sawn timber had constructed a pyre. Once he had been happy there was sufficient wood to create enough heat he had unceremoniously dumped the body of the assassin (failed) on top of it. Rambo had then poured all six gallons (keeping it real Imperial) on the body and, after warning me to stand well back, had lit it.

5

Wooomph! It had gone as the petrol vapour ignited and we had both had to step a few more paces backwards because of the intense heat. The stench had been sickening.

"Do you fancy some toasted sarnies? I've got a few left in my bivvy," Rambo had flippantly asked.

I had declined. Mesmerised by the orange flames I had stared at the body as first the clothing, then the flesh and finally the internal organs had gradually burned away. After some time, I had no idea how long, I had been drifting in a world of my own, the flames had died down until eventually only glowing embers had remained. And a set of bones.

"Great!" I had said. "Just what we want! Another fucking set of bones from another fucking murder victim!"

"Easy, boy!" Rambo had said with a 'stop' hand signal. After a pause he had cocked his head towards me. "Aren't you going to ask me what the hammer is for?"

"Go on, then," I had said, "what's the hammer for?"

Rambo had held up an index finger. "Watch."

Rambo had cut off another small branch, cleaned off any shoots to make it into a stick and with it had skewered the skull through one of its eye sockets. Gingerly he had lifted it off the rest of the skeleton and had touch-tested the skull with his fingertips.

"Shit that's hot!" he had said and had let the skull slip off the stick and onto the ground.

Taking the hammer, with the sole of his right foot forcing the skull into the ground to keep it steady, Rambo had proceeded to smash out all the teeth.

"Do a lot of dental work, do you?" I had asked. "Fillings? Crowns? That sort of thing?"

Rambo had shaken his head. "Extractions. I only do extractions. Right! That's the lot! Now," he had continued, cupping all the teeth in his hands and juggling them gently because they were still hot, "no one is going to identify him by his dental records!"

I had been able to see his impeccable reasoning.

"Right, boy," he had continued. "Not unless you want to make this lot into a necklace, and believe me you don't, take them up to the pit, get my catapult out of my rucksack and fire them as far and as wide and as handsome as you can."

I had fired a lot of things into water over the years as a carp angler – boilies, hemp, peanuts, tigers, black-eyed beans, chick peas, sweetcorn, groundbait, pellets, maggots, pepperami even prawns... but never teeth. Especially charred ones, charred ones thrashed out of a skull with a claw hammer. At least it had made a change from it being a *ballpane* hammer.

Dutifully I had done what I had been instructed to do. Thwack! A front tooth. Thwack! A molar. Thwack! An incisor. Thwack! Another molar. I had walked around the pit distributing charred teeth from various swims with Rambo's trusty catty, each time giving it the big one and going for maximum distance. For the record the molars went the best, which I suppose you would guess easily enough and surprisingly I had managed to skim a front tooth for a couple of jumps. Not a lot of people can claim that as a life experience.

When I had returned to where the pyre had been Rambo had been digging like a good'un. I had instantly been reminded of the two gravediggers I had imagined at Rambo's fake burial, but there had been nothing bogus going on this time. Oh no! It had been far too real, far, far too real.

A fish crashed out near to my middle rod's spot and I was dragged from my reminiscing of gross memories for a few sweet seconds. It was about as much as could be hoped for; relief was inevitably brief and short lived.

Anyway, Rambo had dug for victory – the victory of concealment for evermore – in various locations and had spread the bones as far and wide as I had spread the teeth, but in my opinion, not as handsome. Then he had dug a hole for the embers and disposed of them. By the time he had finished and had disguised the ground at all locations by some cunning landscaping he had pronounced himself happy.

"There! That should do the trick. If by chance anyone ever does try to find him and did manage to track him down to this fishery, unlikely enough in itself, I don't think they'd ever find a single remain. Positive identification is now an impossibility because there's no DNA and he's a toothless wonder! Boy, you're safe! You can relax now!"

Rambo had picked up the containers of fire creation, the cutters of pyre material, the tooth extractor and the implement of earth-based bone-concealment. "Right, let's go."

"That it, then?" I had asked.

Rambo had looked around and nodded. "Yep! I think so. Come on, I want to get my baits back in the water!"

Rambo had walked off in the direction of the pit but I had remained rooted. When he had realised I wasn't following he had stopped and called to me. "Come on, boy."

It had sounded encouraging, like he was talking to a dog. When I hadn't responded he had walked back, put an arm around me and squeezed me. My shoulders had compressed by three or so inches.

"Come on, boy. You've *got* to walk away from it. Tuck the whole episode in the nasty, dirty part of your mind, shut its door and forget about it. The aftermath of a first kill is always a notoriously difficult time, but you've got to get your head around it. Come to terms with it, compartmentalise it from the rest of your life. That's what I was taught in the army, then you'll be ready to kill again if needs be."

"I'm hardly looking to make a career of it."

"Not even for Hollywood?" Rambo had asked grimly.

My whole body had drooped. "God knows. And he won't tell me... You know I'm fucked don't you, Rambo? You know what I'm like for mulling over things, for endlessly chasing tails in my brain. What's it going to be like from now on? I had the psychic premonition that led to me killing this bloke *plus* I've got Hollywood and Sophie to deal with." I had sagged even further. "Do you know the bit that really kills me? The worst bit, the bit I haven't told you about yet?"

Rambo had recognised the desperation in my voice, had shaken his head and had listened grimly as I had told him of the act Sophie had performed on Hollywood. It had been the one bit of the story I hadn't been able to tell him originally. He had said nothing but had taken me back to his bivvy and made me a cuppa. It was then, only hours after I had first squeezed the Glock's trigger when we had discussed our *strategy* and had made our first tentative plans. These plans, well plan, singular, had consisted of one thing and one thing only and the thing had been, and still was, to wait. The plan was to bide our time, much like Hollywood had bided his and allow the dust to settle. Allow the dust to settle on my murder, allow the dust to settle on my relationship with Sophie and to let the dust settle on Hollywood's run of revenge. Then, hopefully, as time elapsed, a clearer avenue of action on all these fronts should emerge. *Should* emerge. As I was all too aware, there are few certainties in life.

Rambo had been philosophical and clear in his thinking as we had sipped his excellent tea and had pointed out that perhaps during the waiting, dependent on how events panned out with Sophie, with any new assassins (God forbid), police investigations (ditto), how I felt on a personal level and so on, I might develop thoughts on *my* revenge. Should I decide to exact any revenge, that is. Rambo had reiterated the choice was mine and mine alone, but whatever I decided he had made it absolutely clear he would help in every way possible. In our minds we had concluded late spring of the following year as a date for possible implementation, should I wish to implement anything. Well, three-quarters of a year had passed and during the time I had developed precisely bugger all regards thoughts of my revenge and what form it might take. However, having said that, there had been a major development.

The major development, and it was a big one, was of deciding – around January actually – I definitely wanted to implement a plan against the odious Hollywood. A cunning, spiteful plan of revenge, brimming with bile and rancour, a plan of massive reprisal and retribution, the more heinous and hateful so much the better! I had stood and took it like a big lemon during his doorstep revelation and now I knew I wanted my own back. The big trouble was I didn't have a clue how or in what way I was going to do it. Still, considering the mess I was in, I was proud of at least getting one decision straight in my head.

To go back a little and as if I hadn't had enough on my plate, what with coping with Hollywood's revenge, my imploding relationship and my dark murderous cloud there had been the world's first pornographic carp fishing video to oversee only days after I had committed Hamworthy's second killing. *Join Hamworthy Fisheries, the finest carp fishing syndicate in Britain. Let the aesthetic beauty of this mature gravel pit both beguile and bewitch you as you fish cocooned in a panorama of unspoilt Kentish countryside. Let its stillness and isolation whisk you away from the stress of modern living as you sit in utter tranquillity angling for English carp to over sixty pounds... unless some poor fucker is having seventeen 9mm bullets pumped into him by the current owner.* To be honest it was something I could have well done without and for once, recently anyway, fate conspired to save me from the ordeal.

Japp had phoned me the day before he was due to come over to impart the tragic news of his leading man, Frans Henk van Herk, being too ill to perform. Japp hadn't expanded on this enigmatic titbit and so I had put it down to some virulent form of galloping knob rot. If it wasn't disease based the chances were it still had to be a major glitch in the same area. Perhaps, I speculated to myself, it was a patent penile problem, a dick disaster, a cock catastrophe coupled with a touch of todger trouble undoubtedly announcing itself in unfocused, flagrant, frustratingly flabbergasting flaccidity. Japp had asked if perhaps he could make alternative arrangements when Frans was better. I had agreed and had asked why he couldn't get hold of another leading man to fill in for Frans.

Japp had been dismissive. "Matthew," he had said in his excellent but accented English, "male leads do not grow on trees even if they are hung like trunks!" It had probably been a good Dutch joke that hadn't survived the translation. "Besides," Japp had added, plunging the pair of us deep into double entendre territory, "he knows how to use his rod well and for this reason we cannot replace him."

I had managed a laugh despite my depression but the silence down the phone had hinted at my misplaced humour.

"No, you don't understand, Matthew. Frans is a fine carp angler, without him we have no one to give a pornographic carp fishing video true authenticity."

"Oh, I see," I had added somewhat sheepishly. "Well, you just give me a ring when he's firing on all cylinders. You're welcome to Hamworthy at any time."

Japp's reply had been swift. "Frans has only one cylinder, but the cubic capacity and the stroke of it are very impressive!"

It had been my turn to let silence drift down the phone. "It was a joke, Matthew," Japp had explained, "you can laugh now if you like."

So with the minor respite of not having to play the gracious host to Japp and his porn stars I had been able to concentrate fully on the bombsite constituting my life. Thank heaven for small mercies. You know, really, really, *really* tiny ones.

In the following weeks Sophie and I had muddled through our personal trauma in a stunned daze. For the millionth time my head had asked how *could* she have done what she had done with that bastard? And *never* done it with me! And then I had told her about Rebecca and Melina. Immediately her demeanour had changed from a person wallowing in self-loathing to one of great indignation. Now it had been her turn to ask why I had acted like I had. Why *I* had wanted to have sex with Rebecca when I had supposedly loved her *and* after all she had put up with concerning the TWTT and my gulag holiday. She had found it galling I had gone away to France to have sex with Rebecca on the proceeds of *her* mother's lottery winnings. She had a point. She had also said she had had a feeling I had played away from home when

Melloney had revealed my pitiful lie concerning Rebecca and this had sub-consciously influenced her decision to fall for Hollywood's charms. In the space of seconds her self-defence mechanism had given her an excuse and, unfortunately, a bloody good one. I had tried to point out, rather pathetically I guess, that she hadn't actually known for *certain* about my affair with Rebecca and – still digging while I was in a crater – Melina, until *after* she had performed with Hollywood. Her disdain had been total and it had been obvious I was on a cliff edge being ravaged by 60x fast forward erosion and had totally missed the point. The point being I was a philandering bastard and why the hell, now she had come to think of it, was I still in her sight. That day I had left the house crestfallen, no mean feat considering the point at which I had started.

When I had returned home in the evening, to find all my clothes on the front doorstep in three large suitcases, I had realised how desperate things were. I hadn't argued with my eviction because to be honest I had wanted out as well. My feelings towards Sophie had been ambivalent; I had been astride the line dividing love and hate. I still loved her and yet hated her. And hated myself. And Hollywood. I had kissed Amy goodbye, tears streaming down my face, had told my only daughter I would be back to see her soon and had thrown all my fishing gear and the cases into the van and had driven to Hamworthy. When I had got there I had walked up to the stock pond and had wondered if – if I filled my pockets full of 4oz inline leads and jumped in – I could successfully drown myself. Then I had remembered I only used 3oz leads and didn't have any fours and gave it up as a bad job. I had then pondered on asking Rambo to shoot me with one of the Glocks. We could have re-enacted anti-terrorist squad officer meets Brazilian electrician in London tube station by way of ex-army, ex-mercenary, ex-gunrunner meets ex-electrician on Kentish gravel pit. The similarities were there but I had dropped the idea. Rambo would never shoot me, not now, not now he owed me for saving his life. If he hadn't shot me for screwing his girlfriend before I had saved his life, he wasn't going to do it now.

That night I had stayed in the clubhouse, I won't say slept in the clubhouse for fear of a conviction under the Trade Descriptions Act. How my head had whirled. How my video replay of recent events had played and rewound in my brain. First one tape; the saving of Rambo, then another; Hollywood and Sophie's sexual dalliance always with him having an enormous smile on his face at his moment of orgasmic delight, then another: Mine and Melina's bivvy-bang, then another; Police investigation into my murder, then another; Me getting assassinated by an assassin, then another; Mine and Rambo's *strategy* (a bit short and boring), then another: Mine and Sophie's relationship with Amy always crying in the background. Play and rewind. Change tape. Play and rewind. Change tape. Play and rewind. Change tape. Play and rewind. Change tape... you get the general idea. In the morning Rambo had turned up and I had told him of my homeless state and in an instant, after commenting on my shit-like appearance, he had offered me a bed at his place.

"Do you flush the toilet after a dump?" he had asked. I had nodded. "Good. I'm sure we'll get along just fine. Consider it a temporary placing until you sort your life out."

Nine months later I was still living with him and still flushing the toilet after a dump. Maybe there was a connection there somewhere, or maybe it was something deeper.

My middle rod suddenly bleeped. A liner? A fish feeding on my scant offering of carefully applied free bait? I thanked the Delkim for distracting my mind for a few precious moments and with the acknowledgement the distraction was gone.

Living with Rambo hadn't been too bad. About once a month he had said, "Want to do anything about Hollywood, yet?" I had said no and he had nodded and I had gone back to churning things over in my mind. Then in the New Year, after he had given me a set of Nash Nitelites for Christmas he had asked again and I had said yes. Then he had asked *what* I wanted to do and I had told him I didn't know.

"I think I'm going to stick with the dynamic ideal something will turn up," I had explained. "You know, I'll sort of follow my nose, let things drift along and somehow it'll all gel together and things'll work out into a plan of breath-taking evil."

Rambo had shrugged. "With you, boy, anything can happen and most likely it will. It's a pity you can't control your psychic powers a bit better. Has it ever occurred to you how weird it is that you managed to see my certain death and yet couldn't see Hollywood's nasty little plot?"

I had given him a jerk back of my head and a snort. "Has it *ever* occurred to me? You *are* taking the piss? What else do you think I'm doing at the moment? Apart from eating a bit, sleeping even less and occasionally visiting my daughter?"

"Going fishing?" he had offered.

I had fished a lot it had to be said. Fishing had been my one outlet, my one thing I had 'done' in a physical sense. In retrospect it had probably saved me from going round the twist and back again, although secretly I doubted as if I was as sane as I had been in the past. (And you have to go back to *before* the SS days and the TWTT for that statement to work! And that was yonks ago! Frightening! Sometimes I'm amazed I'm not institutionalised.) All through the long dark nights of winter I had sat in my blacked-out bivvy, in the cold, all alone, with many a blank session my only reward. It seemed apt. Even if I had known Rambo had been fishing somewhere else on the pit, or another syndicate member, it had made little difference. The feeling of total isolation from the world, of all else being cut off from me, in both a fishing and a lifestyle sense was complete – and scary. Ironically this is one of the attractions of session carping, but the difference for me was it never ended with my packing up. As I had fished, my mind had run its course and had decided all my problems appeared to be unapproachable at the current time. So I had left them, left them to drift and I had bided my time, waiting, waiting more in hope than expectation for something to turn up.

My middle rod violently exploded into unexpected life with an eardrum perforating one-noter. I scrambled out through my bivvy door and hit the take, my first one in thirty-eight sessions. Hamworthy *wasn't* a winter water. I felt the unfamiliar and yet familiar heave of a bent rod.

"You in, boy?"

I looked over my shoulder in surprise at the person who had spoken. As usual it was British Army camo-clad. "Hello, mate. I didn't know you were here."

"Just arrived. I heard your Delkim as I was walking round to see you and legged it the rest of the way."

The carp started to kite around to my left. "Couldn't dip my left-hand rod could you?" I asked.

Rambo obliged, flicking his eyes up at me as he dealt with the rod. "You'll never guess what, Japp's just phoned. He couldn't get through to your mobile, he said you had it turned off."

"Nah, the battery is dead. I couldn't be bothered to charge it," I explained giving the kiting carp some major side-strain. "What did he want?" I said with interest

"Apparently Frans has recovered from whatever it was that was bugging him and he wants to come and shoot the video next week."

"Next week! Blimey! That's short notice." I managed to halt the carp's run and gained some line. "Still, whatever, it's no problem, I'll give him ring after I've landed this beastie."

"Make sure you do land it! You've earned this fish. Jesus, you've waited long enough for it!"

"That's true."

"Funnily enough I also saw those two girlfriends of Hollywood's this morning," Rambo added casually as he watched my fish-playing expertise from close quarters.

My ears pricked up. "What the two stunning looking, lap dancing, ex-international gymnasts, who were also bisexual nymphomaniacs?"

"That's the ones."

"I wonder if they're still involved with the bastard?" I asked.

"Dunno," admitted Rambo and we lapsed into silence.

Although I never said anything to Rambo I secretly wondered if my waiting for something else, as opposed to a run from a carp, was over as well. Rambo's two nuggets of new info had caused a little cog to whirl inside my head, which in turn made a widget go 'snick' and fit snugly into its housing. I had an odd feeling, a very odd feeling, one I hadn't had for some considerable time, which it intimated the start of my rather haphazard, make-it-up-as-you-go-along game plan might just have begun.

Chapter 2

The thirty-seven pound common swam away strongly in the clear water. I watched it intently until it dropped out of sight. I turned away from the water and looked back at Rambo who was putting my camera back into its case. Being a bit of a Luddite the camera wasn't digital but an SLR with a thirty-six shot slide film in it.

"How many shots have I got left?"

Rambo rolled his eyes, took the Eos back out of its case and glanced at the external LCD panel. "Seventeen!" he answered gleefully. "My, my! The same as a fully loaded Glock!"

I eyed Rambo's mischievous grin and gave it a weary curl of my top lip. "*Thanks* for reminding me. I had *actually* managed to forget for a few minutes while I was playing and landing the common."

"Sorry, boy," said Rambo, although it was highly unlikely he was. "Some people join the Foreign Legion to forget, so the saying goes, whereas you, you catch carp to forget."

"Precisely the reason why I *haven't* been forgetting!" I said in a self-deprecating manner. It would have been my thirty-ninth blank on the trot if not for the thirty. "I don't necessarily have to *catch* them," I added nonchalantly. "Earlier on I had a line bite and forgot for at least three seconds."

Rambo's mouth twisted in recognition of my crud situation. "Hamworthy's not a winter water, we both know that. Disregarding the fishing aspect, the more important thing is the need for you to be able to make closure, boy. *That's* what you need rather than the odd lapse in your constant retrospection… or an upper thirty common come to that. I know we're going over old ground here but you *do* need something to enable you to draw a line under the whole sorry mess and to let you move on. You need it to let you finally deal with all your worries sufficiently so you don't have to keep going over the past. You *badly* need to get back to normal, boy. I mean, look at you."

I glanced down my nose at my slimy sweatshirt, slimy tracksuit bottoms and scruffy trainers. If I had to wager, although the price would be evens at best, the trainers would have got backing in the significantly stinking stakes – provided the pants weren't running.

I rubbed a chin covered in the advanced stages of stubble turning into a beard. "I *am* fishing," I protested.

"Some might say you're camping with rods out…"

"Have you been reading those magazines again?" I interrupted.

Rambo was undeterred. "But ignoring that technicality and ignoring your clothing, undoubtedly hideous as it is, I'm talking about the thing claiming to be a body underneath it."

I looked down again. "What do you mean?"

Rambo's eyes widened and he gave a little snort of derision. "What do I mean? What do I mean? *Jesus*! For a start the vagrant wino look doesn't really suit you *and* you're a bag of bones, boy!"

"Please. No more bones."

"What do you weigh?" Rambo insisted.

"Fucked if I know," I answered.

"Fucked if *I* know. But what I *do* know is it's a bloody darn sight less than it used to be! Remember, I see what you eat, or rather I see what you *don't* eat and it's a lot!" Rambo went silent and his eyes locked onto mine. "You look ill, Matt," he said with feeling, "and I don't like to see you this way." He was serious and trying to help. He always called me by my proper name when he was serious or really cared about something.

In all truth it hadn't escaped my attention. Every time I cleaned my teeth or could be bothered to shave – which hadn't been for well over a week – a gaunt, pale face with dark-rimmed eyes stared back at me. And I *had* lost weight – over a stone and a half – and seeing as I was on the slim side to begin with this had pushed me well towards the Japanese prisoner of war/supermodel/marathon runner end of the physique spectrum. I was turning into *Michael*, for God's sake! Look at the facts! He had committed murder and so had I, he had run the syndicate and I was still running it, he had been eaten away, physically and mentally by past events and I was being eaten away, physically and mentally by past events. All I had to do was buy a wheelbarrow full of 4oz leads, fill up my pockets, chuck myself in the stock pond and *voila*! Two identical life stories and all the tenses could match! I could do it if I wanted! I could flop into the stock pond with more lead on me than a scrap metal dealer and sink like a diving submarine! After all, suicide was only an introverted form of murder and I had managed that!

I was as thin as Michael had been when he was alive, as mentally taut but without the rat-like appearance – apparently I was more 'vagrant wino'. Whatever, perhaps the pair of us had invented a new medical condition, one with a potentially zero survival rate. For the sake of it, let's call it 'Hamworthy Syndrome'; a type of grating cerebral tinnitus that gets on your tits so much you would gladly top yourself to get away from it. I ground my teeth having rejected suicide even if I could do it and decided I wanted to make the survival rate fifty per cent. I had seen first hand what could happen to disaffected souls – there *was* something after death in certain circumstances – and I didn't want to end up haunting Hamworthy Fisheries. I could picture it now, the suicide committed, ex-owner drifting aimlessly around the pit with only the odd waft of fish slime coupled with a hint of blue light and the screech of a Delkim pre-empting his ghostly appearance.

'That spook's a skinny fucker,' the members would say, no longer in need to show their deference to me. Aggravated I would click off their free spool mechanisms and turn down their alarms in a wraith-like rage and whirl around their bivvies whispering subliminal messages to disturb them, like; 'Your rigs are tangled,' 'Your bait's crap,' 'You're in the wrong swim, bonehead,' and 'I'm going to gaff you by the bollocks, slit you open like a kipper, rip out your vital organs with a meat hook, strangle you with your small intestine, spoon out your eyeballs and turn them into pop-ups, numpty boy.'

Whether the quality of life in survival would be worth the effort, having rejected the alternative, remained to be seen. At the moment it was borderline, being alive was hard going – much like fishing Hamworthy through the winter – only the fishing *had* kept me as sane as I could dare hope. Hamworthy *was* something to live for, in spite of the long haul over the winter. The winter that was now over, I reminded myself. Fishing-wise things were looking up as the thirty-seven common had proved.

The only person I knew *alive* who looked nearly as bad as I did – ill, undernourished with an air of on-the-edge desperation, was Sophie. There was no true consolation in seeing I wasn't suffering alone – although I was glad I wasn't – but the truth of the matter was it only succeeded in further emphasising what we had had together and what we had lost. She was suffering from Hamworthy one-place-removed Syndrome. On average I went and saw Sophie and Amy once a fortnight. The conversations between my daughter and I were more loquacious than any I had with her mother and each time our eyes met we saw betrayal reciprocated and the awful physical effects of it.

"I just don't feel like eating," I mumbled to Rambo. "And it's a real struggle to sleep, what with the old video-in-the-head stuff."

Rambo nodded and looked away. He had tried to help during the time I had shared a home with him, bless him, he really had. Okay, so he hadn't exactly offered to *cook* me much but he was forever offering to nip down the chippie, order a pizza, get a takeaway or microwave some gunge in a plastic carton with a film lid. Generally I just didn't fancy any of them. Maybe our bachelor lifestyles were in need of a female's touch, either that or a non-celebrity chef on 24-hour call. If it had been a *celebrity* one, God forbid, I could see the Glock having a say in matters. Rambo had also talked to me at length over and over again concerning my mental problems and serious issues only with no real fortune. Maybe I needed 24-hour professional counselling more than a chef – maybe both. I wouldn't have wanted the counsellor to die of hunger, the poor parasitic bastard. In the end Rambo had wearily conceded the only person who could help me out of my psychotic hell and restore my formative physical and mental health was myself. QED I was up shit major inland waterway without so much as a semblance of the beginning of a sailing vessel, let alone an implement to propel it. The healing process within had yet to start, and yet, the odd feeling...?

15

"So where did you see those two stunning looking, lap dancing, ex-international gymnasts, who were also bisexual nymphomaniacs?" I enquired changing the subject as I fitted a fresh boilie to my recently successful hair rig.

Rambo blew out his cheeks. "Yesterday morning. I nipped down the tackle shop to pick up some hooks and swivels around three in the afternoon and saw the pair of them going into the wine bar down from the tackle shop."

"Did they recognise you?" I enquired as I wrapped a cut off strip from a PVA bag around the hair to hold it tight and tangle free to the hook's shank.

"They never saw me here so wouldn't recognise me, although I was clocking *them* through the binoculars all the time they were around Hollywood's bivvy. They were only on Hamworthy for a session after Michael died weren't they? For the short period when that prick Rocky was lording it and Hollywood was so cock-sure and waiting for his inheritance. I wonder how Rocky's arm is?" Rambo laughed, obviously looking back with fond pleasure at how he had snapped his arm like a broom handle and left him nursing a compound fracture. He dragged himself back into the present. "The girls looked good, though. Especially the dark one."

I concurred by nodding, cast out my marker float, whizzed out a few boilies with the trusty catty and with alarming accuracy dispatched the boilie alongside it via my Ballista Slim. I feathered down the 3oz, not-capable-of-drowning-me-in-the-stock-pond lead and felt it touch down with a clunk.

"They were a hot pair, all right," I eventually said tightening down and putting my rod into my buzzer head and rear rest. "*Very* sexy pair of ladies." I clipped my hanger onto my line and gave it a little tug to pull the line nice and tight. "Not that I do sex any more."

"I hate it when people do that," Rambo observed.

"Do what? Not have sex?"

"Set their indicators with their alarms at full blast. Poor etiquette, you know, boy. Plus it ruins the tranquillity."

I gave him a dismissive wave. "One of life's minor worries. I didn't hear you moaning about the noise the Glock made when I was playing at being the cavalry."

Rambo grinned. "Now that *was* music to my ears, whereas your alarms are barking dogs at two in the morning territory. On the other hand, my alarms are a gently gurgling stream."

"But your alarms are the same as *my* alarms," I pointed out. "We're both on Delkims!"

Rambo wrinkled his nose. "It's a bit like smelling your own farts and then having to put up with somebody else's," he explained.

"An odd analogy," I told him, "but I can see where you're coming from." I wound in my marker float rod and propped it against a bush. "Talking of not having sex, do you ever think of Melina?" I asked.

Rambo eyes narrowed a little and his head quivered into a series of shakes. "No. She came into my life, stayed for a while... and pissed off. Shagged my best mate while I was doing her sister and that's the end of it."

Ignoring Rambo's little jibe I cut to the chase. "It will be if Pup ever finds out what you and Melloney did behind the clubhouse!"

Rambo laughed. "Ironic isn't it? There I was swearing not to lay a finger on Melissa, even if I was on a shagging hat-trick, so it wouldn't ruin our bait rolling source and all the time Melissa was going to clear off with Brad and Pup was up to no good with Melloney. And still is up to no good! Amazing how she's stayed with him."

And it was amazing. Pup was still married to Melissa, although she was swanning around the States with the millionaire angler of her dreams, and Melloney, the youngest sister, had moved into Pup's house of multifarious odours and taken her place. Melina, though, had simply moved on and out of our lives. To be honest, I was pleased. Having the sister I had bivvy-banged floating around the local area wouldn't have been good news seeing as Melloney was keeping in touch with Sophie. My reasoning was that secretly I hoped her disappearence would help Sophie forget about what Melina and I had done. Secretly I knew I was deep in delusion because I hadn't seen Hollywood since he had turned up on my – slip of the tongue – *Sophie's* doorstep and I hadn't forgotten about *him*! I don't suppose Sophie had forgotten about Rebecca either and she was firmly ensconced in France. Secretly I knew my secret thoughts were bollocks, but at least they were secret and therefore saved me the ridicule I would undoubtedly get should I choose to share them.

"We'll have to go and get some more bait from Pup soon," I said. "It's a shame no one dropped out of the syndicate this year because I'd have let him jump the queue and he would have got in."

Thankfully all the current members had re-joined this season thus saving me from the dilemma of screening would-be new members. One dropping out would have been fine because I liked Pup and it would have suited me to be able to have offered him membership, but unfortunately it wasn't to be. My sixty, caught on the last knockings of the charity fish-in, may have had something to do with the one hundred per cent renewals! The subs money was handy for obvious reasons and I had used the Hamworthy account for my needs rather than taking any money from the joint account Sophie and I had. The financial implications of a permanent split from her were grim, but I had never mentioned anything to do with money when I had seen her and so far neither had she. I suspected she too was biding her time, waiting to see what would happen and whether she could ever forgive me and give our relationship another go. It was how *I* was viewing matters. The policy of waiting for something to turn up applied to both my strategy and to my family life. Not very scientific but you never know your luck! Delusion *again*?

Rambo smiled. "Yeah. The charity fish-in got him back into carping, all right." Rambo halted and considered. "He'd have needed to splash out on some new equipment to avoid having poor kit credentials, though. His gear was at the awkward age of not being old enough to get away with true classic retro and not new enough to satisfy the modern tackle police."

"You can talk," I said eyeing up Rambo's usual ensemble.

Rambo gave me a little twirl, his boots digging into the turf as he did so. "Classic British Army camo, boy. Fit for a king!"

I was about to say 'Yeah, a fucking blind one!' when the rod I had only recast ten or so minutes earlier rattled off on a mission. Winter was well and truly over!

"Show off!" Rambo commented as I ran to my rod and struck.

I leaned the rod back into the air and looked up at the tip to see it curving gracefully towards my adversary. My pulse had quickened and I was absorbed into a world where the only thing in existence was the confrontation between myself and the carp on the end of my line. The slug of adrenaline coursing around my circulatory system enlivened me and my brain was focused on one thing: Land this fish!

Rambo, seeking to encapsulate the moment in a traditionally and universally accepted format, asked the appropriate question. "Feel any good?"

With the parameters enforced we were set firm in the unwavering, rigid re-enactment of carp fishing custom and so I was duty bound to answer thus; "Yeah, feels like a decent fish."

Now whether the fish did turn out to be decent – hardly unlikely at Hamworthy – was partially irrelevant because this is what you say when your mate asks you if the fish you have been playing for all of two seconds is a decent fish. It may turn out to be one, in which case everything is hunky dory. But what if it isn't? What are the rules and guidelines? For instance it may turn out to be what we call in the trade a 'pisser' or a 'pastie'. This scenario can acceptably be dismissed by commenting on how hard the plucky little blighter had fought at the start of proceedings. Overestimating fish size during the playing of a carp can happen to us all and the angler who had claimed an erroneous whacker need only be suitably admonished. On other occasions the capture may turn into another species. A pike for instance – acceptable in terms of being mistaken as a carp should the take have been fast enough: a tench – equally so within two seconds but not after said time has elapsed; a bream – not acceptable because this really should have been picked up on the take and definitely within two seconds of playing it; a diving duck – a big no-no as you should have noticed the submerging swine over your baits and wings feel different to fins; and finally a sunken branch – don't ask me how the indicator moves and then you hook into a branch – I haven't a clue. Just recognise it for what it is and that the stubborn 'dead' resistance is a large lump of ex-tree and *not* the water's big mirror – if you don't, people will end up naming you after a certain Enid Blyton creation – amongst other things.

I was spared such angling banana skins because I was fishing Hamworthy Fisheries, the finest carp syndicate in Britain, and I *knew* it was decent carp. What I didn't know was how decent. My mind tried to remember how the sixty had felt and what the thirty-seven had felt like in comparison to that and what either of those two felt like in comparison to what was heaving on my rod at the moment. I gave up and applied some side strain as Rambo dipped my left-hand rod again.

"You're getting good at doing that," I said cheekily.

The whole dynamic of our relationship had changed over the years. I would never have dreamed of saying anything so lippy when we had been fishing in the TWTT simply because, at the time, I was shit scared of him. Now due to our long period of friendship and the sharing of some amazing adventures we were much closer and fear had long been displaced by friendship. Subsequently, to cap all that had passed previously, I had saved his life by gunning down his would-be assassin – by virtue of a psychic hat-trick triggered off by Alan's phone call – and our total bond seemed complete. He was my best mate and I was his. And now I was living with him, but not in the sense of the pair of us being a couple of arse bandits. Some might accuse me of being a time bandit – in the fishing sense, not the Terry Gilliam film sense – since I had fished more than my fair share of late, fair enough; but bum banditry was *not* on the agenda. Nor ever would be, I hasten to add, even if I had – temporarily – given up on the heterosexual variety.

The pair of us weren't living in the original flat where we had made bait all those years ago, we were far more upmarket. We were in Rambo's lovely suburban four-bedroom detached. A fine house purchased on the proceeds of his dodgy past and aided by his faked death and the extra money he had gained because of it. I had wondered briefly when I had moved in, because I had more pressing things to worry over, whether Rambo had been sharp enough to have life insurance on his death and whether he, as another alias, had been the beneficiary. When I had asked he had said, "Of course, I'm not stupid." You had to hand it to him he was on the case, yet, without me it would have ended there and then on the banks of Hamworthy Fisheries. The scales of our relationship had swung considerably back towards me but he was still the driving force, the 'can-do kiddy' when it came to action, like it had always been. Like it would always be.

"Why thank you. Nothing gives me more pleasure than helping you land fish when I should be away trying to catch my own," Rambo replied sarcastically.

"I know," I said in a similar vain, "that's why I thought I'd better catch another one while you were still here!"

Rambo gave me a smile and the pair of us shut up, his eyes following my line to where it disappeared into Hamworthy's depths. The distance from us to where my line cut the water gradually diminished as I retrieved line by carefully pumping and winding in. At twenty yards out the water boiled and rolled over, pulled into a vortex by powerful invisible fins. Despite Hamworthy's gin-clear water the fish remained elusive, as it was too deep and too far out to be sighted. My clutch leaked a few inches of line as the unseen fish tried to make good its escape clickclickclickclickclickclickclick-click- click- click- click- click- click- click- click- click... click... click. The pressure soon told and I quickly put a foot or so back on the spool followed shortly by another couple. And then two more. We saw the fish in tandem. "Common!" we exclaimed in unison.

"And a good one," said Rambo enthused. "Looks bigger than the last one!"

Out of the corner of my eye I saw Rambo catch something moving in the corner of his eye and he glanced back whilst instinctively moving his hand towards his trouser belt. I knew Rambo had one of the Glocks tucked in there. Once bitten twice armed – only this time about the person *not* in the rucksack.

"All right, Alan?" Rambo asked over his shoulder and his hand relaxed.

I swung a swivelled shufti and confirmed it was Alan. *Three* people in one swim at Hamworthy! Christ! It was like Piccadilly Circus! Alan was the syndicate artist responsible for painting all the wonderful portraits of forty plus Hamworthy carp. These portraits, comprising beautiful watercolours of both flanks, were annually updated onto the impressive Hamworthy forty plus poster, the one where each new forty was named by the successful angler. Alan was also the person the ghost had first tried to contact but had failed due to his inability to convincingly hear her voice from a world beyond the living. The experience had left him feeling frustrated and he had hoped I would be the one to make a connection. He had been right but I had lied to him and hidden the truth. He clearly had a dormant talent for hearing – she wouldn't have tried to contact him if it hadn't been the case – but his aptitude hadn't been sufficient, so she had had to wait for my first night and my superior, occasional adeptness. Alan was the one syndicate member outside of Rambo and I who had believed, certainly still did, in Hamworthy being a haunted pit. The rest had scoffed – if only he and the others knew the incredible truth! Better they didn't.

Because of this belief in the ghost, once I had become the owner of Hamworthy, I had avoided interaction with him where possible and had cut him short simply to duck his troublesome questions appertaining to Hamworthy's apparition. Coincidentally it was Alan's phone call that had kick-started my psychic brain into its third major piece of mystic action. My brain briefly registered a question other than the one about landing a carp and I wondered what the hell he wanted and what had made him come and find us.

The fish suddenly made a powerful run along the margin to the right and picked up my right-hand rod's line for a split second causing its Delkim to complain audibly at its temerity for doing so. I turned the fish. To my side, Rambo eased my net into the water and stood waiting to impart his crucial input at the correct time. The fish rolled in front of the pair of us. The third viewer wouldn't have seen this because he had decided to watch at a reverential and respectful distance. Alan was a decent old boy and I vowed if I ever by chance turned up at his deathbed I might consider telling him the ghostly truth. *If* I could have it in writing he was definitely going to die. I applied a little more pressure and the carp's head broke the clear water and it gulped in air. I was winning! With dogged determination the common got its head back down and motored for a few yards. I turned it yet again and it rolled, giving us the benefit of a look at its large, broad golden flank.

"It's a forty, boy," remarked Rambo.

I was loath to argue, it certainly looked it. In a few moments time, unless the hook pulled or the line snapped, or, going a little bit out on a limb, I died of a heart attack, or, going even further, the space-time continuum suddenly fractured and all existence warped itself inside out and popped – a little like a light bulb breaking – into a huge black nothingness, I would find out. Thankfully none of these individual adversities happened, and none paired up – which was nice. I daresay it would be quite possible to die from a heart attack prompted by the horror of a hook pull on a big fish and the line snapping could easily make you feel as if the whole universe had imploded.

I eased the common's head over the edge of the net and once the carp was within its confines Rambo slowly lifted the carbon handle and she was well and truly caught. Thirty-eight blanks and then two fish in a quarter of an hour! I clenched my fist and my brain said 'yesss!' Rambo gathered the net and effortlessly lifted the common onto my still wet unhooking mat. We both bent over the enormous fish, its golden scale-perfect side glistening in the mid-morning sun.

"I told you it was a decent fish," I said to Rambo.

Rambo chuckled and whispered clandestinely in my ear. "Perhaps your psychic powers are making a comeback, boy."

"I wouldn't bank on it," I hissed. "Thirty-eight blanks and then two fish in a quarter of an hour!" I explained turning to Alan who had now decided it was okay to come over and get a closer look. "The last one was a thirty-seven but this one looks a bit bigger."

"Really! Excellent fishing young man! Well done!" Alan said to me cheerily although his eyes couldn't mask how deeply unsettled he was by my appearance.

I hadn't seen Alan around for some considerable time, not since the charity fish-in. Our fishing sessions hadn't coincided during autumn and Alan was most likely of the age where long hours in a pitch black bivvy freezing his nuts off had lost its appeal. He was also probably well aware, seeing as he had fished the syndicate for years, that Hamworthy wasn't a winter water and therefore knew that spending long hours in a pitch black bivvy freezing his nuts off would most likely be done whilst blanking. This combination of events had kept us apart and now Alan's 'artist's eye' had chance to peruse the full onslaught of my physical deterioration over the last nine months in one huge shock-horror exposé. I just hoped he put my 'vagrant wino' dishevelment down to the trauma of thirty-eight blanks, an overexposure to bivvy-life with all its attendant dietary and ablutionary problems rather than anything else he might have got wind of. My personal problems, acts of murder and body disposal antics were *not* for membership consumption.

Rambo fussed with the weigh-sling and eventually zeroed the scales to his satisfaction. The common was duly wrapped in the sling and hoisted up on my new Nitelite scales. I watched the flickering pointer with fascination.

"Go on, Alan," I said beckoning to the artist. "You call it."

"Oh, right. Okay."

Alan looked pleased to be asked and he quickly took out his glasses from a scruffy case he had pulled from a trouser pocket, perched them on his nose and looked carefully at the dial. "Forty-one pounds and eleven ounces! This may well be another one for me to paint!" Alan took off his glasses and spoke directly to me. "Get some good photos, Matthew, and then you can check them against all the previous poster commons. Tail shape is often a good way to identify commons if there aren't any obvious blemishes."

Rambo, who had been peering into the common's mouth, added his opinion. "There are no fresh hook marks, the mouth's perfect. I reckon it'll be another new forty. I can't imagine this fish having been caught at over forty before because its been some time since it was last hooked. And look at its mouth, it's full of leeches. The fish are obviously just waking up and coming out of winter torpor." Rambo got up from his knees. "Anyway, enough of the detective work. Never look a gift carp in the mouth, eh?" He gave me a narrow-eyed stare. "So, what are you going to call it?"

I scratched a cheek. I was still fascinated in the bundle of light-green worm-like things hanging onto the inside of the carp's mouth. I dragged my eyes away. "Provisionally, seeing as we're not one hundred per cent sure, I'll call it... let me think... um... God, I don't know... Wormtongue? That'll do, leeches in the mouth and a Lord of the Rings character. See, I did get round to reading the book, Sophie..."

My voice petered out and I remembered what I had so glorious forgot for ten, maybe even fifteen minutes. My stomach tightened into a familiar knot. Fifteen minutes was fifteen minutes, though, and not a period of forgetting to be forgotten or sniffed at. My longest break yet I should say, for when I was awake, you see sometimes – if I was lucky – I could get two consecutive hours' sleep before waking.

"I'll get the camera," I heard myself saying. I went to my bivvy and pulled it out of my rucksack and took it from its case. The LCD panel showed '17' on it as Rambo had teased and as I noted it, abruptly and right out of the blue, a new worry came hurtling through some outer part of my brain, arrived at its epicentre and became focused into a conscious thought. Bullets! Seventeen bullets!! What had happened to the bullets? Where *were* the fucking bullets I had shot? Sweat beaded on my forehead. My head thumped as my pulse pounded through it. How could I have possibly overlooked the whereabouts of the bullets? All the hours and hours of meticulous introspection and I had forgotten them! An icicle slipped inside my shirt collar and ran down my spine. I staggered outside the bivvy gagging to question Rambo on this most serious breach of concealing my murder, knowing full well I couldn't due to Alan's presence.

"Here you are, you take them," I told Rambo as I handed him the camera. My voice sounded to me as if it was at the end of a long tunnel and I had to force myself to concentrate on what I had to do next. My head swimming, I knelt down and eased my left arm under the common's flank that was touching the mat and spread my fingers around the uppermost pelvic fin and with my right hand grabbing the anal fin

I lifted the hefty fish. Rambo clicked off a few photos before I told him that that would do and gladly put the fish down.

"Can you put it back for me? I don't feel too good," I whimpered to him.

Rambo, his eyebrows scrunched in concern, nodded brusquely and did as I asked. I turned to Alan who was looking at me with a mixture of worry and non-comprehension.

"Are you all right, Matthew? You don't look very well."

A waggled a hand at him. "Too many late nights in a bivvy," I said trying to play down things with levity. Alan made an 'ahh' shape with his mouth and raised an index finger but looked unconvinced. His expression quickly changed to one of social embarrassment, one I had seen from him before. Shit! Not more ghost inquisitiveness. Not now, please!

"Um…" he started none too promisingly. "I actually came here to see you for a specific reason this morning."

"Oh," I answered back.

"Mm," he reiterated.

"Eh?" said Rambo who had just returned from releasing Wormtongue – it was bound to be a new forty, logic dictated.

"I was just saying to Matthew," Alan clarified, "I actually came here to see him for a specific reason this morning."

"Oh?" said Rambo.

"Mm," I confirmed, nodding to Rambo, the dialogue fairly fizzing between the three of us.

"Look at this," said Alan passing me the latest edition of Carp-Talk magazine.

I took the weekly magazine from him and looked at it. He had folded it back from somewhere around the middle and the two pages revealed consisted of a host of snapshots of large carp caught in the last week or so.

"There," he said pointing.

"It's that prick, Darren," said Rambo who was looking over my shoulder. He read the photo's caption verbatim. "'Darren Armstrong with a 35lb 7oz mirror caught from a private syndicate in Kent. Darren had a great season last year banking over thirty twenties and eight thirties from this venue. His latest fish, caught on a single hook bait eighteen millimetre Fusion boilie fished at eighty yards to a gravel spot, is his biggest so far and provided a great start to his new campaign.'"

"So," I shrugged. "The little shit always was publicity hungry, you said so yourself."

"It's not that," Alan said.

"'Eighty yards to a gravel spot'! That's bollocks!" said Rambo.

"No, it's not that either. Look!" Alan pulled out an old colour print from his pocket and gave it to me. The picture was of him holding a high double. "Can't you see? I put this fish into the stock pond because it was below the twenty-five pound limit."

23

Having checked the photo for evidence of death – a habit I still had from when we had photographed Michael with Swansong – and not found any, I twigged what he was getting at. A low whistle from Rambo meant he had seen it as well. It was the same carp. Darren and Alan were holding the same carp. It had grown somewhat, but the scale pattern of the virtually fully-scaled mirror was irrefutable.

"You see?" said Alan. "They didn't steal our fish to sell them, as I suppose most of us assumed, they took them to stock another venue. Another syndicate. One I'm pretty sure is being run by the delightful Gary James!"

Hollywood! The bastard! This was *definitely* it! We were off and running – it was game on.

Chapter 3

It was another ten or so minutes before Alan finally left us, although it felt like it was considerably longer. The burning question in my head still raged as fiercely only now it had others alongside it jostling and vying for attention. Once Alan had gone and after I had sincerely thanked him for bringing the matter to my attention, I locked a desperate stare onto Rambo's eyes.

"Bullets!" I said with immediacy. "I *forgot* about the bullets! What happened to the *fucking bullets*?"

Rambo rolled his eyes as he had so many times previously when confronted with what he considered to be a slack comment on my behalf. "Have you *only* just thought of that?" he asked in a highly derogatory manner. "Fucking hell! You wouldn't be much good as a part of a clean-up crew."

My immediacy shrank back to a mood more akin to lying on a beach in a hot climate sipping a cold drink eyeing up attractive members of the opposite gender in skimpy swimwear. "As a matter of fact… yes!" I answered with a little indignation and a lot less intensity.

"Well, to answer your question… I picked them up."

"All of them?"

"All of them."

"Every single last one?"

"Every single last one."

"Wow! You *are* the kiddy!"

"I was nearly the *dead* kiddy, but seeing as you gave me a bit of a leg up in the form of a timely brutal shooting the least I could do was dispose of the body… and pick the bullets up."

"So I can stop worrying about the bullets?"

Rambo gave me an old-fashioned look. "You? Stop worrying? Ha! It would be nice to think so. But like death, taxes and the occasional terminal rig tangle, some things are inevitable." Rambo gave his nose a wipe with the back of his hand. "I wonder if old Alan's right with his theory that Hollywood started a syndicate with the fish he organised to be nicked from here."

I was inclined to think Alan was. "It was the same fish in the two photos wasn't it?" I said. "They could have been taking fish from here for years before we were on the scene to stop them. They may well have taken enough fish to start up another syndicate. We never really found out the numbers did we? When Michael wrote me the note he assumed, like Alan and the rest of us, that because Alan the fish farmer was involved Hollywood was flogging them back to him. Perhaps this Alan's a carp angler as well and wanted in on a new fishery, one based on proven high quality stock. Then again, perhaps he was just getting paid to help with the transporting of fish." It was my turn to play with my nose and I briefly squeezed the tip of it between my thumb and forefinger. "Having said all that it was a bit dumb of Darren to publish a photo of one, especially in Carp-Talk, lots of people are going to see it." I stared into the distance, voicing my thoughts as they formed in my head. "Strange. Very strange. A really stupid mistake when you think about it. I can only assume his ego got the better of him."

"Or Hollywood is arrogant enough to let him publish it because he thinks he can get away with it." Rambo proffered. He too gazed out over Hamworthy's watery expanse for a few seconds. "He was a cocky fucker all right, willing to push his luck right to the wire. Who knows, a few more years and Michael might have pegged out naturally and if he had kept things on the straight and narrow he'd be the one who owns all this and not you." Rambo turned his focus onto me. "But he couldn't wait could he? I reckon he must have set his stall out to nick fish right from the time they started putting the undersize ones into the stock pond." Rambo let out a heavy breath. "Talking of which you'll have to do something with the stock pond fish this year I'd have thought. It'll need draining and you'll have to decide what to do with the fish that are in there."

I nodded. Something else to do and sort out, still, it was probably a good thing. The more things I had going on in my head the better. Then there would be less capacity left for mulling over the past. Wishful thinking? I hoped not. The two fish I had caught, Rambo's sighting of the two stunning looking, lap dancing, ex-international gymnasts, who were also bisexual nymphomaniacs, Japp's phone call and Alan's visit had galvanised me. The last nine months spent in dreadful limbo seemed to have ended with these minor incidents and the odd feeling I had had earlier had been underlined by Alan's discovery. Looking back I had been a right wimp, what with wallowing in my own misery, being paralysed into non-action by events and struggling to get my life into gear. It was similar to how I had started off running the syndicate. I had managed to turn the corner then so perhaps I could do the same again. Admittedly, the bend was much tighter this time around with unforgiving cliff edges on either side waiting for me to go off track – waiting for me to plunge headlong to my doom – so I could only hope I could pull it off again.

I suppose what I *really* needed was a successful plan of revenge with step-by-step guidelines for me to follow – like say; A) Locate Hollywood, B) Take short section of 1½" black iron tubing to location, C) Batter the fucker to death with said tubing, D) Dispose of body in first available half-full builder's skip, E) Get away with it. Realistically I knew there was little chance of it panning out exactly like this because 1) It wasn't going to be that simple, 2) In my heart of hearts I knew it was sure to be a random, suck-it-and-see (insert your own pornographic carp fishing video joke here) make-it-up-as-you-go-along affair and 3) There probably was a 3 only I couldn't think of it at the moment. All I could say was the plan, although there wasn't one as such, had started. I felt sure of it. Haphazard, follow-your-nose, see-what-happens-next, bide-your-time was still its central theme and despite there not being a single alphabetically listed item to go on, it *had* started. The feeling was too strong to be wrong. And there was another strange feeling as well.

"Rambo," I said at last.

"What's up, boy?"

"I think we're on our way."

"Oh? What the revenge strategy? Excellent!" Rambo exclaimed with a slight malevolent grin on his lips.

"Yeah. I'm sure things are on the move. I had a feeling earlier when you mentioned Japp phoning up and you seeing those two stunning looking, lap dancing, ex-international gymnasts, who were also bisexual nymphomaniacs. Combine those two with Alan's little discovery coming to light and it all kind of fits into a semblance of a start. I haven't got a *clue* what we're going to *do*, but whatever it eventually turns out to be I'm sure we're at the beginning of it. And guess what?"

"What?"

"I've got another weird feeling in my guts."

"What's that?" asked Rambo in a voice hinting he wasn't particularly fussed if he found out.

"I feel hungry!"

Rambo's manner changed instantly. "Then eat, boy! *Eat*! You need it!" he exclaimed enthusiastically.

"But I've run out!" I moaned. "I didn't bring much because I haven't been eating much."

Rambo screwed a huge fist into a ball and waggled it at me. "Rrrr!" he raged. "How old are you?" He looked around himself, presumably for food, dismissed my bag of boilies and grumbled. "I'll go and get some of mine. Here," he lobbed me his mobile, "you phone up Japp and organise this video shoot."

By the time Rambo had returned in his van – a brand new Fiat Scudo he had purchased in February – I had spoken to Japp and the arrangements had been sorted. Rambo took out his cooking equipment from the side of the van, courtesy of its sliding side door, and held up various tins of food for my consideration.

"The ravioli, thanks," I said giving him a thumbs up. "I've just spoken to Japp, they're coming over next week. There'll be him and Frans, Nikki, Lola and Steffi are the girls and a bloke called Arnold who's the camcorder guy. I hope you don't mind but I said they could all stay at your place. Japp reckons three nights with three days' filming and it'll be in the can, or on the tape, DVD... whatever format they use for that type of thing."

"It'll be a bit late now if I say it isn't, won't it?" said Rambo already heating the ravioli on his stove.

"It's not a problem is it?" I asked wondering if I had put my foot in it.

"No, course not. Six of them plus us two shouldn't be a problem, so long as they

27

don't mind sleeping on bedchairs or on the deck." Rambo gave the ravioli a violent stir. "I'm surprised there's only going to be one bloke. Frans is going to have his hands full with three women to take care of."

"It won't be much of a porn movie if he hasn't got his hands full!" I remarked.

Rambo smiled and tested a bit of the ravioli. "Let's hope he's up for it now he's recovered from whatever it was that was the matter with him… in more sense than one!"

"The first of many poor jokes," I said. "I wonder if Japp will let a syndicate member have a little cameo role in the film. It might even be you… or me!"

Rambo looked unimpressed. "Huh. I *don't* think so. I don't want anyone videoing me performing, in a sexual context or any other come to that, thank you very much. And as for you…"

"Yes?" I blurted as Rambo's sentence hung in the air.

"If you turn sideways no one will be able to see you. If your dick's standing to attention you'll look like an upside down zip! You must have to walk around in the shower to get wet you're so skinny!"

"I'm not *that* thin," I argued.

"Eat this," Rambo said handing me the steaming ravioli. "It'll double your bodyweight."

I took the aluminium billycan from him and forked out the first little pasta envelope and put it in my mouth. "Hew! Huck me! Hat's hot!" I gasped through an open mouth as I forced my breath over the burning piece of pasta.

Rambo put his stove into his van and slammed the sliding door shut. "That's the general idea, boy." He walked a few paces back towards me. "I'm going to go and get myself set up and try and catch a few fish. There's an English sixty in there," he nodded towards the pit, "with my name on it. You've had one and I want one as well! I'll see you later."

"Okay, mate, good luck and thanks for the grub."

"Mobile!" said Rambo holding out a flat hand.

"Oh, yeah." I pulled Rambo's phone out of my pocket and gave it back to him. "There you go."

"Cheers, boy. You look after yourself and don't catch too many," Rambo said as he turned back towards his van. As he got into the driver's seat he warned, "I'd get your phone on charge if I was you, then you can text the membership about the porn shoot. If you don't tell them there could be an uprising."

"There might be an uprising of another kind when I do," I said. "There you go, there's another corny joke to add to the collection."

"Bye," Rambo said dourly and he shut the driver's door, started the van's engine and pulled off around the grass track.

I went and sat down on my bedchair and ate the rest of my ravioli – all of it. My stomach felt strangely full and a little less squirmy because of it. Once I had finished eating I went through the rigmarole of re-casting the rod that had stopped my run of blanks firmly in their tracks and was soon fishing three-up and at maximum capacity. When ten minutes had passed and I hadn't had another take – talk about wishful thinking – I returned to my bedchair and aided by the food inside me started thinking *forward* towards meeting Japp and his female entourage. Although I wasn't doing sex at this present moment the titillating prospect of seeing a carp fishing porn video being made – and actually living with the cast for a few days – did arouse interest. (There's another one!) From there I moved on to a totally different area and considered what possible evil fate I could get to befall the awful Hollywood. Half an hour later, having come up with a big fat zero, I was still lying on my bedchair and thinking about Alan's vigilant discovery in Carp-Talk until, amazingly, I drifted off into a deep peaceful sleep. When I awoke six hours later I felt refreshed and knew I was on the road to recovery. How strange. The demons were still there – a couple of fish, one can of ravioli and six hours' kip couldn't possibly have exorcised them – but they were a little more controllable and now I had something to look forward to. The possibility that I could have revenge, and through it the issues that lay between Sophie and myself might in some mysterious and undecipherable way be resolved, was marvellous.

I guess looking forward to stuff, whether it is the weekend, a fishing session, a holiday, even something mundane like a TV programme, was an integral part of the modern human condition. Stuck at work and having a rough day? Well in four hours, four days, four weeks – whenever – it would be a whole lot better because something nice was going to happen after that time. Wishing your life away, to a certain extent, it was true but it was how a vast percentage of people made sense of their way of life. And I had just re-discovered it. I couldn't alter the past but I could alter the future – predestination *could* go fuck itself with the rough end of a pineapple. I wondered why I hadn't been able to get to grips with this simple concept earlier. I mulled over the cliché of 'time being the great healer' and decided it was pretty true to a large extent. It seemed my personal requirements in terms of an adequate package of the stuff had passed and had therefore allowed me to partially move on – combined with a few apparently innocuous happenings. Whatever it was I would take it, take it with both hands and hang onto it as tight as I could.

As dusk approached I wound in and walked back to the functional wooden clubhouse and put my phone on charge. I also needed to use the toilet and as I washed my hands afterwards I examined myself carefully in the mirror. Rambo had been correct; I did look a tad 'vagrant wino'. I speculated as to whether I could stretch my demeanour to 'disturbed genius', seeing as there was an impressive list of psychologically damaged – yet highly intelligent – individuals throughout history who had teetered on the brink of complete breakdown. I pulled down the dark puffy bags under my eyes to see the bloodshot nature of the whites of my eyes. No, I would never be able to carry 'disturbed genius' off, not to the casual observer nor to the highly perceptive one. I was simply a misfit, a freak, an ordinary bloke who had occasional extraordinary insight, which had allowed me to witness and to do things… no other human had ever done? I didn't know. Who had read the mind of a fish? Who had made contact with a bona fide ghost? Who had managed to foresee a small section of the future as accurately as I? No one? A few? A hundred? A few hundred? A few hundred people out of all of the Earth's millions and millions of people? I had no idea.

I wondered what the chances were of ever meeting another who had the gift of brief and uncontrollable foresight – if indeed there were any others. Sure there were those who claimed they could see – the TV mediums and clairvoyants – but they were a confidence trick weren't they? They were a bunch of pseudos who could baffle and bamboozle the emotionally vulnerable with their slick style and clever questioning patter. They couldn't be real could they? Of the people I had met, Alan had a drop of it in him, hence the ghost's attempt at communication and I could remember reading an interview with Chris Yates where he had mentioned how he had felt something inside, something to direct him towards catching a fish. He had said it had manifested itself as a kind of inner voice that had not used words. He had described it as a feeling of urgency that would have made him ill unless he went to a specific place and thus resolved the feeling. I could relate to the feeling ill bit, if not in the same context, and it was a similar type of thing, if somewhat less spectacular than what I had achieved.

I blinked my eyes to make them moist because they had dried out under my lengthy examination. Perhaps I ought to offer myself up for scientific experimentation. To a vivisectionist who could chop my brain into wafer-thin slices in order to spot the abnormality which had given me the 'gift' for want of a better word. I shuddered and moved away from the mirror. Bugger that. It had started with Wim's LSD tab and I would rather live with it without ever understanding it than go through any investigative – and most likely uncomfortable – invasive procedure. I wouldn't have minded offering Hollywood for vivisection; they could slice *him* up into Rizla-thick portions for all I cared – and without anaesthetic.

I locked up the clubhouse and wandered back to my swim. I decided to do the night and stay fishing until I had passed the time of the two takes earlier in the day and then come back, get my phone and text the membership about the porn shoot. I reasoned I would get a few messages back worth a laugh or two. I smiled to myself as I sucked in the fresh evening air. The sun was now low in the western sky and I would have to get cracking to have my three rods all nicely placed before it was dark. I quickened my pace and wondered if Rambo had caught anything and then thought of how he had been kneeling with his big hands clasped behind his head with the asylum seeker's gun pointing at his head. And then it was on with the video of my seventeen-bullet assault and the terrible exit wound at the back of his head. By the time I had re-run it and it had finished I was at my swim. I checked my feelings. Yes. I definitely felt a bit better and the re-run hadn't been so vivid and worrying as before. Fewer questions flooded my brain and the ones that did were less acute. Matt, I told myself, you're on your way back, son. Back to where was a little unclear but my heart and soul and my murderous cloud of worry were all a little brighter as I set to my task of arming my three rods.

When I had completed the task and all was ready for the night I slumped back onto my bedchair, took off my trainers, sniffed them, swore at the obnoxious odour and tucked myself into my sleeping bag. Within minutes I was asleep and I never awoke until nearly two hours after the dawn chorus had been sung. Surprised at my long sleep I untangled myself from my sleeping bag, unzipped the mosquito mesh that formed an inner bivvy door and stumbled into the daylight. The morning was clean and fresh and the world felt as if it had been renewed – as if all the dirt and grime from yesterday had been scrubbed from its surface. Heavy dew sparkled on the long green grass and it soaked my grubby trainers within a few strides of walking on it. I turned to face east and the strengthening sun's rays felt warm on my face. I breathed deeply. Spiders' webs, their intricate design emphasised by the morning's moisture, attracted my eye and transfixed me – caught in a web indeed.

A Delkim beeped unexpectedly and I turned quickly, not to see the beginnings of a run, but a Kingfisher perched on my left-hand rod. The tiny bird looked too vivid to be real with its iridescent blue back and wings complemented by its orange/red belly seemingly on fire in the morning sun. I was beguiled by the bird's beauty and I stood as still as I could, my eyes soaking up the splendour of its vision. All too soon the bird was gone and only a wobbling rod tip remained as it flew off to find its breakfast in the form of a small fish. I felt hungry too, very hungry as it happened. In fact I felt so hungry I couldn't hang on any longer, this unfamiliar feeling in my stomach was a call that needed answering. I wound in, left *three* wobbling rod tips and flew off to find my breakfast in the form of parasitic feeding off a certain well-resourced camouflage-clad man mountain.

"Don't eat *all* the cornflakes," Rambo warned after I had tracked him and his food down to the south-east point swim. "And don't use all the milk either."

"Okay, mate," I said pouring out a big bowlful of cornflakes and dousing them liberally in fresh milk from Rambo's coolbox. I spooned the cereal into my mouth as quickly as I could and soon demolished the whole lot. "What else have you got to eat?" I asked.

"I've got some chicken sandwiches but I was saving them for…"

"Oh, they'd go down a treat…" I paused and gave Rambo a look.

"Like Nikki, Lola and Steffi I expect," said Rambo on cue.

"Nice one," I said rummaging for the sandwiches. "There's mile after mile of material in this you know." I sunk my teeth into the brown bread and fresh chicken. It tasted good. "I wonder why any woman would want to get involved in the porn industry?" I asked with a full mouth (that's it, you're getting the idea – Nikki, Lola and Steffi – full mouth; nudge, nudge, wink, wink or nudge, nudge, wink, wank. Whatever.)

Rambo shrugged. "Maybe they don't. Maybe it's a last desperate option. When we're all sitting together drinking hot chocolate and eating digestive biscuits before toddling off to bed, in a sleeping sense, you'll be able to ask one of them and find out."

"I'd be too embarrassed," I said. "How would you ever broach the subject? You couldn't say, 'What's it like getting shagged left, right and centre every day of the week and lots of people getting to see it? I wouldn't fancy it myself to be honest but I was just curious as to how you got involved with it?' You couldn't say that, could you?" Rambo shrugged. "I mean it's hardly likely to be on your school or Job Centre's vocational list is it. I can't imagine there are evening classes or NVQs for the porn industry. I can see why a bloke might want to do it, the obvious reason coupled with an exhibitionist's streak to show off a large God-given talent, if you get my drift. But a female?"

Rambo exhaled slowly and puffed out his cheeks. He seemed to be doing a lot of it lately. "You're feeling better aren't you? That brain of yours is starting to work again."

I stopped munching and thought. "Yeah! I guess I am. Much better. It's not closure but I've moved on."

"Yeah," said Rambo gravely. "Moved on to eating my bloody food and pestering me with stupid questions I don't need to know the answer to."

"I was just trying to see the female motivation." I explained. "I hope it's nothing nasty, like exterior force or exploitation. I wouldn't want to think Japp had anything remotely to do with those sort of things."

"I'm sure he wouldn't," said Rambo. "But as a long shot have you considered the age old reason for most things?"

"What, sex?" I asked.

Rambo's eyebrows twitched heavenwards in agitation at my stupidity. "Possibly the male angle to a degree but no. *Money*, boy! The wedge, the spondulicks, the loot, the dough, the filthy lucre, the dosh, the moolah, the mazuma, the…"

"Yeah, yeah, I see what you're getting at. Licks dicks for the spondulicks, takes it in the head all for the bread. Very appropriate."

Rambo shrugged again. "Like I said, you'll have to ask. I'm sure they won't be the shy and retiring type that are easy to shock."

"Got any biscuits?" I asked. The sandwich was gone.

"Chocolate or plain?"

"*Chocolate!*"

"Christ! I don't know. In the coolbox, right-hand side."

"There's a Mars bar in here. Just the one," I said peering into the coolbox. I angled my head upwards to look at Rambo. The look said more than the question.

"Take it!" he said with exasperation. "Take the fucking Mars bar and *eat* the fucking thing! Then clear off, text the membership, go home, to *my* home, have a shave and a wash and get some food of your own before you come back here. And bring some extra back for me."

I bit into the Mars bar. "Don't worry, I'll reimburse you." I paused for a little contemplation. "I think I will pop back to your place, there are a couple of things I need to do and I'll come back later."

"With the replacement Mars *barzzz*."

"Bars?"

"Accumulated interest, boy."

"Right, got you. Look, I'll see you later. Text me if you catch a sixty… um… if anyone wants to fish in my swim when I'm gone, let them. I'm going to leave my gear set up but I don't want to be accused of swim hogging. It's not how a syndicate leader should operate," I said.

"I'll let them know, don't you worry," Rambo assured me.

Having filled my stomach and offloaded my leadership requests to my lieutenant in the field I walked back around the grass track towards the clubhouse and car park. I popped in and picked up my phone, locked the functional wooden clubhouse back up and went to my van. Soon I was driving up the farm track and out onto the roads. Rambo's house was forty-five minutes' drive away and, as I had so many times before, my driving shifted into a semi-conscious state of autopilot. A minimal part of my brain drove my van and the rest ran through the latest developments, the foremost of which was my sudden dramatic physical and mental improvement. To be honest I was both taken aback by them and hugely relieved. All my prior worries and doubts were still there but had sunk back away from the surface that comprised day-to-day living. Simply it meant I could function without the paralysis of what had gone on before and begin to rationalise what I might do to fully expunge myself from the disaster of Hollywood's revenge. A thought struck me and at the next junction I turned the opposite way to the one I should have taken to go directly to Rambo's.

I followed the winding road for fifteen minutes or so until I turned off again, this time following the signpost to the small town where I knew my destination was sited. I was taking a chance going there – that was obvious – a Health and Safety Risk Assessment Matrix would categorise it as a grade 3 severity of harm (break of limb, 3 days + off work) times by a grade 3 likelihood of harm occurring (possible/may occur) to give an overall rating of moderate. I was minded to put it into tolerable territory, maybe even trivial. My 'vagrant wino' 'disguise' would be a useful aid for a start and he would never have seen me before not unless Hollywood had any photos of me *and* had bothered to show them to him. Take a chance, Matt. I had to go for it – omelettes, breaking eggs and all that.

I spotted the shop on my left-hand side and swung the van into the small car park to the rear. The Koi and Carp Shop, 28 Fellows Rd – the address was there in my head from the original stocking invoice, one of many invoices amongst the paperwork given to me by Mr Furlington when I had succeeded the late Michael Brown. I got out of the van and wandered around to the shopfront and went in. In the first section were four large oxygenated tanks with koi carp of differing sizes specific to each one. Being an angler I went and looked at the biggest ones, like you do, and was suitably impressed. The fish were beautiful. Several were predominantly white but with large patches of black and orange on their bodies and all were upper doubles. There were also two other fish, both considerably larger, scaled exactly like a common carp only orange in colour – not the bright orange of the patchwork koi but a more subtle, softer orange. These two orange giants looked to be pushing thirty and, despite being only a few feet away from them in perfectly clear water, I still struggled to be able to hazard an exact guess at their weight.

No one was in this section of the shop so I walked through an archway into another section. In here was the paraphernalia of keeping koi in a pond – filtration systems, pumps, Durapipe fittings such as bends, tees and couplings, pond liners and literature telling you how to put it all together should you be mad enough to try without professional help. There were sacks of pellets, other types of fish food, ornamentation to place around the pool and lots of tanks of much smaller fish including the bottom end of the market, win-it-in-a-plastic-bag-at-the-fair goldfish. After perusing the small fish and smiling at the young woman who was standing listlessly behind the wallet-relieving counter, I walked into a third section.

The third section was full of photos of anglers holding carp. A large poster announced 'Some of the carp caught from waters stocked by our English strain of carp'. My heart palpitated as I scanned them looking for clues, wondering if any Hamworthy carp and anglers were present. They weren't. I searched for a sighting of Rocky, Darren or Hollywood only to find they were missing presumed not wanting the publicity. Why had Darren submitted his photo to Carp-Talk? It was question I couldn't hope to answer at this precise time.

"Can I help, sir?"

The voice jolted me from my considerations. "Just looking, mate," I said to the voice.

The voice was one belonging to a male in his early fifties. He was short, thickset with a full head of curly hair showing the first signs of greying at the edges. He smiled at me. I smiled back pondering on whether this lump of shit was the person who had help steal fish from my pit – even if, technically and pedantically speaking, I hadn't been the owner at the time. "Impressive fish, eh?" he remarked nodding at the photos.

"Too right," I enthused. "And these are all fish you've supplied to various different waters."

"That's right," he said proudly.

"So you breed and grow them on and when they're big enough you sell them. Is that how it works?"

"Basically. We breed them and grow them on and sell on the shooters to waters where quality fish are required."

"*Shooters*?" I asked.

"The faster growing fish from a batch all the same age," he explained.

"Oh, I see," I felt a need to justify my being in his shop. "I'm a carp angler, you see. I've just come back from a session," I looked down my nose at my slimy sweatshirt to emphasise the fact. Like I needed to, he could probably smell me at a range of fifty yards. "I've just popped in for a look. I'm thinking about putting a pond in my garden. A poor substitute for having my own lake, I guess."

The voice laughed. "It's most anglers' dream, isn't it? To have their own private water. Unfortunately acquiring the lake or the land to dig one is the killer. It costs so much money nowadays. Quite a few farmers are diversifying because they already have the land and can change its type of use easy enough. A lot of our customers are farmers who are setting up day ticket lakes. They're just starting to get savvy to what carp anglers will pay if a lake's got a good head of carp in it. Stick in the odd thirty and ten to twenty notes a day is the going rate."

I nodded. "It's all right if you've got the money to set it all up and the carp fishing boom remains onwards and upwards." I decided to have a little dig, a tiny careful piece of minute excavation. "Mind you, day ticket lakes that have just been dug in a field are not really my cup of tea. Don't get me wrong, I'll still fish them if they haven't been filled with foreign fish, but I prefer more mature waters." The voice nodded vigorously and I hoped I had pressed one of his 'hot' buttons mentioning foreign fish. "Personally I'd like to get into a decent syndicate if I could. Somewhere nice, good fish, sensible membership – I'd pay good money for that. Getting in one's the bastard… Don't know one do you?" I asked jokingly as a faked afterthought.

The voice laughed. "Oh, I know a few. Actually I've supplied the fish for several locally."

"Wow! Really?" I exclaimed hoping to sound suitably impressed. "Any vacancies?" I asked nudging the voice with my elbow in a jocular fashion.

"I doubt it. They're all full up," the voice said bluntly.

"Always the way," I said and held fire for a second or two. "I saw some books in the other part of your shop. Have you got one giving a step-by-step guide to making your own pond? Something straightforward, written in layman's terms?" And one on plotting revenge plans as well. That would be useful.

The voice considered this request – probably because he could smell money in it – a bit more thoughtfully. "I think I have. Let's go and look."

I followed the voice out to the other area and he quickly scanned through a pile of books before picking one out. "This one's good. Expensive but very thorough and detailed." He flicked through the book showing me a lot of colour photos of a koi pond in various stages of construction. It looked a lot of hard graft and expensive – very expensive. "We sell all the materials shown in here as well," he added.

"Looks good," I said becoming aware things were sliding away from me. I wasn't getting anywhere in the direction I wanted to. "How much is it… er? Sorry, I don't know your name."

"Alan. It's twenty-five pounds."

So it *was* you. You scumbag! Then on another tack I thought; twenty-five quid for a fucking book! Who would spend twenty-five quid on a fucking book? Ten pounds ninety-five was bad enough! "Okay, I'll take it." Apparently *I* would pay twenty-five pounds for a book in the vain hope of extracting some useful information from a fish thief.

"I'll get you a bag," said Alan and he went off to the girl at the till and spoke to her. When he returned I gave him the twenty-five quid and didn't say 'While we're here, just to say, *don't ever* come on my pit again and try and help nick my fish from it, all right? Otherwise, I should warn you, my mate will make your eating of hospital food a foregone conclusion.'

"There you go," said Alan handing me the plastic bag with the book inside.

"Cheers," I said. "Thanks for your help."

"No worries. Look I probably shouldn't do this but…" Alan quickly wrote down a telephone number on a piece of paper and popped it in the bag. There you are sir, something for the weekend. My eyes widened. "Try this guy, he's got a relatively new syndicate up and running and there *might* be a place going. Tell him Alan told you about it."

My heart was banging like a drum and the question had to be forced out. "Thanks, Alan. Appreciate that. What's the bloke's name?" I attempted with cool nonchalance.

"Gary. Gary James," said Alan.

"Is the venue far from here," I gasped.

"No," said Alan. "It's on the same estate as the Broomham day ticket venue.

I knew where it was! "I know, on the B2068."

"That's right," Alan confirmed.

"Nice one! Thanks very much, you've been very helpful. If I go ahead with the pond I'll come and see you for the materials."

Alan gave me a genial wink. I would rather it have been because I had poked him in the eye with a bankstick.

Chapter 4

"Hello, Matthew," Japp said as he shook my hand vigorously, "good to see you again."

"Likewise, Japp," I said smiling at the friendly Dutchman. Was there ever a Dutchman who wasn't friendly?

Japp's bright orange national team football shirt – seemingly as ubiquitous as Rambo's camo clothing – reminded me of one of the koi carp's markings I had seen in Alan's shop a week or so ago. The memory brought with it a glow of satisfaction at my duping him into finding the whereabouts of Hollywood's syndicate. Rambo had been impressed with my cameo-like piece of acting when I had told him, although we had yet to evaluate how this new information could be incorporated into our *strategy*. No change there, then.

During the week I had also sorted out the application process for the Section 30 I would require to move the fish from the stock pond. Once this had been done to everyone's satisfaction I had been in contact with a local angling club, who were keen to purchase the carp and help with their removal and transportation. A provisional date had been set provided I received the necessary documentation from the EA. The members had been sent a text concerning the filming of the world's inaugural pornographic carp fishing movie informing them the water would be closed for the duration and their subs reimbursed accordingly. The replies I had received were lacking in original wit – not as I had predicted – and were deleted forthwith!

"Rambo!" said Japp offering his hand. Rambo pumped it enthusiastically and I saw Japp wince slightly.

"Good to see you, Japp," said Rambo. "How's Wim? Out of rehab yet?"

Japp gave a tight-lipped grimace. "Out and trying to stay clean. It isn't easy for him… as a family we are hopeful he can be strong."

"Get him on PCP and he'll be as strong as an ox," I chipped in – rather stupidly in retrospect.

Japp gave me a cold stare. "He's already tried it. It took eight of us to hold him down."

"I'm sorry," I said chastened. "It was a dumb joke. Mouth working before brain engaging as usual."

Japp smiled and the tension evaporated. "I know, no problem, Matthew. How are Sophie and your daughter…?"

"Amy," I reminded him.

"Yes. Amy."

"We're going through a trial separation at the moment," I told him. "It's a long story, one I don't especially want to tell and one with which I'm sure you wouldn't wish to be bored."

Japp looked genuinely sorry. "That is a shame…" he said and his words hung in the air a bit like a delayed traveller hangs around an airport departure lounge – listless, trapped, forever looking at his watch. I nodded and Rambo nodded. Japp nodded in sympathy with our nodding. We should have all been in the back window of a naff car dressed up in dog outfits. Eventually the aeroplane was boarded, taxied down the runway, took off and the words were gone. Whether it was to crash into a mountain killing all occupants or arrive safely at its destination remained to be seen. "Come and meet the others," said Japp.

The three of us walked from Rambo's doorstep down to the driveway. "You found the place, all right?" I asked Japp.

"No," said Japp casting me a quick glance. "We are still looking. Your directions were hopeless."

Rambo thumped me in the kidneys and I sped ahead of Japp on the momentum of the punch. "You asked for that one, boy!" he said gleefully.

"Ugh! If you've ruptured my spleen I'm suing," I whined.

"Just a tap," said Rambo. By the way his voice tailed off I knew his interest in the possibility of my shattered internal organs had ceased and had been usurped by the Chrysler Voyager – with darkened windows – parked on his drive. The pornmobile was in town. Suburbia's curtains would soon be twitching and being peered around if they weren't already. Out of fascination for metering my theory I quickly checked next door's upstairs' windows. Nothing! I felt a mild stab of disappointment. Still, I argued to myself, they were probably out at work and once word or sighting got around things would be different.

Japp smacked the flat of his hand on the MPV's roof. "We are here, guys. Come and meet your hosts!"

Like a mysterious alien ship in a woeful old-fashioned 'B' movie, one of the side doors clicked and slowly moved backwards down the length of the car. The suspense was killing me. What *were* they going to look like, these beings from another world? A little melodramatic in concept but it *was* an out-of-this-world lifestyle they led. Once the door was fully open a man – not a creature from outer space – got out from the side passenger seat. Another man from the middle seat followed him. The occupant of the third seat spanning the Chrysler's middle row, a woman, got out through the door on the far side and she walked to the rear of the car and opened the tailgate. Two other women got out through the open tailgate and the five of them approached the three of us.

Japp introduced Frans and Arnold to Rambo and me first of all and we all shook hands saying our hellos. In doing so I committed the graceless, social faux pas when being introduced to a male porn star – that of staring intently at Frans' groin. When I did eventually wrench my eyes off his crotch it was to see Steffi – as it turned out

– scowling at my actions. To show my idiocy wasn't tied to a single gender I then gawped at her bosoms when I took her hand. It was purely an attempt to assess its likely silicone composition, but I have to admit it may not have come across as such. Nikki and Lola followed Steffi and I mentally forced myself to stick to eye contact only before I made myself look any more stupid than I already had.

I hadn't been sure of what to expect from this adult production cast. I had imagined many things apart from the one resounding facet now manifesting itself. Ordinariness! They all looked like ordinary attractive human beings in ordinary clothes doing ordinary things, which, of course, was exactly what they were. How odd I should have thought otherwise. It would change when the filming began – *then* they would slip into a mystical minority group – but until that time they reverted to type.

Over the next hour or so the eight of us sat and talked in Rambo's living room and we all got to know each other in a superficial way. Frans was clearly a keen carp angler and very much up to speed on all the latest tackle, bait and methods. He asked Rambo and me many questions about Hamworthy, including the tricky one of how I obtained such a magnificent water – I glossed over it somewhat – and said how keen he was to try and catch something during filming even if it was on borrowed tackle. His biggest hope was to get a take during filming as he saw it as the ultimate in authenticity – a *proper* take in a carp fishing porno video. I doubted if patrons of the finished video/DVD would really care – I had yet to see hardly *any* carp fishing videos with genuine takes in them, let alone a smutty XXX version!

I put Frans down as a bit of a carp angling altruist, in his early thirties, tall, of muscular build with long dark hair, pleasant looking and in possession of a cock conservatively estimated to be at *least* the size of a MCF 8″ Swordfish spod. This man *wasn't* going to be a Gardener Pocket Rocket! Strangely, at least to me, Frans informed us he was married, stranger still, after he had, Japp slyly nudged me and put his thumb down hard on the coffee table as he gestured at his leading man. A printed circuit board in my skull went, 'Does not compute. Does not compute.'

Arnold was older, balder and browner. Despite being only into his late forties his skin had the texture of a Brazil nut and was a similar colour. He either went to a tanning salon in eight-hour shifts, used fake tan from a bottle or spent every conceivable moment he could spare sitting in the sun. Arnold soon confirmed it was the sun he worshipped as much as any Druid alive or dead. In truth it was obvious his tan wasn't out of a bottle because his skin showed the aging effects of excessive UVA and UVB rays all too readily. Despite the inherent risks of overexposure and his dislike of sun lotion Arnold liked to be outdoors as frequently as possible and so consequently his input into the films he shot invariably led to the suggestion of al fresco sex. In a field, in a swimming pool, around a swimming pool, on a beach, on car bonnets provided the cars were outside, anywhere, in fact, where the sun shone. His leading man might stick it where it didn't but as long as he stuck it where it didn't in a place where it did, Arnold was as happy as a pig in shit. Arnold was looking forward to filming at Hamworthy and he hoped the sun would shine and make his video both bright and beautiful. I wondered if overexposure to too much sun and too much staged sexual activity had addled Arnold horribly. Arnold looked longingly out the window all the time we were inside Rambo's house and kept glancing at his watch, no doubt dreading the inevitable sunset.

Steffi was originally from Germany and was a typical example of the Aryan race from which she descended. She had short blonde hair, very blue eyes and just the slightest hint of hardness in her otherwise attractive face. She wore no make-up and sat scrunched up on the settee chewing gum looking mildly disinterested in everything and everyone around her – although I did catch her arching what seemed to be an eyebrow of disbelief at Rambo now and then. Japp had known her for only a year and she had appeared in just a few of his adult films. Steffi was disinclined to tell much of her past and the little information we gleaned about her came from the man in the orange shirt. The most interesting piece of trivia to crop up was the remarkable statistic that during her eighteen appearances comprising her adult film career she had taken it up the arse no less than twenty-two times... actually I just made that up and it's not true at all. Steffi was a German enigma machine.

To counteract Steffi's non-participatory approach the two other girls were much more lively and gregarious. Nikki and Lola were long time acquaintances of Japp and had appeared in many of his titles. Both the girls were Dutch, and I thought, very pretty. Nikki had brown hair, dark eyes and was petite, while Lola's hair was jet black, probably dyed, and she was much taller. It was difficult to ascertain what their figures were like because, as with Steffi, the girls had opted for loose, baggy clothing – the type of outfit you might slob out in. It made little difference, I told myself smugly, because I knew I would find out eventually!

Nikki and Lola chatted in English less erudite than Japp's or Frans' but of a similar standard to Arnold's. It was more than sufficient to hold a decent conversation and I got the impression Steffi understood every word but couldn't be bothered to contribute. We talked about lots of silly stuff, none of which had any bearing on what the girls and Frans did for a day job. I certainly wasn't going to be the first schmuck to bring it up and I daresay Rambo felt similar, therefore, rather ironically, sex was a taboo subject. It was a bit odd really because any other time when three women and five men talked in a group it could have been a central theme. I put forward a theory to myself proposing that if you were doing it all day the last thing you would want to do was to talk about it in your spare time – a busman's holiday of sorts.

Once the little get-together had run its course and Japp had decided it was time to get things organised, Rambo and I helped him and Arnold get all the equipment out of the Chrysler. This constituted lighting rigs, camcorders, clothing, adult props and everyone's personal possessions. There was too much expensive gear to risk leaving it in the car overnight so all the filming equipment was left in the hallway and the personal possessions taken to where the five guests were going to sleep for the three nights. Nikki and Lola were in Rambo's double bed. (When I had first seen it I had ribbed him for being optimistic enough for having one in the first place. He had explained it was all in the crusade for a good night's sleep – a likely story if ever I had heard one! However, it had motivated me to ask myself if he would ever find a long-term girlfriend to fill it – or if he wanted one.) Steffi would take my single bed where I had been sleeping for the last nine months since my eviction and the rest of us would sleep on bedchairs. Rambo and I would go into the third bedroom, Japp and Arnold in the fourth bedroom and Frans on his lonesome in the dinning room.

When I asked Frans if he was all right sleeping on his own he told me he was. "My wife would be much happier to know I am not sharing," he said. "She gets very jealous."

Before my stupefaction could take hold of my windpipe and throttle me, his mobile rang. "It's her," he whispered as he noted the incoming call. "Hello, darling. How are you?" he said into his mobile in English.

While Frans was on the phone Japp passed me with a huge bag belonging to Steffi. "See what I mean, Matthew," he said motioning towards Frans. "There is a man under his wife's thumb. She will phone him anything up to ten times a day to check up on him. To make sure he is not getting himself into any mischief... She's American!" he hissed as he struggled by me as if it explained everything.

"Hold on," I said catching Japp up and grabbing the other end of the bag. I started to help him lug it up the stairs. "What do you mean she's checking up on him to make sure he doesn't get into any mischief?"

"You *know*," said Japp as we turned the half-landing. "To make sure he is not playing away."

"What, in the sense of other women?" I asked confused.

"Sure," Japp confirmed. "They have only been married two years. She is the jealous type."

I dropped my end of the bag onto the floor of the upstairs hallway and placed both hands on my hips. "What *are* you talking about?" I cried. "He's a porn star isn't he?"

Japp considered this. "I would not say he was a *star*, more of a porn journeyman!"

"But she *knows* that? She knows what he does for a living?"

"Sure she knows."

"And she's phoning up to keep tabs on him?"

"Yes."

I wasn't getting it. "Why? She knows he's going to be porking other women, doesn't she?"

Japp's head wobbled up and down. "She wants to make sure it is only the ones he is getting *paid* to 'pork', as you put it."

My head rocked back as if someone had pushed my forehead. "*Bizarre!*" I exclaimed.

"Her name is *Betty*," Japp informed me with a look hinting this was significant. I must have blinked eight times in a second but said nothing. Japp continued. "It is a job, Matthew. It isn't an ordinary job, that is true, but whatever you may imagine it to be it is just another way of making money. *Good* money. If you are the right type it isn't a bad way to work but you must remember ordinary human emotions and day-to-day realities still exist... I can think of a lot harder ways to make a living!"

"Running a syndicate for a start!" I said jokingly. Japp looked away and scratched the back of his head, pinching his lips together. "What?" I said.

"It's nothing," he lied.

"Yes it is!" I argued. "Come one, say it! I won't be offended," I offered, wondering if I would be.

Japp took a deep breath and clasped a hand onto my shoulder. "I have to say, my friend, it does look as if running your syndicate has taken a lot out of you. You look too thin... and very tired."

"You should have seen me a week ago!" I informed him. "At least I'm shaving regularly now, eating fairly regularly and even sleeping fairly regularly. Believe me, mate," I said with deep sincerity, "I'm looking *good* compared to what I have looked like! And I'm *piling* the weight on. Two pounds in the last week!"

"And this is all stress related from running your syndicate?" Japp was incredulous.

I decided to lie. "Yes. And because of it my relationship with Sophie has gone downhill and that's only made things worse. It's been a vicious downward cycle."

Japp offered me a gentle non-Rambo-like jab to my shoulder. "I'm sure you will work things out and get back together."

"Thanks," I said and thought; don't put any bloody money on it. As I did so one of my heartstrings suddenly went 'ping' because I thought of Amy and I blinked a welling of tears away as quickly as I could. Fortunately Japp never noticed or was clever enough to give the impression he never noticed and his counselling was over. "Let's get Steffi's bag into her room. I don't want to upset her, she can be a bit difficult at times."

By late evening we had eaten a Rambo-inspired meal – a local Chinese Takeaway – and all the beds and bedchairs were ready to have their respective occupant slump into them. There was a hard day ahead tomorrow – at least from Frans' point of view and in keeping with the running joke there had better be – or he was going to get some serious grief from his employer! Before turning in everyone had taken turns to do their ablutionary duties in the two bathrooms. As I came out of the first floor one, having cleaned my teeth and had a piddle, Steffi beckoned me into her bedroom. Somewhat taken aback and feeling decidedly uneasy I went in. She was sitting on the bed and she looked at me with her piercing blue eyes.

Steffi pouted her lips and ran her immaculately manicured nails through the shock of bright blonde hair on her head. "Sis is your bed normally, yes?" she enquired, her German accent reminding me of the M & Ms. I nodded. "You don't sleep vitt ser big army guy, sen?"

My brow furrowed. "*No!*" I said with indignation. Apparently I not only looked rough, I looked gay with it.

"But you live vitt him?"

"I live with him because I have… *temporarily* split from my partner, my *female* partner, and my *daughter*," I said feeling as if I had to justify myself.

"Your voman srew you out because of your affair vitt ser big army guy, sen?" she persisted.

I sat down next to Steffi on the bed. "No. *No!* You've got it all wrong," I explained trying to get the truth across to her. "We're just friends, *best* friends. We go back a *long* way, believe me. We've had some amazing adventures Rambo and me, I can tell you. All to do with fishing, which I know sounds crazy, but it's true. Only you *wouldn't* believe me if I did tell you because they really *are* crazy."

Steffi's gaze held me. Her eyes bored deep into me. "You are too sin. Too skinny. You look like you haff AIDS."

"There's not much chance of that," I said flatly. "I haven't had sex for *nine* months! And I don't do drugs. Well, not on purpose. Japp's brother Wim once gave me an LSD tab when we were fishing in France and I had this really weird trip… but I haven't touched anything other than lager since and I haven't touched *that* for months." I gave her a cursory nod. "*You're* the one who ought to be worried about AIDS."

Steffi gave an unconcerned shrug. "Ve are all checked every monz. Until ve are clear Japp von't let us make ser film." Her eyes did their trick again. They really were the most penetrating blue eyes I had ever seen. "So. You are not gay?"

I laughed. "No, I'm not gay and nor is Rambo."

"Has Rambo a girlfriend?" Steffi asked.

"No," I told her. "He did have one for a little while… then she had sex with me while he was having sex with her sister. It all got a bit complicated to be honest."

Steffi eyes sparkled. "And you are still friends?"

"Oh yes. We survived that little debacle easy enough," I informed her.

"But ser one vitt your female partner didn't survive?" Steffi asked. She was sharp.

"It wasn't only that," I said dolefully.

"Sere vas anozzer?" Steffi asked in surprise.

"Another from a few years ago," I replied. "I had wondered if I'd ever live to regret it and I guess now I do."

"Do you still love your partner?"

"I do and I don't," I answered honestly. "Unfortunately she was unfaithful to me as well. Unfaithful in a way I can't forget, with *someone* I can't forget."

Steffi nodded and to my surprise she took my hand and stroked it. "I'm sure sings vill vork out okay… now I must go to sleep and rest," she said. "I expect I vill haff a lot of ser cock sucking to do tomorrow and I vould like to read a little before I turn off ser lights."

There was no answer to that, so I didn't give one. I gave the briefest of acknowledgements, left Steffi's room and went into the third bedroom, pulled the door to, eased myself onto my bedchair and snuggled deep into my sleeping bag.

"All right, boy?" asked the huge hulk under the sleeping bag adjacent to me.

"Not too bad," I replied.

"Good." Rambo turned over inside his bag. "Had any thoughts about Hollywood's syndicate?"

"I had one," I admitted. "To wipe out the entire stock by either some form of poison or by introducing diseased fish. Not a very good idea. Bit crap, really."

"Yeah," Rambo concurred. "Those fish don't deserve to die, it's not their fault they're in the wrong place."

"Once I'd thought it through I came to the same conclusion," I said.

"Best to sleep on it," said Rambo.

"Yeah. Something will come to mind eventually… Have you put the alarm on?"

"Yeah."

"See you in the morning."

"See you in the morning, boy."

My last notion before I drifted off to sleep – I was really getting the hang of it again now – was we did sound a bit like a married couple. I grinned to myself under the sleeping bag in case Rambo could hear it and wanted to know what it was I was smiling over! Rambo *married*! I couldn't ever imagine *that* happening!

By ten o'clock the following morning the whole entourage was at Hamworthy Fisheries. To Arnold's undisguised delight the day was perfect with a blue, clear sky and warm, bright sunshine flooding the beautiful Kentish panorama. Arnold had already had his shorts on when we had left Rambo's house and now we had arrived his first course of action was to take his shirt off. The texture of Arnold's skin, coupled with his obvious need for a fix of sunshine, made him take on an almost reptilian air. As his dark brown body soaked up the sun I was instantly reminded of the iguanas of the Galapagos Islands, sunning themselves on a rock to build up sufficient body heat to go swim in the sea – only Arnold was building up sufficient body heat to go wield a camera at five adult film actors.

Japp had let out a low whistle when he had first gazed upon the pit and Frans' jaw had gaped equally. The pair of them had bombarded me with questions all appertaining to carp fishing. What was in here? What was the biggest? What was the average? What swims produced? What was the depth? What was the bottom like? What tactics worked? What was the going bait? And then Frans' phone had rung and his wife had bombarded him with a different set of questions. When, finally, he had convinced her what he was about to do constituted the actions of a genuine day's work – in *his* line of business, naturally it wouldn't have added up should you have been a car salesman or long-distance lorry driver – she had hung up.

Once his phone was silent I asked him a question. "Is this the first time you've filmed with any of these girls?"

Frans nodded. "Yes, the first time with Steffi but not Nikki and Lola."

"Does that make it any more exciting? You know, doing it with someone new?" It was only idle curiosity but I had to ask.

"No," said Frans emphatically. "And you can tell my wife I said so when she next phones up."

Eventually the fundamental reason why we were at Hamworthy came to the fore and Rambo and I were told to set up a set-up just as if we were fishing for real, which in fact we would be, or rather Frans would be. As we did this Arnold did some preparatory camera work with Japp and Frans. This consisted of getting the opening shot where Frans was supposedly driving to his fishing venue. The three of them filmed this section on the mile long farm track and around some of the grass perimeter track. Next they got Frans to unload his gear out of the back of the vehicle and start to set it up. After only a few seconds of this Arnold cut to the completed set-up as done by yours truly and Rambo.

An idea tripped into my head and I asked myself whether we might make the final credits for doing so. Clearly we wouldn't be accredited with something as lofty as Producer, but perhaps we could be construed as being Fishing Consultants, or more specifically Executive Bivvy Erectors (add in running joke no.28), Bedchair and Buzzer Bar Anti-gradient Establishers, Alarm Head and Indicator/Swinger/Hanger Co-ordinators, Sleeping Bag Consultants, Team Leader Boilie Stop Inserters and Riggers, NVQ Level 3 Free Spool Mechanics, Terminal Tackle Tiers incorporating overall Rig Design and Application Management and finally Senior Rod Ring Aligners (a Disability Priority Position most suited to the applicant having just the one eye, a permanent squint, or at a push, being completely able-bodied, having two eyes but with ownership of an eye-patch). The list of menial tasks required in sorting out equipment for a carp session set-up were virtually endless and could easily be parodied in the style of Guardian-advertised, governmental employment opportunity bullshit, where so very little could sound so very much *and* so very pompous.

On a different angle we might receive our name check by way of Mr Henk van Herk's Bivvy Arranged by Matt and Rambo, Mr Henk van Herk's Bait Application Applied by Matt and Rambo, Mr Henk van Herk's Tactical Nous and Overall Carping Campaign Conducted by Matt and Rambo and Mr Henk van Herk's Line Aligners Aligned by Matt and Rambo, which was all very amusing and very preposterous. What I *didn't* want to be, and I'm sure Rambo felt the same, was Chief Lubricant Squeezer, or, even more hideously, Principal Body Fluid Moperupperer – most ghastly of all I didn't want to be construed by the cast as Apprentice Voyeuristic Bystander. I reckoned I would settle for a credit of Background Venue Supplied by Matt Williams and Rambo Ramsbottom. That would do nicely.

Frans insisted on casting the three rods we had ready and baited for him by himself – all to spots indicated by the collective wisdom of Hamworthy's first lieutenant and myself. Frans ripped the longest spot off a treat – one pushing ninety yards – and showed good accuracy on the two other shorter placed rods. Arnold captured all three casts on the camcorder and also recorded Frans parking his bum on the bedchair placed adjacent to the bivvy.

"Cut!" yelled Japp. "How was that looking Arnold?" Arnold gave a gesture to show it was fine and eased his face up towards the sun and closed his eyes. He was a human sponge sucking in the sunlight. "Good," said Japp. He turned to Rambo and me. "Now we need to do our first bit of proper action. Steffi will be first, she'll be someone walking around the lake that gets talking to Frans and... well I think you can guess what happens! We try not to make the plots as complicated as The Matrix!" Japp looked at his watch. "If she ever gets ready in time. Where *is* she?"

The girls had stayed at the clubhouse to get ready and were meant to be driving back to the swim in Rambo's van. I had offered to be chauffer but Steffi had insisted she could drive the Scudo and they would rather get dressed and made-up on their own and in private. I hadn't argued. I looked at my watch. We had spent well over an hour and a half getting all the gear ready. Surely it didn't take so long to put on whatever was soon to be coming off and a bit of make-up? I had a quick scan around. Rambo was now talking to Japp and Arnold, almost certainly about carp fishing, so I sloped off to have a chat with Frans while we waited for the arrival of the female cast.

"Are you okay, Frans?" I asked him.

Frans rubbed the palms of his hands together expectantly, his face pulled in a broad grin. "I am looking forward to this. Very much," he said excitedly.

I winked at him. "What because it's your first time with Steffi?"

Frans' face clouded for a second and he looked puzzled. "No. The *fishing*. I am hoping if I can make a big effort we can get all the filming done in two days rather than three. Then we can fish for a whole day. *Properly*! Without all this other nonsense going on! Japp has agreed!"

I think it would be fair to say – although I didn't have a mirror handy to verify it – I was the one looking most puzzled. Here was a guy who was getting paid good money to have sex with a stunning blonde-haired beauty – who was no doubt going to do lots of rude things to him *and* act as if he was the most fascinating, amazing stud she had ever been with – and all he was worried about was getting in some carp fishing. Role reversal or what? How many carp anglers got in plenty of fishing yet sat on their bedchair dreaming of the kind of woman Frans was shortly to be thoroughly investigating?

"Aren't you interested in the sex?" I queried.

"Not really," admitted Frans. "I have to be interested in the sense I can perform adequately but more than that... no. Carp fishing is what interests me the most. When this trip is over I am fishing in a weekend meeting on a big lake near Eindhoven, near a tiny town called Westerhoven. It is an unusual lake, very different from here." Frans looked at me and his eyes lit up. "You could come! You and Rambo," he said avidly. "It is not far to drive, only three or four hours from the Channel Tunnel. Yes, you could come. You must come! I will introduce you to my Dutch carping friends." Frans' enthusiasm turned to sudden reverence. "If we are lucky," his eyes darted left and right, "The *Eye* will be there!"

Before either of us could further the conversation Frans' mobile rung. "Shit!" he said. "It is Betty. Here," he said giving me the phone, "you talk to her. Tell her I am on the job."

Thanks a bundle, I thought. Barking Mad Betty was all I needed. I looked at the phone as if it was a dog turd capable of chiming the Nokia ringtone and held it gingerly to my ear. "Hamworthy Fisheries, home of the finest carp syndicate in Britain. You're through to the owner, Matt Williams. How can I help you?" I said.

"Frans, honey. Is that t'you?" drawled an American voice on the other end.

"No, Madam," I said playing up my part. "This is Matt speaking. I'm looking after Frans' phone for him."

"Oh… You playing voices with me Frans?" Betty demanded. I assured her I wasn't. "Oh, gee… So you're the Brit guy, right? The one who owns the puddle in England?"

"Gravel pit," I corrected her.

"Gravel pit?" Betty proclaimed. "You mean there's no warter? Just a great big hole filled up with a bunch of gravel stuff. How can fish live in a hole with no warter?"

"There's water," I said. "It used to be filled with gravel but they dug it all out…"

"Who dug it all out?" asked Betty before I could finish.

"Aliens," I said deadpan.

"No shit?" said Betty.

"They left everything spotless," I informed her.

The phone grunted at me. "What's Frans up to?"

"He's on the job," I dutifully explained.

"Tell him that's all he better be on!"

"I shall pass the message on ASAP, Mrs Henk van Herk." I hit the phone's red button ASAP. Fucking hell! I wondered what redeeming features Betty must possess to enable her to be married to someone as affable as Frans – then Steffi turned up with Nikki and Lola and I gave up due to the distraction.

Steffi looked nothing short of sensational in an obvious and sleazy way with her ridiculously short, tacky skirt and open to the navel, bosom-revealing top. She walked barefooted to where Japp, Arnold and Rambo were standing while I looked on feeling acutely aware of my relief in banning the rest of the membership from the shoot. If people wanted to look at the finished video fair enough, but to have had even more bodies here involved in lechery would have been a disaster. As it was my reservations of being a voyeuristic bystander at the video's conception, so to speak, were rising – and *not* anything else, before you ask!

These three young women, these three apparently ordinary young women, who had become acquaintances, were soon going to cease to be women. They would soon cease to be individuals of the female gender and become purely objects of male fantasy and would be used as such and expected to act as such. Were they empowered by their choice to use their bodies as they wanted or was it something more sinister? Why were they here? Why weren't they earning a living in a more traditional way? Why had their lives veered off in the direction they had? I doubted if I would ever know. Thankfully all three of them seemed relaxed enough and happy with the situation. There was no intimidation from Japp or Arnold, all concerned were consenting adults and it seemed as if individual choice had put them there. I exhaled slowly and told myself I was probably getting too touchy over it all. Even so, I wouldn't want *my* partner wrapped up in the porn business and despite the fact it was clear Betty was a complete nutter, I could empathise with her predicament.

By the time I had dragged myself out of my little vortex of windy worry the filming had started. Steffi casually strolled along the banks of Hamworthy Fisheries, virtually unclothed – like you do – and became involved in a little light conversation with Frans the carp angler. (Used to happen to me all the time in my younger days!) She sat on his chair. He sat beside her on the grass and they talked some more. She pouted. They talked some more. He made a pass and they kissed. Surprise, surprise, all of a sudden and just like that her top came off – and then Arnold stopped them and reset the scene with a better camera angle. Frans soon took off his top after having thoroughly manually examined Steffi's pert, silicone-free breasts with tongue and fingers and in due course peeled off the rest of his clothes. Steffi's bedside prediction to me of her likely workload was proven to be accurate. Although Frans was probably bigger than a MCF 8″ Swordfish spod Steffi took it like the pro she definitely was – until Arnold stopped them to get a better camera angle.

After some prolonged deep throat action, and obviously happy the fellatio content of the scene was sufficient, Japp directed Steffi to take her skirt and thong off. Ticking off the boxes comprising a porn scene Frans now began his penetration routine – God knows how many times he had done it, but I suspected the involvement of a Wychwood Superlight 3 leg bedchair was unique – until Arnold stopped him in his tracks to put the two of them into a different sexual position and got himself a better camera angle.

During this Rambo walked over to me. "I don't feel right about this."

"Me neither."

"Shall we leave them to it?" he suggested.

"I think so. You know what's going to come next, or rather you know *Frans* is going to come next and you just know who he's going to come over. We can always watch the video when it's all done and dusted, *if* we ever feel the need. Let's go and have a walk round and see if we can spot some carp." Rambo twitched his head and we started to walk back to the grass track. "We're just going off for a while," I said to Nikki and Lola. "We feel a bit embarrassed hanging around and watching. We'll see you later." The girls smiled at us and waved goodbye. I wasn't convinced they had totally understood our English, or if so, had understood our embarrassment. "Well, mate," I said turning to Rambo as we sidled off. "How do you fancy going fishing in Holland for a long weekend?"

Chapter 5

It was only nine o'clock in the morning but it was unusually warm – in the low twenties centigrade. Advocates of global warming would be banging on their drum again and the tabloids would soon be running 'Phew, what a scorcher!' headlines if it lasted another day. The obligatory hosepipe ban was already in force from months earlier. Me? I keep on spraying my CFC-based propellant aerosols into the atmosphere and turn Rambo's carbon dioxide producing boiler up to maximum when he's not looking – the sooner Britain got to the predicted South of France climate the better! I made some tea and took a mug of the steaming brew over to Frans who was crashed on a bedchair. It was the very one – the Wychwood Superlight 3 leg bedchair – on which he had fornicated with Steffi, with Nikki, with Lola and then with Nikki *and* Lola two days earlier. It was also the very same bedchair on which Nikki and Steffi had performed their obligatory one-a-movie lesbian dalliance scene. From the bedchair's point of view I imagined this probably made a welcome change from its usual type of customer – a static carp angler whose only occasional dynamic movement was to cock his arse and fart on it.

As far as I could tell the bedchair looked pretty smug with itself having secured its place in carp fishing tackle history by being such an integral part of the world's first ever carp fishing pornographic movie. However, its smugness was overshadowed by the man who was now – thank goodness – only sitting on it. Frans had an overwhelming look of supreme satisfaction stamped on his face. He had done it! Not only had he shagged himself senseless and crammed three days' worth of leading man porn stud action into *two* days – which had afforded Japp and him a twenty-four hour bash on Hamworthy Fisheries, the finest carp fishery etc. etc. – he had also caught one of its inhabitants at half seven this morning.

One and a half hours earlier Frans had been a gibbering mass of excitable schoolboy as he had landed his first English carp – a stunning 37lb 6oz fully-scaled mirror. Now it was chill-out time. With the pressure off and his tasks fulfilled – 1) Porn movie completed: check and 2) Catch English carp: check – he could sit back, relax, drink the tea I had made him and when it took his fancy, phone Japp to wind him up over the fact the orange-shirted pornmeister was still blanking – provided his phone wasn't being monopolised by the grating tones of Betty, the wife-from-hell.

Frans and I were fishing the south-east point swim two-up whilst Rambo and Japp were sharing the swim at the north end of the lake near to the old wood where I had been contacted by the ghost on my first Hamworthy overnighter – although I had never mentioned it, like you don't. Later on, once they had roused themselves, the three girls would be coming down to see us along with sun-worshiper Arnold. I could imagine Arnold was cajoling them and nagging them at this very moment to get their butts into gear and get the hell out of Rambo's house and into the beautiful sunshine.

I had wanted to fish with Frans when the twenty-four hour window of opportunity had arisen for the simple reason that as Rambo and I had decided to whiz off to the unusual venue near to the small town of Westerhoven, I was intrigued to find out more about The Eye. Frans and I hadn't had any chance to discuss the trip other than to confirm our place on it. It hadn't taken much to convince Rambo – and me – that a quick-fire blast into Holland for a weekend's worth of Dutch carping would be fun. I had asked Rambo if he fancied it and he had said he was up for it if I was. I had said I was up for it if *he* was and so, what with *both* of us being up for it, we had decided to go. When we had told Japp and Frans they had seemed pleased and said they would look after us in reciprocal fashion, like we had them, and all would be hunky-dory and sweetness and light in the garden.

"There you go, Frans," I said handing him his cuppa. "Feeling good?"

It was a question that didn't need answering because Hamworthy had worked its magic once again and had gained another convert. Although Frans hadn't managed a genuine take during the filming of the porn video I had managed to get his fish from this morning on the principal camcorder. Arnold had thought of leaving me the camera and Frans had sagely worn the same clothes so as to create the illusion of continuity. We were in a different swim from the one where the smutty action had taken place but clever editing would cure any discrepancy on that count. Frans catching had been the cherry on the cake, or if you're not partial to cherries, then the icing. Overall, the whole venture had been a right result in every aspect and the fish was the crowning glory of 24-carat authenticity. Japp had been very pleased with the way things had gone even before Frans' fish and he had told me in confidence he had never seen him so motivated or perform so well. Flippantly I had told Japp it was patently obvious Frans wasn't going to go around getting paid top money for screwing lots of exciting women unless there was something in it for him. It was obvious he had needed the true incentive of twenty-four hours' of carp fishing on Hamworthy at the end of it to get him truly interested. Japp had laughed and had agreed I was probably spot-on.

Familiarity breeds contempt and although Frans showed nothing but respect for the girls off-camera – it had to be different on-camera unfortunately – it was a lesson in how people's priorities and attitudes could be changed by what they perceived to be a chore. Frans having sex with women for money had apparently become relatively mundane and humdrum to him, whereas given a day on Hamworthy and a chance to catch one of its carp, induced a major adrenaline rush for him! His gushing excitement and final climax at landing the carp he had hooked was surely as fulfilling as any orgasm! With the boot firmly on the other foot I tried not to get blasé over Hamworthy and what it offered, yet I doubted if I was as reverential as I should have been over Frans' upper thirty. To me it was just another carp of mid-size for the water because, to put it into perspective, I had had a sixty. (I *had* told Frans about my sixty, you have to tell fellow carpers stuff like that – it's in the rulebook.) It all went to underline the old adage of familiarity breeding contempt and different things floating different boats.

"Feeling very good," said Frans. "I am so pleased to have caught a fish." Frans looked at me and carried on. "You and Rambo are good anglers, I could tell, and I wanted to prove myself, prove *I* was a good angler also. Do you understand what I mean?"

I did. As soon as you fish with someone new, or with an old friend on a different venue there's this extra need to prove you can catch. To prove you are a capable carp angler. The very nature of fishing makes this impossible to achieve some of the time, but if everyone is blanking then it makes life a little easier. Everyone is in the same bait boat as it were. However, once one person has caught then the pressure is definitely on – especially if it's your mate! Japp was undoubtedly feeling the magnified effect of this because up until this point he hadn't had a snifter. Having said that the two local experts were also lagging behind the supercharged Frans! But I *had* caught a sixty. Once. Last year. I don't want to keep on keeping on about it – it's the equivalent of a prile of threes in a game of brag, that's all.

"I'm chuffed you've caught one," I admitted donning my benevolent fishery owner's hat. I sat down on my bedchair, which was adjacent to Frans' one. I sipped my tea and casually eyed his bedchair for stains – tea, coffee, cup-a-soup, superglue, spunk, that kind of thing. "The Eye," I asked him. "A big fish is it?"

Frans shot me a serious stare. "No. The Eye is a *man*! A very *special* man! A very special carp angler, one who Japp and I have only recently been admitted into his close circle of friends."

My mouth turned down at either end and I nodded. "What's so special about him?"

Frans took another mouthful of tea, swallowed it – I was reminded of Sophie, *not* Steffi (less visual impact) – and he turned to me. "He can *see*," he said.

I stared at Frans wondering if he was taking the piss. The earnest look on his face told me otherwise. "What do you mean, like, *really* well?" I asked moronically.

Frans' eyebrows dipped together. "No. He can see ahead. Into the distance."

I thought I understood. "Oh! You mean without binoculars! Has the eyes of a hawk, that sort of thing."

"Into the *distance. Ahead*!" said Frans getting agitated at my non-comprehension. Clearly there was something being lost in the translation here.

"*I'm* looking into the distance," I said making a great play of standing up and holding a hand to my forehead to shade my eyes. "*I'm* looking ahead. It's not *that* clever!"

Frans wiped his hand across his brow – his furrowed brow. "Sorry, Matthew, my use of English is letting me down. He can see ahead in *time*."

"*What*?" I said staggered.

"It's true. Every now and then he gets to see into the distance…"

"You mean the future?"

"…Yes, *that* is the word. The *future*," Frans confirmed.

Thunder rumbled in my ears. "How does he do it?" I heard myself ask.

"He gets drunk," said Frans, "on a drink called absinthe and the ingredients within the drink affect his mind and give him special powers. It doesn't work every time but when it does he usually catches a big fish."

The thunder faded into the distance. A piss-head carp angler. Maybe this wasn't the revelation I had hoped it was going to be. "And that's all he uses it for? To try and catch carp," I asked dubiously. "Does he mention what's going to happen in the future *before* it happens or does he just say he predicted something in the past once it's already happened?" I asked sceptically.

Frans shrugged. "I only know of things he has said will come true in fishing. His house was broken into six months ago and I do not think he saw *that* coming." Frans fell silent for a second and then continued. "But I was there when he used the absinthe, in his bivvy with him, and he said he could see where he would catch the big mirror when the wind was in the right direction." Frans looked down into his tea and then back up at me. "And you know, Matthew, he caught it. He caught it in a swim he moved to, to get on the end of a big wind from the south."

"Oh," I said vaguely while my guts churned. It was the mirror image – if you pardon the pun – of my capture of the big one from Lac Fumant. And as for the bit about his house getting broken into, well, I could relate to that all right. Hollywood had burgled a great big chunk of my life away and I hadn't seen it coming either. If what Frans was saying was correct The Eye could be the person I had been asking myself about in the clubhouse a short while ago. Either that or he was a very clever manipulator like the pseudo psychics on the box. I mean, how many anglers had moved onto the back of a big wind, whether by premonition, by having a hunch or simply previous experience? Even so, if it was the former then was he a genuine misfit like I was? Were his intermittent powers akin to mine? Could he, *would* he, be able to help me in my plan of revenge in some strange and mystical way? Would he be able to give me some tiny pointer from the future that could guide my cobbled together plan? And what if the future he saw wasn't what I wanted it to be? What if he couldn't see the future at all?

As always I was getting way ahead of myself. All I could realistically ask at this point in time was: Was this another small step in my haphazard, don't-know-where-this-is-all-leading-to plan of revenge? The intangible feeling I had encountered earlier that had gradually amounted to something the size of a poor excuse for a molehill via the sighting of the two stunning looking, lap dancing, ex-international gymnasts, who were also bisexual nymphomaniacs, Alan's spotting of Darren in Carp-Talk and my remarkable Oscar-winning performance in fooling Carp Thief Alan into giving me Hollywood's mobile number and the whereabouts of his syndicate, had now enlarged itself. It had graduated to a respectable molehill, one any self-respecting mole would be happy to put its name to.

Unfortunately molehills were *not* enough. I had plans to make a fucking great big mountain out of it – the trouble being I didn't really know how to set about it. Still, I needn't be too hard on myself, compared to how I was a few weeks ago I was doing fine. The video replays were under some semblance of control, I was eating and sleeping much better and the plan, as such, was under way.

As I sat next to Frans I realised two trips would have to be made before Rambo and I left for Holland and my chance to meet The Eye. One would have to be made to Pup for some more bait and one to Sophie – to see my little Amy. Unfortunately of late she was growing up without me and I felt a deep pang of regret because of it. I had had such high hopes of my fatherhood directly after her birth and it had all gone sour in the last year. I was certainly not turning out to be the father I had hoped. And it was all Hollywood's fault... coupled with a fair bit of mine. I had to admit bonking Rebecca and Melina had *not* been the most astute move I had ever made in my life, it was just that at the time it was so tempting... and I was *so* weak.

"What's absinthe," I asked dragging my attention back to The Eye and his favoured method of crystal ball gazing. "I know it's a drink but that's about all."

Frans looked blank. "I do not know more than you," he admitted. "When you meet The Eye you can ask him, he will not mind."

"If he's on the stuff at the moment he'll know I'm going to ask him and he'll have an answer off pat for me," I said jokingly.

"I do not think it works like that," said Frans. Before I could say 'Don't I know it!' Frans' mobile warbled its familiar tune. Bloody hell! Betty was on the blower *again*.

"Yes, still fishing, my love... with Matthew. Nobody else... Japp is with Rambo at the other end of the lake... yes we are coming home tomorrow... yes... love you... bye."

Frans put his phone down and I had to ask. "What does Betty do, Frans? Where did you meet her?"

Frans pushed his mobile from hand to hand. "Betty was a stuntwoman. I met her when we were filming on a large Hollywood film set. 20th Century Fox were making an action movie where Betty was the stunt double for Cameron Diaz and we were using the set to film our movie after they had finished filming for the day. I don't know how Japp managed to arrange it... but he did."

My mind whirled at the thought. There was Betty doing her cunning stunts and there was Frans amongst the girls with the age-old spoonerism. "What was it? Love at first car crash or where you smitten by her backward somersault death fall off the high veranda?" I asked grinning.

Frans' face took on the look of one reminiscing. "She was the one who saw *me* in action. I think she liked the size of my..."

"I get the picture," I said hastily.

What a bizarre clashing of lifestyles – a stuntwoman and a male porn star! I wondered what their kids would do should they ever have any. I laughed in my head; I couldn't see Frans and Betty getting on to many reality TV shows where job swaps for two couples were the order of the day. Cue daytime TV presenter, 'Our second couple, couple 'B', are Mr & Mrs Bland. Mr Bland is a paperclip facilitator for a large accountancy firm and Mrs Bland is a librarian. Now in our show not only do the couples swap jobs but the male of couple 'A' does the job of the female of couple 'B' and vice versa. Mrs Bland, tonight, let me assure you, you are in for a *big* surprise!'

I looked out into the blueness of Hamworthy's waters and saw a fish roll around in the margin to my left. A minute later a different carp did the same and then another and then yet another. A short time later two more fish crashed out in perfect synchronisation and the tempo gradually increased until there seemed to be a fish moving out of the water every ten seconds or so. At last I twigged it – the carp were spawning! I had speculated as such in my bivvy during the previous session and now it had come to pass. The water was now warm enough, the wind and light were now right and the spawning areas – and evidently there was one over there where I had been looking – were suitable. This latest blast of warm weather had kick-started the carp into action. I phoned Rambo and asked him if there was any sign of spawning activity up his end of the pit. He said there wasn't but he did inform me of a different kind of activity. Steffi, Nikki, Lola and Arnold had arrived and were keeping him and Japp company.

"Is Arnold sunbathing?" I enquired.

"Yeah," said Rambo. He lowered his voice. "And the crinkly old fucker's doing it bollock naked."

Partially miffed as I was at the remainder of the company's decision to visit Rambo and Japp before Frans and myself, I thanked heaven for the small mercy of not having Arnold's entire body, genitalia included, inflicted upon my delicate retinae. It was the sort of thing that could force you to want to rip out your own optic nerves with a pair of forceps or to perform the same operation with the red plastic disgorger – 'Free with this month's magazine!' – you keep in your tackle box, forever unused, 'just in case'.

I hung up. "The others are with Japp and Rambo," I told Frans. "Arnold's sunbathing naked!"

Frans looked at the sky. "There would be no point doing it with clothes on. It is a free world."

I didn't want to get sucked into a discussion on the merits of the individual's choice within a state-imposed rule of law, nor to argue the toss over anything whatsoever being free in the materialistic, capitalistic, coporate-globalism western consumers found themselves enmeshed… so I let it ride and kept my gob shut. The Dutch – so bloody tolerant! In fact so *bloody* tolerant as to almost, but not quite, make them bloody intolerable!

"I doubt if we'll catch anything else today," I told Frans instead. "The whole place has become sex-obsessed lately!"

In retrospect, eight hours later, I would be proven to be right.

It was sometime after the eight hours had elapsed. Rambo and I sat in two of the three seats in the cab of his new Scudo van. The empty one had previously been occupied by Steffi and was vacant now because she had just nipped across the road to buy some chewing gum. We sat parked on double yellows and waited for her to return. It was six in the evening. The others were probably already at Rambo's house by now, getting changed in preparation for us to go out for a last drink together. Steffi had opted to return home with us after we had stopped fishing at Hamworthy while the other five had travelled back in Japp's MPV, which in itself was a little surprising. Maybe she had had enough of Arnold. Whatever. As I had sagely predicted no other chances had fallen to any of our rods and Frans' early morning fish had been the solitary success in the twenty-four hour session. It would have been nice for Japp to have pulled one out but it wasn't to be – the carp had had other things on their minds.

I had a humorous theory as to why the carp had started to spawn and it had nothing to do with the criteria I had considered earlier. I ran it up the flagpole to see what Rambo thought. "I reckon all the carp got turned on by watching Frans and the girls do their stuff!" I said to him. "That's what started off all the spawning, you know. It gave them the horn!"

Rambo gave me smile. "You could be right, boy. Who knows?"

The van went silent. I looked across the road to the small newsagents where Steffi had gone to buy her gum. "What do you know about absinthe?" I casually asked Rambo.

At that moment a group of six teenagers in hoodies and baseball hats crossed the road in front of the van. They were loud and yobbish, pushing and shoving each other and swearing at the top of their voices.

Rambo eyed them with cold disregard. "That it makes the heart grow fonder," he said with idle distraction.

"Very good," I said watching the group arrive at the far pavement. "You should write that one down and repeat it at your next dinner-party. There's nothing like a bit of droll adroitness to impress a hostess."

"And that was *nothing* like it," Rambo stated.

I laughed and continued to watch the group of teenagers. One of them spat on the pavement to try and make himself look tough. The group sauntered along towards the newsagents; they were all mouth and attitude. With fatalistic timing I saw Steffi emerge from the newsagents just as the group of yobs arrived directly outside the shop's entrance. Her effect on the group was instantaneous. They stopped dead in their tracks and leered at her and then surrounded her. The biggest one of them looked like he said something to her and I could see Steffi's mouth moving as she said something back. The big one tried to grab Steffi's bag only she wasn't having any of it and wrenched it from his grasp. I could see it was going to turn nasty very soon.

"Look out! Trouble!" I barked at Rambo who couldn't see what was happening because he was on the far driver's side and the shop was slightly to the rear of my passenger's window. "Those yobs are hassling Steffi."

Rambo was out of the van and around to my side by the time I was out the door and as we ran across the road I saw Steffi karate kick the biggest yob right in the mouth and then spin through three hundred and sixty degrees and – Eric Cantona style – flatten one of the others with a perfectly timed kick to the solar plexus. By the time we had reached the pavement she had downed two others with a karate chop to the windpipe and a swift right knee to the gonads. When Rambo decked the fifth one with a bone splintering straight right to the nose it almost seemed superfluous.

Not wanting to be left out I told the last one standing to "Fuck off out of it!" which unsurprisingly, he was only too glad to do.

"Christ!" I exclaimed surveying the carnage of the future manhood of our country (God help us!) "Are you okay?" I asked Steffi. It was a dumb-arse question because she was fine – it was the boys cuddling the pavement who were in trouble.

She waved a dismissive hand. "Sure. No vorries. Soze little shits don't bozzer me!"

By now three of the yobs had managed to stagger to their feet and, after staring at Steffi with wide-eyed incredulity and on seeing Rambo in close proximity, were getting the hell out of it as quick as they could. Rambo's victim was still out cold and the lad who had taken it in the nuts was writhing in agony in the foetus position. There was the small hope he could now never father children and pass on his moronic genes to yet another snot-nosed scumbag kid. My heart beat a little lighter at the prospect of it.

"Where did you learn to do *that*?" I asked again.

"My life has not been easy," Steffi said enigmatically whilst running her hand through the blonde hair sitting atop her pretty but slightly hard – bloody *well* hard as it turned out – face. Her blue eyes sparkled. I glanced over at Rambo who was staring at her with a look I had never seen on his face before. I think it was awe. I had never seen Rambo look at anyone with awe, a couple of carp possibly, but not a human being!

"You were *fantastic*, girl!" Rambo told her.

"Sank you." Steffi looked him up and down and then at the comatose one with the broken nose. "Nice punch, big guy."

I felt it was time for the mutual admiration party (street division) to move on. "Come on, let's go," I said, "before the law turns up or anyone else starts asking too many questions."

I have to admit the reasons for my saying this were hardly selfless. Although, as usual, I hadn't laid a single, aggressive finger on anyone, I was mindful of my black cloud scenario coming back and biting me in the arse. I definitely didn't want an officer of the law interrogating me! I might crack under the strain and admit to my one-way seventeen-bullet Glock gunfight. We ran across the road, jumped into the van, Rambo made heavy with his size thirteen – or whatever they were – army boots and the Scudo van screeched away.

"How did you learn to fight like that?" asked Rambo as he wrestled the van around a junction.

Steffi bit her bottom lip and seemed to be weighing something up in her mind. After a few seconds she answered. "Boz my parents ver killed in a car crash vhen I vas only fourteen," she began. "Sey had led a very Bohemian lifestyle, I sink ser vord is. I had no birs certificate, ser ausorities knew nozzing of me and I had no ozzer family. Ve lived many kilometres from ser nearest big city in a rented, remote house in ser country. I had to grow up very quickly, to look after myself. I had to live, to earn money to buy ser food, sey had left me vitt nozzing. I vas a young girl all on my own, very scared but also very determined. I did vott I could… used vott God had given me." Steffi stopped. She had tears trickling down her face and she wiped them away quickly as if our seeing them would indicate a weakness on her part. My heart reached out for her. What she was divulging was her deepest, darkest secret and I knew exactly what courage it took for her to tell us and how much the memory and recollection must be hurting. I could empathise. I had more than my fair share of dark secrets. Now composed she continued. "It vas horrible but I had no choice. I vas pretty and men liked me, so sey paid, and I survived."

I felt sick for her. Poor Steffi. Could this sort of thing still happen in a country as affluent as Germany? Was there nowhere the young, tragically orphaned Steffi could have turned? Was there nothing or no one who could have helped her and stopped her having to sell herself so very, very short? Apparently not. I looked at Rambo whose countenance was grim. He stared ahead at the road and the whiteness around his knuckles as he gripped the van's steering wheel told a little story of its own.

Steffi wiped away the last remaining patches of moisture on her face and continued. "East Germany vas a very poor country before ser unification. I did vott I had to do, learnt how to protect myself by learning karate and moved to ser Nezzerlands vhen I had saved enough money and vas old enough. My line of vork changed a little for ser better and I met Japp and it vas better still. It vas safer, a more controlled situation, it vas good money and I vas less at risk." Steffi stopped and considered what she had told us. "I'm sorry, I'm upset because of ser attack and ser sad memories."

"Don't you worry, girl. You let it all out. You're amongst friends here," said Rambo. He took his eyes off the road for a second and looked over at Steffi. "You know, my life story is a bit similar to yours, girl" he confided in her. "I lost both of my parents by the age of sixteen but I lost one of them before I was only two days old." Rambo shook his head slowly. "You see, I was such a big baby at birth my mum died because of it."

It was, literally, a killer of an opening statement. I had briefly heard Rambo's sad tale before, early on in Sophie's pregnancy I think it was, and to this day it was still the only part of his earlier past life he had ever told me about despite our long friendship.

Rambo continued. "What a thing to grow up with… killing your own mum! What a nightmare! She was in labour for such a long time giving birth to me complications set in and she died two days after she had safely delivered me into the world." Rambo's voice was hushed and almost drowned out by the drum of the van's engine. "She was the mother I never knew," he said disconsolately. "The only way I could find out what she looked like, what she *had* looked like, was through family photos. It creased me up as a kid I can tell you and it meant my dad had to bring me up all on his own. Sixteen years he looked after me with no help from anyone. It must have been hard for him what with working and running a home on his own. He never did go out with any other women, never made any effort at all. I don't think he ever truly got over losing mum. Then one night he went out for a ride on his motorbike, his only other real love, and never came back. Killed at the age of forty-two. Lost control on a corner and smashed headfirst into a lamppost. Killed instantly and with no insurance. Like I said, I was only sixteen the time. My world fell apart and to escape it I went straight into the army from school. Dad hadn't thought about money either, or providing something for me. We lived in a poxy little flat that he rented and he had no savings. I don't suppose he had planned on dieing. Who does at forty-two?" Rambo turned to Steffi again. As his eyes came off the road I inwardly prayed *we* wouldn't crash on a corner and end up wrapped around a lamppost. "That was all *I* could do to earn money," he told Steffi. "To go in the army. You see that's what nature had given *me*, a body as strong as an ox, a determination to never be poor again and an inbuilt ability to fight. Oh yes, I learnt to fight as well! To fight and to kill! There's no disgrace in using what you've been given, girl. No disgrace at all. You did what you had to do. Just as I did what I had to do."

To my surprise Rambo put out his left arm and wrapped it around Steffi's shoulder and pulled her close to him. Although technically it would have been impossible to have pulled away from it – I was all too familiar with the grizzly bear-like power of Rambo's physical shows of affection, playfulness, annoyance and such   it was obvious Steffi didn't want to. She snuggled up to him and we sat in silence for the rest of the journey back to Rambo's house.

Shamefully I have to own up to spending it sneaking furtive glances at the pair of them and wondering if Steffi was going to be The One – the one woman in the whole world who could capture Rambo's heart. Assuming the callous bastard had one that is. Going by his past track record of killing people legit, moving onto killing people for money, superseded by the indiscriminate selling of instruments of destruction which killed people in droves and finally – before retirement in a faked death – ripping off and killing the people to whom he had sold the instruments of destruction, made it look unlikely. Trouble was you could cite his paying off my mortgage whilst in prison, years of being my guardian angel *and* not killing me after having sex with his girlfriend to counterbalance the argument for a lack of a compassionate ticker. Maybe his heart hadn't been ensnared due to the age-old adage of not meeting Mrs Right. Was Mrs Right a slightly hard-faced blonde-haired, blue-eyed, East German porn actress who could fight like Bruce Lee? If she wasn't The One I doubted there ever would be one – a highly speculative thought but a genuine one nonetheless. In retrospect maybe Steffi had fancied Rambo from the start and I had read the signs wrong. Of all the mad combinations a couple could boast – porn star meets ex-army, ex-mercenary, ex-gun running, ex-arms dealing, camouflage-clad, murderous man-mountain who had faked his own death was surely one of the most outlandish – the two of them did have a common thread appertaining to similar past life experiences. A match made in heaven or one forged in the depths of hellish long-past experiences?

I could remember him saying in the past how he had shied away from loving someone because it made him vulnerable. His mantra had been to stay alone and to look after himself. He hadn't wanted any easy targets like a partner or children should some lumbering killer from his shady past come to try and get equal with him. He had even told me how some girlfriend of the past had said she was pregnant in order to trap him and tie him down and Rambo – in typical Rambo style – had fucked off out of it without a backwards glance. And yet it *had* happened, he had been vulnerable! Despite his solo, solitary, single-handed, separated, unescorted, on his own, no pillion passenger, Jack Jones philosophy – if it hadn't been for me – he would have been shot dead on the banks of Hamworthy Fisheries, the most violent carp fishery etc. etc. Okay, he had been distracted at the time by sex with Melina – but it hadn't been love. The electron microscope analysis, I quietly told myself, would be better spent concentrating on The Eye and not on The One. I tried to turn the dimmer switch on my brain down a few notches. Oh well, at least it was getting back into its old routine and edging out the video replay shit for which I was more than grateful.

I watched the scenery fly past the van's window and, due to the faulty dimmer switch – no surprise there – another feeling started to edge its way into my stupid head. Now Rambo had arched out his huge left arm and placed it around the willing Steffi, I had started to become a tad uncomfortable. The physical gap between her and me on the double seat and the close contact between her and Rambo spoke volumes. Phrases like 'three's a crowd', 'gooseberry' and 'spare prick at a wedding' shuffled through my consciousness. Although I would hesitate to use the word 'romance' – especially when applying it to the two people in question, who, through no fault of their own, had been guided by fate and survival instinct into becoming a blue movie actress and a killing machine – it was evident some kind of attraction at some sort of level seemed to be manifesting itself. My mind dithered and boggled. I felt I was in the way, conspicuously in the way, of them getting to know each other better. If the van had had a roof-rack I would have offered Rambo the opportunity to bungee-strap me to it so I could get out of their faces. The fresh air would have done me good as well and might have blown some of the crap out from between my ears.

That evening after we had drunk to the success of Hamworthy Fisheries' (the most seductive carp fishery etc. etc.) inaugural pornographic carp fishing movie, Japp's

MPV left for Holland. Inside it were Japp, Frans, Arnold, Nikki and Lola. Steffi stayed with Rambo and me. The two of them slept in the large double bed while I went back to the room Steffi had originally slept in. In the morning Rambo and I were up well before Steffi who was partaking of a lie-in. Over the breakfast table I knowingly asked him how the previous night had gone.

"We only slept together," Rambo said as he munched on his cornflakes.

"Yeah. I know. How did it go?" I asked again.

"Just slept," Rambo reiterated.

"Just slept?"

"Just slept."

"What no…?"

"No," Rambo confirmed.

"Oh!" I said a little mystified.

"Yeah," said Rambo. "She wouldn't let me have sex with her. Not on the first date."

"You should have got your camcorder out," I scoffed. "Then you might have fooled her into having your wicked way."

Rambo gave me a scary frown. "Easy, boy," he growled. "That's my girlfriend you're talking about."

Chapter 6

Rambo's white Scudo van flew along the A16 French autoroute with ease. He had chosen the JTD version with its 109 bhp output over the bog-standard engine for such an occasion – the occasion on this particular instant being a short blast across northern Europe to fish a venue in Holland. It was Friday morning and still disgustingly early despite the fact the trip down to Folkestone and the Channel Tunnel crossing had already been safely negotiated. I glanced at my watch. It was just after 5:30am and we had been up since two. I felt knackered. I closed my eyes and eased myself back into my seat thankful I didn't have to do anything because Rambo was driving and Steffi was navigating. I re-opened my eyes after a few minutes to see we had just passed the junction for the A25. Through the window I was listlessly peering, Dunkerque, the town of the British Army's World War II retreat, was only a few miles away northwards.

Travelling – the scourge of going anywhere to do anything.

I had heard people comment on how they enjoyed travelling, when they were going on holiday or partaking in an event, and how they thought it an integral and important part of the whole experience. Well, bollocks to that theory. The sooner some clever bastard invented a matter transporting device guaranteed to put you back together in the exact reverse order of how it took you apart the better in my opinion. Travel! You could poke it! Poke it on planes, trains and automobiles. Poke it even in something as opulent and mindlessly luxurious as Rambo's new van.

I resisted the temptation to ask Rambo 'are we there yet?' I wriggled my arse in an attempt to get comfortable and, having failed, pondered on the technical and logistical difficulties in shifting a van full of fishing tackle and three humans at atomic level by revolutionary transporting beam across Europe. I surmised that even if you could fathom it out, even if you could achieve an engineering miracle and pull off the implausible, something would still go wrong. Something crucial like your right arm being transposed with your left leg, or even worse, your boilies going off and their flavour being lost to the infinite ether. Even boilies as awesome and as hardy as the ones we had with us. For the record and for all you baitheads out there, we had Pup's latest air-dried specials – as rolled by Melloney – and fortified with his new 'killer' flavour. For the first time since before the TWTT we weren't going to be fishing exclusively on our trusted red bait and it left me feeling a little exposed and a little spooked.

Pup, however, had been adamant when Rambo and I had visited him at the house of a thousand rampant rampaging flavours. "This is the bait for you," he had enthused, holding up a handful of dirty brown boilies to my nose. "Smell them!"

I had smelt them, Rambo had smelt them and Pup had then dealt them to Melloney, who had looked at me as if I had committed a felony, when I had said, generally, they didn't do anything for me in terms sensory.

"Noooo!" Pup had exclaimed in the style of Luke Skywalker discovering Darth was his daddy. "You're *wrong*! They're the business!" Pup had said proudly. "It's the first bait Mel and I have developed together and they will be perfect for a trip overseas. I can make them rock hard, air-dried and they'll last a week, no sweat. Ha, no sweat! *Literally*, no sweat… *and* they'll catch. Trust me. Plus they're a *bottom* bait, a *bottom* bait as legendary as my pop-ups!" He had shuffled over really close to me, invading my personal space. "Look at the indentations," he had said grabbing a single boilie back from Melloney and holding it up to the light. "They're perfect in terms of regularity of size and placement on the boilie. It's a newly designed rolling table I've had made up and it's working a dream. These boilies will fire as straight as a die from catty and throwing stick *and* you'll haul like a pantechnicon." Pup had eased back away from me and had cuddled the boilie to his chest. "I'm afraid I can't tell you what's in the bait as far as ingredients go, *or* what the flavour is… just *trust* me! I know a good boilie when I see one," and he had lifted the boilie back up to his eye-line, "and I'm looking at one right now! This bait is *revolutionary*! If you put this bait out on the streets it would bring down the government!"

In spite of Pup's gusto I had spoken my mind rather truculently. "They don't smell *much*," I had told him, "and I can't really put my finger on what it is I *can* smell. Sort of, I don't know… I'm not too sure about them… what do you think Rambo?"

Rambo had been equally unsure. "Hmm, our red bait *is* very good," he grabbed the revolutionary, indented, dirty brown bottom bait boilie from Pup and sniffed it again. "Nope. I can't tell you what it smells of. It's a vaguely savoury, meaty type of smell…" Rambo had looked up at me, his face a picture of consternation and he had sniffed the revolutionary, indented, dirty brown bottom bait boilie again. "With a hint of fruit! A weird smell!"

"No one has *ever* fished with a bait like it," Pup had reiterated.

"I *like* our red bait," I had whinged. "I feel confident using it. I don't want to go away to a strange water and have to step back in time and start worrying whether my bait's any good. I've been there, done that, got the tee-shirt, got the sweatshirt *and* the fucking bandana!"

"I'll tell you what," Pup had said taking the boilie back from Rambo – imagine a mother taking back her newborn son from a mistrusted uncle and you'll get the picture. "I'll make you up fifty kilos of each and you fish one alongside the other and see which one comes out on top. I'll only charge you the same as your red bait and won't say *anything* about you not letting me into your syndicate this year!"

"They all re-joined!" I had said. "There was *nothing* I could do."

"Couldn't you have kicked one of them out for a rule transgression?" Pup had countered.

"Only if one of them had… but everyone behaved. To be honest as long as they can come up with the money I can see it being a case of 'dead man's shoes'."

Pup had flicked the boilie up and down repeatedly by thumb-springing it and catching it. "Then *kill* one of them!" he had said. He had probably been joking.

"You want to get in my syndicate, *you* kill one of the members… or get someone to kill one for you! Just don't let me find out you were behind it!" I could have added a murder on Hamworthy Fisheries, the finest carp fishery in Britain for *homicide*, was nothing particularly new. "You *are* next on the list, I promise," I had said by way of a sweetener.

Pup had smiled, and flicking the boilie right up to the ceiling, had said. "I *suppose* I can wait… why you can't make another place available and increase the membership by one, I'm not too sure!" Pup gave me a narrowed-eyed smirk. "Maybe one day you'll want something bad enough from me… *then* I'll have my lever! Now. What size shall I make them?"

I had ignored Pup's statement on leverage and considered the question. "Fourteen millimetres" I had ventured.

Pup had frowned. "I'll make them twenties. Right! Sorted! Come and have a look at my new Method mix."

I had gone to protest only to catch Rambo giving me a little shake of the head. Twenty millimetres it was! I had been outvoted! We had followed Pup out of the room into another and had been shown his new Method mix. Afterwards he had showed us his new rolling table and so it had gone on – we had been subjected to wave after wave of enthusiastic discussion and explanation concerning all things appertaining to, relevant to and central to bait. It appeared as if Melloney had even further galvanised his desire to create the world's finest carp fishing baits and if Pup and Melissa had been an unlikely pairing then Pup and her younger sister, Melloney, seemed even more so. Rambo and I had left with the fifty/fifty deal Pup had haggled us into taking and three days' later Rambo had picked up the hundred kilos of air-dried boilies. Two twenty-five kilo bags of the familiar red bait, two more twenty-five kilo bags of an unfamiliar dirty brown. In two sacks nestled round, red twenty-millimetre confidence – in the other the dirty brown unknown. Pup had an excellent track record but would the pair of us bottle it when it came to casting out? We *had* promised. Seeing as it was a three rod venue I had decided to go two red/one dirty brown until something else – i.e. results – told me different.

Oh, and one more thing had happened. Rambo and Melloney *hadn't* mentioned the fact they had had sex – which was a big relief for the three of us who knew. What the mind doesn't know the heart can't grieve over. (How grimly I had hung on to that little truism only to find out the mind has an uncanny knack of finding shit out!) Whatever, Pup didn't know and our boilie source was still on tap!

The road rushed beneath our wheels.

Our directions on the one hundred and eighty or so mile bum-numbing trip we had to make through mainland Europe was as follows; the A16 followed by the A18 towards Oostende, the A10 to Gent, the A14 to Antwerp, around the southern route of its ring road to eventually pick up the A21 proceeded by a very short section of the A67 towards Eindhoven. Before we hit Eindhoven we had been told to come off at junction 32 to Eersel and to follow the N397 to Westerhoven. Once we were in Westerhoven and we had phoned Japp on his mobile, he would come out and guide us to the venue. On the map it looked a piece of cake and we hoped to reach the venue near the small Dutch town of Westerhoven well before ten. If all went well and we didn't get lost and end up in Brussels, Amsterdam or Siberia we would rendezvous with Japp, Frans, the other Dutch anglers, and hopefully The Eye, in time for a midday bivvy set up. The fishing would then take us through to Monday morning when it would be time to pack up and – hooray! – drive all the way back.

I looked over at Rambo and Steffi. Now they *were* lovers. I could sense it in their interactions, their movements and their words. The tiny signs were there – subtle and intangible they were fragile pieces of human conditioning – yet to the lucid observer ones so easily read. I could read the subtle signs of love. The biggest one being when Steffi had brazenly told me at the breakfast table one morning how she had fucked Rambo's brains out all night. He had been so wasted from the night's activities he had stayed in bed until ten in the morning and she had decided to talk to me about it because – I don't know – the telly wasn't on, or the paperboy hadn't delivered the newspaper and she had nothing to occupy herself with. It had been a *bit* of a giveaway as far as subtle and intangible signs of human conditioning went and was distinctly *not* an insinuated or enigmatic one. More akin, I thought – going with the sign thing – to having a set of traffic lights eased up your rectum, ones only recently taken down on a frosty, freezing night. On the whole – rather than *up* your hole – I was pleased for the pair of them. Seeing as I was Rambo's best mate – one who was currently split from their long-term partner – I was glad to feel that the pleasure of seeing him happily involved with a woman was only *slightly* marred by the alienation I also felt due to their new partnership.

The van motored on, gobbling up the *kilometres* (when in Rome etc. etc.) on the relatively uncrowded tarmac. Despite my reservations concerning travelling, driving on the continent sure beat parking on the M25. The whole motoring experience abroad was altogether a much better deal than at home – for instance buying diesel was a lot less of a wallet-lightening event. Britain was too small with too many cars and was too expensive – that was the trouble. Our car population was similar to that of the French, yet France was four times the area of the British Isles and you didn't need to be Einstein to realise we were far more prone to gridlock because of traffic density. Another problem was the British government appeared to promote a culture of attack against the motorist without offering any other form of transport as a viable alternative. It seemed anxious to clobber the motorist with punitive taxes on fuel, outrageous parking costs, money-making Gatso speed cameras and in doing so managed to successfully disenchant the vast majority of law-abiding drivers.

I reckoned what we needed was a new expansionist policy – an empire perhaps – somewhere to enable us to spread out and ease the strain on our creaking green and pleasant land. Somewhere we could claw back a bit of territory and space and – while we were at it – somewhere we could dig up some cheap oil. Jocularly, I wondered why we hadn't thought of it earlier and then, equally jocularly, I remembered that, oh yeah, we used to rule a quarter of the Earth's surface! The trouble was the old colonial and empire days brought with them a lot of baggage – the baggage of guilt.

To some thinkers it almost seemed to be a sin to even mention Britain's past and its culture. And as for being a patriot, now you *were* asking for trouble. I daydreamed that if I ever got round to writing a series of books about my adventures, to go with the one I wrote in gulag-central, and was to put a St George's Cross on the front cover, I would probably be declared a racist by some liberal lefty elitist tosser.

A racist? I wondered if I was or if Rambo was. I was pretty tolerant – except when it came to assassins posing as asylum-seekers! If he hadn't been an assassin and had been an asylum seeker my initial reaction on seeing him would have still been one of hostility –although I would have obviously stopped short of pumping him full of bullets! But would it be so wrong for me to question why we, as a country, should financially support an outsider when we couldn't support our own people properly? Charity starting at home was hardly racism, more a common-sense point of view and one shared by many people.

In our defence – if accused of being xenophobic Little Englanders – Rambo was now sleeping with a German girlfriend and we were going fishing in Holland with Dutch friends. Why we were as good as genuine Europhiles. We had Euros in our pockets, could say 'hello' in French, ate Belgium chocolate, were driving an Italian van and had thrashed (cough!) two Austrian M & Ms in a carp fishing contest. The European dream was alive! One big happy family! One size fits all! One fucking great trough of taxpayer's money and enough highly paid un-elected bureaucrats to sink a committee-designed, bits-of-it-made-here, bits-of-it-made-there, multi-state-venture battleship!

On second thoughts maybe the European dream was a nightmare. On the positive side we weren't fighting wars in Europe any more; there was no need, we could piss off to the middle-east, team up with Captain America and do it over there! No point in shitting on your *own* doorstep and making a nasty mess!

Going back to baggage, the three occupants of the Italian van had more than their fair share of the personal variety. To boot: the spasmodically clairvoyant, adulterous, assassin-killing fishery owner; the orphaned, Eastern European, karate expert, porn star actress and the ex-army, ex-mercenary, ex-gun running, ex-arms dealing, camouflage-clad, murderous man-mountain who had faked his own death. You wouldn't want to meet *us* walking down a dark alley at night *or* round a dark gravel pit!

I looked out of the window and the road signs had turned to a rather bemusing bright orange from the previous blue. The place names looked very unfamiliar. We were in Belgium! No customs, no stopping, no nothing – Europe was our non-bordered playground! The only notification we received for crossing a border was a text message on our mobile phones welcoming us to our new network! One big happy family!

Not *all* families are happy. My one isn't at the moment but I was working on it. I had visited Sophie and Amy the day before we had left for Westerhoven. To begin with the atmosphere between Sophie and I had been as tense as had been the norm – only this time I had made a real effort to try and alter it. To put it in a succinct phrase, I had apologised. I had said sorry for what I had done with Rebecca and for what I had done with Melina. It had felt as if it was the right thing to do – it hadn't before – and the right time – ditto – to do it and so I had chomped on the bullet and had said the words. Remarkably Sophie had apologised back for sucking Hollywood's dick and swallowing the lot – not in so many words you understand – but we both knew what she was talking about. The atmosphere had lightened a little and I had told her why I was going to Holland.

I had told her I wasn't going just for the fishing on its own. I had told her about The Eye and how I hoped my meeting him would somehow pave my way to a plan of revenge – a plan of revenge to wipe the smile off Hollywood's handsome face. Sophie had been shocked, like I had, to hear of someone else who – allegedly – had the gift of foresight. She had been so shocked it had almost matched my state of stupefaction when she had whispered to me with quiet venom, "Do it, Matt. Get the bastard back for what he's turned me into and for what he's done to us."

Although unable to exactly pinpoint *what* Hollywood had turned Sophie into – in her own judgement – I knew instantly she hated it.

Grimly I had nodded. "I won't let you down, not like I have in the past. I'll pay the bastard back, I swear on Amy's life."

So no pressure there then!

It had been a defining moment, and one that had put our relationship in a seminal state. The road ahead to Getting-it-back-together City was undoubtedly long, arduous and difficult, but before there had seemed to be no road at all – and now it appeared there might be. Consequently we had sat down, she had made me a cuppa and I had cuddled Amy on my lap and we had talked. Talked properly for the first time since Hollywood's killer knock on the door. Feeling able to do so at last and by keeping a tight rein on my Hollywood/Sophie sexual liaison flashback facility, it had all flowed out of me. The shooting of Rambo's would-be assassin, the disposal of the body, my inability to sleep or eat, the horror video replays in my head, my weight loss and the pornographic carp fishing movie. (This had momentarily threatened to upset the applecart and paralyse my momentum until I had told her of Frans, Arnold, Japp, Steffi and how she and Rambo had, against all odds and all rationality, started to become a couple.) I had told her how I had gradually pulled through to something approaching normality – only approaching mind you, I didn't want to lose the sympathy vote altogether – and how my tenuous, crap, no-plan-at-all plan had come into fruition.

Sophie had been horrified at my grizzly seventeen bullet shooting and had shuddered at the details of how Rambo had disposed of the body and I the teeth. She had listened intently to my tale up to the point where I had walked through her door an hour and a half earlier. I think part of her had been impressed by how I had saved Rambo and I had felt her warm to me when I had apologised profusely over my inability to see Hollywood's revenge coming. "I can't control it, Sophie," I had told her. "It comes when it comes. I can't make it happen, as much as I wish I could."

I had told Sophie how – now I had a purpose and a sort of a plan – I had improved both mentally and physically of late. She had told me how something similar had happened to her. She too had managed to pull herself back from the brink and we had both commented on how we looked better physically than we had a month earlier. For Sophie's part it had been the desire to not let Amy suffer which had turned her around and had led her to start a rehabilitation of sorts. Inwardly I felt now we had conversed and aired a common desire in terms of retribution on Hollywood – the plan I had sworn on my only daughter's life to make happen – the future held hope. The future, or at least a small part of it, I was banking on The Eye being able to see.

"What do you want to do to him?" Sophie had asked enquiring of my bottom line philosophy on Hollywood. "How do you want to exact your revenge?"

"I honestly don't know," I had admitted. "Something horrible, I suppose. Ruin his syndicate or something, take something away from him he holds precious."

Yes, my precious, lop his dick off we will. I had thought of saying it, briefly, and had dismissed it as too near to the boner for Sophie's consumption – even if she had consumed it in the past.

By the time I had left her and Amy I had felt, and still did, much more positive. Hollywood had become our adversary, our sworn enemy and our foe – perhaps more truthfully our scapegoat. The bond between Sophie and myself, one tiny thread of it, reached out and re-tied itself. Now if only I could truly stop seeing the past and her with Hollywood and his goading smile and she could stop looking at my terrible indiscretions with Rebecca and Melina we could be onto something. I was under no preconception as to how feasible all this was going to be, but I was sure my revenge was the key. Make it happen and things could really progress – and I *had* promised.

The pressure of my promise had made me consider how Rambo was dealing with having a sexual relationship with a porn star actress. If I thought I was under the cosh promising to get even with Hollywood, then what sort of demands was *he* under every time they had a bit of nookie! I would have to ask. Not now, though, not while he was driving, I didn't want him blowing a gasket and forgetting to *tenez la droite* even if we were on a motorway.

The trick was, I guess, to convince yourself the past was gone, that it was totally unalterable and set in stone despite how painful the recollection of it might be. Whatever had gone had gone – and there was diddley squat you could do about it! It was a trick I had only just recently acquired the knack of doing successfully to a small degree. It was the *future* – alterable and not set in anything – that could help to alleviate the visions of the past. Supposedly. Well, it had bloody well better be! If not I was in more trouble than a drunk, comatose, horizontal, under-endowed Scotsman wearing a displaced kilt with nought else on underneath who was being attacked by a flock of early birds all keen on getting the worm! I prayed to the God I didn't believe in for the salvation of the future and it being a panacea for the past.

"You all right over there, boy?" Rambo asked. "You're very quiet."

"Just thinking, mate," I answered. "A bit of idle speculation to help pass the time. I was just..."

"That's all right, boy," Rambo said cutting me off. "I don't want to know what's rattling around in that barmy brain of yours, you keep it to yourself." Rambo lent forward a little and looked around Steffi. "But if you *do* get wind of anyone else trying to kill me, then you'd better let me know." The Glock magically appeared from out of nowhere and Rambo held it in one hand, the other gripping the steering wheel. "I'm tooled up and ready this time!" The look on my face must have spoken in volumes. "Steffi knows. I've told her *everything*," Rambo said casually.

"*Everything?*"

"I might have left *some* of it out," Rambo conceded. "There's too much to remember all of it... but I think I got the bulk of it."

"Fucking hell," I said sarcastically. "I'm surprised you've had the time. Steffi's only been with you a week!" I have to admit I was trying to conceal my reservations of Rambo telling our dark secrets to Steffi so readily. What *was* he playing at? The more I thought it through the less unsure I was as to how sensible he had been. New love or new lust had warped his sense of judgement!

Steffi laughed and gaffed me out of my considerations like a conger eel being hoicked violently unto a boat. "It's a crazy story, Matt. I vas not believing it to begin vitt, until Rambo said yes it's true. You don't haff to vorry, your secrets are safe vitt me." She cocked her head slightly to one side and gave me a glowing smile. "You are a very strange man vitt a very strange life. Mine is unusual but you, you are in ser different league."

As she was saying these words Rambo was winking at me behind her back and mouthing 'don't worry' and giving me a thumbs-up. He was up to something or nothing, I had no idea which, and I decided I would have to go with him and keep my gob shut until he and I were alone and he could explain fully.

As for Steffi's assertion that I was in ser different league, well, I was top three Premiership by anyone's reckoning. I gave her a smile and a shrug and went back to brooding and looking out the window. Rambo and Steffi started jabbering away to each other in hushed voices and I slipped back into my little self-absorbed world. I was an oddball; there was no denying it, short of actually doing so and therefore being in it – denial, that is. I mean, how many anglers would have spent the night before a trip abroad surfing the Internet after shoving the word 'absinthe' into a search engine? Not 'carp tactics for foreign waters', not 'crayfish', not 'poisson-chat', not 'brothels near Lac Cassien' and not 'complicated rigs for big, clever carp'. No sir, not me! 'Absinthe' had been the word entered into Google's search engine and it had been an enlightening evening.

Seeing as I had only known one solitary fact concerning absinthe – it was a drink, thank you, I'll pick up my prize as winner of Mastermind now – and Google had thrown up 2,700,689 pages, which would have taken me until I had keeled over from death by old age or repetitive information brain seizure to research thoroughly, it wasn't surprising the experience was enlightening. More like information overload and then some. Who the hell put all this stuff on the Internet? I had expected a few articles on absinthe, not the best part of three million pages! But it wasn't just absinthe it was *anything*! Absolutely anything from absinthe to zig-rig via magneto-hydrodynamics was there to be researched. Jimi Hendrix, Postman Pat, Attila the Hun, Scooby-Doo, Albert Einstein, worm breeding, Beano albums, boiler output capacities, DIY medical diagnosis, degree dissertations, bomb making, penis enlargement patches, cake recipes, how to convert old computer motherboards into Klingon-style cloaking devices, the world's biggest everything, the world's smallest everything, the world's longest everything, *everything's everything*, it was *all* there. The trivial, the historical, the banal, the scientific, the disgusting – the whole fucking lot – the whole sum of human achievement and vile degradation was available at the click of a mouse – *if* you could find it. And somebody somewhere – a multitude of somebodies somewhere – had posted all you could ever hope to know or find out in a lifetime. Amazing. There were even carp fishing forums where passionate, intelligent, articulate anglers could argue into the early hours of the morning on the subject of their choice – or slag each other off in glorious anonymity!

Anyway, back to the absinthe. The Eye's preferred tipple to induce him into foresight, which allowed him to predict where large carp might be caught and – if I could persuade him – where my plan might lead to, had an interesting history. According to my research absinthe had risen in popularity during the late 19th century when grape phylloxera had wiped out two-thirds of the vineyards in Europe. Only the very rich could afford wine and so 'la bourgeoisie' – artisans, tradesman and the like – had looked for an alternative and the alternative had been absinthe. Its popularity grew and the drink slotted in snugly alongside the emerging Bohemian culture due to its strong alcoholic content and its supposed mythical heightening of the senses. Who knows, perhaps Steffi's ancestors had been absinthe drinkers. Many leading lights of the time had drunk absinthe, among them Pablo call-me-the-cubism-kid Picasso, Vincent where's-my-ear-gone? Van Gogh, Oscar the-only-gay-in-the-village Wilde, the eminent short-arse Toulouse-Lautrec and Edgar Allen Poe, a morose fucker who wrote horror stories and died a clichéd death penniless and as an alcoholic at the tender age of forty, to name but a few. As Oscar might have said 'although Edgar was lying in the gutter he was looking at the stars, only trouble was the stupid bastard was face-down staring into his own vomit'. What a wit.

At the height of its favour the cocktail hour in the cafés of Paris became known as 'L'Heure Verte', *The Green Hour* and the drink itself was nicknamed 'La Fée Verte', *The Green Fairy*. (The only green fairy I could think of was Arjen Robben in a Hibernian shirt! All complaints from Chelsea fans, of over *two* years standing please, you bandwagon-jumping fools, to the following address…) The drink itself – surprise, surprise! – was coloured green. Even *I* had managed to suss that one out fairly quickly!

As absinthe rose in popularity to huge levels of consumption, public hysteria mounted over the drink's mysterious effects. This was primarily fuelled by concerns of alcoholism, alcoholic poisoning and the drink's effect on the human mind – a Swiss farmer called Jean Lanfray had supposedly run amok and shot his entire family while under the influence of the drink. Or alternatively the chocolate crop may have been poor, who knows? – and consequently public pressure caused the authorities to act and absinthe was banned in much of Europe. It appears looking back from a century on much of the hysteria and research into absinthe at the time was poor and other factors were significant in the supposed problems of absinthe drinking. Like getting pissed on other drinks for a start. Since then, due to a more objective approach, the original bans of the early 1900s have been lifted in some Western countries. Spain, Denmark, Andorra, Czech Republic and Portugal now produce it commercially and the legality of making absinthe (to strict procedures) has also been reaffirmed in most places except in the States. (We'll all laugh now at a country where the only criterion needed to get hold of a handgun is a pulse yet you *can't* buy a green drink!)

I discovered it was only as recently as 2004 that the Swiss parliament had lifted its ninety-six-year-old ban on absinthe, but then in a wild moment of insanity simultaneously placed one on cuckoo clocks and not taking sides in world wars (not true but the absinthe ban bit is). Absinthe is now generally not viewed as a controlled substance – like marijuana and cocaine – but is controlled as a food, hence the strict procedures over its making and how much of each ingredient can go in it.

This background stuff was all well and good but what I wanted to know was; why did the drink aid The Eye to see into the future? Apparently the original concoction was devised by a certain Dr. Ordinaire (made up name, got to be) in 1789. It was he who mixed the elixir of the plant wormwood (Artemisia Absinthium) with other herbs and alcohol to produce one hundred and thirty-six per cent proof rocket fuel. Through a series of bequeathed requests, sales and marriage the formula ended up with Henri-Louis Pernod and he made the first commercial example of absinthe.

However, it is the wormwood that gives the drink its alleged psychoactive effect. Wormwood has an essential oil – come on you bait buffs, you've heard of them! – containing the toxic chemical, thujone, and it is this when combined with ethanol (drinking alcohol) that gives the drink its psychoactive effect. Amongst all the reams of stuff I printed off there was much conjecture over how potent a psychoactive drug absinthe was, or is. The drink made today has levels of thujone considered safe (those damn strict procedures), but there are still a few rogue bootleg distillers, mainly in Switzerland, who were cranking out 'the good stuff' with a much higher level of thujone than was legal. In *Switzerland*! I mean how bizarre is that? I didn't think Switzerland had people who committed crime! I could imagine a few cases of excessive yodelling and being a smug git on skis, but bootlegging dodgy booze? Hallucinogenic booze! Shocking! Still, I was happy to wager The Eye was on the good stuff wherever it came from!

As with all fabled drug taking there was associated paraphernalia in taking the substance and drinking absinthe was no different as it had its own peculiar ritual. It was usually taken by slowly pouring iced water through a specially designed slotted spoon on which a cube of sugar had been placed. The cold water would dissolve the sugar and the solution would trickle into a glass containing neat absinthe. The sugar helped mask the absinthium and other oils and as the water and absinthe mixed it clouded to an opalescent white with a tint of green. This effect is called 'louche' and is where the essential oils are able to disperse in the water, usually at a ratio of five parts water to one part absinthe. Finally, when you got round to actually drinking the bloody stuff, I found out the taste of absinthe was similar to liquorice. Lovely!

As I had trawled through the mass of information the predominant thought I had had when Frans had first mentioned The Eye was still to the fore. Simply the single notion that whereas The Eye used absinthe to kick-start his trip to finding big carp, I had inadvertently kick-started my capture of Lac Fumant's big mirror by swallowing Wim's LSD tab. Talk about tripping to the carp fantastic. The similarities were stark and the questions had rushed forward to be answered. Did it happen every time he used absinthe? Had he 'seen' different events other than carp related ones? If so had he contacted or been contacted by the 'other side' – the netherworld inhabited by the ghosts of the dead? Had he 'seen' without the use of the drink as a psychic starter-motor like I had managed to do? Could he control and predict when it might happen if he had managed to by-pass the use of absinthe? Unfortunately from what little info I had gleaned from Frans the answer to all the questions seemed to be 'no'.

Most importantly, and the question at the top of the list, was would he be able to 'see' for me and help cement my plan of revenge into something more solid than my fluid, fluctuating, flaky, frivolous, formless, fickle, function-free fortuity-fest? And if he could, would he be arsed to do so? On those last two questions I had no idea as to the answer.

Once these concerns had been addressed more minor enquiries of the carp orientated type could be levelled at The Eye – ones such as what bait was he on when he was pursuing his absinthe-ascertained quarry and what rig did he use? And while we were on the subject, what bait would *I* be on, and would Pup's confidence in the revolutionary, indented, dirty brown bottom bait boilies be realised?

On a personal level, seeing as I had treated myself to a new Fox Euro Easy Dome – the old Apotheosis was getting a bit brittle and leaky – would I be able to set up my new bivvy without looking a right numpty? In the catalogue the set up time was given as three minutes. I mean, I *ask* you! *Three* poxy minutes! Did they give a Fox employee four hundred goes and then recorded his PB? A stiff zip on a cold morning with uncooperative fingers could take three minutes to undo – and that was the zip on the carrying holdall! Reading the instructions could take up to a week and digging out the bank level enough to take a big bivvy plus hard standing for your barrow even longer.

A cordial warning – bivvy manufacturers keep your set up times real!

Coincidentally Rambo also had a similar thing to cope with i.e. his two-man (read one man, one woman) Fox Continental Easy Dome, purchased to house him and Steffi over the long weekend. Set up time? Go on have a guess... Nope! *Four* minutes! Did that include getting planning permission from the local council to put it up? Four minutes! It would take four minutes just to put up the shelves and install the central heating. Ah, well, all these questions and more were waiting to be worked out when we had whizzed our way to Westerhoven.

I couldn't hold it any more. "Are we there yet?" I asked.

"No!" cried Steffi and Rambo in unison.

"Ve are close to Oostende, zough," Steffi informed me.

I lifted my chin in acknowledgement and glanced across at the map she had on her lap. For all my mental perambulation and time consuming introspection, we had moved a couple of measly inches along the A18. The next time I was on the Internet 'transportation of matter' was going to be the subject to get Googled. Inwardly I half expected someone might have the answer already but had been bought out by the oil companies – or murdered by them and the laboratory of the successful inventor torched to a cinder. Maybe I ought to check out 'conspiracy theories' and 'industrial espionage' while I was at it.

Chapter 7

Rambo was now having to *tenez la droite* for real. The motorway was behind us and the narrow single carriageway we found ourselves upon had snaked itself across the flat countryside for the last twenty minutes. Steffi, the proverbial rose between two thorns by way of the Scudo's three-seat arrangement, had ably navigated us to the junction where we had turned off the motorway. The driver's seat, so amply filled by my muscular, camouflaged-clad buddy, now hugged the kerb and it was I who was in the prime position to watch the oncoming traffic. Roundabouts as opposed to huge ring roads were now being taken in an awkward, more involving anti-clockwise direction and right-hand turns involved no crossing of traffic whereas left-hand ones did. Rambo's adjustment to this proper 'N' road continental driving, as opposed to the less trying motorway bombing, was made relatively easily thanks to him only having to follow the car in front. The car in front belonged to Japp, adult entertainment entrepreneur, brother of drug addict Wim and above all else a keen carp angler. We had made our connection with the orange-shirted Dutchman as planned and our venue was less than five minutes away. We were nearly there!

Excitement mounted in my stomach – either that or it was my bulging bladder begging for relief – and I waited for the first sight of our home for the weekend. Japp's equally orange indicator flicked on and off and we emulated his manoeuvre and turned off right into an even narrower road lined either side by flat-as-a-pancake fields. The fields had the beginnings of green shoots sprouting out from the rich coloured earth and I idly wondered what the crop was. In national stereotypical thinking mode I decided it was most likely marijuana, or if not, tulips. What did I know? I was unfamiliar with the rural and agricultural ways of heavily subsidised farming. For all I knew they could be genetically modified crops and the air I was breathing at this very moment was laden with carcinogenic spores and pollen, the causality of which deemed it possible I would struggle to see out another clean pair of pants – another clean pair of pants I had remembered to pack.

Japp turned left down a tarmac track and stopped at the five bar gate barring his progress. He jumped out of his car, waved to us and undid the padlock and chain securing the gate and pushed it open. Some things are constant and familiar even when abroad. Japp got back into his car and both vehicles drove through the gate. Although I was expecting Japp to stop and re-lock the padlock he didn't and we followed him further down the track until we reached a bungalow-sized blockwork building with a flat roof (shades of Hamworthy's functional wooden clubhouse) and a large hard standing area adjacent to it. We had arrived at the venue's car park and we were the only ones present.

At the furthest edge of the car park there were some trees and I guessed somewhere beyond those trees would lay the lake we were going to fish. Proving me correct Japp kept driving towards the trees and it wasn't until we were right up close to them that he stopped, turned off his engine and jumped out once again. Rambo killed the Scudo's diesel and I was out the passenger door quicker than an amphetamine-taking rat down a greased, vertical drainpipe. Whereas I was usually happy to slump into a chair when I had been on my feet all day, now I had been on my arse all day the reverse was the case. I stretched my legs and back luxuriously as I walked towards Japp and breathed in the pleasantly warm, possibly spore-laden carcinogenic air.

Philosophically speaking what else can you do in such an industrial and commercially tainted world? You've just got to chance it, haven't you? Keep on breathing, keep on eating and drinking and pray your contamination provokes only a slow burning form of cancer, hope the clean pants will easily come into play and the payback will only hit at around the age of eighty-nine by which time the chances are you'll have stopped worrying – or forgotten what it was you were worrying about.

"Nice spot!" I said to Japp in my best, forced Sussex 'old young'un' vernacular.

Japp gave me a withering look. "Yes, Matthew. It is very pleasant here. You wait till you see the lake. You won't have fished anywhere like it. Come. We can have a look before the others are starting to arrive."

I went back to Rambo and Steffi who were still in the van and opened Rambo's door. I saw Rambo's hand move off Steffi's thigh as I did so. "We're going to take a quick shufti at the lake before the others arrive. You coming?"

Rambo nodded eagerly. "Too right, boy." Steffi nodded as well.

The three of us caught up with Japp and he led us through the trees without saying another word. Once we had passed the trees there was a thirty-yard wide band of scrubby grass, which at its edge dropped away steeply to a depth of four or five feet to what I can only describe as a mini beach – a shoreline of greyish sand onto which the gin-clear water of the lake lapped.

We all jumped down onto the sand and stared across the lake. It was big. At least two to three times as big as Hamworthy and although I had fished enough 'three acre' day ticket venues in the past which had turned out to be the size of a couple of tennis courts, this had to be sixty to seventy acres' worth of water.

I bent down and scooped up the sand. I rubbed it between my thumb and index finger. It was very coarse-grained and when it was dry I imagined it would have been virtually white. Looking out into the margins the water was crystal clear and I could see the sand perfectly until it dropped into a blue mass as the water increased in depth. Even if the place was chock-a-block with feeding frenzied carp, there was no way this water was ever going to be anything but dead clear.

"Is it all sand?" I asked Japp.

Japp waved an expansive hand across the horizon. "All sand. Every centimetre is sand."

I was looking at the blue mass only a few rod lengths out. "Is it deep?"

"Very. You see here?" said Japp pointing to where I had been looking. "Eight metres. In the middle, in some places, fourteen and fifteen metres."

"You could still make a hell of a lot of egg timers from what's left," I said.

Japp laughed. "The sand is too big for that, I think, Matthew."

"But it was dug out for a reason?" Rambo said. "It must have been dug out to be so deep."

"Sure," said Japp. "It really is no different from your gravel pit, Matthew, only instead of gravel it is sand. Sand dug out for the making of roads and other works."

I nodded and soaked in the panorama. The lake was virtually a rounded-off oblong, had no islands and with no defining features other than on the left-hand side at halfway distance was a point jutting out into the lake by fifty to sixty yards. It was impossible to tell how much width this spit of land had to it because it was reed-lined, as were other areas of the margins – only they were the exception rather than the norm. More typically in other areas of the lake there were mature trees much closer to the water's edge than in the swim where we were now standing. It looked as if the trees were within a yard or two of the drop off that led down to the sand. The drop off itself was visible in all the areas of the lake I could see from where I was standing and it looked fairly uniform at four or five feet. However, this did mean none of the trees were close enough to the water's edge to create a margin feature. The only feature around the edges was the patchy reeds and if the water was as shallow by these reeds and stretched out as far as it did where I was now standing, it would be physically impossible for any carp to get into them. My first impression, although the lake looked nice and was unusual in being all sand was it was big, by my standards, featureless as such, intimidating and *hard*. I couldn't see us bagging up – Pup's supersonic boilie(?) or not. *One* fish from the weekend would be a result from my way of thinking.

"What's the stock like?" I enquired, praying Japp didn't say there were six fish but they *were* all forties.

"There are a lot of carp in here," he started, which I mentally marked down as promising, "*but* there is also a lot of water for them to hide in. If you get in a good swim and fish well I would expect you to catch," Japp wobbled his head from side to side like a wonky seesaw, "three or four fish. It isn't as hard as it looks *but...*" Japp breathed in deeply (he would be dead by the time he was eighty-four if he wasn't careful) "there *are* a lot of bream in here." He pointed a finger at the three of us. "*Don't* fish with pellets!" he warned.

The dreaded 'buts', (plural) had been laid on us. I looked uneasily out of the corner of my eye at Rambo whose jaw was clamped shut and whose lips were thin and straight. They started to curl upwards. "Good job we're on a hundred kilos of rock-hard twenty-millers, then!" he said laughing.

Rambo was spot on. Good old Pup, I thought, my confidence rising slightly. If it had been left to me I would have had fourteen millimetre baits only he had insisted on us going bigger. Big enough, I hoped, to stop the bream gobbling up our bait. As I considered our good fortune on the metric boilie front I laughed inwardly at our crazy mixture of carp fishing measurements. Boilie size – millimetres. Boilie buying weights – kilos. Line breaking strain – pounds. Line diameter – millimetres. Line spools – mainly metres. Fish weight – pounds and ounces. Water size – acres. Casting distances – yards. Hooklengths – inches. Rod lengths – feet and inches. Rod test curves – pounds. Rod rings – millimetres. Flavours – millilitres. Leads – ounces. What was that all about? I had no idea and now I had thought of it I wished I hadn't.

"Come and have a look at your swim," said Japp thankfully distracting me.

"The swims are all sorted?" I asked with a tinge of astonishment.

Japp nodded. "Yes, Matthew. We have ten other anglers coming plus you two and me. Thirteen in all, so not so many for such a big water. We have already agreed amongst ourselves where we will fish and I have chosen a swim for you and Rambo."

I was mightily impressed with this organisation and the fact no one had taken to issuing a back street beating or a date in court to sort out the perennial problem of who was fishing where. I was also thinking about something even more important – to *me*.

"The Eye is *definitely* coming?" I blurted.

Japp eyes glittered. "Yes. Yes he is. We are lucky. He has only lately become an acquaintance of Frans and myself and I am looking forward to seeing him fish again. He is an unusual person."

I flicked a tongue tip over my top lip and said as easily as I could. "That's great, I wanted to meet him too." What I didn't add was 'because I'm relying, some might say rather stupidly, on him supplying me with a small chunk of the future I can then use, in an unspecified and as yet unknown manner, to wipe the smile of the face of a certain person I detest'.

Japp also didn't add. 'Personally, Matthew, I think you would be better off using a baseball bat rather than a piece of the future. It is more solid. The future, especially in the purely clairvoyant format, is rather will-o-the-wisp whereas a *baseball bat…* well, you can bludgeon the fuck out of someone with a *baseball bat*'. He slipped out of character towards the end – my input I'm afraid.

"Actually I think it is *him* who is really wanting to meet *you*," Japp did say.

"Eh?" I answered.

"Yes," assured Japp. "When I told him how you have caught a fish of nearly thirty kilos in *England* he was impressed. And when I told him how you caught the big mirror at Lac Fumant, how you told us where it would be caught, how big it would be and in what weather, he was very, *very* impressed. Especially when I told him *why* you were able to do this remarkable thing."

"Wim's LSD tab?"

Japp nodded. "You two are very alike. That is why he wanted to fish near to you," Japp paused. "Although I think The Eye is more eccentric than you. You English have an expression for it, I think." Japp paused again. And stayed paused.

"Well?" I enquired, as it seemed Japp needed a little push – like when your Scalextric car used to get stuck on the duff bit of track.

Japp breathed in deeply once again. I downgraded his life expectancy to death in his seventies! "I have been told by some he is a nutter. Having met him once… I would agree. Others have gone so far to say he *is* a fucking nutter. I do not know him well enough to say whether I think he is so bad…" Both mine, Rambo and Steffi's eyes burned into Japp demanding a subjective opinion. Japp quickly wilted under the onslaught. "Okay," he said resignedly. "He is a fucking nutter… or he sounds like one. You will find out what he is like in real life soon and you will have the best chance to find out if you agree because he wanted to fish near to you. I guessed you would also want to be near to Rambo and Steffi so you four are going to fish on the point. Let us go and look."

My heart surged with excitement and intrigue. I love it when a plan comes together. Okay, so it was a plan coming together that might help me get a plan to come together – fair point – but whatever way you looked at it, it was good news. *Excellent* news. Rambo raised his eyebrows at me to show he understood the implications of what Japp had said and we followed him off to the point – the swim you would obviously pick as an angler new to the water with no knowledge other than what was set before your eyes – after I'd had a quick pee against one of the previously passed trees. As I whizzed up the tree I wondered if The Eye's brain was more addled than mine or whether Japp was just being polite. Either way it didn't matter a jot if The Eye could come up trumps on the future. It was the old fine line between genius and madness. 'You don't have to be mad to fish the point swim… but it does help!' to paraphrase the corny office wall slogan.

After a ten-minute walk we arrived at the point and I saw it was even larger than I had previously thought. It stuck out into the lake a good seventy yards, maybe a bit more, and despite narrowing slightly at its most extreme end was forty yards in width. There were three clear swims, one at the furthest end, the very tip of the point and two others thirty yards back from the tip almost back to back – one facing east and one facing west. The tip end was a south facing swim and the one to soak up the sun. Arnold would definitely have liked it. All three swims had been cut out of reed-lined margins, the depth of which was three yards. The openings were nice and discreet because whoever had cut them had refused to get carried away with a scythe and had kept them to an environmentally and aesthetically pleasing three to four yards in width. It was easy enough to see the depth of the water to several yards past the reed line and it was shallow, not even a foot, and as I had suspected. The reeds were not going to feature as a feature. Once past the shallow water the lake turned deep blue just as it had at the original spot where we had looked at it. Seven metres of water Japp told us, and both Rambo and I had converted it into an approximate twenty-one foot of water – like you do.

"Aren't there *any* shallower areas, apart from the edges?" Rambo asked with a tiny hint of desperation.

"No," said Japp emphatically. "Not on this side. On the far side there are some places where the shallow edge goes out much further and reaches maybe two metres in depth. It does produce fish, usually at night. In my opinion to have one of those swims is perhaps the best on the lake because you have a better choice of depth – two metres and eight metres. Here you have seven metres and if you can cast far enough from the furthest point, nine metres. The deepest point is in the middle up at the far end, a hundred metres from the bank."

"What tactics do you reckon on?" I asked. I wasn't proud. Local knowledge is king.

"Beds of baits will sometimes work," Japp informed us. "Fishing for one bite at a time with much smaller amounts is also a good idea to try. No pellets, otherwise you will catch lots of bream as I have in the past," Japp pulled a face. "Although you will probably still catch them in any case, even with boilies." Japp rubbed his chin with the inside of his hand. "Bright single baits will sometimes work as will a mid-water pop-up." A big grin spread across Japp's face. "I can't think of any more methods apart from the Method but the bream again, you see!"

I gave Rambo a rueful smile. "Try everything, mate. That's the answer!"

"I think you're right, boy," he agreed.

Japp looked a bit sheepish. "I am sorry I cannot help more. There is no method that works all the time on here, you must try to find what will work for this session."

"No worries, Japp. We know what you mean," I assured him.

"Just do not be worried of the depth," Japp stressed. "These fish feed in eight metres of water no problem, they are used to it. It is their home. Remember, a twenty-five kilo carp is a possibility from here."

Twenty-five times two equals fifty. Fifty pounds – right remember that – twenty-five times point two is five, add five to the number I just worked out – fifty – that make fifty-five. Fifty-five pounds. Got it! My brain could understand fifty-five pounds as a fish weight but not twenty-five kilos, yet I was happy knowing I had fifty kilos of boilies to dispose of. Flipping heck! I wished I had never got tangled up in the imperial/metric dilemma.

"Nice fish," I said with authority even if I could have faked it and guessed it without the mental arithmetic. You know 'big' but not exactly sure *how* big.

"Sure," agreed Japp. "And if you drink absinthe with The Eye maybe you will see where to catch it!"

"A bloody lot of good that'll do if I see the fish in two metres of water!" I joked.

Japp's face dropped a little with a touch of hurt. "I thought these three swims would be the best taking all things into mind..." he started.

I walked to him and grabbed him round the shoulder. "Hey, Japp. I'm only *joking*, mate! These swims are *great* and I really *did* want to fish with The Eye and Rambo as well. Thanks for sorting it out. We appreciate it. We're just pleased to be here, aren't we Rambo?"

"Absolutely, boy. Spot on," Rambo confirmed giving Japp a wink.

Japp looked relieved. "That is good... I was worried for a second... Do you want to start to carry your gear round?"

"Carry it! Aren't we having it dropped off by helicopter?" I exclaimed.

"This isn't Hamworthy Fisheries, Matthew. There is no track for a car, let alone a landing place for a helicopter. You have to carry your gear."

Two hours later, when I had finally managed to bump all my stuff round, I was even more acutely aware of the fact – Hamworthy Fisheries, the finest carp fishery in Britain, for not dieing from a tackle-carrying related heart attack. Why the fuck hadn't I invested in a motorised barrow as well as a new bivvy?

"I'm knackered," I moaned to Rambo as I fell into my stalker chair, the one designated as my sitting-outside-the-bivvy-in-the-sun-during-the-day chair.

Rambo, whose face reflected the gut-busting effort involved in shifting what felt like four tons of fishing tackle over three-quarters of a mile in twenty-five degree heat by leaking a solitary bead of sweat on his forehead, laughed disparagingly. "Three hours earlier you couldn't wait to get on your feet, now you're collapsing unto a chair."

"Times change," I answered flippantly.

Rambo laughed again and wandered off to his east-facing swim to put the finishing touches to his set-up while I looked over the water that was 'mine' from my west facing one. We had left the tip of the point to The Eye on Japp's advice (he liked the swim) although the great soothsayer had yet to arrive. I could now see and had seen several other anglers starting to lug their stuff to their respective swims and I didn't envy them one bit. I stretched my legs out and rested. Another half an hour and then I would start to get the rods sorted. There was no rush, we were all going to meet up at the blockwork building for introductions at around two and only after we had concluded would the fishing start.

I cocked my head back to look proudly at my new bivvy. I had managed to negotiate my virginity at putting up the Euro Dome without ripping it, breaking a pole, ruining it in some other manner or pushing one of its pegs through a major artery. 'New-bivvy-numptyism' had been avoided and I was glad of it. The spider leg-like 'click-in' poles of the Euro Dome were unusual in design but had been easy to erect (but *not* in three minutes!) although like all new bivvies the thought of ever packing it away as neatly as it had come out of the original bag seemed a distant prospect. (I reckon all the tackle companies use origami experts to pack their stuff.) Rambo had succeeded likewise with his new, similarly designed, bivvy/marquee Continental Easy Dome – it was much bigger than mine (oo-er missus) – and with no little help from the willing Steffi. As well as helping him set up their temporary home – a poignant moment I can tell you – she had also carried a fair amount of tackle and had proved herself to be well fit in the athletic prowess sense of the word. She had easily kept up with Rambo and like him didn't seem to have suffered any energy drain whatsoever. Yours truly, on the other hand, was shot away – I had to face it, I would never get to play the alkaline Duracell Bunny and was destined forever to be a clapped out zinc chloride.

Going back to my comment to Rambo, times *do* change all right and his life looked to have been turned on its head by Steffi. To be honest I had never seen Rambo behave so oddly – so oddly for *him*. When I had spotted the pair of them walking back hand in hand to the Scudo to pick up another ton of tackle each, I knew life was never going to be quite the same again. Rambo had found The One and I had found The Eye – *if* the bastard ever turned up. I wondered how long the pair of them would want me kicking around Rambo's house cramping their style. I felt sure Steffi would be moving in period and Japp would be looking for a new female porn actress. The prospect of me playing gooseberry to the pair of them didn't exactly enthral me or fill me full of unbridled happiness. If I did move out where would I go? Where would I live? There was no way I was going back to live with my parents.

Briefly I imagined myself dying old, alone and in a bivvy with rods uncast for the last five years due to crippling arthritis. Sod that! A little part of me desperately regretted the actions that had contributed to my current single status – if only I had shown more commitment to Sophie when it had really mattered. The thrill of illicit sex with others had long since faded and all that was left for me now were the dire consequences.

If Rambo had recoiled from commitment in the past and had been scared of the vulnerability he might feel should he ever love another person, then it appeared as if Steffi was the ideal girl. Like Rambo she had fought and learnt to fend for herself from a tender age and the school of hard knocks she had attended had moulded her into an independent woman who could beat up a group of yobbos, cart heavy fishing tackle for miles without complaint, give perfect head *and* do the splits. No wonder Rambo had fallen for her – she seemed perfect. *If* you could get your head around dealing with her porn actress past. Evidently it seemed he was more than man enough to cope. I considered whether in a few hours' time she would be getting *her* head around his wedding tackle after having carried his fishing tackle. Of course she would! On the whole I would have to say she was the perfect woman for him. As it said in the corny old country and western song 'There's someone for ev'ryone and Rambo's love was Steffi, In her arms he was always provin' he was a man, One day while he was fishin' the Yobbo boys came callin', They took turns at Steffi... They had the shit knocked out of them'. (Kenny Rogers: Coward of the County, my Mum bought it, that's how I know the song... honest.)

Steffi *was* tough. She might even be able to beat up Rambo – now *there* was a thought – possibly in the voluptuous style of a James Bond female adversary, you know, crushing your windpipe with a pair of velvet-skinned, muscular, cellulite-free bare thighs *and* mocking your pathetic attempts at escape in an East European accent. Shit! I hoped Steffi wasn't a plant, a spy, and an accomplice in Hollywood's Machiavellian plot Part II. A hot sweat overcame me for a brief second and I was transported back to Hollywood's orgasmic smile of delight as Sophie played out her wicked act of betrayal. Please God, no! I wriggled my shoulders in a horror-scene shudder and tried to get a grip on myself.

And Japp reckoned The *Eye* was a fucking nutter! Look under the surface of my calm, (?) normal (??) exterior and have a look at the mess *I'm* in! Well, at least it was in less of a mess than previously now I had a plan to sort it – *if* the fucking nutter turned up. If he didn't I was in serious trouble and my hopes were as sunk as a rowing boat hit by an Exocet, as sunk as a 3AAA waggler loaded with a 6oz bomb, as sunk as a Mafia corpse, as sunk as a very heavy dense thing chucked into the Mariana Trench – the bit called Challenger Deep.

I forcefully turned my attention to things more carp orientated. The nearest swim back down the lake from me was well over two hundred yards away. Even if I launched one straight back down the lake with the very best – read 'very average' – cast I could muster, I wasn't going to be interfering with anyone. In my mind I was going to marker float three distinct areas and fish three different bait application ideas on each one until one proved better, if indeed it would, than the others. A PVA bag to a shortish range mark, a big bed at middle distance to which I could easily catapult the twenty millimetre boilies – I reckoned this to be seventy yards out – and a single hookbait attack on maximum range, say ninety to one hundred yards. I hadn't decided which bait was going to be used in which circumstance – I was waiting for inspiration – probably in the form of last minute panic.

I had to admit to being slightly intrigued as to what Pup had put into his 'revolutionary' boilie. It certainly didn't look revolutionary, far from it, and it didn't smell revolutionary – what ever a revolution smelt like – just odd. Pointedly I reminded myself how Pup *did* have a great track record, how he had proved himself to be sage on the matter of boilie size and how you bet with gross folly against the boiliemeister on his own domain. You never know, I told myself, I might even push the boat out, go in for a penny in for a pound, take a chance and have a punt on fishing *two* rods on the dirty brown bait. Carp fishing – talk about living on the cutting edge of decision making!

I mulled it over. Yes! Decision made. *Two* rods on the revolutionary, indented, dirty brown bottom bait boilie it was – the single hookbait and the PVA bag attack! This would be my starting off policy until fish movement, fish action, successful tactic discovered by me – or by others and then related to me – or complete desperation forced me to do otherwise. The third or was I got pissed out of my tiny little mind on absinthe, sussed the entire universe and bagged-up big time. I looked up at the vacant south facing point swim. Where in damnation *was* The Eye?

Chapter 8

I zipped up the mosquito door on the Euro Dome and took my trainers off. I eased all the laces out of their eyeholes, yanked up the tongues of both shoes so they remained slack and were therefore easy to put on in an emergency – i.e. a take – and tied a loose bow in them. This action was purely force of habit and I had to remind myself more suitable footwear was needed because on this venue the trainers were redundant due to the shallow water in front of my swim. I would need wellies to wade out and net a carp successfully should I hook one – only not *too* far otherwise I would be stepping off into the deep end and seven metres of gin clear water – and it was my trusty ancient black ones I put at the zip end of the mozzie door. With myself all set on the run-in-the-middle-of-the-night front I embedded myself into my sleeping bag.

The very early start, the journey, lugging all my stuff from car park to swim and then helping lug all The Eye's stuff around to the point had finished me off. I needed some kip! What I *didn't* need was a night's worth of attention from a shoal of bream with abnormally large, twenty millimetre boilie capacity gobs. Snot City at two in the morning was a grim prospect. I snuggled down and my mind – after having been briefly diverted to the smile on Hollywood's face and the hideous exit wound to the head of Rambo's would-be assassin – fixed on The Eye. He had finally arrived – fashionably late – when we had gone back to the blockwork building to meet up and be introduced to the other anglers.

The predominantly Dutch group of carpers were a nice bunch of guys and mine and Rambo's friendship with Japp and Frans meant we were immediately treated as if we were long-lost pals. It had been handshakes all round coupled with polite, mainly carp fishing orientated chit-chat. I had mentally winced at all the new names – all the new foreign names – needing to be associated to new faces to provide decent protocol. In the end I had given up knowing full well I would never remember even half the names and would have to plead forgiveness. Consequently I had settled for enthusiastic conversation where it had been possible and where it had been foiled by language difficulties either Japp or Frans had acted as translators once summoned.

Frans had been especially pleased to see both of us, and it was he who had given Rambo and me – rather theatrically and definitely with the intention of playing to the gallery – a copy each of the world's first pornographic carp fishing DVD. Subtly entitled 'Lakeside Pleasure', the sleeve notes briefly described how 'carp angler Frans catches more than he bargained for on a beautiful lake where the local girls are more interested in high energy sex than taking in the view'. On the front cover was a photo of Frans, Nikki, Lola and Steffi seductively draped on or near to the

Wychwood Superlight 3 leg bedchair set against a backdrop of bivvy and other carping paraphernalia. Now there *was* a cover to grab the fishing/non-fishing public's attention! If I had mused about putting a St George's Cross on the front of a book should I ever write my life story, I further theorised I might even put a picture of a beautiful girl surrounded by tackle on another one! A good selling point, although I doubted it could be quite as suggestive as Japp's version.

On the inside of the DVD's jewel case tucked away in the small print of the credits both Rambo and I got a mention: 'Special thanks to Matt and Rambo for all their help' it said. My heart had burst with pride – *that* was something to be proud of, something to show the grandchildren and impress the neighbours at dinner parties! Of course, if I had been on the front waving my todger like a lasso and had commanded a starring role, it would have made even *more* of an impression – but beggars (read; average sized dick anglers) can't be choosers!

The sight of the DVD had brought catcalls of delight from the other anglers and a ripple of lusty applause. Frans had bowed in mock appreciation whereas my first reaction had been to glance at Steffi who was standing alongside Rambo. Had any of the others seen the DVD and therefore *her* in action? Or were most of them still to realise she was one of the cast? There was no ambiguity as to whether she was in it or not due to the cover and Frans might have showed a fair few of them already – all that was needed was an observant eye. Most likely he had already told them a female member of the cast was going to be present over the weekend. How awkward for her and typically I had wondered how she had felt being so close to her public. Normally she would have been a detached fantasy figure to all who had seen the film, but here she was now, in the flesh, in a carp fishing situation – in the very scenario covered by the DVD. Reality and fantasy had blurred together and maybe a few of the anglers might be hopeful she would act as she had in the DVD and brighten up their lives considerably. If they had they were going to be disappointed. I had just hoped they would keep very discreet any secret desires they might harbour and control how they acted and treated Steffi. Otherwise I could see someone ending up with a knuckle sandwich or a karate chop to the windpipe. Japp wasn't stupid, I had told myself, he would have told them the score with Steffi and Rambo – luckily it had appeared to be the case.

You had to ask, or I had, what had gone through Rambo's mind at that juncture – had he thought about the possibility of the others having seen her in all her glory? Even worse – when he had shaken Frans' hand a few minutes earlier – there was a man who had recently done just about everything there was to do in a sexual context with his girlfriend. To me the whole situation had seemed incredibly awkward and fraught with problems, but if Rambo and Steffi had been embarrassed, or had felt a little indifferent concerning the situation neither of them had shown it and thankfully all had gone swimmingly. I worry too much at times.

The group of anglers clearly knew each other very well, although I had the impression it was a pleasant rarity for them all to congregate and fish a venue simultaneously. Accordingly the atmosphere was relaxed, friendly and many anglers had seemed to have much catching up to do over who had been doing much catching. Once I had relaxed over my concerns for Rambo and Steffi's feelings, I had to admit it felt good to be amongst like-minded individuals and keen, decent carp anglers. The fishing time in front of us looked as if it was going to be a pleasant experience even if fish might be hard to come by. The prospect had warmed me and when I had cast my mind back to my gruelling winter on Hamworthy with all its attendant troubles, I had felt even perkier. I had clawed my way back from the depths of despair and thirty-eight consecutive blanks to catch and I was determined to do the same here.

I had to try and see through my rather – objectively analysed – rash promise of revenge I had vowed to Sophie as well. If I could pull it off things could get even better still and my worries over rattling around Rambo's house might diminish, nay, disappear! You see there was the possibility, the *slight* possibility, I could go back and live with Sophie and Amy. Did I want to? Could I cope? I wasn't one hundred per cent sure but superficially the answer seemed 'yes'. If I could pull off a suitable revenge I might be able to go back and forgive her – provided she would forgive me and *let* me go back! I had resolved to do my bit as I had stood in the car park and see how things faired. Another tiny step in the healing process had dropped into place aided and abetted by a carp fishing session abroad.

If Rambo and I had been treated as long-lost friends then The Eye, after hammering into the car park, skidding to a sideways halt and leaping from his car, had been greeted as a deity. Rather disturbingly he had immediately walked directly over to me before greeting anyone else – after getting a surreptitious nod from Japp to point out which one I was – and had kissed me forcefully on the forehead. This action had cause even more catcalling than the DVD and had provoked howls of laughter.

"Man… at last!" he had gasped as he held my head between the palms of his two hands. "A kindred spirit."

I had been touched in a rather embarrassed this-really-is-not-a-gay-thing-at-all way and had promptly empathised with the wide-eyed madman standing before me. The Eye was thin, of medium height, had an electric shock of gravity-defying, spiky, sun-bleached blond hair, (not dissimilar to Steffi's) murderous aqua-blue eyes (as opposed to Steffi's penetrating ones) – which contrasted nicely with the bloodshot white parts – and a clichéd vein permanently throbbing at both temples. On his left wrist he had platted three or four lengths of green rig tube and knotted them together to make a friendship band. Around his neck had hung a small, green plastic coated pendant lead suspended on green rig tube. Green for absinthe, I thought? All he had needed to complete a full set of ethnic carp tackle jewellery was a very politically incorrect pencil marker float stuck through his nose. Regardless of his superficial adornments – as someone once said some people would hang a dug turd around their neck if it were made of gold – the empathy had come from seeing a version of my earlier self. One I was only very slowly recovering from, thus enabling me to blossom into a slightly less disturbed version. The Eye was still at the stage I had been a month or so earlier and it was clear the gift of foresight lay as heavy on The Eye as it did on myself.

As well as The Eye's disturbing physical appearance and odd line in jewellery his movements had been jerky and rushed, particularly his bird-like head movements, and his speech was quick, text like in form and prone to leaping off at tangents in mid-sentence. In short any characteristic you could lay at the door of a person aspiring to be a professional, corporate sponsored fucking nutter, The Eye had it in spades.

"We'll speak, man. We've words to swap," The Eye had told me before reluctantly moving off to meet the rest of his posse. What I hadn't realised at the time was we would make a start at word swapping while I had helped him bump his tackle round to the point swim. After he had chatted to his buddies he had asked me to help him and considering what I was going to ask *him* to do for *me*, I could hardly decline… and hadn't.

It was during the knackering process of shifting his stuff – it was my *second* load – when I had gleaned some facts about him. The Eye, born of a Dutch mother, sired by – well, he wasn't *too* sure, (nor was his mother) but most likely an English punk rocker she had met at Glastonbury one year – was only twenty-three. The first thirteen years of his life had been spent living in a commune in England before his mother had upped sticks and headed for the Netherlands – in search of drugs and a better life – and had stayed there ever since. This mixed upbringing had left him fluent in two languages and fully embracing of the 'alternative' lifestyle. (There seemed to be an awful lot of alternative lifestyles kicking around of late, what with The Eye and Steffi. Frans, Japp and their porn entourage were hardly what you might call 'normal' and although I was slightly more conventional I wasn't exactly an average geezer – and nor was Rambo!)

At sixteen The Eye had discovered both carp fishing and absinthe. He hadn't explained how but had said originally there had been no interconnection and the two had been independent revelations. It was when he had inadvertently combined the two during a drunken overnight session the fun had truly begun. That fateful night had seen The Eye successfully look forward in time and spot the whereabouts of the lake's largest inhabitant, and in the morning – after he had sobered up enough to move swims and chuck a line in the water – he had caught it.

At first he had put it down to chance, to an odd, amusing anomaly, yet somewhere in the back of his mind there had been the inclination to try it again. This had been due mainly to his great enthusiasm for drinking absinthe and a similar determination to find out if he had unveiled an incredible carp-catching phenomenon. So, he had tried it again, and it hadn't worked. Undeterred he had tried it another time and it hadn't worked. He had tried once more – no joy – and then again with the same result – bugger all. Twice after those miserable efforts he had given it his best shot and again had achieved nothing other than complete inebriation as well as the long journey into absinthe-dependency. The following attempt, however, had come up trumps and The Eye's first twenty-kilo fish had been caught as a direct result of his ability to see into the future. He *did* have foresight and it had been fuelled by bootlegged, thujone abundant, Swiss-made absinthe – the one rider being it wasn't there on tap, to mix the metaphor, like the switching on of a light. How I had related to *that* part of his story!

Not exactly being the shy and retiring type, word – mainly his own to begin with – had spread across the Dutch hard-core carp fishing grapevine concerning his achievements. With each successive – although spasmodic – absinthe-aided capture, his star rose ever higher within the select circles it was talked of. His nickname soon followed and The Eye was quickly regarded as the top man in his field. When I had asked him why I hadn't heard of him before he had told me the commercial mainstream was for 'cunts' and 'pussies'. The Eye didn't sell out, man. The Eye was keeping *below* the radar. The Eye got *his* respect from the people who *he* respected – that was good enough for him – and only those deemed sufficiently 'cool' ever got to hear of him. By default it appeared I was 'cool', which was nice, seeing as I'm now into my thirties and getting to be a bit of an old git!

One minor disconcerting thing, from my point of view, was The Eye's habit of talking about himself in short stark sentences in the third person. In my humble opinion this was one of the first signs of being a bit of a nutter, but in truth it paled into insignificance compared to the rest of his outlandish behaviour. The lad was barking all right and you didn't need a degree in psychoanalytic assessment to see it. To put it into context I thought he had come across as being one swivel short of a rig, one length of elastic short of a catapult and about six tent pegs, two poles and a groundsheet short of a bivvy. In fact he was the nuttiest fucking nutter I had ever clapped eyes on. Nuttier than a binge-eating squirrel's stool, nuttier than a vegetarian health food shop and nuttier than a Boeing spare parts warehouse *and* (this is the best bit) *I* was relying on *him* to help me pull through on my plan of revenge against Hollywood – although I hadn't yet plucked up courage to ask.

The question that begged to be asked was; who was the more mentally unstable? Him for being a fucking nutter or me expecting a fucking nutter to deliver what he had never delivered before – a glimpse of the future unrelated to carp fishing – and with only one crack at it. Reading between the lines The Eye's hit to miss ratio, if he wasn't prone to exaggeration – and he seemed to exaggerate *everything* – was one in six. Still a remarkable feat – seeing as I'd had three hits in around twice as many years – but still not an average you would want to bet your house on. Not over a single three night/four day session. Ruefully I had admitted I might be betting exactly what the adage offered – my house – and to make it even spicier my family as well. Scary!

"Oi! Boy! You there?" Rambo's voice wrenched me from my thoughts.

"No," I hissed. "I've flung myself in the deep end. That fourteen metre spot."

Rambo's huge dark silhouette crouched outside my bivvy in the small porch section of the Euro Dome. I unzipped the mozzie door and immediately heard one of the little bastards whine past my ear. "What's up?" I asked.

Rambo's outline wiped its nose a little self-consciously – even in the dark I could tell. "I thought I needed to come over and explain," he said.

"Oh," I said. "What, about how you've told Steffi my life story?" I was on his case straight away.

"Yeah," Rambo admitted. "Only I haven't," he immediately negated. "She's got this thing about us not having any secrets. I think it's her way of wiping the slate clean and making a fresh start..." he began by way of an explanation.

"What with you?" I interjected.

"Yeah. With me."

There was silence.

"And that's what you want, is it?" It was a rhetorical question because it was obviously what Rambo wanted otherwise he wouldn't have told her my life story. Only he hadn't. Apparently. Call me confused but never call me late for dinner.

"I think so, boy. I know it runs a bit against the grain and everything I've ever said and stood for but..." Rambo paused, groping for words which wouldn't fail him. "I've never met a woman like her. She's suffered in the past like me and come out the other side unscathed and strong. I respect that, I really do." I could tell this was a difficult speech for Rambo and an equally demanding concept for one of life's natural loners. Renouncing a personal religion often is. "You see, she's beautiful, she's tough *and* she's unbelievable in bed! Okay, so she looks good when she's acting but believe me, boy, she's even *better* when she's doing it for real!" I nodded in the gloom. I could well believe it. Rambo carried on. "I *can* love her and not worry about it! I've given it a hell of a lot of thought since things developed between us and I *can* do it! I *can* fall for her, *have* fallen for her if I'm honest, because she's the most street-wise woman you could ever hope to meet! Any trouble and she'll fight her way out of it! Make no mistake about it, boy! She's a black belt in karate, you saw what she did to those little shits the other day. Plus I can teach her so much more... She's got the other Glock, now," Rambo added in a throwaway tone. "The one you used to blow away you-know-who."

"Oh, right," I said quietly.

"But don't you worry, boy, I *haven't* told her about that! Not the killing! I told her about the ghost and all the other stuff," Rambo let out a resigned puff of air. "Christ, it took *forever*! I'd forgotten just how much carnage we've been through... but I *didn't* tell her about Charlie getting charcoaled and you plugging my would-be assassin. I also didn't tell her why it all happened. I left that one episode out... pretty much everything else she knows. I have hinted that there *may* be a few sad bastards out there who might *quite* like to put a bullet in my head... but I made it sound low key so I don't *think* I put the wind up her unnecessarily."

I wondered if Rambo heard my eyebrows lurch upwards like a pair of snatched hangers at this little gem of an understatement. There was no comment so obviously not, which, on the whole, was a good thing. Rambo continued. "We'd made a pact of no secrets when we decided we both wanted to give it a go together, which I've more or less kept to... the trouble was, so much of what has happened to me in my non-army and non-mercenary days has involved *you*! By definition you came into the story rather a lot."

"That's fair enough," I said. "I don't mind." What else could I say? Still, a small part of me was pleased Rambo had held back the shittiest card in my deck. The fear of someone somehow finding out would have been only increased slightly by her knowing, but even so it was better she didn't – providing she *wasn't* Hollywood's plant and was going to lace Rambo's cornflakes with a truth serum and then forward all the incriminating evidence onto him! "Does she know I'm trying to sort out a plan of revenge to wipe the smile off Hollywood's face?"

"Yeah," Rambo confirmed. "And she offered to help in any way if she could."

"That's nice of her," I said genuinely. "Is she asleep?" I asked.

"Sound asleep," Rambo confirmed. "It's why I nipped out to have a quick word. I didn't want you fretting or saying something out of turn when it wasn't necessary." Rambo's voice sounded apologetic. "It's the first chance I've had to get over to you and speak to you alone."

"Thanks, mate. I appreciate it," I said solemnly.

Silence gripped the night air. If my life had been a magazine article my buzzer would have screeched into life on cue to fill the void. I would have rushed past Rambo, knocking him on his arse as I did so and played in a fifty. The silence held firm. Magazine articles – they're all bollocks, unlike books.

"I suppose things really have changed for good this time, boy," Rambo propositioned, to himself as much as to me. "Before Steffi it was always you and Sophie with *me* as the loner, apart from my short time with Melina and my one-off with Melloney. They didn't really count. It's not like it is this time." Rambo snorted gently. "Now *I'm* with Steffi and *you're* on *your* own... temporarily," Rambo quickly tacked on to try and make me feel better.

"It's called irony, mate," I said with a trace of bitterness. I gave myself a quick reprimand and told myself to grow up. "I'm pleased for you, Rambo," I continued in a much lighter vein. "I'm glad you've met someone you feel good with... you just remember if it wasn't for me and the TWTT you'd never have met her!"

Rambo laughed. "That's true, boy! It's one hell of a long story going right back to the meeting at the Black Horse. I should know, I've told most of it to Steffi!"

"One thing I *was* going to ask..." I began slowly.

"I know what it is," said Rambo quickly diving in, "because I'd ask it as well. It's what's the score over all the other hung-like-donkeys men she's ever been with and the thought of other porn viewers wanking themselves silly over her, isn't it?"

"Yeah," I admitted, "something like that. Not phased by it?"

I heard Rambo pull the night air into his huge chest cavity. (Death at sixty-nine for him! Or more likely from the exertion caused by doing it!) "It's a bit odd having

Frans fishing over the other side knowing he's had her *and* I've now got visual documentary evidence of it in the form of a triple X DVD plus the others she's made… but there you go! Nothing's perfect in this world and I'll settle for what I've got, besides, Betty copes, just about, and Frans is still in the business. In any case it's all dated BR – Before Rambo."

"And Steffi isn't still in the business?" I asked, ignoring Rambo talking of himself in the third person. I would let him off – it was all new ground for the poor sod, this proper relationship lark.

"No," Rambo replied emphatically. "I can't alter her past but I can shape her future." Rambo's sage words hung in my bivvy for a while. It was a lesson I had taken a long time to get to grips with. "We'll have to tell Japp for certain, although I'm pretty sure he'll have already guessed… he'll understand and I'm sure he can find someone to replace Steffi easily enough." Again I nodded in the dark and things went silent until the mozzie buzzed my earhole. "I'm going back to bed," Rambo whispered. "I'm shattered and I'm sure you are as well. I just wanted to set the record straight… scream out if you hook one."

"Will do," I said and Rambo stealthily slid off into the night without another word.

I re-zipped my door, ruthlessly hunted down the mozzie who had gatecrashed my bivvy with the light from my headtorch and squashed him flat between my palms with a sharp clap.

"Gotcha! You bastard!" I exclaimed with delight far too disproportionate to the act. And on that high note of achievement I wiped my hands clean and slumped back onto my bedchair. Almost as soon as my head hit the pillow I fell into a deep sleep and began to dream.

It had been a funny dream, in what way I couldn't quite put my finger on, because to be truthful I couldn't remember much of it. It hadn't been one of my soul-consuming ones from the past with its usual list of characters and the only bit that stuck had been the last part. For some reason Rambo had been punching David Beckham in the face for pulling out of a tackle in the 2002 World Cup and Wayne Rooney had been pestering me, asking whether I thought his metatarsal was going to get better in time for the 2006 World Cup. I had been sitting behind what looked like at least ten rods. 'Wayne,' I had said. 'How do I know? Your best bet is to keep reading the newspapers and the colour supplements, I'm sure you'll find out from them! What? No, I can't come and play cards. I'm not budging from these rods in case I get a take.'

Beeeeeeeeeeeeeeeeeeeeeeeeeeeeeeeeeeeeeeeep! Beeeeeeeeeeeeeep! Beeeeeep! Beep! Beep! Beep! Beep! Beep! Beep! Beeeeeeeeeeeeeeeeeeeeeeeeeeeeeeeeeeeep!

My dream went 'Pop!' like a cartoon's onomatopoeic script.

I woke up, my heart pounding. The take in the dream had corresponded with a *real* one – my subconscious run had been mimicked by reality! If I could pull that one out of the hat on a regular basis I would be laughing! Muzzy-headed and with hands shaking I yanked on my wellies as planned, unzipped the mozzie door and blundered through it only partially stumbling as my feet caught on the inner door's five-inch upstand. As I ran the few yards to my rods I could see it was the right-hand rod's buzzer making all the noise. The bright blue LED shone in all its more-expensive-than-a-red-one intensity, casting a ghostly light on my three rods until I snatched up the Ballista Slim (in burgundy – tart) and lent into my first ever Dutch carp. Pup, the old bastard, had done it again! The rod I was now wielding against a solid resistance was the PVA attack rod at short distance, the one I had baited with a single twenty millimetre revolutionary, indented, dirty brown bottom bait boilie hair rigged to a size 4 Talon Tip along with a small bag of boilie coup d'état crumb.

Behind me I heard footsteps and a light momentarily danced across my face. I glanced round to see a figure with a Cyclops-like three LED headtorch shining directly at me.

"Whoa! Matt! You in, man?" the figure cried. It was The Eye.

"Sure am!" I confirmed feeling proud of my first take on the new venue.

"The Eye heard the buzzer. The Eye was awake. Couldn't sleep. Having one off the wrist! *No* man! *Just* kidding!" The Eye laughed. His light flickered down at my feet. "*Bla*ck wellingtons! For a *black* soul," he said slowly.

"Black wellingtons because the shop never had green ones," I told him, somewhat thrown by his line of patter.

"Bought black even if they'd *had* green. You've a black soul, man. The Eye's seen it in your eyes. The Eye can tell," The Eye said with deadly sincerity.

"You're probably right," I admitted as I tried to focus on what the fish on the end of my line was trying to do to escape me instead of thinking; 'boy', 'man', wouldn't anyone ever again call me 'Matt'? What *had* happened to my angst and acne-ridden teenage section of life? It was passing me by in giant steps in terms of how people addressed me. As for the black soul? The Eye *did* have a point – it matched my black cloud of murderous worry. "Can you dip my other rods?" I asked The Eye.

The Eye stepped backwards as if threatened by something sharp and pointy. "Sorry, man. No can do. It's one of The Eye's things. The only rods The Eye touches belong to The Eye. Bad karma for the next life."

Well, he *was* a lunatic, or well on the way to being one, so what else did I expect? Pushing The Eye's non-participation to the back of my mind and with the anti-reverse on (as always, I play'em off the clutch, me, backwinding's for Noddies – light blue touch paper etc. etc. and watch Standard Carp Fishing Argument no.8 explode into life) I held the take rod in my right hand and dipped the two other rods as best I could with my left hand, realising the shallow water combined with the sudden twenty-foot drop would compromise the effectiveness of doing so. On cue – unlike the absent run during Rambo's earlier silence – the fish ploughed straight through my middle rod and pulled line off my universal bite 'n' run converted (patent applied for, but not, I suspect, by Gary Bruce – more fool him) Emblems. I applied serious side-strain in an attempt to bully the fish back away from the middle rod but as stipulated in Sod's Law, section 14, paragraph 5.8 the fish came back having looped the line. Quickly realising what had happened I eased in the bite 'n' run converter to the forty-five degree angle so I could pull over the bail arm and then pushed it fully into its housing. The line from the open spool jagged off as the fish powered away once again taking two lots of line with it – I had to admit, this type of thing seemed to happen to me quite often when I was playing fish of late.

The Eye stood and watched me struggle, his headtorch's beam jumping from spot to spot as his interest guided it. Personally I was terrified the chafing of the middle rod's line would cut through the one attached to my first ever Dutch carp despite it being on an open bail arm. For several minutes I battled to gain the upper hand constantly fearful all would go horribly slack and I would be left with an empty hollow feeling inside my stomach – 'gutted' being the technical phrase. Fortunately Lady Luck smiled on me and all held firm.

"How's your karma thing on landing nets?" I asked The Eye.

"No grief. The Eye'll net her," he said and on grabbing my net waded out into the shallow water. As he did I noticed The Eye was barefoot.

The Eye's headtorch shone onto the clear water and as if by magic, or by design of a carp wanting to be in the limelight, a large mirror rolled directly in its beam. She was almost ready. The Eye expertly sunk the net, bided his time until the opportune moment and as the mirror glided over the front edge of the net he hesitated for a split second and then up he lifted and in she went!

"Nice one, man," said The Eye laconically.

"Nice one, The Eye," I said, which sounded ridiculous – as ridiculous as Bono congratulating U2's guitarist on an excellent riff.

I could see the middle rod's line wrapped over a few inches above my anti-tangle tubing, so I downed the rod with the fish on it and bit through the main line. I took the rod out of the way and propped it against my bivvy and miraculously pulled out the loops and pseudo-tangles from the middle rod and managed to put it back on my buzz bars and reset the hanger and alarm. I quickly did the same with the left-hand one. While I was doing this The Eye had carefully placed the mirror onto the unhooking mat I had pegged out earlier and had removed my Talon Tip. He held the rig and anti-tangle tubing up to me. Pup's revolutionary, indented, dirty brown bottom bait boilie was still hanging on by a thread, the boilie stop now well embedded inside it on what looked an extra long hair.

"Good fish," The Eye stated. "Upper thirty. Not one The Eye's seen before." He smelt the revolutionary, indented, dirty brown bottom bait boilie in a series of quick, noisy sniffs. "Unusual bait. Not one The Eye's *smelt* before."

I took the rig from him without passing comment and set about weighing the mirror. I wasn't sure what I was trying to achieve by making no comment. A certain cool credibility? An enigmatic persona? Whatever it was The Eye seemed fascinated and he watched me with a disconcerting closeness as I weighed in the mirror at a chunky 37lb 14oz. Afterwards I got him to photograph it and The Eye took a photo on his own digital camera so he could show his mates and have a record of this latest possible 'new' capture. With The Eye holding the sacked fish in the water I quickly went and told Rambo of my success. He came back with me to take a look at the mirror having already been told the vital nugget of information. The revolutionary, indented, dirty brown bottom bait boilie had struck first!

With the mirror safely back in its deep watery home and Rambo safely back in his deep roomy bivvy with his chic, pervy Steffi, I was all set to make up a new rig for the successful PVA attack rod. The only thing was The Eye was still hanging around, hanging around not saying anything, but nevertheless still, by all appropriate elucidation, hanging around. Somewhere in the back of my cranky brain I started to think of the kiss on the forehead he had given me, and with it, its dreaded connotations. Dear God don't let it be so bad I prayed!

"Are you okay, The Eye?" I asked thinking what the fucking hell did *that* sound like?

"No, man," The Eye admitted.

Aye-aye, I thought, The Eye's up to his eyes in it. In *what* was the crucial question.

"Well, fire away, mate, anything you want to ask, go ahead," I said inviting the question and thinking here we go, hold tight for a fast ride this time!

"The Eye's gotta ask, man," The Eye said, his eyes popping and widening in my headtorch. "Did you *mind-meld* with the fish? Before you caught it?"

"No," I said flatly. "I have done in the past. I think Japp has told you... Lac Fumant?" I ventured.

"Yeah. With an LSD tab?" The Eye answered. Japp had told him all right.

"That's right," I confirmed. "We spoke earlier when we were shifting your gear how you've managed to do something similar, only using absinthe. I used an LSD tab, although to be honest at the time I thought it was a headache tablet." The timing appeared appropriate and so I struck out tentatively on my quest. "What we *didn't* discuss were other things. Incredible things!" I said in a voice conveying deep mysticism.

The Eye's head seemed to wobble and his skinny body shivered. "What other... *things*? You gonna *tell* The Eye, man?" The Eye said his voice rising in tone and volume at what sounded like his desperation and thirst for knowledge. "You're the only one The Eye knows can do this shit!" he gushed. "The Eye's met no one else!"

I felt as if this was definitely my chance. As I read it The Eye saw me as a senior figure with regards to reading the minds of carp and other such – as yet undisclosed – improbable nonsense. Rightly or wrongly he held me in some form of esteem – he was young, ten years or so younger than me and I calculated he assumed I could tell him more than he might know or be able to imagine. It was time to strike while the iron was hot, even if it meant telling another person about my darkest secret. Sometimes you have to give to receive.

"If I tell you *everything*, *everything* I know and *everything* I've ever done concerning all this foresight stuff, will you help me try and see something I can't see on my own?"

As I asked him the moon came out from behind the clouds for the first time and bathed him in a soft moonlight. I saw The Eye pull the long, thin toes of one foot across the sand. "Okay, man. *Deal!*" he said. "Go to The Eye's bivvy," he motioned. "*Man*, The Eye needs a drink!"

"Just let me get my receiver box and I'll be with you."

Chapter 9

With my Delkim receiver box tucked into my belt – as opposed to the two Glocks that were almost certainly tucked under Rambo and Steffi's belts – I made my way down to the south facing point swim. It took all of twenty seconds. When I got there The Eye was brewing up under the moonlight and he gestured towards his sitting-outside-the-bivvy-in-the-sun-during-the-day chair. I parked my shattered body onto it. Despite being knackered the adrenaline rush left in my system from the capture of my first Dutch carp, plus the anticipation of my forthcoming pitch to The Eye, kept me highly alert. Tiredness receded on a wave of nervous energy and I sat and watched The Eye make a brew thanks to the now cloudless night sky and a nearly full moon. The sun's reflection on our orbiting neighbour made visibility good without the aid of artificial light. I looked at the moon's reflection on the water and was reminded of the beginnings of the mind-meld at Lac Fumant. I would be re-telling the story again pretty soon.

"Tea?" The Eye asked starring at my wellies.

"Yeah, that'd be nice."

"Milk?"

"Yeah, great."

"Sugar?"

"No thanks."

The Eye stirred the milk into my mug and handed it to me. "What's the worst thing you've ever done, man?" he suddenly asked, his eyes fixed on my wellies. Maybe he had a black rubber fetish, or a black soul one – the wellies were black rubber *and* had black soles, whether the black soles had a black soul I had no idea.

I grasped the red-hot mug, taken aback by his directness. It wasn't an easy question to answer so I decided not to. "You can decide," I told him, "once I've told you my story." The Eye's head jerked in a bird-like peck, which I construed as a nod. "But I'm only going to tell you if you agree to help me see something in the future."

"The Eye's *already* said yes, man," The Eye reminded me.

"Sorry," I said feeling a bit stupid. I had just wanted to re-iterate the terms. Perhaps I should have drawn up a contract on the back of a PVA bag and got him to sign it in non-water based ink. Keep this somewhere dry Mr Furlington and don't go putting any goldfish in it. "Shall I start?" I asked The Eye.

"Drink first," The Eye said, so we drank – slowly, because the tea was very hot.

When we had both finished – without another word being spoken – The Eye rinsed out the mugs and rather alarmingly stripped off his shirt and lay face down on the ground, his arms spread out straight on either side. "Now. Fire away, man," he said, "while The Eye soaks up the lunar energy."

"Right…" I faltered being somewhat put off by his strange actions. It was a bit off-putting trying to tell your life story to a prostrate, semi-naked fucking nutter who was moonbathing! The Eye was a night-time Arnold! "Can you hear me okay?" I ventured.

"Check."

"You won't fall asleep will you?"

The Eye sprang up and turned a fearsome look on me. "Listen, *man*," he said his voice wobbling with emotion. "The Eye's waited *fucking* years for you! Someone like you! This is *big* to The Eye! Like a sixty, man!" and with that he turned round, hit the deck and spread-eagled himself stomach down on the sandy ground. A sixty *was* big. Hands up all those who have caught one… I thought as much… I don't want to brag but my arm is just coming down now.

"Right. Sorry," I said apologising for being such a tool. "Okay…" I began uncertainly, "here goes. Perhaps to start off with I should mention it goes without saying I had *never, ever* had any sort of premonition of any sort before all this malarkey started. Not as kid, teenager, grown man… *nothing*! I did think once a set of carp catch weights in a diary might be the right numbers for the national lottery, they weren't incidentally. Luckily someone else close to me did have the right numbers, and basically it all started from there. I'd just come out of prison, you see, for blowing up some arsehole's bivvy… you don't need to know *that* part of my story," I hastily added, "only to be aware that he fucking asked for it, the bastard! Anyway, when I came out…" And so I was off. For the next few hours I carried on with my tale of going to Lac Fumant on Sophie's mum's lottery win and the eventual mind-meld with the big mirror right up to the killing of Rambo's would be assassin via my meeting of the ghost and solving the mystery of her murder.

I recalled it as deeply as my memory permitted me and actually surprised myself with small details I thought I had forgotten. I told him *everything* I thought relevant to what I was eventually going to ask him to help me with; the characters, the relationships, the cheating, the lying, the laughs, the companionship, the revelations, the life-altering shocks, my closest thoughts, my closest desires and my closest evaluations. In short I spilt the whole fucking lot out. I spilt my heart and guts out to a twenty-three-year-old absinthe drinking clairvoyant carp angler who, through the whole amazing saga – it *did* sound utterly amazing when told in one sitting – had lain face down in the sand, had never uttered a word or a question for the entire duration but who had, conceivably, soaked up thirty litres of lunar energy, or whatever the fuck you measured lunar energy in. "And that's why I need *you*," I said, Judge Williams coming to the end of his summing up. "I need you to try and help me see something that'll allow me to plot a plan of revenge against Hollywood. Preferably something vile and horrible… but I guess most of all, something I can make happen without any trace or implication leading back to me." I stopped. There. My tale was told, my throat was now sore and another human knew of my murderous dark secret.

The Eye never moved to begin with until his arms came in and he started, much to my consummate consternation, to do press-ups. With quick efficiency he reeled off twenty and then lithely turned himself over, sat on his arse and pulled his knees up to his chest, linked his hands across his shins and stared at me. I stared back.

"Is that all *true*, man?" he inquired.

"On my daughter's life," I assured him.

"*Shit*! Fucking hell! *Freaky* shit, man!" The Eye said his spiky hair flicking back and forth in a moonbeam. The Eye seemed unable to control his emotion/excitement – whatever it was – and suddenly jumped to his feet, pulled back both shoulders in a kind of ghastly shudder and proceeded to walk back and forth in quick tight little lines. A few yards one way, a couple of strides the other, then back again and so on. The balls of his feet turned up little mounds of sand as he did so. He scratched his head, pulled at his stud earrings and wiped his face with his palms so hard he pulled and distorted his features grotesquely. When he was close enough to me I could make out goose bumps all over his body. He thrust a handful of splayed fingers through his hair. "*Aaah!* Fuck *The Eye*, man!" he said his voice rising in tone and volume. "That's *well* freaky! *Ssshhhit!*" He turned, came right up close to me and faced me, his eyes blazing in the moonlight. They were so wide and popping I could see the moon's reflection in them. "*How* can you live with that knowledge?" he implored.

"It wasn't easy," I acknowledged, "especially right afterwards… but other things are even more pressing now."

The Eye's right hand went up to his forehead and rubbed it while its thumb kneaded a temple. I could see he was having trouble getting his head around all the implications I had tried to get my head around after it had happened to me. "*Talk!*" he barked. "From… the *living*… to the *dead*! From the *womb* to the dead!" he exclaimed.

Truthfully it was a heavy one – a right shocker in fact – the ghost knowing an unborn foetus in a womb wanted to be named Amy. Amongst all the other impossibilities how could it possibly be? Beyond any stretch of anyone's imagination how could it be? Spilling it all out again and watching The Eye try and grapple with the repercussions of my tale made me realise how fantastic my story really was. In a way it was a story that needed telling. Telling to the whole world if it would listen, and surely much of it *would* listen, and be only too glad to listen to a man that had talked to a real ghost! It was the revealing of all the other accompanying stuff I wasn't so keen on going public!

The Eye walked away again still trying to square in his head what he had heard. It obviously had a momentous meaning to him, whether religious or personal I wasn't sure, because it seemed to have hit him much harder and made him react far more intensely than Rambo, Steffi or even Sophie – and she had been *severely* shaken. Eventually The Eye stopped walking and he looked up at the moon before turning his vision onto his bare feet. His shoulders sagged and then they started to heave up and down and I realised he was crying – silently to begin with until the sobbing became audible. Soon he became completely overwhelmed, his whole body wracked by the release of intense emotion, he blubbered and wept uncontrollably. To be honest I was at a loss what to do and settled for thinking it was a good job he never had a bait in the margins because what with the noise he was making it would have spooked any half sensible, union card carrying carp. It wasn't a particularly helpful thought, I decided, so I walked over to The Eye and put an arm over his bare, bony moonlight-impregnated shoulder.

"Makes you wonder doesn't it?" I said with true conviction.

"So *many* questions, man," The Eye sobbed.

"So few answers," I admitted. "All I can say is, and this is the conclusion I've come to after more thinking than you can imagine, there is something after death. To me, and this is only my personal interpretation, the ghost was locked in a twilight world between us and wherever she should have been. Once I'd communicated with her and Rambo and myself had exposed her murderer, making Michael top himself in his oxygen deprived zipped up bivvy, she left it… to a better place? Let's hope so. To heaven? A parallel universe for souls? Who knows? But now both you and I know there's definitely *something*."

"It's enough," The Eye said becoming calm. "The Eye thinks she went into another life. A rebirth. A transmigration."

"A *rebirth*? *Transmigration*?" I asked, not sure what he meant.

"Buddhism," The Eye stated. "The self is not permanent, man. Karma judges our good and evil deeds for reward or punishment in another life. Reach the Noble Eightfold Way, man. Break the chain of karma. Then its Nirvana."

I patted The Eye on the shoulder. "Yeah," I said, completely pig ignorant of what he was mumbling on about. All I knew was Glenn Hoddle had bombed out of the England job for spouting on about how the disabled had been bad in a previous life and Kurt Cobain had blown his fucking brains out with a shotgun – thus ending *his* version of Nirvana (oh, well, nevermind.) Somehow I doubted if this was what The Eye had in mind.

"So, what's my most evil deed? The one to go with my black soul?" I asked.

"You *don't* get it do you, man?" The Eye said eyeing me with wide-eyed lunacy.

"Eh?" I said not getting it – not getting within a million light-years of it.

"A *rebirth*, man," The Eye stated slowly.

"Yeah… you reckon the ghost, according to Buddhism, would rebirth…?" I shrugged my shoulders. "And?"

The Eye put both his hands on my shoulders, I could feel them shaking. "Your *daughter*, man. The ghost *told* you she wanted to be Amy. She said you are my beloved friend. That's what Amy means, man. *Aimée*! French for beloved friend. The woman who died was reborn as your daughter. She transmigrated. Her soul passed into a different body. The body of your daughter. Metempsychosis, man."

It was my turn to shake and for my jaw to go as slack as a dropback on a heavy indicator. I had *never* thought of that! But then not knowing the slightest thing about Buddhism, I wouldn't have. But he *was* right! The name did mean that, Sophie had told me it along with the meaning of a couple of other names she liked – now there was one bit of the story I *had* forgotten! It was my turn to feel cold and shivery and my flesh turned to the consistency of a chicken's just out of the supermarket's cling film and Styrofoam packaging. Much more of this moonlight and it'd be the same colour. Pole-axed I sank to my knees in instalments and let my forehead sink onto the sand. Now I was embracing all these new religions I wondered which way Mecca was.

"Only a theory. We've opened up each other's eyes. *What* a night, man! What a night of discovery!" The Eye stated.

I lifted my gritty head up from the floor. "So will you help me, help me try and plan my revenge?" I gasped, still in shock from The Eye's supposition.

"Sure, man. You should be with your daughter. And her mother. It's how it should be. Tomorrow night you and The Eye will drink absinthe. We'll try and meld our minds and see the future. See what it might bring."

"Thank you," I croaked and saw The Eye staring at the black soles of my wellies. He walked over to me and stood alongside me, over me, as I knelt.

"Black wellingtons for a black soul," he whispered quietly. "You should never have slept with Rebecca, man."

"But Michael's forced suicide? The shooting of the asylum seeker? Wanting to maim Hollywood in some yet to be defined hideous and hopefully incredibly gruesome way? Doubting Pup's new revolutionary, indented, dirty brown bottom bait boilie?" I said, craning my neck to look up at the young nutcase who had just dumped a bombshell of a hypothesis into my already cratered life.

The Eye threw away a hand. "Nah! Fuckers asked for it! Hollywood's *asking* for it!" His voice turned lower and more menacing. "*The Eye'll* be asking for *bait!*" He turned and walked away a few yards from me, stopped and stared up at the moon, arching his back as he did. I was convinced he was going to start to howl.

"Oooooooowwwwwwllll! Ooooowwww, oooowwww, oooooooowwwwwwllll!" he cried at the top of his voice. What do you know? I was right!

"Let's hope we can give it to that cunt, Hollywood!" I said venomously under my breath as I watched The Eye bark at the moon. "And you can *have* your bait!" I meant it too, more than anything I had ever said in my entire life – and I'm not talking only of bait for once. Revenge! I wanted to dish out revenge, not boilies!

The Eye howled three more times and, his werewolf-like lust sated, returned to where I was still on my knees. "The Eye's going to bed, man. The Eye'll see you in the morning. Thanks for confirmation. Buddhism is real! Real cool, man!"

Chapter 10

"So, *are* you getting up sis morning, Matthew?" Steffi asked, directing her question from outside my bivvy. "Or are you going to stay in bed all ov ser morning?"

"The second one," I mumbled to her – she might have heard, who could tell and for that matter who cared? I was deep in sleeping bag territory, undercover, well comfy, knackered from a night's worth of sleep deprivation and with a knot in my guts. It was like old times, although I was none the better for it! Whatever impact I had made upon The Eye with my story, *his* theory of rebirth had been at least as devastating to me. To be honest I was still reeling from his one statement, crash-course in Buddhism and the fresh notion a woman murdered by the ex-owner of Hamworthy Fisheries had been reborn as my daughter. What *would* her mother say? I would have to tell her – not yet though, best left till later when the impact of imparting such information could be of more use to me. I'm a cynical Simon sometimes.

I made another decision. "I'm not getting up until I get a run," I informed the ex-porn star, this time much louder.

The words had no sooner left my mouth than Rambo turned up to hear them. "Ha!" he goaded me. "That means your buzzer will be rattling off any minute now, boy, because, and this is the crucial part, you're a lazy bastard who wants to stay in the sack!"

Just as Rambo completed his sentence The Eye's bare feet appeared in my vision as I had begrudgingly managed to poke two eyes out from under my bag and was looking through the opaque mozzie door. "Bound to happen, man," he said. "Temptation of fate."

"Ve haff a vord for zat type of sing," said Steffi. "*Schicksalsschwer.*"

"How do you spell it? I'll make a note," I said sarcastically, "so I can casually drop it into conversation the next time I'm in the tackle shop asking for camouflaged presentation foam."

"S… c… h… i…" Steffi began.

I never did get to hear how you spelt… whatever it was that Steffi said because my Delkim – undoubtedly triggered by the desperately unappealing prospect of a lesson in German linguistics – took the easier option and decided to decibel itself the hell out of it. This left me with the socially embarrassing situation of having to get out of my warm, womb-like, (*don't* mention wombs and unborn foetuses… touchy subject) all-enveloping, super cosy, cuddly, comfy, commodious and above all *fully zipped up* sleeping bag in front of an uninvited audience. Once this tricky hurdle had been surmounted there still lay ahead the tasks of getting on the wellies – a form of physical sudoku – and *then* getting past the four-foot thick, solid high-tensile steel, combination locked door, aka the bivvy's mozzie door. Should I ever progress so far there was finally the small incidental of hitting the take and playing in a carp. To be honest the prospect would have been more appealing in the pitch black and pouring rain as opposed to under the full glare and scrutiny of three pairs of eyes.

Stoically I reminded myself carp anglers have no choice in the matter and every run should be treated with the due excitement it deserved – whatever the time, whatever the conditions, either climatic or physical. Besides the noise emanating from my Delkim was having a galvanising effect and a nervous energy was starting to course through my body. The old 'Pavlov's dogs' theory was working again!

I ripped open the sleeping bag like the Incredible Hulk going green and flexing his muscles, made the executive decision *not* to fuck about with the wellies, heaved open the zip and blundered through the mozzie door with all the skill and precision of an overweight drunk being ejected from a nightclub by two muscle-bound bouncers. Haphazardly I ran through my three observers in a body-at-ninety-degrees-to-legs, socks-on-ice stumble.

"Excuse me!" I said glibly and proceeded rather foolishly, once I was past them – probably because I had got as far as I had without major mishap – to crane my head back towards them while explaining, "I'm late for my take!" This last piece of posing was quite literally my downfall and a ninety-degree body to legs aspect went very quickly to one of being over-square and, as I lost complete control, I nose-dived into the shallow water with a spectacular splash… and started to aquaplane. Luckily my head crashed in to my rear buzz bar pole and it stopped me from skimming out into the lake's considerable depths.

As I lay dazed in the shallows, feeling the ascending progress of cool water being absorbed by clothing recently toasted inside a warm bag, I can confirm buzzer noises *are* transmitted into water. My left ear, being submerged, could verify the scientific fact of water being a superior medium to air for the transporting of sound waves. You see, basically, the buzzer noise in my left ear – the one in water – sounded louder than the laughing that was winging its way through air into the right one. If there ever is a certificate to pass to allow you to go fishing – and let's face it, the way the Health and Safety Directives are booming you'll need written authorization to take a shit soon – this subject is bound to be part of the curriculum… so mock ye not and take note!

As quickly as I could I struggled to my feet and hit the left-hand rod. The one fished as a single hookbait – the single hookbait being Pup's revolutionary, indented, dirty brown bottom bait boilie – at ninety yards. I tried to regain my composure – not easy when you've got seventy-five per cent clothing saturation by lake water – and concentrate on getting the carp I had hooked safely into a landing net. I might have made myself look a right spanner, but if I could get to grips with this carp, wrench it from its watery home to hammer out another result, I would be back on the level. It would bolster my confidence, clamp down on the piss-taking – in fact I could really drill it into everybody how good I was – and all those who saw it would say, 'Don't get agitated, Matt. Be still, son, be calm, we know you're not a tool at all'.

"Nice bivvy exit, boy," remarked Rambo still choking with laughter.

"Almost as good as your one at Lac Fumant when Spunker laid down that turd for you to step in," I reminded him.

"Hmm! Fair point," Rambo conceded sobering up. He turned philosophical, "Thinking about it, how many carp anglers are there who *haven't* had a spectacularly comical bivvy exit? Can't be many. It's the rush of blood combined with all the other factors... the element of surprise, the shock, the disorientation, for any number of dubious reasons, and the shear panic. Mind you," Rambo gave me a withering look, "I doubt if there are many who could top what you just did."

"Just remind me, how many runs have *you* had this session?" I pointed out.

"Bitchy, bitchy," Rambo gently chastised despite the big grin on his face.

"Aren't you going to ask?" I said to him.

"I guess so. Does it feel any good?"

"*Mahoosive*, mate," I replied.

"It'll need to be after the earlier debacle," Rambo suggested and added quietly in my ear, the one that wasn't still full of water, "and we *don't* want The Eye losing his respect for you."

I was just going to point out the likelihood of one banana skin bivvy exit ruining The Eye's regard for me was slight when Rambo's stomach started to sound similar to a Delkim receiver – one hidden behind a sturdy jacket. Rambo snatched apart his camouflaged jacket as if yanking apart a pair of hideously patterned curtains and, unsurprisingly, revealed a warbling Delkim receiver box (red LED latching) *and* the handle of a Glock 17 poking out of the top of his camouflaged trousers. Unusual beltfellows but then Rambo is an unusual type of bloke.

"Pup's boilie!" he stated simply. And on imparting this nugget of information disappeared so fast an outline of his British Army camouflage pattern hung in the air for a second before it swished off to catch him up.

The Eye picked up my landing net while lazily watching the rapidly receding man mountain hoofing it over to his rod; the one perched on the red LED buzzer. Steffi followed her new man dutifully some yards behind.

"Just The Eye and you, man," The Eye said in his truncated style holding onto the landing net, the handle of which was planted firmly in the white sand at his bare feet. He looked less edgy this morning, lethargic even. I tried to put my finger on it – ah, that was it, The Eye looked shot away. The Eye's eyes looked like piss-holes in the snow. Maybe all that soaking up of the moon's energy had worn him out.

"Like tonight," I reminded him.

"The Green Fairy's ready and waiting, man."

I nodded. Despite being partially distracted by what a passer-by might make of the last few seconds of our conversation, I knuckled down to playing in a carp hooked at, what was for me, long distance. I carefully eased back my rod in a slow pump and then wound in the gained line. I imagined Rambo to be doing something similar. I kept on pumping and winding, concentrating on not being too heavy-handed and pulling the hook out. I gazed at my rod tip as I eased back, watching it curve against the sky. As I did I mused Pup had certainly pulled another rabbit out of his bait hat – and a bottom bait at that. Although Pop-Up Pete translated into a nice acronym Bottom Bait Pete was crud. Still, the boilie was clearly anything but crud and was the most crucial point.

Although I was clueless as to whether anyone else had had anything, three takes all to Pup's self-styled revolutionary boilie augured well – especially as we'd had nothing on our normally prolific red bait. Curiosity caught the carp angler and I wondered what was in it. Even The Eye had said he had never smelt anything like it before. Maybe I would give Pup a ring if I managed to land this one and tell him the good news. Yeah, a good idea – he would appreciate it.

After five minutes or so of gentle but persuasive pumping, the hooked carp was coaxed back to within twenty yards of the bank. Now it was closer I could get a better feel for its size. Although I had blagged Rambo over how big it was, now I was within a much smaller yardage of my piscine adversary it did feel a hefty beast. The fight it was giving was slow and purposeful combined with a latent power. This fish was a plodder – a deep plodder – and on this venue deep plodding was a thing it could excel at. The carp, seemingly happy all the long line nonsense was done and dusted, decided, definitely, deep plodding it was. For the first time since I had made contact with the fish it started to mosey – in a deep plodding style – to the left. All the time I had been pumping and gaining line it hadn't kited at all but had come virtually straight in. Now, however, it appeared as if the rules of engagement had altered. Slowly, forcefully, it shifted from directly in front of my swim to thirty yards up to my left. If it went much further it could start to swim around the point and feasibly deep plod through The Eye's lines. I had to act pronto! Carefully I edged out to the very end of the shallow ledge in my swim. Ruefully I noted if I felt wet now then one more stride and I would be fully conversant with the meaning of the word 'submersed'... or 'drowned'. I applied side strain to turn the fish only to see my clutch tick off the line as my rod hit its test curve.

"Here we go!" I muttered to myself and jabbed the rod's butt in my groin and clasped the spool with my left hand. The rod lurched to the left, partially straightening and I was convinced the line would either snap or the hook would pull as everything hit maximum stress. Remarkably neither happened and the fish turned.

The Eye's keen fishing brain saw it all happen and instantly realised the score. If there was a defining moment in my appreciation of this young man's knowledge of carp fishing this was it. He knew. "Good, man," was all he said. It was ample.

I gained line easily as the fish moved towards me and as it did I hoped it might also move up in the water. By the time it had reached the point where it had decided to deep plod up to the left I was disappointed to note it was still deep plodding – not mid-water plodding and absolutely *not* surface plodding. I was mindful of a repeat of the previous carp's escapade and wondered if it was time to dip the other two rods, not that it had made any odds last time. I knew The Eye wouldn't lay a finger on them as he had decided touching other people's rods – for what reason I wasn't too sure, perhaps he considered it poor carping etiquette – was crap karma for the next life. Crap carp rod karma – try saying it with a mouthful of individually cut boilie stops held in between your lips.

As it turned out once the fish had gone barely a yard past the point it had previously turned at, it did so again. I was left staggered by its cheek and in time honoured traditional carp fishing phraseology I can hereby announce, without any fear of contradiction, that 'I couldn't do anything about it' and was 'powerless to stop the carp's surging – but slow – run'.

As before the fish plodded up to my left to the spot where, once again, I thought it was shit or bust time. I gave it the big'un, *again*, got away with it and managed to turn the carp. The fish and I repeated the next instalment of the fight as it swam back down towards me and left me to wonder whether the carp in question liked doing what it was doing as a form of exercise. A carp into circuit training, now there was a novelty. I was inclined to crack this little joke to The Eye and so looked over to him only to see his eyes closed, body slightly inclined towards the up-ended landing net, which he was still gripping with his left hand, his head dropping and his jaw slack.

"The Eye," I said gently. Nothing. "The *Eye!*" I said a little louder. Still nothing. Despite knowing it could cost me a big fish I shuffled back through the shallows to get closer to him. I cocked a dry ear at him and then pulled away in total perplexity. He was *snoring!* Not very loudly, in fact very quietly with soft, virtually inaudible snorts, but snoring he was! The fucker had fallen asleep, upright, on his bare feet, hanging on to my landing net handle while waiting for me to wrestle control from a deep plodding behemoth. Okay, so I had taken a bit of time playing the plodder… but not *that* much!

I considered what to do next and decided that despite The Eye being skinny I couldn't manage manipulating him *and* the landing net as an ensemble – you know, using him as a handle extension. It also concerned me The Eye might be some while waking up, for all I knew he might turn into Rip Van Winkle, grow a beard and still be there in winter. Consequently I shuffled back to the edge of the shallows and set to the task of getting the carp somewhere near ready to net, and then take it from there, which was pretty much my entire life philosophy of late.

Equally I decided there was no point in trying to wake The Eye up just yet. The way things were going it could be *hours* before the carp was ready to net and the poor sod evidently needed the kip. My worries over his sleep were hardly altruistic – I wanted him fresh as a daisy for tonight! For tonight we were due to see the future, to scan the distant horizon for forthcoming events – allegedly, hopefully, possibly, optimistically and so on. Come to that I needed to be as fresh as a daisy for tonight! I puffed out my cheeks and ruefully admitted the information each of us had passed onto the other had taken its toll in the form of yet another sleepless night. Who needed a shoal of bream with abnormally large, twenty millimetre boilie capacity gobs when you had reciprocal revelations to recite?

"You still mucking about with your one, boy?"

It was Rambo, back from what I presumed to be his first capture of a Dutch carp on Pup's revolutionary, indented, dirty brown bottom bait boilie.

"Afraid so," I admitted. "This fish is a powerful mother-fucker, all right!"

Rambo must have noticed the inert The Eye. (Look, I know it sounds ridiculous, just go with it, it is the bloke's nickname!) "What's up with him?" he enquired jogging his head towards The Eye.

"He got bored waiting, so he's powered down and gone into a coma," I explained.

"Can't say I blame him, it's been over twenty-five minutes."

"Sorry. I didn't realise there's a time limit on it."

"We leave on *Monday*," Rambo reminded me.

"Be a pal and get the net, will you?"

Rambo grunted and went and unwrapped The Eye's fingers from the net's handle and took it away from his grasp. Miraculously he didn't awake, even more miraculously he stayed upright. Rambo walked out into the shallows alongside me armed with my net and the pair of us looked back at The Eye, still asleep, still snoring and still vertical. "Funny lad," remarked Rambo. "What's holding him up? Gravity?"

"Could be skyhooks… could be a twenty-foot scaffold pole piled into the sand running up his trouser leg… or it could be that small anti-gravity rig tubing friendship bracelet on his wrist. Korda make them. No need to climb trees, you just hover above the lake fish spotting."

"Don't start," Rambo warned. "Come on, you've thirty-four eight to beat," he said indicating it was time to get my carp-landing head on.

"I've already beaten it!" I told him reminding him of my earlier capture.

"You know what I mean."

"What do you know about Buddhism?" I asked Rambo changing the subject.

The fish was deep plodding in a four-yard circle now – on the short reps having done the longer endurance stuff – and we were at the stage of a Mexican standoff. The fish wasn't plodding up the margin towards the point and I wasn't gaining any line, all in all it seemed a good time to engage Rambo in the latest gut-knotting facet of my life.

"Not much," Rambo admitted. "Buddha? Short, fat, bald bloke from India, wasn't he? The one who started a slightly mystical religion appealing to the Western hippy set and fashionable celebrities who think Christianity is too boring. That's it really," Rambo offered.

"So you don't know what it entails, its teachings, its beliefs, its ideology?"

Rambo curled up a top lip. "All religion is bollocks in my book. I've seen first hand that more people have died fighting over religion than anything else in history and that includes *money*! In my opinion there's fuck all to it, science and man's knowledge has made it irrelevant… until, that is, this mate of mine met a ghost and made me think twice…" Rambo's voice petered out.

And?" I prompted.

Rambo shrugged. "I thought twice, realised I could think to infinity and not come up with any definitive answers, eventually tucked it to the back of my mind, got on with living and tried to ignore it. What else can you do?"

"Fuck yourself up over it?"

"That's *your* forte, boy. Not mine… anyway why are you asking?"

"Well, last night I… hold on it's started taking line again. Going straight out this time. I tell you, I've hooked a nuclear sub. Christ! The power!"

"Or according to The Eye, *Buddha*, the power?"

There were no flies on Rambo – once I thought I had seen the marks where they had been but I had been mistaken. "Something like that. It's stopped taking line now… chance to put some back." I started to pump and wind again and had the feeling I was shifting the fish up in the water for the first time during our extensive struggle. "As I was saying, last night I told him my life story from when I came out of the gulag, *including* the bit you didn't tell Steffi." I checked Rambo's face to see his reaction – a mere hint of a nod. "I felt I *had* to put him in the picture before I could ask him to help me… and after I'd told him… it *is* a hell of a long tale as you said, he hit me with a theory."

"Being?" Rambo said a little wearily for my liking.

"I don't know how much he's into Buddhism… a lot I think, for instance he wouldn't touch my rods to dip them when I was playing my last fish because he said it would give him bad karma," Rambo rolled his eyes at this. "Bad karma for the next life," I explained.

"Oh! We get *another* one do we? That'll be nice," came the caustic reply. "Do you get to choose? I'll be someone rich and powerful who leads an energetic and fascinating life if it's all right by you. Or do you come back as an ant and get your guts squashed out of you within the first month of being hatched by some fat fucker's size thirteen trainers?"

"I'm not *too* sure on the exact details… I don't know fuck all about it either," I conceded. "The Eye knew," I continued still pumping. The fish was getting very close in now. "How you can break the cycle of rebirth and achieve Nirvana through the Eightfold Way or something…"

"You're rambling, boy. Get to the point," Rambo said curtly.

"What before this fish does?" A huge mirror rolled on the surface and stopped my sarcasm dead in its tracks. "Whoa!" I exclaimed.

Rambo turned to me with a big grin. "*Mahoosive*, boy! Spotter's badge for the call!"

My heart was pounding wildly, mainly due to the size of the carp we had both seen and also partially due to the fact I was going to lay the reason of my latest sleepless night on my best buddy. "In a nutshell, The Eye thinks the ghost, the soul of the woman who Michael murdered, was reborn as my daughter, Amy. *That's* how the ghost knew the name. Amy. *Aimée*, French for my beloved friend."

"Is that it?" said Rambo with a look of disbelief on his face.

"Well... yeah," I admitted somewhat deflated by Rambo's under whelmed response.

Rambo scowled at me and then gestured towards the upright The Eye. "He's a fucking nutter! Look at him! He's standing there asleep! What *else* did he do or say last night?"

I licked my lips. This was going to sound bad. "He moonbathed to soak up lunar energy... face down in the sand that was, for the whole duration of my story... in all around three hours."

"*And?*" demanded Rambo who knew he was on a roll.

"He did some press-ups and barked at the moon... like a werewolf in a 'B' movie."

"And that friendship bracelet," Rambo continued, still not finished. "*Not* made by Korda, *not* containing any anti-gravity properties, in fact making him slightly *heavier* if anything, but undisputedly made of rig tubing. Along with the little lead bomb necklace."

I answered in a sniff and looked out to where my line cut into the water. The mirror boiled the surface on cue.

"Land the fucking fish, eh?" Rambo suggested. "And then I'll repeatedly punch you in the face until you see reason. You'll thank me in the end."

"What. When you stop?"

"No. When you see reason."

"I'll have two black eyes," I whined. "I won't be able to see *anything*."

"Seeing reason is a state of mind, it's not a visual thing. Come on! Get on the case. Steffi's promised me bivvy sex when I get back!"

"Don't kneel on any mixer, it'll cripple your knees," said the voice of experience.

"Oh, that's right! Bring *that* up! How you had sex with my last girlfriend!" Rambo mocked.

A huge white mouth gulped in a mixture of water and air less than half a rod's length in front of me. It wouldn't be long! Finally, after one of the longest carp versus me battle I had ever experienced! Hang on in there hook! Rambo placed the net in the water and while The Eye slept peacefully on only yards away and while Steffi got ready to apply extreme sexual excitement within a monogamous relationship rather than in a porn movie, I played out the last few seconds of my epic battle with the deep plodding behemoth.

A little run there, easily turned. Up to the surface and more air and water gulped. A thrash and head back down only with little power... all looking good, Houston. Back up to the surface the deep plodder came and this time it rolled onto its flank as

I manoeuvred the mirror towards the net, the net my best mate and fishing buddy was wielding. Over it came and with a deft, effortless lift the plodder was mine. Oh yes! Bring it on!

Rambo scrunched the net with his massive right hand and lifted it up along with the fish. As we paddled through the shallow water Rambo turned and prodded The Eye hard in the solar plexus with the landing net handle. The Eye startled into consciousness.

"Oi! The Eye!" barked Rambo. "Remember when you saw him try and swim in six inches of water to get to a run? Here's what he swam for," Rambo informed The Eye as he flicked his head towards me.

The Eye blinked and focused on the huge bulge in the net. "Yeah! The Eye *remembers*, man! Must have crashed out. Too much thinking last night. Wasted me. Your story, man! Your freaky story!"

The Eye walked over to where Rambo and I were unhooking the deep plodder. Lying on my unhooking mat with the net's folds eased away from its huge body and so affording a perfect view, the deep plodder was indeed a beast of magnificent beauty. Large, erratically placed scales dotted the broad flank and although the fish was very dark in hue near its dorsal fin its colour lightened to a vibrant orange/tan either side of the lateral line area and ran to a yellowish white belly. It was a stunner – a very, very big stunner. The best compliment I could give the fish was it looked the equal of any from Hamworthy Fisheries, the finest carp fishery in Britain etc. etc.

"Wow!" stated The Eye. "Cool fish, man. Phone the others."

While Rambo and I (not *The* Eye, me) prepared to weigh the deep plodder, The Eye rang several people and told them to, like, come take a look, man. I don't think I would have been too keen to wind in during what was clearly a feeding spell, but The Eye insisted on sacking the fish until the others could come. Of course, the weight of such a beautiful and fantastic creature is utterly immaterial. Whether it weighed twenty, thirty or even forty pounds made absolutely *no* difference. To have caught and seen it, to have had your photograph taken holding it in all its wondrous magnificence was ample – much more than ample. A lifetime's worth of memories and the photos to go with it were reward enough. This was why it was so strange to hear the edge of desperation in my own voice.

"Well... come *on*. What does it *weigh*?" I badgered Rambo as he hoisted up a zeroed-in set of Nash Nitelites, a weigh sling and a creature carved from a solid lump of wild natural beauty.

"Have a guess," Rambo teased.

"I don't *want* to guess. I want to *know*," I pleaded. "In any case, if I guess what I think it might weigh, *might* weigh, it might stop it weighing it."

Rambo gave me one of his looks. "So you're saying that you guessing... shall I hazard a little guess myself?" I nodded impatiently. Rambo loved all this. "You guessing this fish to be over a certain, shall we call it... *strategic* barrier, because that's what you're hoping against all hope it *will* weigh, might somehow stop it weighing over said strategic barrier... even if I, or you, *haven't* said it. Go on, say it!"

"But..."

"*Say it!*"

There was little point arguing. "Is it over fifty?" I said grudgingly. There – that had fucked it right up! Forty-nine fifteen here we come! Forget all the other crap I said earlier – I *wanted* a Dutch fifty.

Rambo turned the Nitelite's face towards me. "Fifty-six pounds dead! If I'm not mistaken a foreign PB. It's bigger than the Lac Fumant mirror isn't it?"

"*Yessss!*" I cried, though not specifically to Rambo's enquiry.

Rambo sacked the fish for me and The Eye offered to stand barefoot on the edge of the shallows – where I had played out the epic battle against the deep plodder – in order to hold the sack's string as the fish recovered in the deep water.

"What's the difference between The Eye and a bankstick?" Rambo whispered to me before he dashed off to get his camera. I glanced quickly at the painfully thin human holding the string lead to what could be construed as a drowning dog. I shrugged and pulled a face, saying nothing.

"*Exactly*! See you in a sec."

As Rambo jogged over to his bivvy I whispered. "A bankstick can't see into the future?"

The photo shoot did marvels for my ego. Frans, Japp, The Eye and two other Dutch lads, whose names I had forgotten, were knocked over by the deep plodder, which I was now thinking of as Deep Plodder. As far as bankside lore could establish the fish hadn't been caught for six seasons and then at a weight in the high thirties. Consequently, its growth and re-emergence was staggering to all who had fished the venue over the years. To me it was equally as staggering. I received the plaudits from all with good grace, had my photo taken – smiling of course – with Deep Plodder and returned the magnificent carp safely back to its deep, clear, sandy bottomed home. Everyone lingered for a while and after a while eventually drifted off.

"Well done, Matthew," said Frans. "It was worth coming to see such a carp."

"Thanks, Frans," I said shaking the offered hand. "And thanks for inviting me!"

"We won't ask you back again!" joked Frans.

I laughed and waved him goodbye.

"I must also go now to see if I can catch something too. I don't want to blank here as I did at your water. I will see you later, Matthew," said Japp.

"Okay, cheers, Japp. I'm sure you'll get one. Thanks for coming round."

The orange-shirted Dutchman laughed. "My pleasure. A fantastic fish, I wish I had been lucky enough to catch it."

Once Frans and Japp had departed I turned to Rambo and Steffi who had delayed her preparations for bivvy sex and had come to have a gawp at the Deep Plodder. Rambo spoke first. "Right. We'll leave you in peace, boy."

"Okay, mate." I smiled at Rambo and at Steffi. "What do you think of your first fishing trip, Steffi? Enjoying it? Can you see why we go?"

Steffi scrunched her face. "A little… if you can catch ser carp. It is nice being in ser outdoors, vitt ozzer friends who like ser same sing. Yet I am sinking zat none ov ser ozzers have had a fish, sey must be bored out ov sere minds." She looked lovingly, or something pretty much of a similar vein, at her large camouflaged partner. Rambo – a partner. How weird was that concept? Steffi continued. "Ve haff each ozzer to talk to, ve can haff sex if ve vant. Vott do you do if *you* get bored? If you vant to talk? If you vant to…"

"*Don't* go there," I warned. "*Don't* go near the five-fingered bivvy shuffle, please!"

"No. Let's not," said Rambo. "Come on, Steffi. Let's leave Lord Worryguts alone. He's got a big night ahead of him tonight." Rambo looked towards The Eye who was still skulking in my swim. "Eh! The Eye. The future's bright, the future's green, eh?"

Although I doubted if The Eye was especially *au fait* with British mobile phone ads he seemed to get the nuance of Rambo's comment. "Too true, man," he concurred.

I hoped it was true as well or I was totally and truly buggered. "I'm going to phone up Pup and tell him his revolutionary, indented, dirty brown bottom bait boilie is the mutt's nuts in a minute," I informed Rambo. "He'll be well chuffed."

"Say I'm impressed as well," said Rambo and with the request he turned Steffi's shoulder away from me and began walking her back to his bivvy.

"I *wonder* what they're going to get up to?" I said to a grinning The Eye who was sufficiently mentally stable to realise what I meant. "What time tonight for the absinthe mind-meld, mate?" (How many times had that sentence ever been spoken?)

"Nine. Get some sleep before. Eat a little before. Psych yourself, man," The Eye told me.

"Will do. Nine it is. Have absinthe, will time travel!"

I gave The Eye a thumbs-up and nipped into my bivvy to get my mobile. When I came out he was still there, his head nodding as he drew a little circle in the sand (Belinda Carlisle, circa late1980s, ex Go-Gos) with his big toe. I looked at him. He looked at me. "Yes, The Eye, what is it?" I asked sounding like a schoolteacher.

"Man. Bad karma ask. Gotta think of *this* life a bit… can The Eye have some of your bait?"

I gave a little snort of laughter. "Sure, no worries." What else could I say? Giving him it might rack up some good karma points for me.

I gave The Eye a couple of kilos in a spare plastic bag and he went away as happy as a sand boy. No harm in keeping your local clairvoyant and soothsayer sweet. Besides, if he didn't come up with the goods tonight I could just flatten him with the draught from a shaken unhooking mat and take them back, you know, before I fell into total wretchedness and I slit my wrists with a pair of braid scissors.

I went back in my bivvy and worried over the plausibility of Amy being the ghost reborn, of getting some decent kip and an evening kick-off to a mind-melding match with The Eye when pissed on absinthe. But before I did, I made a quick phone call to a certain bait-roller back in England. I could smell his house down the phone.

Chapter 11

At a quarter to nine I reeled in my three rods making the conscious decision to re-bait them all with the revolutionary, indented, dirty brown bottom bait boilie supplied by Pup when I next cast them. Pup, the mean lean Melloney shagging/boilie making machine, had been gracious in receiving my rave review of them by phone earlier and had only said 'I told you so' about nine times. The idea to re-bait all three rods with the revolutionary, indented, dirty brown bottom bait boilie was hardly a huge step in carp bait application strategy – I would have been a bit of a muppet *not* to do so – but if The Eye and I (I know) could come up trumps with a little astute absinthe assimilation, then an altogether different strategy might finally materialise. The long awaited 'wipe the smile off Hollywood's face' strategy could soon be mine! Pause while I cackle sinisterly in the style of Sideshow Bob/demented evil genius. Tonight was the night. Success meant I could strive forward; failure… well, failure was simply too dreadful to contemplate. I wanted Amy back full time and I *had* promised her mother to sort out Hollywood. Me and my big mouth!

My something will turn up, wait and see game plan had done me proud so far – it had turned up Darren's photo in Carp-Talk, the two stunning looking, lap dancing, ex-international gymnasts, who were also bisexual nymphomaniacs in a bar (not *quite* sure of the significance of that… but watch this space), the realisation of a Hollywood run syndicate filled with Hamworthy fish, plus its whereabouts and, last but not least, The Eye. The Eye was a commodity so rare and so precious it was one I had wondered, back in the depths of my depression in Hamworthy's functional wooden clubhouse, if it could ever exist. It had, it *did* – I *wasn't* alone, there were two carping clairvoyants and tonight we would join forces and look into the future. Allegedly.

I was apprehensive – *very* apprehensive. Tonight was my one chance. My chance to grab a future vision by the throat and shake it until it supplied me with the next vital step of my haphazard plan.

I put the third rod back on the buzz bars, hook safely latched onto rod ring like the other two and went and had a pee. Once relieved I glanced at my watch. Five to. This was it. I zipped up my bivvy door to keep the mozzies at bay (they seemed to have suddenly exploded into a multitude of whining flesh eaters from the previous evening) and wandered down to the point swim where The Eye was fishing. The Eye had caught his first carp of the session around midday and there were no prizes for guessing what bait he had caught it on. You had to hand it to Pup; he was a genius when it came to things round and smelly. It gnored away at me not knowing what was in his revolutionary bait, but whatever it was it did seem as if it was something extraordinary. What *could* it be? You would have thought with all the energy and commercialisation going into the modern era bait business every corner and every aspect would have been covered. Apparently not. Pup had found something new and quite rightly was keeping his pack of fifty-two aces close to his chest.

They say the proof is always in the pudding and I'd had it confirmed by Japp an hour ago – the only fish to have come out so far had all been on the revolutionary, indented, dirty brown bottom bait boilie. Our reliable red bait, in spite of Rambo fishing it for a whole day on two rods and me on one, had blanked, and so had all the other baits the other lads were using. Coincidence or wonder boilie? You decide – I knew where my money was placed. I reckoned if Pup was as good at sex as he was at coming up with new bait recipes it was no wonder Melloney had moved into the house of a thousand flavours and replaced her wayward, eloped-with-a-millionaire-angler sister, Melissa.

I craned my neck around The Eye's bivvy's opening. "The Eye?" I said softly.

The Eye's head shot out at an unlikely angle, his lead pendent necklace acting as a plumb-line and accentuating the fact by running down his arm rather than the centre of his chest. "You eaten?" he asked unexpectedly. A vein pulsed at each temple and his eyes were even more shock-horror wide than they had been when he had screeched into the car park earlier and when he was gawping at his thirty-six pound common! He had killer's eyes all right, scary, murderous, aqua-blue eyes sitting somewhat perversely atop a body lacking the physical presence to scream 'killer death machine psycho' at you! If you could have stuck his head on Rambo's body it undoubtedly would have provoked a 'life sentence waiting to happen' observation. The Eye's hair was nice though, constantly denying gravity in its cheery, spiky-blond upstanding manner.

"Yep," I told him.

"You slept?"

"Fitfully, this afternoon."

"You got your chair?"

"No," I admitted with my first negative of our opening dialogue.

"Get your chair, man," I was told.

I went and got it. "Chair, check. Check, chair," I said imitating my dad imitating Tommy Cooper, once I had returned with it. The Eye, being a whippersnapper, virtually a decade younger and therefore not having the remotest idea what I was on about, looked at me as if I was a fucking nutter. To keep things on an even keel I looked at him as if *he* was a fucking nutter. Admittedly this was how I had been looking at him from the first second I had clapped eyes on him, but he hadn't taken umbrage, or hadn't noticed, and to be truthful I hadn't expected any different. I had presumed one of the aspects of being a fucking nutter was you didn't notice people looking at you like you were a fucking nutter *because* you were such a fucking nutter. Whereas, naturally, I saw The Eye looking at me like I was a fucking nutter – and recognised it straight away – because I was patently *not* a fucking nutter. Some might see that viewpoint a little differently. All correspondence on the back of a dead herring, please. Not a red herring… that would put me right off the scent.

"Sit on it, man. Sit and chill," I was instructed. And with that The Eye's head disappeared back into his bivvy.

I sat but didn't chill – I was far too hyper. I let my eyes wander in the last knockings of daylight and was pleased to note The Eye had wound in his three rods as well. The last thing I wanted to happen was to be on the cusp of some futuristic revelation and for a buzzer to go off and rip us both back into the present reality! You can say things like that and mean them with a couple of big fish under your belt.

From The Eye's swim the far bank was visible and I now knew it was Japp who was fishing almost exactly opposite the point swim. Japp had picked one of the swims where the water was shallower, but as at Hamworthy was struggling to get a take. *Everyone* was struggling to get a take if they weren't riding the wave of Pup's towering wall of water i.e. the revolutionary, indented, dirty brown bottom bait boilie!

The Eye reappeared with a small, gunmetal coloured bivvy table upon which, once he had erected it, he placed four large, mottled red scented candles. I knew they were scented because I could smell them – elementary my dear Watson – and I could smell them even though they weren't alight. The Eye soon remedied the situation and lit all four. However, much like sniffing a boilie your mate has given to you with the express instruction, 'Go on smell that, guess what flavour it is?' I couldn't quite put my finger on what the candles smelt of – not specifically. Fruity… fruityish – you know what it's like.

I watched the four orange flames flicker in the capricious zephyr of the evening. The Eye had set the bivvy table down in front of my chair, my sitting-outside-the-bivvy-in-the-sun-during-the-day chair that neatly converted into my sitting-outside-the-bivvy-under-the-moon-during-the-night chair. (What an awesomely adaptable bit of kit it was and I fleetingly felt as if the marketing men had missed an opportunity.) The Eye got his chair (ditto as mine) and put it down on the other side of the table so the two chairs were facing each other. After he had done this he went back to base bivvy.

Perusing his chair and its relationship to the table and to mine I began to think silly thoughts with the intent of taking my mind off the scary momentousness of the next few hours. What might we do to break the ice and set the mood before the main event of the evening, that of chasing the future? Perhaps we were going to have a game of chess before we started, I mused. One where the chess pieces had been painstakingly individually carved from redundant hanger bodies during the lean times between takes. (Christ! I could have gone into mass production during my winter on Hamworthy!) The King… Terry Hearn? In bad taste, Steffi and Frans would make good pawn/porn and as for The Queen…? Fill it in for yourself – libel's a nasty old business.

I moved on, dismissing the chess option because even draughts was too cerebral for me! It could be we were going to embark on a just-for-fun arm wrestling match. I had no sooner thought this than dismissed it. No. The bivvy table looked marginally more flimsy than The Eye's arms and a physical tussle didn't strike me as being his kind of fun. A grin stretched my face. I knew what it was! It was going to be a game of blow football to start off, one with two straws and a dirty brown twenty-millimetre ball. We would both try to blow it into each other's goal – candlesticks for goalposts *and* floodlights – until one of us died from an asthma attack or the candles burnt down so much the ref had to abandon the game due to floodlight failure and a severe lack of goalposts. When The Eye returned he placed a distinctive green bottle and two empty glasses on the bivvy table. Two other similar green bottles and a rucksack went down on the ground by his chair. I knew now it would be none of the things I had thought of earlier – it would be straight to the drinking.

"Is that where your nickname came from?" I asked The Eye, gesturing towards the label on the bottle of absinthe – the label with a huge singular eye staring out from the centre of it.

The Eye nodded. "Bootlegged Swiss absinthe labelled as legal French absinthe!" He winked and smiled, but the smile soon disappeared from his face. "The Eye's not sure how this is going to work, man," he warned me as he sat on his chair. "Not with two."

As he spoke he unzipped the rucksack with shaking hands (think; trying to tie on a piece of mixer while a forty hoovers up your free offerings just yards away from you). The Eye was evidently feeling the pressure as much as I was. From the bag he took a smaller bag of sugar cubes, a flask and one of the peculiar spoons I remembered seeing on the websites when I had trawled them for absinthe info. He placed them all on the tiny bivvy table. I picked up the spoon and inspected it. His was like a very ornate cake slice lifter, it had a middle groove with a pattern of circular and diamond shaped cut-outs on the flat spoon part – which had upturned sides – while the handle had a slight kink in it a half inch away from the spoon end. I placed the slotted spoon over the glass. The rim sat neatly into the handle's kink whilst the spoon's tip marginally overhung the glass. It balanced perfectly. I remembered from my research that the sugar cube would be placed on the centre of the slotted spoon and iced water would be poured over it into the glass containing the absinthe. How ritualistic!

"What do you normally do when you're on your own?" I asked him.

The Eye scratched at his spiky hair and began to count out the list and point at the items on it with a tremoring index finger. "Table. Chair. Candles. Swiss absinthe. Cold water onto sugar, into absinthe, drink it. See what happens, man."

I nodded. It was hardly scientific. Besides, there was precious little science to explain what the pair of us had achieved in the past or what I desperately hoped we *could* achieve in an hour or so. "Are the candles for the ambience, you know, a special type?"

The Eye nodded his head. "Yeah," he didn't explain or expound.

"I see," I said, not seeing at all. I lifted up the green bottle. "Is this stuff very alcoholic?"

"Ninety-five per cent, man."

I let out a low whistle. "Shit! Don't you get pissed before the thujone works?" The Eye gave me a longer than usual wide aqua-blue eyed stare. I got his drift. "I looked it up on the Internet before we came," I told him by way of an explanation.

"Swiss-made absinthe, man. Shit loads of wormwood."

I nodded and wondered if I was going to become another alcohol/drug fatality statistic. I would find out soon enough, especially as The Eye had now opened the bottle and was pouring a measure into each glass. He proceeded to trickle cold water from the flask over the sugar cube on the spoon. I watched the green liquid in both glasses turn to an opalescent greeny-white.

"Here goes, man," said The Eye. "Here's to the future. The next step in your freaky story."

"The future," I said, raising my glass and I downed the contents in one. A liquorice taste hit the back of my mouth – not the greatest flavour sensation I had ever experienced – swiftly followed by the question; Had Hollywood's spunk been similarly disagreeable when it had hit the back of Sophie's mouth? It was this knotty conundrum that caused my body to shudder, only The Eye thought otherwise.

"Tastes weird at first, man. You'll grow to love it."

I chastised myself for getting sucked off (bad choice of phrase) into my place of personal demons – I really *had* to put the Sophie/Hollywood thing into the lockable 'nasty' compartment Rambo had told me about or the prospect of being a re-united family was distant. I hoped I would once I had wiped the smile off his face.

Trying to concentrate on the events in the present leading to hopefully snatching a glimpse of the future rather than the past (it's like a fucking grammar lesson all this) I watched in fascination as The Eye's eyes grew calmer with each glass of the good green stuff. By the fifth glass they looked almost mellow and his eyelids had drooped enough to lose his lunatic look. Fuck knows what mine looked like, they felt heavier, yet my head was *lighter* – I felt as if someone had been pumping helium into my right ear.

"How many's it take?" I asked The Eye.

He poured out another two glasses with a steady hand. A *very* steady hand now I come to mention it. "For The Eye it's usually eight or nine, if it's going to happen. Just remember it doesn't happen every time, man." The Eye cranked his head around this way and then that way on his skinny neck. "Oh, man," he confided, "The Eye feels *well* loose, now." Not too loose, I hoped. I didn't want his bloody head falling off! "*You* might feel it quicker, not being so used to it."

I nodded. I was feeling it all right. My status as a hopeless manager of liquor was in no danger of being rescinded. I was getting pissed pretty quickly... but there *was* something else and it reminded me of my trip on my trip to Lac Fumant.

'Heightened perception' was how I would describe it, a very strange feeling of oneness with everything – use The Force, Matt – and a higher degree of understanding. Not that it stretched to knowing what Pup was slipping into his revolutionary, indented, dirty brown bottom bait boilie unfortunately, but certainly other, almost as intriguing, secrets were less inaccessible than before. (Like *anything* is *more* intriguing than a wonder bait ingredient!)

My eyes stared into the flickering orange candles now comprehending the chemical combination of a substance with oxygen accompanied by the evolution of heat and light, a soft orange light. I could feel the molecules carrying the scent of the candles after they had travelled to my nose and were dissolved in mucus before drifting to my olfactory epithelium. Here ten million smell receptors reacted to the dissolved chemicals and sent a message to my brain; the candles smelt of... *grapefruit!*

"Why the fuck do the candles smell of grapefruit, The Eye?" I asked in only a slightly slurred voice.

"They're an energy candle, man. Grapefruit is a smell of energy, like clove or coriander."

I wasn't impressed. "How much energy can there be in a fucking *grapefruit?*" I said starting to laugh. "All it does is *sit* there until someone eats it!"

"If it was at the top of a hill and you gave it a push it'd roll, man. Really roll. Keep on rolling until the hill ran out," The Eye answered.

"That's *potential* energy!" I cried. And then not being too sure of my old physics schoolwork I added the rider. "Isn't it?"

The Eye downed another glass. "No idea, man. School wasn't The Eye's thing." The Eye shut one eye and looked down into his empty glass. "Nothing was The Eye's thing until The Eye found absinthe and carp fishing," he explained. He looked up at me with slits for eyes. "And do you know all the time The Eye sat and fished The Eye thought of what The Eye could find to make sense of the world. And the only thing The Eye found was Buddhism. And when The Eye saw into the future The Eye thought maybe the soul *can* move on out of a body, survive on its own. It made *some* sort of sense, man... more than anything else. And then you, man, you and your story have proved it right... at least to The Eye. You've proved it right to The Eye." He poured himself another glass and ran the cold water from his flask over yet another sugar cube.

I stared at him, the skinny bastard with his rig tube friendship bracelet, lead pendent necklace and good hair. High, low, medium, gas mark 6, whatever he was on, he was different under the influence of absinthe. Relaxed and with his truncated pattern of speech and jerky head movement virtually gone, he was The Eye Mark II. Instinctively I reached out to him, like I had tried to do many times before to Amy, not with a hand, not with physical touch, but with my mind. I pushed and pushed harder... and gatecrashed The Eye's mind.

First impressions? Fuck me, what a mess!

116

Hopes, fears, desires, needs, philosophies, temperament, aspirations, opinions and memories were strewn haphazardly – even more haphazardly than my wait-and-see-what-comes-up-next plan – and utterly randomly across The Eye's mind. It was disorganised, dysfunctional, disconnected, disarranged, disturbed, distinctive and yet disarming – it *wasn't* disagreeable, disastrous, disaffected, discouraged, disengaged, disgusting or dishonest. The Eye's mind was like the bedroom of a likable, yet frustratingly untidy, child and its consciousness rose up to meet mine. 'Welcome aboard, man,' it 'said' – not in words as such because we were beyond the need for such rudimentary means of communication – but by mind-meld telepathy. I watched The Eye's version of a personal Internet with the sum knowledge of all his experiences, thoughts and phobias rotate around me as if I was at the hub of a carousel. Above the carousel was a large bright canopy, a huge umbrella from where The Eye's 'words' emanated. This was his entity; this was what made him, 'him', and below it span the images of his life, his thoughts, his everything. Ironically having a carouse had given me access to The Eye's mind's carousel.

Random images of things, people, experiences and concepts fluttered by on the carousel; an image of his mother, one of his younger self, a group of young adults looking down on him, a large carp, his first sexual experience, a black smudge, a car accident, a blazing row with a girl, an absinthe spoon, fishing tackle, a black smudge, fear of company, of speaking, love of fishing, love of nature, fear of commitment, fear of the drudgery of work, a black smudge, shyness, social embarrassment, embracement of Buddhism, a whole world in fact – The Eye's world – passed before me like a deck of playing cards being flicked, each card an almost subliminal exposure before the next in a rat-a-tat-tat quick-fire parade. I concentrated and searched for what I was looking for, but there was no search engine facility here, no Google button to click. I needed help. Instantly The Eye's mind grabbed one of the spinning, revolving images and held it out for me to see. There it was. I recognised it as *the* thing I had been looking for… a vision of the future, one leading to the capture of a large carp.

Frantically my mind leapt onto the carousel and chased it, chased it through all the disassembled, random, kaleidoscopic memories and thoughts that whirled and spun and constituted The Eye's mind. Maybe all minds were like this, I didn't know, this was the first time I had melded with a human – compared to the mirror at Lac Fumant it was staggeringly complex. My mind weaved in and out, in and out of The Eye's mental existence, chasing the vision of the future as I circled endlessly, swimming against the revolving tide of The Eye's other experiences. The black smudge was the one thing to keep constantly appearing whereas all the other events were random and unique – even a life as young as The Eye's had masses and masses of data storage. I dodged under a day out at the beach, side-stepped a driving lesson, avoided a dislike of Indian food and connected to the vision of the future and forced upon it *my* vision of Hollywood – grinning smugly on my doorstep as a distraught, crying Sophie lay broken on the hallway floor.

'The bastard, man,' The Eye 'said'. And suddenly, astonishingly, quantum leap style, we were out of The Eye's head and flying over the land at supersonic speed to arrive high above a lake. With a vertigo-inducing dive we plummeted downwards to view the picturesque scene of a large, English, rhododendron and tree-lined estate lake. The scene of English perfection was marred only by where a large tree branch had fallen into the margin next to what was an obvious swim. Two men stood in the swim and looked out to where a third man was arriving across the water in a sturdy wooden boat powered by a small petrol outboard motor. I recognised them all. The two in the swim were Rocky and Darren; the one in the boat was Hollywood. Here was the glimpse of the future I had dared to hope I could see. I watched the scene from the future play out before me as I had watched the scene of Rambo's would be assassination – only this time the medium was The Eye's mind.

I saw Hollywood feather down the engine via its twist-grip throttle/steering handle and then stop it. The wooden boat glided alongside the large branch and came to rest as the friction between branch and hull took its toll. Hollywood retrieved a hidden petrol chainsaw from the bottom of the boat, started it up and proceeded to cut up the large branch in complete silence. I could see the future, not hear it. Hollywood wielded the chainsaw with consummate ease. He was obviously well practised at using such a dangerous tool and as he sliced the branch into more manageable pieces Rocky and Darren manoeuvred the lumps onto dry ground until gradually, piece by piece, the swim was made snag free.

Mesmerised I watched as future Hollywood jumped onto dry land, cranked up the chainsaw yet again and cut the pieces pulled from the water by Rocky and Darren into foot-long sections. Once completed and while the two landlubbers piled the logs neatly in an area away from the swim Hollywood turned his boat around, placed the chainsaw safely in the bottom, climbed in and started up the outboard motor with its rope pull. With the engine running he sat himself on an integral plank running across the boat's breadth and settled down for his tiny cruise across the lake. As he twisted open the throttle and pulled away from the bank something must have caught his eye in the water, a fish perhaps, and Hollywood quickly got to his feet to gain a better view only for him to stumble over the chainsaw. As he lost balance his hand revved the twist-grip throttle to maximum as well as yanking the steering handle to full lock. The boat lurched hard to starboard and the extra movement coupled with a loss of balance caused him to pitch head first into the water. With glee I watched him disappear under the surface and the boat drive itself over the top of him and run on a long arc before thumping into the bank. Hollywood was still underwater; the dork couldn't swim!

Alerted by the splash I couldn't hear, Rocky ran into the water and dived in, himself disappearing under the water. Transfixed I watched huge amounts of bubbles break the surface shortly to be followed by Rocky and, disappointingly from my viewpoint, a gasping Hollywood. Rocky powerfully hauled the soggy Hollywood up onto the bank where my nemesis coughed, spluttered and threw up some lake water.

After a short burst of violent coughing, reaching and spitting Hollywood calmed down and a large smile spread across his still handsome face. Mission *not* accomplished! With blinding speed the vision pulled away to a large bush situated in what appeared to be a coppice some thirty yards from the swim. Behind the bush, in full camouflage regalia, Rambo and I hid and watched!

Confusion grabbed me. This wasn't what I was expecting to see, not now or not when I was in the future, when I was actually there. This was no good! This *hadn't* wiped the smile off Hollywood's face at all! All he was to get was wet! And – I realised with horrifying panic – the vision was fading! The power of the absinthe was weakening and it was my fault! I couldn't hang on to the revolving vision of the future for any longer. I tried; grimly I tried, with all my resolution and all my might to hang on, but I couldn't and I seemingly fell out of the vision back into the mass of spinning, individual collectiveness that comprised The Eye's mind. The black smudge came by again.

'Can you see that?' I 'asked'.

'See what, man?'

'The black smudge.'

'What black smudge?'

'There! There it goes again. It's the only thing I've seen twice. I keep seeing it.'

The Eye told me he couldn't see it so I made a conscious decision – about the only one I could make considering where I was – to try and look at it to find out what it was. I felt as if I hadn't long left. My ability to stay within The Eye's head would soon be over and as I figuratively waded through the kaleidoscope that was The Eye's mind I knew I had to act fast. Luckily I soon found it.

The black smudge turned out to be an optical illusion. It wasn't randomly reappearing here there and everywhere, it was staying still. It was staying still but only appeared to me when there was a brief gap in The Eye's stream of images. It gave the *impression* of movement, but in fact there was none. I edged closer to it. It was a black smudge. A deep black smudge and whereas colour and vibrancy spun all around it, it appeared lifeless. A dark, brooding, deep black smudge of inert nothingness. I stared at it and swore I saw, at the very edge of its indistinctive blurred, smudged outline, a pinprick of darkness appear across the colour it blotted out. Realisation! It was *growing*! A dark, brooding, deep black smudge of *active* something. With a vast feeling of disgust I watched it sitting on some part of The Eye's brain – dark, brooding, malevolent… *malignant*. I knew what it was and the shock of it jettisoned me out of The Eye's head and back into my own.

I saw the moon and the stars. A mosquito whined by my ear and I immediately collapsed face first onto a flimsy bivvy table smashing it to pieces in the process.

Chapter 12

I had awoken ten minutes ago, or had come round – I wasn't *too* sure which route I had taken, but the end result was the same. The ten minutes I had been 'up' I had spent slumped in my sitting-outside-the-bivvy-in-the-sun-during-the-day chair, still in the point swim next to The Eye's bivvy, feeling dazed and sorry for myself. My face and head hurt like hell and I couldn't see properly. My mouth felt kind of funny as well. Whilst grappling with these newfound physical manifestations – although not very successfully – a certain ex-porn star and my numero uno buddy, Rambo, turned up. The female part of this blooming relationship started to ask me trick questions.

"My gott!" said Steffi her hand cupping her mouth. "Vott haff you been doing to look like zat?" she asked in horror.

While the cogs of my brain ground forward by a microscopic amount the camouflaged one answered for me. "Diving face first onto a bivvy table by the looks of it," said Rambo surveying the debris of an ex-bivvy table. Trying hard, but dismally failing, to contain the amusement in his voice he continued. "It's the wax in the hair and ears I'm having trouble getting my head around." Rambo came up, bent down and sniffed me. "Hmm. Fruity... fruityish! Can't *quite* put my finger on it. Come on, boy, illuminate me."

"Gratefruit," I mumbled – I knew what was wrong with my mouth by now. It seemed I had two lips each the size of the back tyre on a sports bike and not far off the colour I suspected, only without the tread pattern – I hoped.

"Did The Eye perform plastic surgery on those lips, boy? A grapefruit flavoured injection of special wax collagen to give you the old trout-pout so preferred by today's sad generation of superficial morons," Rambo quipped.

I tried to explain. "No. Ind-eld. Collast on gihhy table after. Hucked. Totally hucked. The Eye's totally hucked as ell."

"I can see The Eye's totally fucked as well," said Rambo, "because I'm looking at him hanging over his bivvy like a jumper chucked over a washing line."

Rambo was right. The Eye *was* hanging over his bivvy, hanging over his bivvy exactly in between two of the main poles of his Trakker Armo MKII with neither a foot nor a hand touching *terra firma*. I was going to suggest to Rambo he take a picture of him and offer it to Trakker as a promotional shot – one to extol the virtues of its robust construction and inherent strength. A bivvy with a safe roof to crash on is always useful after a hard night's mind-melding on illegal, Swiss-made, bootlegged absinthe and could well make a good selling point. Unfortunately my lips hurt too much so I didn't bother. I tried to sniff but my nose was blocked by the congealed blood caked on its inside. I felt like shit, the only plus point being I hadn't thrown-up and given my track record with alcohol – coloured green or otherwise – this was an almighty bonus.

The shit feeling was, fortunately, now my brain was functioning enough to rationalise such things, all head orientated. I attributed this in a three-way split to the duress of a mind-meld coupled with the mother of all hangovers and the physical impact of slumping face first through a flimsy bivvy table – to begin with – before impacting upon the bivvy table's main back-up. I am referring, of course, to the ground.

I looked at my watch with a depth perception bordering zero due to my right eye being shut – swollen shut. *That* was why I couldn't see properly! At least its colour probably matched my lips. I felt it tenderly. The eyebrow above it felt swollen as well, swollen enough to give a Neanderthal a run for his money. It was eight in the morning. With my one good eye I looked around to see if there was somewhere I could crawl off to, lick my wounds and pass out in private for a few hours.

My bivvy. I *needed* my bivvy. Sanctuary. And a comfy bed.

"Oi going to ged," I said pointing vaguely to the distance. "Don't eel to good. Look ater The Eye or e. I'll ell you all agout it later." And with those heroic words I got up, took my sitting-outside-the-bivvy-in-the-sun-during-the-day chair, waved all offers of help aside, and staggered back to my bivvy, chucked the chair on the ground, unzipped the mozzie door and collapsed on my bed. It felt so comfy. In an instant I was asleep. My rods, naturally, remained uncast.

When I awoke or came round, I still wasn't sure which, for the second time in the day, I felt a bit better. I felt well enough to notice my arms, my bare arms from the warm night before, were covered in mosquito bites. I reasoned if my arms had been bitten there was a good chance my face had been attacked as well. I scratched my itching arms and went to ask Rambo to have a look.

"Nope," he insisted. "Not one. I reckon you must have slept on your face and that piece of good fortune saved you from having your face eaten off, or…" during the pause I gave Rambo my best one-eyed 'well-come-on-then-let's-here-the-latest-piss-take' stare, "the sight of your ugly mug was so gruesome it scared them off and they decided to make do with your meatless arms!"

Steffi tut-tutted. "You are zo horrible to him, Rambo. Vy are you zo horrible to your best friend?"

"*Horrible?*" said Rambo astonished. "This is TLC isn't it, boy?"

I winked at him and the lights went out. For a split second I panicked and thought I had gone blind. "It's called sarcasn," I explained gaining my composure. (I could just about bear my lips to touch each other now.) "Us gest riends use it all the tine." (But not enough to pronounce an 'F', 'V','P', 'B' or an 'M'.)

"British humour. Tch!" Steffi said unimpressed.

"How's The Eye?" I asked.

"Mosquito bites to the back of the neck, the arms and to the feet, especially the soles. Apart from that he's racing. He came round just after you'd crawled back into your hole, gave himself a good scratch and started fishing like he was on a mission. He told me the union between him and you was the second most fantastic thing in his life *and* he was onto a carp." Rambo gave me a look and the hint of a rise at the corners of his mouth made me guess what was coming next. "Buggery in a bivvy was it?"

"No it gloody wasn't guggery in a gihhy!" I said. "It was ind-eld i gratefruit scented candlelight." I gave Steffi and Rambo a far away look – how far, I couldn't tell you, because of my depth perception being temporarily offline. "And we saw the uture, The Eye and e… and I saw sonething else as well," I said lugubriously thinking of the dark smudge. "Sonething horriggle."

If Rambo was thinking of saying 'gottle of geer, gottle of geer' he jammed the words up in his throat because of the inflection in my voice. He could tell I was serious.

"What was it, boy?" he said quietly.

I looked at him and at Steffi biting her bottom lip. "The Eye ight e dying," I said slowly. "When I was in his head I saw a tunour, a grain tunour."

Rambo was horrified. "A *brain* tumour? Are you *sure*?"

I nodded. "I saw it growing."

"Does he know?" Steffi asked gravely.

This time I shook my head. "He couldn't see it. I asked hin ih he could gut he couldn't."

"So what happened, boy?"

I raised one eyebrow. Neanderthals could never have shown surprise. "I'll tell you."

So I told them. I was getting good at telling these stories, re-capping the events of my life, even when impaired by a speech impediment.

When I had finished Rambo was the first to comment. "Only *you* could tell me a story like that, boy," he said slowly shaking his head. "You can see why I've stuck with him can't you," he said turning to Steffi. "Despite all the introverted, endless, trawling, neurotic self-analysis, plus the occasional big carp, there's always a new revelation waiting just around the corner. You're weird, Matt. Very weird… and not a *bad* carp angler, which, at the end of the day, is what we are all to be judged by."

"Oh, sure," said Steffi with a bit of German sarcasm.

"What about the vision?" Rambo asked. "And what about The Eye's tumour? You'll have to tell him, tell him to go get it checked out. You might have got it wrong."

"I hote so," I said masking my inner thoughts. Inwardly I knew there was no chance of me being wrong, it was purely a question of curability. "The ision," I shrugged. "I'n not sure how it can helt."

"Intervention!" said Steffi. "You haff to intervene to change vott you saw! If you don't your vision vill be ser future and sis Hollyvood vill be okay. I can't remember its title now but I am sure I haff read a book vhere someone does somesing similar. I vill find out vhen ve get back to England."

I was at a loss despite Steffi's assurances. "Gut how? Aybe he'll get Weil's disease fron the water and die fron that."

Rambo gave me a sceptical look. "Rats are immune to their own piss, boy. It ain't going to happen. Steff's right, at some stage in the future you've got to *do* something to change the version of the future you've seen."

"What ih the uture is set in stone? What ih I can't change it?" I said.

Rambo went to open his mouth but stopped. I suspected he was about to remind me how I had intervened before, intervened to save his life, only he couldn't because of Steffi's presence. If he had, I would have pointed out the vision I had seen of him, after being jump-started into it by Alan's phone call, had been *exactly* as it was in reality. If I had seen Rambo being shot by the asylum seeker and *then* had managed to change it by my intervention, I would have felt confident I could do it again. That hadn't been the case; I had merely arrived on the scene at the end of my vision and had altered what was going to happen later, *not* what I had seen in the vision. If I was to exact my revenge on Hollywood I had to *change* what I had seen. It was a completely different situation.

"We all have choices, boy. Fate might push us one way or another from time to time but we choose the road we go on. You *have* to believe that or we'd all go loopy," said Rambo. "You've got to believe in free will."

I nodded weakly, a list of problems racking up on top of my headache. I didn't even know *when* this vision was going to happen – although apparently I *would* because I was there, there with Rambo, in full camouflage regalia, which in itself pointed to forethought, prior knowledge and planning. And if I chose not to go? I suppose that at least did prove the vision could be changed. Conundrum with a capital 'C', or what? Fuck me, I thought, this future lark was fraught with problems – even with an advanced screening! What I needed to do was to go and cast out, unwind and heal. I would make a start and deal with the most pressing problem later.

I made my excuses, returned to my swim and slowly, very slowly started to get into some semblance of a fishing mode. It wasn't easy due to my physical roughness, the vagaries of the vision and the necessity of my having to be the harbinger of such terrible news to the poor The Eye. I set to casting three rods baited with three twenty millimetre revolutionary, indented, dirty brown bottom bait boilies onto the spots I had fished earlier. (Just as an aside next time you're fishing, just for a laugh, try baiting up with boilies and a catapult with one eye shut, or putting a boilie stop through a hair loop. It's horrendous!) My accuracy was, consequently, how should we put it, somewhat below par. My sight deficiency, coupled with my crushing headache and impending improbable tasks ahead, will hopefully allow all you carp heads out there to let me off when I admit to my parallelogram baiting pattern on the middle rod not being *quite* as tight as it should have been. Call me the Scattergun Kid.

"Uck it," I quietly said to myself. "That'll do." And if any of you have *never* said that – not even *once* – then I don't believe you!

I dozed throughout the warm, sunny day, made myself a fair few cuppas and drank them through my tender lips. Gradually I recuperated and began to shake off the hangover caused by the absinthe. I was tempted to go and see how The Eye was doing, but every time I was I shunned the notion because of what I had to tell him. To be truthful I was desperate to see him and ask him 'how was it for you?' even with the associated connotations of Rambo's 'buggery in a bivvy' jibe. I wanted to exchange notes, to see if it had appeared in the same way to him. To see if he had witnessed some tiny facet I had missed making it more useful. Somehow I doubted it. We had been linked, melded, we would have seen it the same way... and yet The Eye *couldn't* see the black smudge.

I suppose we *had* achieved what I had set out to do – apart from the inconclusiveness of the vision. In truth I hadn't a clue what I had been expecting to 'see' in any case, perhaps I should count myself lucky I had managed to see anything at all. After all, it was only a once in a lifetime chance. Uneasily I wondered how long The Eye's lifetime would last and then spent the next half hour worrying whether he had seen a black smudge in my head, one *I* couldn't see.

In retrospect it was evident the absinthe had made something happen to me as well as The Eye because I had slipped into him very easily when it had come down to it. (His *head*! Oh, for God's sake! Slipped my *mind* into his head!) I had never been able to do a human-to-human mind-meld before – in actuality I had only managed *one*, with the Lac Fumant mirror – and I had tried plenty of times with Amy. I would have to make a point of finding out The Eye's absinthe supplier and have a private dabble with it. You never know, I might be able ascertain if his theory of the ghost being reborn into Amy had any credence – *if* I could get inside her little head and provided a small remnant of a past life existed in its new body

Of course, I still had to relay this latest implausible piece of information to her mother. Feasibly not a bad thing, it might possibly help unite us, provided I kept my promise to her and my revenge came to be reality. How to make it happen, though...? I went over the vision yet again – I was on familiar ground here – and pondered, brooded, meditated, cogitated, deliberated and generally mused and mulled over it in a carp-angler-alone-in-his-little-world kind of way. I came up with nothing.

My mobile rung and woke me up. It was Pup. "Had any more?" he demanded with infectious enthusiasm.

I told him since I had last spoken to him I had lent some of the revolutionary, indented, dirty brown bottom bait boilie to a bloke called The Eye and he'd had one on it. I also reported as far as I was aware all the fish caught had been on his bait, two by yours truly, one by Rambo and one by The Eye. I tempered this glowing report with the fact I had been out of commission for around twelve hours and so wasn't fully up to speed on the latest catch situation.

"What do you mean 'out of commission'?"

"A git to uch to drink," I said sheepishly.

"Are you drunk now?" said a disgusted voice.

"No!"

"You sound it. You're a bloody disgrace, Matthew Williams! You're there to fish, not drink! To catch more fish on my revolutionary baits."

I couldn't explain what had happened, I couldn't face it. I had told enough tales on this session already and my lips were still in Sum 41 track territory. "What's in it?" I asked trying the old diversionary tactic.

"Wouldn't *you* like to know," Pup said garrulously. Hah! Pup never could resist talking bait.

"That's why I'n asking," I replied.

"Get me in Hamworthy Fisheries and I might tell you," he said cheekily.

"What Hanworthy Hisheries… the hinest carp hishery in Gritain?"

There was a pause.

"Mmm. That's the one," said Pup slowly.

"I'll see what I can do, gut I can't romise anything."

There was another pause.

"You got drunk and fell face first through a bivvy table didn't you?" Pup proclaimed.

I pulled my mobile away from my ear and stared at it in glorious mono-vision. There was more to Pup than met the eye. Even my one eye could see that. If Pup were to meet The Eye then The Eye would see there was more to Pup than meets the eye. "Aybe," I admitted returning the phone to my ear.

"You blokes *never* learn, do you? Look, I can't hang around talking to you and your smashed up face all day, I've got fifty kilos waiting to be mixed *and* I'm on a promise with Melloney. I'll speak to you later. *Try* and behave for the rest of the session, eh?"

Pup hung up. "Sure thing, goss," I said grumpily to the dead phone and, still slightly peeved at his amazingly correct deduction, I went and sat and waited for a run – like you do.

When I didn't get one – like you don't – after some four hours, I realised it was time to force myself to do the right thing. I grabbed the nettle by the horns, grasped the plunge, took the bull and went to meet The Eye just after tea-time, with, I might add, my Delkim receiver safely clipped to tracky bottoms. I was shaking like a drum, my heart was pounding like a leaf; my metaphors and similes more muddled than a Ritalin withdrawn ADHD diagnosed kid's sweet bag at the pick'n'mix counter. Nevertheless, I walked up to The Eye's point swim.

He gave me a wonderful smile, underlining his blazing aqua-blue eyes and my heart sank at the prospect of what I had to tell him. His head jerked down to his watch. "In time, man. The Eye was going to phone. In five." And he held up a palm full of fingers to me. "Watch!" The Eye vigorously scratched his left arm leaving red weals along its length and fixed his gaze on his rods.

I did as I was told and halted my tracks, glad of any distraction from and postponement of my cruel task. As I stood and watched I heard footsteps and voices murmuring behind me. I turned round to see the entire group of anglers on the water turn up en bloc, including Steffi and Rambo. Japp came up to me and only smiled fleetingly at my battered countenance. I guessed he had heard how it had happened.

"It is show time, Matthew," he whispered. "The Eye has seen… and we've all come to see it."

While we had spoken the crowd of carp anglers had formed a horseshoe shaped line around The Eye's swim, one deep, so no one had to endure restricted viewing – I was the only one suffering from that condition! I immediately clicked on what was going on – Rambo had said The Eye was on a mission and onto a carp. The Eye was living up to his publicity and to his name. The show was soon to begin and we were all in the front row seats. The anglers stood with excited expressions on their faces, nudging each other here, whispering a few words there, enthralled and spellbound by what they were going to see. The Eye moved towards his rods, a smile of utter certainty on his face. He pointed to the right-hand rod, gesticulating his finger over it so there could be no mistake of intent, no ambiguity, no blurring of identity whatsoever. He held up one finger to his audience. Several of the anglers checked their watches, me included.

"If he's fucked up and got it wrong it's going to be a case of car crash carp fishing," Rambo whispered.

I was homed in on The Eye's right-hand rod's indicator. My good eye never left it. "He hasn't," I said.

"The minute is almost up," said Japp.

A complete hush fell over the group. The Eye, who was to the right side of his three-rod set-up so as not to obscure anyone's view, flicked a glance right-hand rodwards. Was there a scintilla of doubt in that glance? No. Fifteen more seconds passed. Another glance. *Now?* The Eye widened his eyes at his audience and began to mouth words. With only one eye I struggled to make out what it was straight away, but when I picked out The Eye mouth 'eight' and heard several other voices say it in accented English, I knew it was a countdown to blast off!

"Sheven! Shix! Five! Four!" chorused the Dutch group at the top of their voices. A shiver of naked excitement ran up my back. My lips still hurt too much to shout but I was in there, mumbling to the best of my ability. "Three! Two! *One!*" they all screamed.

Delay of a nanosecond.

Deeeeeeeeeeeeee! Deeeeeeeeeeeeeeeeeeeeeeeeeeeeeeeee! The Eye's right-hand buzzer erupted, on cue. Thirteen anglers and one ex-porn star also erupted – into delirious applause.

"Eye! Eye! Eye! Eye! Eye! Eye! Eye! Eye! Eye! Eye!" we hollered as The Eye, after a florid thespian-style bow, hit the take. The take he had previously seen as a vision of the future during an absinthe bender – after I had vacated his head and slam-dunked the bivvy table with my face. Briefly I thought I really ought to offer to buy him another one before I felt the wave of collective adrenalin surge through all of us and we screamed and bayed like a group of football supporters whose team had scored a late winner. People were jumping, clapping and cheering like lunatics – lunatics watching a fucking nutter. Steffi had jumped into Rambo's arms, her legs astride his waist, and was punching her fist into the air, Japp was jigging around in his bright orange football shirt doing a dance that could only be described as 'eclectic', Frans had just cut off a call from Betty without even speaking to her and was whistling and clapping and the other blokes, whose names I still couldn't remember, had started doing a Mexican wave; up and then back down the horseshoe line their bodies made. It was brilliant and I too, was swept away by the euphoria of seeing something as mind-blowingly preposterous and unlikely as a bona fide, on time, on rod, one hundred per cent legit, predicted carp take.

I had seen numerous exciting heart-jumping sporting events over the years and up there with the best of them was The Eye getting his predicted take at a sand pit near Westerhoven before an invited audience. Wow! And they say fishing's 'boring' and 'passive'! What *do* they know?

While we cheered and clapped and danced The Eye quickly won the day on the carp playing front and soon guided the fish safely into his net. He had played it with much bravado and I suspected the sneaky git had seen he would land it, otherwise I doubted he would have been quite as cavalier! (Was that a bad omen for me changing *my* vision? Was Rambo wrong about personal decision-making? Was that fish destined to stay on the hook *whatever* The Eye had done? If so, I was shafted.)

Once the battle was over the crowd immediately invaded the pitch and swarmed over to him offering handshakes and pats on the back. The palms of well-wishers' hands pummelled the Eye's skinny body and as usual it was the one from Rambo that jolted him the most. When it came to my turn, in the interest of him taking no further physical punishment, I shook his hand. "Well done, The Eye! Antastic stuh! Glad I could get here to see it, even ih it was through one eye!"

The Eye was in a chatty mood. "Fell out of The Eye's head, fell through The Eye's bivvy table, man! The Eye was gone, too. Ended up on The Eye's bivvy roof. Fucking mozzies ate The Eye alive! The Eye saw though. Saw like The Eye had never seen before. Saw your vision. Saw that carp," he said pointing to the lovely mirror Japp and Frans were preparing to weigh.

"I saw sonething else," I said sombrely.

The Eye's murderous, aqua-blue eyes widened even further. "What?"

I licked my fat tender lips. "Do you eher get headaches?"

"Did you see how much it weighed?" said Japp excitedly to no one in particular.

The Eye's head shook with the distraction. "What, man?"

"Did you see how much it weighed?" Japp asked again, nodding towards the scales – the scales Frans was trying to hold steady as they suspended the large carp and weigh sling.

"Over twenty kilos," The Eye guessed but his look of happiness had gone and his brow was furrowed.

A cheer sprang up as Frans shouted. "Twenty-one kilos exactly!"

I looked away from The Eye to Rambo and raised my one working eyebrow. "Big," he answered. "Over forty-five pounds!"

The Eye shook my shoulder to regain my attention. "Why d'you ask, man?"

"Do you?" I insisted.

The Eye's head dropped and his spiky blond hair levelled itself at me. "Last couple of months," he said to his feet. His head came back up and there were tears welling in his aqua-blue eyes. They no longer looked murderous – they looked scared. "The black smudge thing?"

I averted his stare and nodded. "I saw sonething growing in your head," I explained. "And where it was there was nothing, just glack. No inages, no nenories, no thought… nothing. You should go to a doctor and get it checked out, just to ge on the sahe side. I'n sure it'll ge okay."

The Eye blinked away his tears. He looked young, vulnerable and frightened. "Don't lie, man. What do *you* think it is?"

I rubbed my hand round the back of my neck. Oh shit! "I'n not sure…"

The Eye put his hand on my shoulder again. "Man, The Eye waited for someone like you. Been great. You're story has made The Eye believe… Tell me the truth, man."

With fat bloated lips, one eye swollen shut and seemingly a million mozzie bites, I told him the truth. I told him I thought it was a 'grain tunour'. There. It was done. The last time I had been a bearer of bad news Watt had attacked me on hearing of his being cuckolded, The Eye though, had only nodded gravely.

"Thanks, man," he said and he turned to go and have his photo taken with a large carp. I suddenly wanted to ask if he had seen anything in my head but I didn't have the nerve. I'm sure he would have told me if he had.

Chapter 13

"Maybe you *could* have chosen a better moment... then again when *is* a good time to hit someone with a downer like that?"

My eyes, my *two* eyes, turned away from Rambo and, with *both* eyebrows raised, I looked out across my home venue, Ham – m, m, m, m – worthy Fisheries. My lips were back to normal as well. If The Eye's medical problems turned out to be as easily rectified as my cosmetic facial damage we would all be laughing.

"I guess so," I admitted. "It did kind of ruin his moment of glory. Leaving it for another half hour wouldn't have made any difference."

"Don't go beating yourself up over it, boy, hideous news as it was, it *has* given him an early opportunity to do something about it." Rambo gave me an earnest look. "You've got enough on your plate as it is. Your dish of revenge!"

I flicked my head backwards in synchronicity with my rolled eyes. "Too bloody right! There's *this* to wade through for a start!"

I waggled the paperback I was holding; the one Rambo had brought me fifteen minutes earlier, before chucking it onto my chair – the chair I used for absinthe drinking and sitting outside the bivvy in the sun during the day. The book's strange cover landed face up, showing off its title and the peculiarly named author. I had never heard of the book, or of the author, although I had to admit that counted for little. I had never been an avid reader – unlike Steffi. A well-read ex-porn star! One who read in a language different from her native tongue! Unusual to say the least!

We had been back from Westerhoven for two days and were now fishing Hamworthy. Well I was, and shortly Rambo would be. He was just playing at camouflaged delivery boy at this precise juncture. On returning from the Dutch sand pit both of us had been extremely keen to subject our syndicate water to an onslaught of revolutionary, indented, dirty brown bottom bait boilie. The results from Westerhoven had spoken for themselves. After The Eye's impressive one-man carp fishing clairvoyant show, the one I had effectively hosed down with ice-cold water to end on a chilling note, things had improved dramatically on the fishing front. I had caught four more fish, all thirties, and Rambo had captured another three. The Eye, despite his fishing head being severely disrupted by my disconcerting news, had also caught three more. In fact fish started to be caught all over due to the mysterious phenomenon of a water 'switching on' manifesting itself during the last twenty-four hours of our stay. The big difference was no one apart from the three of us, myself, Rambo and The Eye, had had multiple captures. Can you spot the connection?

Whatever Pup had put into his revolutionary, indented, dirty brown bottom bait boilie *was* the business. His prior claim of 'if it was let loose on the streets it would bring down the government', was no longer as unlikely as it had first seemed. I secretly reckoned if Rambo could whiz half-a-dozen of them from his trusty catty straight into warmonger Blair's face – and come on, who wouldn't like to see *that* happen? – we would have a new government equally as useless, self-serving, hypocritical, nest-feathering and corrupt as the last in no time at all. Naturally if he did you would have to ask yourself the age-old question 'Why fucking bother?' and on answering it plummet straight into depression at democracy's devastating demise. And politicians wonder why the percentage of those who vote is dropping!

But, in all seriousness, you see my point. Take away the inconsequential cast iron conclusions of a morally vacuous, insipid, crony-ridden, egotistical, vain, repugnant government and focus on the *real* issue – we were on a going bait! The best one *ever*! Sometimes in life you have to prioritise and sort the wheat from the chafe. The government, any government, were chafe and Pup's revolutionary, indented, dirty brown bottom bait boilie was superwheat. Superneat, supersweet (not in taste but in contemporary vernacular) and a supertreat – apparently – for carp!

The boilie was something special! Statement. *Fact.* This was the thing we had taken home with us when we had left... *and* a spare bottle of absinthe The Eye had given me in appreciation for me telling him he might be dying from a brain tumour. He *was* grateful, if you can ever be grateful for receiving such a terrible life-threatening piece of information. It was the timing which had left me feeling uneasy and it had left a bad taste in my mouth. Either that or it was because I had tried to suck the poison from the legion of mozzie bites on my arms, in a foolhardy attempt to quell their interminable itching, as soon as my lips had been up to it.

We had left the car park after saying our goodbyes to Japp, Frans, The Eye and the forgotten names and had motored home without a hitch in Rambo's Scudo. On our departure, a tearful The Eye had promised to phone as soon as he could drag himself away from fishing and get to a doctor to confirm or deny my bad news. He had asked for, and I had given him, something else, something he had *wanted* to hear – Pup's phone number. The Eye had promised he would be on the revolutionary, indented, dirty brown bottom bait boilie for years to come and everyone present had verbally agreed and then had secretly wondered – like I had – if there was to be a somewhat bleaker future in store for him. And I don't mean Pup not supplying him with the boilies, I mean a bleaker future in terms of there not being very much of it left for him.

It had been on the journey home when Steffi had said the thing she had been wracking her brain to remember had been retrieved. She *had* read a book that might help me make some sense of intervening in my vision to somehow alter it. She had remembered its title and who had written it. She would buy it for me, she had told me, and would give it to Rambo so he in turn could give it to me. She had been as good as her word and the bloody thing was now lying on my chair – lurking, bugging me – waiting to be read.

"I'd get on with it as soon as I could, if I were you," Rambo advised. "You never know when the future you saw in the past will turn into the present."

"Don't start all the tense nonsense, it makes me…" I began.

"Tense?" Rambo quipped.

"Perfect," I quipped back. "You've got it in one."

Rambo *was* quite right, though – as usual. I had discussed my vision with him at length and the only clue the pair of us could come up with regarding the timing of when this future event was going to take place was the obvious. And the obvious clue was wind – a lot of it. The chances were the cause of the fallen branch I had seen Hollywood expertly cutting up with the chainsaw was wind. Presumably a gale force wind would, at some as yet unknown time in the future, whip across Hollywood's syndicate water and cause the breaking off of the large branch. Then Hollywood would come along in his little boat, cut it up while Darren and Rocky cleared it, and having finally stumbled in the boat and fallen, Rocky would fish the bastard out none the worst for wear… but wet. It was all very tenuous by definition but what else was there to do other than to check the long-range weather forecast regularly? This morning, on the radio, it had solemnly stated high pressure sat, and would continue to sit, across southern Britain for the foreseeable future. (Foreseeable future! Huh!)

The one other thing we could eliminate from being tenuous was the venue. It seemed safe to assume it was Hollywood's syndicate water but unfortunately assumptions were not good enough. We needed to make a little visit to Hollywood's syndicate, sooner rather than later, and check out the swim I had seen in my vision was on the water we thought it was. The information I had gleaned from fish stealer, Alan, at the koi shop had now taken up its position of some worth. In the next day or so we planned to fish the day ticket venue on the Broomham estate and sneak off for a quick reconnaissance mission. It was a mission fraught with danger, one sight of us anywhere near to Hollywood's syndicate water and he would know we were after him! Dodgy! Still, it had to be done.

In line with the weather prediction the sun currently shone on Hamworthy Fisheries, the breeze was slight, fishing conditions were not at their best and tonight it would undoubtedly be clear and a bit chilly. Takes might be in short supply – so perhaps a book to read to while away the time? If there *was* to be time – I was on a killer boilie!

"Anyway, I think I'm going to go and set up, boy," said Rambo.

"Yeah, okay, mate... How come you were so late?" I looked at my wristwatch. "It's nearly ten."

Rambo smiled. "The love of a good woman!" he stated.

I opened my mouth to make a silent 'ah'. "So, she's the one?" I asked.

Rambo smiled. "I think so. The *only* one. And I *never* thought I'd meet her… How's Sophie?"

"All right, thanks. We had a long talk the other day and I told her what happened with me and The Eye, don't ask me to say The Eye and I…"

"I *won't*."

"I told her what The Eye thought of Amy and the ghost."

"And?"

"Freaked her a bit, although she tried to hide it. I decided against suggesting having a go at mind-melding with Amy, even if I have got the rocket fuel to go for launch courtesy of The Eye."

Rambo nodded vigorously. "Wise move," he said simply.

"I did tell her about the vision. She seems to have hardened against Hollywood even more..."

Rambo cut in with a mischievous grin on his face. "Better than the other way around!"

"Please!" I protested and continued. "She wants revenge as much as me now, I'm convinced of it. She wants the smile wiped off his handsome face as much as I do. It's almost become a crusade. I get the impression it's a test for me, a test for me to right my wrongs and redeem myself... and redeem her at the same time. Once it's done, *if* it gets done, we might be able to let it go of the past at last and sort ourselves out. I hope so, anyway."

"In that case you'd better get your finger out and get with it!" Rambo picked up the paperback and waved it under my nose. "*Read* the fucking book, boy! When you've got your plan sorted come and see me. That's *my* field of expertise, the strategy's down to you! Steffi might be onto something... it's got to be worth a shot. She's no idiot. If she says there's something in this book, there will be."

"I will, don't worry... You know we've got the stock pond to start tomorrow morning. The guys from Folkestone Angling Club are due to arrive at nine so we have to be ready for them. The Section 30 came through okay while we were in Westerhoven."

Rambo gave me a look. "That's not going to be a five minute job. You're sure they're bringing all the necessary equipment?"

"That's what they said. Pumps, nets, waders, pick-ups with tanks and oxygen bottles... they would supply it all, plus four bodies to help as well."

"Dead ones?" Rambo asked tongue anchored in cheek.

"*Alive*," I said pointedly. "Not unless Michael was a serial killer and we find a few concrete shod ones in the stock pond."

"Let's hope we find enough *carp* to make it all worth while," Rambo suggested.

"If the members have been keeping to the rules there'll be enough in there. The stock pond logbook has a lot of entries and I don't think there's any fish stealing going on *now*!"

Rambo laughed. "They wouldn't dare. Not while *I'm* around!"

He was right. They wouldn't dare not unless they had a death wish. I held out my hand. "Give me the book, then."

"There you go, boy. I'll see you tomorrow at seven not unless you catch something horrendous... or I do!"

I took the book from Rambo and bid him goodbye. The man mountain turned and left me safe in the knowledge he had already had sex this morning and I hadn't… like I hadn't for the last God knows how many mornings. I had forgotten what it was like. And when I tried to remember I thought of Sophie and *not* Melina. Significant? Or a bit of mental psychobabble on my behalf?

I gave myself a slap and turned my thoughts towards the cover of the book Steffi hoped might help me. 'Asimov' it said in big letters above a pattern of several elliptically orbiting lights and in slightly smaller ones beneath it was the title, 'The End of Eternity'. Science fiction. Fucking hell! I flicked through it. Fuck me! I was going to read a book with no pictures in it. A book with no pictures in it concerning a genre I had no time for. A genre, I would go as far to say, as one I liked equally to the prospect of stepping in deep, fresh dog shit whilst wearing trainers of the deep-treaded sole variety… And then proceeding home to walk in haste across a recently laid deep-pile, cream carpet to turn on the television in order to find out the football results… And on seeing your team's four-nil loss and subsequent slippage deep into the relegation zone noticing a succession of dark marks on the floor… And a strange smell!

I read the blurb on the back. It was all about time travel. If it had been a handy manual telling you how to knock up a time machine from bite alarm printed circuits, the electrical guts of a fishfinder, a bait boat motor and a power pack it would have been neat. I could have zapped back in time and changed history and made everything hunky dory. But it wasn't. I read the first line, 'Andrew Harlan stepped into the kettle'. Jesus! Keep calm and go with the flow, I thought, so I made myself a brew, settled down into my chair, my sitting outside – you know the one – and read, expecting the mind-numbing drudgery of a book not to my liking or interest.

Three carp and one novel later I had changed my mind. I could see what Steffi was getting at and my original thoughts of nipping back in a time machine to alter the past hadn't been so wide of the mark. As an aside, I wished I knew more than ever what Pup was putting in the revolutionary, indented, dirty brown bottom bait boilie. It was four in the morning and I had just changed the tiny batteries on my LED headtorch to allow me to complete the book. I was on my bedchair now, inside my bivvy and sleeping bag, warm and cosy despite the predicted chilly summer's night. Although I felt tired from the extended reading, nicely interrupted by three takes and three fish, I felt strangely exhilarated. It had been a corker of a session, a short session that had fairly flown by. My gradually escalating interest in the book had gripped me over the time I had read it and the punctuation of catching three cracking fish – one in the afternoon, one early evening and one just into a new day – had conspired to give me a buzz equivalent to the noise you hear standing under an electricity pylon on a drizzly day. I was wired and my brain was alive and squirming with possibilities! Well done, Steffi!

The premise of the book without going into too many details and sticking to the relevance it had to myself was this: The book concerns itself with a world where time travel has been invented. Andrew Harlan is a time traveller, a Time Technician to give him his proper title, who lives in 'Eternity', a place that exists outside of time. The Eternals – a select group of individuals taken from different eras in 'real' time comprise Technicians, Computers, Sociologists, Life-Plotters and Observers – are dedicated to one thing, to insure humankind has the safest and most benevolent life possible. They do this by travelling in time in their 'kettles' to alter history so that catastrophic events are avoided. Through their expertise they decide on making the MNC (Minimum Necessary Change) to achieve the MDR (Maximum Desired Response). For example by moving a canister on a shelf, space travel is not attained in the 2456th Century. This is desirable as the Eternals deem space travel as self-limiting and a waste of energy and resources. Don't tell NASA, they'll only get upset.

The crux of the story is how – to be flippant about it – the Eternals pop into real time, move four grains of sand three inches to the left and avert a world war. The analogy I came up with is it's like you narrowly avoiding a car crash and thinking 'Christ if I'd left home a few seconds earlier that car would have hit me' and the reason you were delayed by said few seconds was your shoelace snapped when you tried to tie it. Consequently you had to juggle the lace to get sufficient equal length and it held you up for those few vital moments. I suggest an Eternal weakened the lace enough beforehand – secretly, in a period between the last wearing of the shoes and this instance – to make it snap and therefore saved your life!

I have to admit it made the hairs on my neck stand on end as I began to realise the book's implications. I had to become a Time Technician! I had to pop into my vision, or as I was beginning to think, sometime *before* my vision, make my MNC and in consequence, in the passing of time, achieve my MDR. *Voila!* Hollywood's face bereft of a smile!

Like the Time Technicians in the book, I *had* to do it without being spotted and without my MNC being spotted – hence my thoughts on the intervention, sorry, my MNC, being done before my vision. Stupidly or not, the book had convinced me it could work, had to work, if my revenge was to be obtained. If you could go back in time and alter the most mundane of things it was perfectly possible, given that you had altered the *correct* mundane thing, that a huge change in outcome could be achieved. Well, it convinced *me* anyway and a positive mindset is a wonderful tool.

As I turned off my headtorch and finally got my head down I mulled it over in my tired mind. I soon conspired to the idea the incident where Hollywood had come so close to permanent harm, when he had fallen out of the boat and into the drink, or when he was using the chainsaw – albeit expertly – was the crucial point. If I could change some minor detail beforehand so he somehow drowned or cut his own throat revenge could be mine! As I drifted off into sleep the only minor detail was what minor detail to alter, when to alter it and how I would ever get into a situation where I could alter it. As is often the case, the minor details were turning into a major obstacle.

Chapter 14

The six-inch diesel pumps had been pumping away all morning and the stock pond's water level had gradually dropped accordingly. In the true accepted tradition of all this type of work Rambo, the four lads from the Folkestone Angling Club and myself had stood around doing fuck all watching it happen. We would have lent on shovels while we waited, only we didn't possess the appropriate Health and Safety certificate to allow us to do so. However, I *did* possess a vital certificate and it was nestling in my tracksuit bottom's pocket – that of an Environmental Authority Section 30 allowing the movement of fish from one identified place to another.

Fortunately all the fish I was selling on to the Folkestone club were being moved to a totally enclosed stillwater. A stillwater, as equally important, that was nowhere near a river flood plain. If we had been moving them to either a river or a stillwater near a river's flood plain, thirty of my beautiful Hamworthy specimens would have had to be killed for a health check test. If this had been the case it would have made the whole exercise futile in terms of financial considerations and, to be honest, far too brutal. I think I would have rather left them where they were than slaughter so many of them – or moved them illegally. Don't say I said that, EA spies and Echo are everywhere!

Earlier, too bloody earlier as far as I was concerned – I'd had a wild, late night book reading session – Rambo and I had run out the large coils of heavy hose with the FAC representatives from the stock pond to the main pit and pulled the pumps into life. The slightly coloured water from the stock pond had started gushing into the gin-clear main pit and from that moment another type of carp waiting game had begun.

The club had brought two pick-ups with them to transport the fish back to their new home and each one had two large tanks sited in the back. These tanks had already been filled by a smaller pump with water from the main pit and were now sitting waiting for the introduction of their temporary visitors. Strapped to each individual tank was a black British Oxygen Company bottle containing – surprise, surprise – oxygen and from them ran compressed airline hoses into each tank. The end of these hoses had been plugged off, weighted to sit on the bottom of its respective tank and the last few feet had been perforated so once the oxygen was switched on it could bubble out and diffuse into the water. It was all very professional and the carp care aspect of it was beyond reproach – provided we could get them safely from the stock pond and into the tanks! The time when we would start to do so was fast approaching.

As I viewed the partially drained stock pond I could now see it was deeper than I had previously thought. A full seven feet of almost vertical bank was now exposed on its western side but with water still in the bottom. On the other side, twenty yards away – the side where Rambo and I had hidden under a bush whilst spying on Rocky and Darren – the bottom was starting to show. The stock pond had a sloping bottom, considerably so, and I could picture this being the side where, many years ago, the mechanical digger had reached out and had dug and scraped towards itself on an incline. A section of aluminium ladder dropped against the western bank with the greatest depth revealed three foot to go. It was time to put on the chest waders, turn off the pumps and go fishing!

Rambo and I were going to help do the 'fishing', right at the so-called sharp end. I felt it was a task we should get involved in, seeing as we were owner and first lieutenant and until the cash changed hands the fish were still my 'babies'! Us two, plus two of the club lads, were going to get into the quagmire that was the partially drained stock pond and hopefully net the fish into a tight area. Once this had been achieved we would pluck the prized specimens from the shallow water, pop them into a weigh sling and pass them up the ladder for placing into the oxygenated tanks.

In conversation it sounded a breeze but in reality it turned out a tad more tiresome. Things got off to a poor start, or to be honest, I did. This was wholly due to my foot slipping on a rung as I went first down the ladder and I fell what felt like – conservatively estimated – one hundred and forty feet into sub zero stock pond water in a reverse belly flop, no twist, not with pike but with carp, in a comic book plunge with a degree of difficulty rated 2.8. Personally I blamed the chest waders.

The shock of the cold water hitting my skin was delayed until it cunningly found the top of the waders and rushed into them with unadulterated glee. I scrambled to my feet and felt my legs become encased in water to just above the knee. As I looked up in shock from my debased position I saw four other people trying not to laugh and one not bothering. Rambo was pissing himself. What with this latest escapade and my tripping up while re-entering the Earth's atmosphere from my mother bivvy-ship at Westerhoven, I felt suitably mortified at my own clumsiness.

"Nice one, boy!" cackled Rambo. "Hope you didn't squash a twenty!"

"My foot slipped," I told anyone prepared to listen to my pathetic, lame excuse. I don't think there were any takers.

An air of silent embarrassment hung over the stock pond – if you discounted Rambo's laughing – as I sloshed my way back up the ladder, took off the waders and emptied them out.

"The pumps do that part of the job," Rambo said wiping away a tear of mirth. "You're meant to get the *fish* out, *not* the water!"

"Ha, ha!" I said dynamically. Social chagrin is not a pretty thing. I felt small, Oompa Loompa small – and silly – a 'wagonload of monkeys' silly.

"How about we lower you down on a rope next time?" Rambo suggested.

"Shut up!" It was plea rather than a command.

"Easy, boy. I'm only having a laugh. Believe me it *was* funny, at your expense, granted… but still funny." Rambo looked away with a wistful look on his face and muttered something about never having a camcorder handy when you needed one.

My second attempt at descending the ladder went more to plan and once I had safely made it down into the water the other three joined me. Ruefully I noticed they had let me go first again, I don't suppose any of them were especially keen to have British carp fishing's finest syndicate water owner land on top of them – even if he was a skinny bastard. Footnote: But not as skinny as he used to be!

Once we were all safely in position (nastily I was desperate for someone else to commit the same faux pas as myself but remained disappointed) the four of us started to manipulate the soft mesh net from the most distant end of the stock pond and to force the carp up towards the ladder end. As we inched slowly down I could both see and feel carp in the water. The pumping of the water, the disturbance of the weed within the stock pond and the large amount of carp in such a confined space had made the remaining water far more opaque than it had been beforehand and visibility was limited to a foot or so. (Funnily enough this season had been the first where weed had taken a bit of a foothold in the main pit. Apparently, despite its gin-clear properties, it had never suffered unduly from weed problems to much of a degree in the past. This season had seen more weed than ever before, although nothing compared to how choked some other gravel pits can become.) By the time we had condensed the carp into an area of a few square yards it was obvious there were plenty of good fish to be taken out. The carp were getting quite stressed now and were bashing into the net, into us and frantically looking for an escape route that didn't exist. Now was time to get them out as quickly as we could.

It was Rambo who nominated himself as chief carp picker – no one argued – and it was he who had four slings tucked into the tops of his waders. While the three of us held the net firm and forced the carp up near the surface he picked off the carp and placed them in a sling. It seemed as if Rambo had an almost uncanny knack of plucking the carp from the water and getting them into a sling with the minimum of fuss. My theory was the carp caught sight of him and thought, 'Fuck this, I'm not messing with that mean geezer' and virtually jumped in a sling of their own accord. The power of suggestion! Once in a sling each individual carp was passed up and out of the stock pond, weighed and put into the tanks by the other two members from FAC. The sling was then re-cycled and Rambo was kept permanently replenished and permanently on the go.

After no more than three hours the stock pond was cleared of all its inhabitants and a quick tot up showed we had removed forty-two fish of which over half were twenties. There were eight high singles and the rest comprised doubles. In all, over seven hundred pound of fish came out, which was going to equate to a whole lot more in pounds sterling! I cocked my hat to the syndicate membership; they had done me proud and had clearly stuck to the rules.

One aspect of the morning's work did throw me and it was the number of smaller fish present. In truth I was surprised at how many there were because to my recollection I had only ever caught one fish of stock pond size in all my time on Hamworthy. Whatever, it had made it worthwhile for me financially and worthwhile for the club as they had purchased a great strain of carp and an adequate head to put into their new water.

With the job virtually complete there was a chance to relax a little so I stood alone in the back of one of the pick-ups and watched the carp in the tanks as the pumps re-filled the stock pond, forcing water in the opposite direction to how they had pumped previously. It was fascinating watching the carp swim up and down at such close quarters in the clear main pit water, seeing how their fins, their mouths and their gills moved. As I casually gazed upon them, absorbed by their movements, I wondered how their tiny brains were dealing with their sudden change of surroundings and how they would cope with their new long term, Folkestone Angling Club owned 'home'. Pretty much how they would have done when they were put in the stock pond in the first place, I supposed. I wiped my sweaty, grimy brow. I decided I would never suss the machinations of the *Cyprinus carpio* brain and as a mind-meld was out of the question I decided to stop wasting mental energy on the subject.

I checked out the filling process to see how it was fairing. The stock pond was now half full, or, as the pessimist would say, half empty. A few more hours and we could wrap things up. Good. I could do with a nice hot shower and a change of clothes; some hot grub wouldn't go amiss either. Appetite – such an elusive commodity in months gone by and now the knack of it was back. I *had* moved on.

Rambo was still chewing the cud with the FAC lads – probably trying to convince them I wasn't quite the bumbling idiot I had intimated with my ladder trick, bless him – and I, with nothing better to do and despite my earlier thoughts, went back to carp watching, this time leaning over the second tank where some of the bigger fish were housed. I watched the biggest common swim with slight agitation around the black plastic tank, occasionally touching the side as if to physically feel the edge of the strange 'lake' it found itself in. Boundaries. We all had them, in different shapes and forms, every living creature did – and yet now and then I could seemingly escape from them all for a short time by virtue of my strange mental 'powers'. I gave myself a wry smile – a fucking lot of good it did me as far as Hollywood was concerned!

I tugged on my ear with a gritty hand. I mustn't be too hard on myself, I had saved Rambo's life – even if Steffi didn't know it – I had nailed Michael as the ghost's murderer and I had wrecked the fish stealing scam. Surveying the evidence it appeared I was useful at helping solve other people's problems but couldn't sort out my own! I bit my teeth together and felt my jaw muscles bulge in my cheeks. Maybe that would change. No, be positive, it *had* to change if I wanted my family back and believe me I *did*. I had promised Sophie I would exact revenge for us both, would wipe the smile off Hollywood's handsome face and in doing so could forever put to bed the image of him ejaculating in... I shook my head and forced the aberration from my mind only for it to come straight back.

I never thought it was going to be easy.

The big common swam up and down, up and down, up and down and my eyes followed it in a trance. Watching fish *is* therapeutic. Tiny bubbles rose from the hose in the bottom of the tank – a myriad of effervescent spheres sometimes swatted away by a vortex of water created by the common's or other carp's fins as they swam through them. Sunlight sparkled in them as they reached the surface. The common's gill covers flared in and out, the delicate red tissue underneath endlessly extracting the oxygen from the water. Bemused, transfixed and preoccupied I asked myself what would my MNC be? What would be my MDR? What *could* I do that might make Hollywood drown or hack his cock off with the chainsaw? What tiny piece of intervention would set up an unfailing chain of circumstances and events so the bastard would end up maimed or dead rather than simply unscathed, wet and alive? Whatever it turned out to be it had better be done with a lot more dexterity, subtlety and discretion than my bomb into the swimming pool this morning!

I dragged my eyes away from the tank and looked up into the afternoon sky. Well, the common didn't know and at this point in time neither did I. What a shame! What I needed was a bit of divine intervention to point out the intention of *my* intervention. Where *would* it come from? I had come so far with my haphazard plan surely I couldn't fail at the last piece of the jigsaw puzzle? The keystone that would make sense of all I had chanced upon found out and deduced so far. In a frightening instant I realised how much the whole blueprint of my revenge plan was still poised, teetering on a knife's edge; on one side fulfilment, my life regained, the possibility of my *family* regained and on the other… abyss. In rig analogy it was critically balanced, suspended in water, neutral in buoyancy – waiting for either a pick-me-up or the ingress of water to sink it to the bottom to be lost in the black silt of failure for all time.

Time passed, like it tends to.

"Matt!"

I looked up. "Yeah,"

"We're just about done. You going to sort out the money with Jack?" said Hamworthy Fisheries' lieutenant.

I nodded. "Will do."

I jumped down from the pick-up and went and saw Jack. Jack was the chairman of the club and as such the senior person present. He had always been my point of contact and the person with whom I had discussed financial implications, logistics and so on earlier in the year. He motioned me to get into the pick-up's passenger cabin. He got in one side and I got in the other.

"Good day's work, Matt," he said as we both sat down. Jack shut his door. The transaction we were shortly to conduct was to be strictly one-to-one. I shut my door in solidarity with his wishes.

"Apart from my unscheduled jump off the ladder," I said.

"The lemming lust is in us all," he joked and then continued in a more serious tone. "I shouldn't worry unduly, we all have accidents from time to time. Last year, Craig, one of our members, cut two toes off with a chainsaw during a work party. All hell broke loose after it happened... he didn't have a chainsaw certificate and wasn't wearing safety footwear. The trouble was it happened on a council controlled reservoir, it was a water we lease rather than own, and the council's Health and Safety officer became involved. It was a complete nightmare. We had to totally alter the club's whole perception of what was and what wasn't suitable work for members to do on a work party. Now we must have designated, qualified people for the more dangerous specific tasks and all manner of safety equipment, safety wear, eye protection, hard hats, lifejackets, harnesses, written procedures, bloody risk assessment forms... not that any of it matters a tinker's cuss if your foot slips on a ladder. All the bits of paper and procedures in the world can't legislate for... that happening." I suspected Jack was too polite to say 'stupidity'. His head shuddered. "Anyway. Money. As we agreed before?" I nodded. Jack rummaged in his pocket and dragged out the grubby piece of paper on which his colleagues had written down the fish weights and numbers they were taking. "Where's that calculator... ah!" Jack found the item on the dashboard and his thick fingers began punching away. "That's what I make we owe you," he said after a while, turning the calculator's display panel towards me so I could see it. I couldn't successfully deny the sight of the four-figure display didn't warm the cockles of my heart – the financially motivated cockles of my heart.

"Seems right," I concurred.

"Cash okay?" Jack asked.

"I'd rather have it in a cheque so I can put it through with the Fisheries' accounts when I submit my tax return to the Inland Revenue, if you don't mind?" I said. Jack gave me a look similar to one I suspect he would have given me if I had pulled down my trousers and pissed into the glove compartment. No – as if I had pulled down my trousers and *wanked* into the glove compartment. "Only kidding," I admitted. "Cash is fine."

"Good," said Jack brusquely. This time he rummaged in an inside coat pocket and yanked out the all time favourite of sly, underhand, cash funded negotiations – the brown envelope. A great big, fat, thick one. "This is our cash fund," he explained. "Day ticket fees, cash memberships, guest tickets... all the untraceable stuff," he said giving me a broad smile. "I'll count it into hundreds. It's mainly in twenties and tenners, so there's going to be a lot of them."

I shrugged. I could wait, besides, buying the morning newspaper with a fifty always agitates the newsagents.

The two pick-ups drove carefully up the farm track, laden with their expensive cargo of high-quality carp. Rambo shut the gate behind them and spun the combination padlock, locking the rest of the world out of Hamworthy Fisheries.

"Been a bit of an eye-opener today," I said.

"Meaning, boy?"

"How much money there is in carp as a commodity and therefore why people choose to take the illegal option… in all its varying forms."

Rambo agreed. "You think what would have been in the stock pond if it hadn't walked all the way to Hollywood's new syndicate. Imagine the amount of fish he's creamed off here during all the Michael years. A fucking fortune, I bet. He must have been cooking the logbook to get away with it… either that or Michael simply left it all to him and never checked up."

"And that's just *our* little bit. Think of what's happened all over the country… all over *Europe*! All over the world!"

"It's like everything, boy," Rambo explained. "Once something gets desirable and enough people want it and the price gets high enough, the scum pop out of the woodwork and try to make a few quid on the back of it."

"What, like you and illegal arms dealing?" I said cheekily.

"*Exactly* like that!" Rambo retorted without a hint of umbrage. "You've got it in one! I thought to myself, why fuck around killing people and risk getting killed when I could just stand to one side and give them the ammo to get on with it themselves… and make a killing on the killing, as it where."

"Someone's cracked that one before," I reminded him.

"We'll have to get a better scriptwriter," said Rambo as an aside before he was back to his central theme. "Although we both know it didn't *quite* work out like that, did it? Some of my dirty work came back to try and kill me!"

I laughed. "*We* know… *Steffi* doesn't! Perhaps you ought to tell her. Maybe she'd like me more if she knew I saved your life."

"She likes you now," insisted Rambo giving me a level stare. "Within the parameters of your occasionally debilitating neurosis."

"You'd be fucking neurotic if you'd been through what I have," I said.

Rambo looked indignant. "Have you ever been shelled at night, dug into a poxy little fox-hole, your friends being killed either side of you…?"

"Well, if you're going to start dragging things like that into it…" I stumbled.

"I am!"

"Fair point," I conceded. "I guess my stuff is more the bizarre end of the pant-cacking spectrum whereas yours was straightforward in-your-face unadulterated violence. I've only blown away the one solitary individual." I pondered on the relative merits of our respective had-it-tough life experiences. "Yeah, you're right, as usual." I conceded and with a flourish pulled out the brown envelope and threw it Frisbee-style at Rambo who caught it. "I'll tell you what, *you* take out Hollywood for me. There it is. Payment in full, cash upfront!"

Rambo took out the wedge of cash from the envelope and ran a thumb across the edge of the notes and fanned them. He let out a low whistle. "Six grand?" he asked.

"Over seven!"

"I daresay we could get it done for less and *still* have change for a set of three rods each, a few hundred kilos of Pup's boilies *and* enough absinthe to take a bath in."

"Nah!" I said dismissing the suggestion with a wave. "This time it's personal, as they say. It's something I've got to do by myself... with as much help as I can get from anywhere else, of course!"

"Talking of which, did Steffi's book help at all?" Rambo asked.

"Yeah. It did," I answered. "I did think I would struggle to even be able to read it to begin with, but once I got started I could see what she was getting at and why it had tweaked something in her memory. I was up till four in the morning reading it last night... in between catching a few fish." I gave Rambo a grin. "That's why I fell off the ladder... lack of sleep!"

"Lack of co-ordination more like," Rambo chipped.

I ignored this. "The mechanics of the book are in my head. The hardest part has still to be worked out though, I'm afraid."

Rambo scratched the stubble on his chin. "She told me the basic gist of it. My first idea was to kill Rocky and Darren, car sabotage or something, and then there'd be no one to fish Hollywood out of the drink and he would drown. Only he wouldn't have been there doing what he was doing if the other two weren't there to help..."

"That's right," I said cutting in. "It's got to be something tiny. Something *very* tiny that nobody notices as odd or unusual, that keeps us right out of the frame and yet changes what I saw in the vision and wipes the smile off the bastard's face. Big time!"

"Something with the chainsaw?" Rambo broached.

I nodded my head. "That was my first thought... not that it's developed any further," I admitted.

Rambo was pragmatic. "Let's not rush things or panic, it's all come together so far..."

"So near and yet so *very* far!" I pointed out.

"I know, boy, but from where we set out you have to admit we've meandered along very nicely and things *have* slotted into place." A look of slight incredulity spread across Rambo's face. "It's all a bit odd really, when you stop and think how contrived it is... still, that's the story of your life isn't it?" Rambo took a deep breath and cleared his mind. "Look, why don't we have a day at the Broomham place tomorrow and at least clear up the point of knowing *where* exactly the swim is that you saw? We've got to put that one to bed first, haven't we?"

I nodded before adding flatly. "It's risky, though. I'm worried about going."

"What, sneaking off to Hollywood's place and getting seen?" said Rambo answering his own question. "Hmm. It *would* blow everything out the water. He'd know you were up to something... or at least *trying* to get up to something if we were spotted."

"It's not *only* that," I said. "There's more!"

"Oh?" said Rambo barely disguising the 'for-God's-sake-what-has-he-thought-of-this-time' inflection in his voice.

"Yeah. It's the thought of fishing a day ticket water as much as anything." I admitted. "The stampede for best spot from the morning kick-off time, instant carpers, three yards between swims, people casting over you, people backfilling with peanuts, people asking what bait you're on, people asking what rig you're using, people telling you how many they caught from your swim last week and how big they go and can they borrow a lead bomb because they've just lost their last one casting halfway up the tree in the opposite margin twenty yards away. I don't know if I can deal with it all at my age after being used to this," I gestured vaguely around myself.

"You poor old sod! You're turning into a carp snob!"

"*Turned*, most likely."

Rambo handed me the wad of money. "Here. Look after the dosh. Let's get packed up and get ourselves home, have a nice hot shower and some food. Tomorrow won't seem so scary after a hot meal and shower."

"Takeaway? My treat," I offered.

"No," Rambo declined. "Steffi'll cook something. You can tell her you've read the book and it's helped. That'll please her."

"Okay, mate. I'll sort your share of the money out once we're back at yours… She won't mind me coming back will she?"

Rambo gave me a puzzled look. "You've been living there for the best part of the last year, boy! Longer than her!"

"I know. Sad isn't it?"

Rambo was dismissive. "It's a phase. You're going through a phase."

I gave a weak little bob of my head. If I didn't get my act together the phase might last me through my thirties. A decade at home with the Ramsbottoms! No way! It wasn't going to happen – Rambo would have kicked me out well before then.

Chapter 15

Imagine the disorientation of being blindfolded, spun viciously on a high-revving roundabout – a roundabout situated, let's say, at the top of a bungee jump – getting pushed off the roundabout, plunging into a bottomless cavern and just as you were certain of feeling the body shattering impact with the ground, the powerful elastic pinged you equally violently back upwards, to the ephemeral hovering point of no vertical movement, either up or down, when suddenly, unexpectedly, you were grabbed by powerful, unseen hands and placed, remarkably, on a roasting golden sandy beach, bungee elastic cut, blindfold whipped off, a bucket of cold water poured down your neck and standing in front of you was your old, loathed, long-dead headmaster who asks you, 'Williams, (substitute your surname) we are *all* waiting. What are nine sevens plus the number of letters in the capital of Denmark… *minus* the valency of oxygen?'

And for good measure times it by seven… no, eleven… I don't know, maybe even a hundred and six. This was the level of disorientation bestowed upon me.

"He looks okay," said Steffi, leaning casually against the front door frame. "He looks okay to me, better to me. It's only because you haff not seen him like sis zat it looks strange to you."

My head swam, not very well, doggy-paddle at best. Much more of this deep end stuff and I would be under, my arse parked on the bottom. "It looks strange, all right," I managed to utter.

"It *feels* fucking strange," said the cause of my disorientation who was standing on the second step leading to the front door.

It was a Friday morning and a little bit of a legend had died. Died at the hands of a woman. Who would *ever* have believed it? Not me. And I had seen ghosts, talked to them and been inside the head of another man, seen his brain tumour and seen the future.

Steffi was unmoved by the negativity. "Vott is ser first sing he vood ask? Sis Hollyvood… Vas sere a big guy dressed in ser camouflage clozs?"

I looked over at Rambo and he looked over at me. Her logic was impeccable. What she was saying was *totally* right and there was *no* counter argument to even touch it. Logically. But what we were talking about here was reneging on the principle of a man's lifetime dress code. What we were talking about – wait for the roar and ebb and flow of pressure in my head to steady – was Rambo *sans* camouflage! Not even Pup's wedding had succeeded on that front!

"I bought ser clothes yesterday vile you vere fishing, and ser trainers."

Rambo and I both looked at the trainers on his feet. To me they looked conspicuously big, white and new, but perhaps not necessarily in that order. To Rambo, judging by the expression on his face, they looked like an abomination similar to the butchery caused by stepping on a landmine and blowing both feet off. The big man continued staring at the two remaining bloody stumps.

"They look a bit new," I ventured.

"Zat's because sey *are* new! Make sem dirty if you don't like sem new! Sey didn't have his size in ser Oxfam shop or I vood have got old vuns!" Steffi said with irritation. "You can't spend your whole life dressed like you are still in ser army!" she added giving the entire game, and her complete agenda, away in the brevity of a sentence.

"It hasn't stopped him up until today," I pointed out when perhaps it would have been more prudent to keep my gob shut.

Steffi came closer to me. I tried to avoid looking at the hint of cleavage her dressing gown afforded me and instead I cowered, waiting for the impending karate chop. Hell hath no fury like an ex-porn star black belt in karate. "I am only sinking of you," she said levelly prodding a finger at me. "If somevun asks and he is in his army clozs, sey know it is him. If not, maybe you get avay vitt it and your revenge can go on."

"I know," I said. Knowing she was lying, that is. Not *exactly* lying, that's a bit unfair; let's say using the situation to promote an issue of hers. The issue being, Steffi, having been in Rambo's life for a matter of weeks, was trying to change him and stop him wearing camouflage all the time. The other even bigger issue was whether he would wear it or not – in all senses of the phrase.

I looked over at the non-camouflage version of Rambo – boy, to use a popular word of his, did he look different – and waited for the outcome.

"Just for today," he mumbled. "Just for you, boy, just to help cover our tracks if anything goes wrong."

"Thanks, mate," I said. "Appreciate that." Now *Rambo* was lying. Not *exactly* lying, that's a bit unfair; let's say using the situation to deny an issue of his.

And so it was we set off at a little after five in the morning for the Broomham day ticket venue with all our tackle loaded into the Scudo van, Pup's revolutionary, indented, dirty brown bottom bait boilie to hand, Rambo in jogging bottoms, trainers and a sweatshirt – much like myself – and him knowing the *real* reason why he was wearing them and me knowing the real reason why he was wearing them and him knowing that I knew the real reason why he was wearing them – his love for an orphaned, Eastern European, karate expert, ex-porn star actress. Things would *never* be the same again. If there was any doubt she was the one, Rambo submitting to only a temporary respite of camouflage clothing laid it to rest there and then. Unequivocally.

Rambo turned the key and fired up the Scudo's engine. As I went to open my mouth I was halted in mid cod-like gape by Rambo's dire warning. "*Don't* say anything about the clothes," he warned, his eyes hard and piercing. "*I* know what's happening, *you* know what's happening… *she* knows what's happening. Let's leave it at that." His voice dropped a few levels of austerity. "Okay, so I never thought it would happen but it has. Times change… people move on," Rambo's eyes dropped from mine and he spoke to the accelerator pedal, or more likely the huge white monstrosity resting on it. "As unlikely as it may seem to *everyone* involved."

I shut my cavernous maw and looked out the window. I waved to Steffi who was still on the doorstep seeing us off – she had been pleased the book she had told me to read had helped – and after a second or two of this I looked back at Rambo. My lips began to part.

"This isn't going to be about the clothes is it?" Rambo asked.

"No."

"Good."

I looked at him again but couldn't stop myself perusing the strange vision at the steering wheel. It had been like this since he had come down for breakfast and we had discussed the day's tactics. All thought simply vaporised in the wake of a *sans* camouflage Rambo. Again I pored over him with the proverbial magnifying glass. Wow! And I never thought I would live to see the day. If we died in a car crash on the way to the day ticket venue my life would have accomplished something!

"It *is* going to be about the clothes isn't it?" Rambo insisted. "Stop *staring* at me!"

"I'm not staring," I lied.

"Yes you are!"

"I'm just…"

"Staring."

I wiped a forked tongue across my top lip. "Do you think we'll catch?"

Rambo aggressively shoved the gear stick into first and pulled off. "Course we'll catch. Pup's killer boilies and our skill… we'll empty the fucking place!"

I couldn't resist it. "*Even* with the spook factor from those trainers?"

Rambo slammed his fist into my shoulder, laughing and swearing at the same. The searing pain miraculously put paid to any more smart arse comments and also took my mind off worrying over how we were going to sneak off from a busy day ticket venue and locate my 'vision swim'. Every cloud has a silver lining.

On the way to the water we stopped at a newsagents. I bought two papers with a FAC slush fund tenner – one for Rambo and one for me. Mine was to read but Rambo used his to rub the print off onto his trainers and tone them down from 'polar bear in a blizzard' to 'albino badger on a grey misty morning'. What a waste of a Daily Sport.

"There!" said Rambo. "Marginally better." He quizzically inclined his head towards me and lifted up one foot. "Fucking light aren't they?"

"Compared to army boots, I expect they are," I granted him. Something in Rambo's eyes told me he was unconvinced this was of significant benefit. I decided to proffer an observation. "You'll be able to get to your takes at least a tenth of a second earlier," I said. Rambo looked down at the trainers and then back at me, his expression unchanged. "Could be crucial," I said supportively.

"I fucking doubt it," he said bluntly.

I wiped my nose. "You're probably right... you look all right, though, mate. I won't deny you look... what's the word? Alien? But that's just to *me*. To anyone who's never seen you before, you look like another ordinary bloke... who's just spent a few quid on some casual sports clothing."

Rambo shook his head in a well-it's-come-to-this-manner. "I knew things would have to change once she moved in," Rambo acknowledged veering surprising off-topic. "But I hadn't expected it to be this particular bit."

"See! You're coming to terms with it already," I said in an upbeat manner. "If she's the one, she's worth it, isn't she? Worth a bit of change and a bit of effort?"

"I guess so," Rambo said and he reached out and grabbed the scruff of my sweatshirt with his mighty paw, hauling me closer to him. "Just don't go telling her I said so!" he warned. Slowly he let me go. My sweatshirt remaining scrunched until I rubbed it flat along with the sore part of my chest where he had ripped out some of its hairs. "I've got *some* dignity you know. She'll have to work for the change. I'm not getting bowled over overnight."

I was about to point out I considered this to be *exactly* what Steffi had done to him but thought better of it. "Sure," I said. "A few special sexual favours perhaps?"

Rambo pulled down the corners of his mouth. "No. There aren't any left... not that I know of, or rather that *she* knows of! Not with only the two of us at any rate!"

I was touched. Love. It can conquer all you know. I read it on the back of a cigarette packet along with the obligatory death warning. A connection? You tell me.

When we pulled up to the fishery gates there were already two more vehicles in front of us waiting for the opening time. Broomham was a seven till dusk fishery and, despite it being six thirty, two other anglers had beaten us to the first choice of swims – if any such gentlemanly agreement existed. If it was going to be how I had imagined in my earlier day ticket tirade, it could quite easily turn out to be the Charge of the Light Brigade once the gate was opened, a handbrake turn and park in the car park, out and on with the tackle and a sprint to the lake for best spot. I hoped not. I had put up with all that sort of nonsense years ago before the SS syndicate and when we were in limbo after returning from Lac Fumant first time – all the naff competing against carp *and* other anglers. The prospect of doing it again, if only for a day, didn't fill me with relish.

I eyed the two other vehicles with disdain and wondered what sort of tossers were sitting in the driving seats waiting to unleash all manner of bedlam upon a water that must get absolutely hammered for six months of the year. With grim realisation I knew I was about to find out because the driver of the second car got out and, after dragging heavily on a fag, walked up to us and knocked on Rambo's window. Rambo wound the window down and for some reason I wondered if he still had the Glock tucked into the waist of his newly acquired jogging bottoms.

"All right, mate?" said our new acquaintance. "Shouldn't be much longer. Nicko usually opens up at quarter to." Rambo gave the briefest of nods, his demeanour bristling with every antonym you could ever think of associated with the word 'affable'. Being out of camo was clearly not doing his disposition any favours. "Been here before?" the smoker asked.

"No, first time," I said, trying to sound enthusiastic while Rambo looked evil personified.

"It's not a bad place," said our newfound fount of information, oblivious to the simmering hulk just inches away from him. "Usually catch a few." He dragged on the fag again. "I had a twenty yesterday, actually."

I tried to suppress a smile. So *that's* why he had come to have a little chat! I could hardly criticise, been there, done it etc. etc.

"You going back in the same swim?" I asked.

Our new friend's face clouded for an instant. "If *he* doesn't," he said gesturing towards the car at the front of the grid.

"First come, first choice, is it?"

"Yeah, usually, not unless you get some arsehole jump in front of you. Most of the blokes are all right."

"There are plenty of wrong ones about. Chav carpers, who needs them?" I said grinning, hoping he didn't have the obligatory Burberry cap on his passenger seat.

"Too right, mate," our friend said sucking on his cancer stick.

I decided – seeing as things were going so chattily and Rambo hadn't flung open the door and beat him into a snot and gore purée – to introduce the subject of why we had come to Broomham in the first place. "We've been told there's a nice syndicate water on this estate somewhere, is that right?"

Our pal took another long drag, exhaled a plume of smoke, dropped his cigarette butt onto the floor and ground it into the tarmac. "Yeah," he sneered. "Been trying to get in myself but no joy. Like all syndicates, it's who you know lets you jump the list and if you don't know anyone you're shafted. Sit on the fucking list for years."

"Tell me about it," I calculatingly empathised. "Who runs it? D'you know?"

Our mate nodded, his tongue momentarily bulging out a cheek. It was my turn to sneer. Fuck me, he was cool and had his finger on the local carping pulse. "Bloke called Gary James runs it. The main access is just up the road from this one, but you could walk through this part of the estate to it, from this water, from the far end of the lake, provided you could climb the fucking great fence he's put around it." Our new pal turned philosophical. "Don't blame the bloke, though, I wouldn't want any of my fish taking a walk down the road."

Only if it was to walk back to where they came from originally, I thought sarcastically. Unfortunately I had to live with the fact, as appealing as the notion was, it would never happen. I would never know how many Hamworthy fish were swimming around in Hollywood's water and I would never get them back. How many *had* the bastard spirited away over the years? Most likely all the original stock were Hamworthy fish. No wonder they were growing big and fuck-wit Darren could ease his ugly mug into the likes of Carp-Talk. I tried to control my bile and find out how far this walk might be, but was foiled by the arrival of the tin god named Nicko. The galvanising effect on our buddy of his turning up was extreme; one minute he was by Rambo's window chewing the cud, the next he was gone, into his car and revving its engine.

Nicko unlocked the gate and we drove through it into the car park, all a little faster than we should, all with an air of slight desperation hanging over us. This was real world carping! The cloistered environment of Hamworthy Fisheries had been shed for a day! We were out in the carping wilds, with all and sundry, fishing alongside the good, the bad and the thick as shit. I flicked a glance at Rambo. If he didn't deck someone today the mood he was in it would be a miracle. I resolved to make sure I was a moderating force on him – we didn't want to draw any more attention to ourselves than necessary.

As things turned out it wasn't half as bad as I had suggested earlier. Within half an hour we were nicely settled into a couple of adjacent swims looking out over the furthest corner of the lake from the car park. Our two other early bird anglers had both opted for middle of the lake swims, which had access to the margins of a small island. I could see why it was a popular feature, not only because of the obvious, but also due to the relative seclusion it offered. No far bank Charlie could cast into your spot!

Our swims were okay considering they were third and fourth choices because both the end bank and far bank were nicely tree-lined with established willows and had no swims in them. The far bank was over seventy yards away while Rambo had an underhand flick to the end margin as he was in the end swim. The next swim down from me on our bank was only ten yards away – a similar distance from the one between Rambo and I – but I doubted if anyone would fish it. The only fly in the ointment was the first far bank swim from the wooded end. This swim was only a few yards down towards the car park in relation to me. An arsehole ensconced in this swim – and I was convinced someone would fish it because it had the obvious features and couldn't be covered by anyone else only ourselves – could cause aggro.

In all honesty I should have fished it, but the main duty of the day dictated I had to fish directly alongside Rambo. If by chance it did remain empty I could cast right over to the far margin while Rambo went against the end margin under the trees. If it didn't my swim was 'open water only' and a bit limited without a written invitation from where Rambo was fishing enabling me to share the end margin by casting well over to the right. However, the old conundrum of where swim bragging rights started and stopped (middle for diddle?) would raise its ugly head if the wrong type of angler fished opposite. Dear me! What a palaver! I had never even thought of such niceties at Hamworthy because no swim covered another, well, not without a bait boat, a big pit reel and a ridiculously unreasonable attitude.

While Rambo armed his first rod – of only *two*! What was it all coming to? Two, not three was the answer! – with the Pup revolutionary, indented, dirty brown bottom bait boilie, I sneaked off up through the trees to see if I could locate the iron curtain Hollywood had placed around his precious syndicate water. As I slipped off I wondered how Hollywood had managed to secure the venue – I knew all about where he had secured the fish stock – because that in itself must have constituted a considerable amount of dosh. Maybe he was in with someone else, the landowner perhaps, or possibly it was a lease deal? Whatever it was he was still perceived as the man who ran it by both Alan, the koi shop owner, and the angler we had met this morning.

For some time, ten minutes or so, I ploughed through a coppice before reaching the fence we had been told of. Although substantial I felt it wasn't an insurmountable problem – I could get my leg over it, even if I wasn't getting my leg over anything or anybody else – it was what lay on the other side that bothered me. A nice little blunder into Darren, Rocky or even shitface himself could wreck everything I had so carefully allowed to trundle along and play itself into place. Equally I had no idea how far away the water was, how big it was or where the swim I had seen in my vision was in relationship to anywhere else. I went back to Rambo and moaned.

"I found the fence. Christ knows where the swim is from there," I whinged.

"You'll have to climb over and find out won't you," Rambo said curtly. "Without being seen." For good measure on noticing my perturbed expression he added. "No one said it was going to be easy, boy... about as easy as wearing these fucking clothes! I feel a right knob!"

"Will you be able to throw me over the fence?" I asked ignoring his whining – I had enough worries of my own.

"Sure. When do you want to go?"

"Not yet. Nicko's bound to be round for his money soon. I'll fish a few hours first and pick the moment. Are you going to come with me?" I asked.

Rambo looked away from his static indicator. "I'll be staying here, boy, looking after the gear and covering for you. I can always give you a ring on your mobile if anything awkward crops up. Put it onto vibration only."

"Likewise," I mumbled somewhat distracted by an angler turning up in the far bank swim opposite.

Rambo followed my gaze and chortled. "Open water for you, boy!"

"Aren't you going to let me cast up the end bank?" I said bottom lip thrust out. "Under that willow tree?"

"I've got a bait under there," said Rambo. "You should have got here first if you wanted to fish there."

"I *let* you fish there!" I proclaimed.

"*You* let *me* fish there!" said Rambo laughing. "I'll tell you what, you wait till I catch one and then I'll move down a bit and I'll let you put one on the end bank. How's that?"

"Not out!" I said with mock grumpiness. "I suppose I'll have to stick two in open water for the time being... you never know it might be a hot tactic." Rambo gave me an eyebrow-raising 'you wish' look and a wide grin. I gave him one back. To be fair the all-new version of Rambo was bearing up reasonably well considering his undoubted accoutrement induced discomfort – I imagined it being something similar to me fishing in a collar and tie with Hessian underwear and new brogues a size too small times an unknown irritability factor of at least several thousand.

I had a sudden thought. "You haven't got the spare Glock with you, have you?"

Rambo briefly lifted up his new sweatshirt to flash me the one Glock. "All authorised carp anglers on day ticket waters should be armed. That means *me* only," he insisted.

"What about the other one?" I double insisted.

"Steffi's got it," Rambo replied.

"*Why?*" I asked a little mystified.

Rambo looked awkward and not solely because of his new clothes. He scratched his head and avoided my stare. The penny dropped. "You've *told* her haven't you?" I said in a voice tinged with slight disgruntlement. "And she's got the other gun in case any more asylum seekers, who are in fact assassins, come looking for you or me and instead of you or me find her. Not that they'd recognise you now, of course," I added acidly looking him up and down.

"Sorry, Matt," Rambo said softly. "I had to tell her. You can see why… I've been sucked in by circumstances, circumstances I've always tried to avoid in the past. You see," he looked down at his sweatshirt, tracksuit bottoms and almost white trainers, "now *I've* got someone I care for as well."

My annoyance withered away and disappeared like a PVA bag dropped in a shallow margin during summer. "That's all right, mate…"

We were both distracted by a splash and the chilling sight of a marker float jauntily popping to the surface under the willow tree where Rambo had his left-hand rod.

"Oh dear!" I uttered dolefully and we both trained our eyes on the angler on the far bank. "Whatever next?"

"You *know* whatever next!" said Rambo.

"The spod?" I theorised.

"Got to be, hasn't it?"

I lifted both shoulders. "That or five kilos of readymades."

The far bank angler cast again. We saw the offending object arc through the air and explode onto the lake's surface delivering its payload of carp grub goodies. Splash-splash-splash went the spod – for that was what it was – as it raced back over the surface in full retrieve. There was a lull while it was refilled and then out it went again. Splash! Rambo slumped into his chair and watched the angler repeat as necessary – as he thought necessary – the whole noisy process time after time after time.

"Casting accuracy is pretty good," I commented as we watched the show.

Rambo, who had his arms folded tightly across his abdomen, seemed unimpressed. "Never even *asked*!" he said as much to himself as to me. "Never even asked where my baits were! The tree is definitely in *my* water, especially as I was here first!"

"Maybe there's an unwritten local bye-law," I suggested.

"Shall I just shoot him?" asked Rambo. "I can't imagine anyone would miss him... oh... looks like the spod bombardment is over. At last!"

Rambo was correct. The spod bombardment was over... only it was time for the catty attack to begin. Thwack! Thwack! Thwack! Out went at least one hundred boilie free offerings and then, finally, the angler cast out his baited rod and with a final flourish set his hanger indicator with his alarms on full volume.

"Fucking hell!" exclaimed Rambo with resignation. "He's worse than you!"

"I wouldn't say that."

"No," agreed Rambo. "On second thoughts nor would I."

Silence, having at last managed to muscle itself to the front of the queue, pervaded.

"That's one rod sorted," I pointed out. "I wonder what's in store for the other one?"

We both watched in bemusement and – in my case – a certain amount of fascination. This was entertainment, of sorts, and because I didn't really care about the fishing too much today it was nearly palatable because of it. As I watched I wondered if it was it going to be a repeat of the last rod or whether it might involve a bait boat. In the end it was neither. The angler opposite promptly left the pair of us dumbstruck as he underhanded out his single hookbait rig, set his alarm, this time only turning it on for a single, testing beep and parked his arse onto his chair.

"I don't believe it!" said Rambo. "Must be a type of loud and silent, little and a lot routine he's giving them. Maybe this boy's a real pro and involved in a game of psychological warfare we can only just begin to comprehend."

I heaved a sigh. "The only thing more surprising is why you didn't shoot him, or at least beat him up."

Rambo tilted his head. "Understated, no ripples, don't draw attention to ourselves. That's the game plan for today, boy."

And with that statement Rambo's right-hand rod ripped off – the one he had cast under the tree and had received the bait bombardment. As Rambo hit the take I walked over to his side and hissed. "And I suppose you think *that's* in keeping with our game plan do you?"

"Go and cast out," replied Rambo, "if you're quick you can get one bait in the water by the time I've caught one."

I turned on my heel and before I tried to do what he had suggested said. "Don't forget, I'm casting up to the tree now."

"Do you *really* want to look so sad and desperate?" came the comment. "Especially in front of an expert."

"Who's that? You, or him over the road?"

152

Rambo nodded his head towards Spodman. "He rang the gong, Pup's boilie did the rest. I'm a mere facilitator in nearly white trainers."

I cleared my throat; despite the sarcasm he did have a point. "I'll go open water."

Chapter 16

"Watch your groin on those spikes. Get impaled on one of those and you'll know all about it... it's made by the Tetanus Steel Company. And can you take your foot off of my face, boy."

"Why, did I step in some dog shit?"

"No. I have this strange aversion to people walking on my nose, that's all."

"You without camo, it's like Superman *with* kryptonite!"

Carefully I managed to ease myself up onto the top of the spiked metal fence via Rambo's body and jumped from it onto the other side. I was in Hollywood – Hollywood's syndicate's grounds – and my heartbeat was in the one-forties.

"Put this on," I was informed by my other-side-of-the-barrier-buddy. "If you get seen, leg it back to here and get over ASAP. Hopefully no one will recognise you. With any luck you'll be perceived as just another in the long list of curious carp anglers." Rambo lobbed over a small piece of black material. I picked it up and saw it was a type of balaclava, black and made of a very lightweight silk-like material. The mouth and eyeholes were separate; my nose would be completely obscured by its material when I got to wear it. I looked at it with disdain.

"It hasn't got 'rapist' written across the forehead and a zip mouth!" I pouted.

"Zip *your* mouth and get on with it!" Rambo said sternly. "The longer you fuck around in there the more chance you have of being spotted. You're behind enemy lines now, boy!"

With a fraught look I put on the balaclava, pushing my ears flat to my head.

"Who's a handsome, boy?" cracked Rambo. "It's a good job you've managed to put a *bit* of weight back on otherwise you'd have looked like a safety match running around."

I poked my tongue out through the mouth opening. "You get ready to bale me out if the balloon goes up," I warned.

Rambo waggled his mobile at me. "Ready and waiting, boy. Now, go find the swim before the weather changes and the big wind comes!"

I gave Rambo my thumbs-up signal, turned away from the fence and made off slowly through the coppice. My heart pounded a little harder as I picked my way through the trees and I felt hot and claustrophobic under the balaclava despite its thin construction. I was truly on my own now. One mistake and the whole teetering contrivance constituting my revenge plan would come crashing down like a house of cards torpedoed by a flung paperback. This was pressure! No big bad buddy to bale me out, no quiet assertive voice of reason to calm and suggest, no big fist to hammer any would-be opponent. No Glock! On retrospect the latter was most likely a good thing as my only killing so far had not created a bloodlust, especially not one with me being directly associated with pulling the trigger. (How far I had come, I reminded myself, the replay of the bullet riddled asylum seeker was no longer number one in-my-head-video, nor was my imagined reconstruction of Hollywood and Sophie's sexual liaison. The thing grabbing me most was the vision I had seen of Hollywood in The Eye's head and how I might change it to wipe the smile off his handsome face.) I was Technician Williams on reconnaissance. The pain I was hoping to inflict on my enemy was spiteful, mysterious – natural even – and above all else untraceable. I hoped the swim in my vision was not of a similar nature.

For fifteen minutes I carried on through the coppice, trying to hold what I imagined to be a straight line from the fence Rambo had so ungraciously helped me over. The coppice was quite open and I could see through it fairly well, a blatant downside for a trespasser such as myself. I stooped a little lower but on tramping forward felt a vibrating inside my jogging bottoms. Shit! The mobile! Quickly I went into the prone position and fished out the offending phone. The phone didn't recognise the incoming number.

I answered in a whisper. "Hello." Who the hell was this?

"Hi, man. The Eye," said a forlorn voice.

To say I could have done without The Eye phoning at this particular time would have been an understatement as big as saying there are adverts in carp magazines. The time and the place were of poor timing and I guessed the subject matter was going to be even worse. I had a good idea what this was going to be concerning and it wasn't pretty.

"Hello, The Eye," I whispered.

"Man. Quiet?" The Eye said with his customary brevity.

"Stalking," I whispered. "Big common but don't worry, carry on. What's up?"

"Been for scan. Was tumour. Caught early. Reasonable chance of cure, man," The Eye sort of explained.

What was I meant to say? Good? Bad? Can I have your rods if you die? I settled for vagueness. "Oh."

"Phoned to thank you," said The Eye. "Without you, too late. If it is… The Eye'll be back."

I was thrown by the pseudo Schwarzenegger line until I twigged he meant how I had provided the evidence to seal his total belief in Buddhism.

"You'll be fine. You've got too many carp left to catch in this lifetime!" I said pathetically trying to be upbeat. "You keep me posted how you're doing."

"Will do… Tried the absinthe?"

"Not yet. I'm waiting for a special occasion."

"The vision happened?"

"Not yet. Soon, I expect."

"Tell The Eye what happens."

"Sure."

"The Eye'll let you get on."

"Okay, mate. Take care and good luck with the treatment. You let me know as well. Me and Rambo are pulling for you."

"Cheers, man."

The Eye hung up, much to my relief. Anytime would have been a bad time to field such a tricky conversation, but doing it while sneaking around in the enemy's den was much worse. I just hoped I hadn't sounded too disinterested. Guilt flooded through my body – poor old The Eye. What a bummer! And I thought I had problems – *The Eye* had problems! In a twisted reversal of the popular adage I realised there's always some poor fucker worse off than you… not unless you really *are* unlucky!

I eased myself back onto my feet and started walking again, heading in what I presumed was the right direction. As I did I tried to fix tiny memory joggers into my brain so I could find my way back. Unfortunately one tree looked pretty much like another and I had a sudden rising panic in my craw. 'Man dies in local wood', was the headline. 'Matt Williams, local part-time psychic and occasional murderer was found dead on the Broomham estate yesterday. His painfully thin, emaciated body was found decomposing in the middle of a coppice where, according to the police, he had been walking in circles for four days. Police suspected Mr Williams' strange behaviour to be sexually motivated due to the odd headwear found upon him. A senior officer implied it was most likely a bizarre tree fetish with confusion of choice leading to exhaustion and subsequent death'. I told myself to keep calm and concentrate, concentrate on forging ahead – straight ahead.

Ten minutes later, shortly after I had convinced myself the coppice I was in was roughly the size of Canada, I spotted something over to my left. Carefully I picked my way over to the object I could see through the trees, which lay a hundred yards or so away. As I moved closer I could see the object was at the edge of the coppice and as far as I could distinguish no more trees were behind it. Eventually I realised it was a boat, a wooden boat. My heart cranked up the tempo again as I prayed I had found the boat I had seen in my vision.

Once within twenty yards it was obvious to me it was *the* boat from my vision. Beyond it was grass and beyond the grass water! The water I could see, not that there was much of it, was in between two huge swathes of rhododendron bushes. Quickly I ran up to the boat and crouched behind it noticing – because I'm observant over such things – the boat had not been left 'hull up' to prevent it filling with rain. The hull sat snugly on the grass and I could tell it had been only recently placed there as many of the grass blades tucked underneath were still green. On my hands and knees I crawled round to the back of the boat and saw the tiny petrol outboard motor lifted on an angle to keep the propeller and its shaft from digging into the ground. I started to kneel up to afford myself a look inside the boat, only before I could, I heard voices. I immediately dived for cover behind the boat catching my shoulder heavily on the gunwale as I did. The boat rocked a little but the grass it was on ensured the movement was silent.

The pain in my shoulder was nothing compared to the experience my heart was undergoing. If I was going to die relatively young and beat The Eye to it – from a coronary rather than a brain tumour – then now was the hour. Gagging for air, sweating profusely, overcome by nausea and with a heart setting the pace for a thrash metal group's new two minute single my mind gyroscoped in an attempt to come up with plausible escape routes. Despite the paucity of control I had over my body, I wasn't mentally incapacitated enough to realise there were none. I was in – as one of my old bosses used to say when I was an electrical apprentice – 'The Sultans' (Sultans of Swing by *Dire Straits*!) and it wasn't a pleasant feeling.

The voices became louder and I shuffled further under the rounded 'V' shape of the hull in a vain attempt at a disappearing act. If the voices had come for the boat I would be discovered and would have no other option than to leg it like I had never legged it before. Thankfully the voices became softer and were gone. I gave it another minute and then cautiously poked my head above the parapet of wooden boat. No one was to be seen. I thanked my lucky stars and tried to regain my composure and stop my shaking.

I turned my attention to the inside of the boat. Someone had evidently been busy in the boat keeping Hollywood's water in tip-top shape, probably Hollywood himself. There were a couple of bow saws, a pair of secateurs and the remains of a rhododendron trimming session with leaves, short stalks and bits of branches liberally scattered in the bottom as if it had been half-heartedly cleared of a large pile of off-cuts. However, most intriguingly there was a green canvas cover doing its official union job of covering up a substantial object. I carefully teased up its edge and with immense gratification saw the chainsaw, a possible primary object on which to later make my MNC to create my MDR and wipe the smile off Hollywood's face. It was all here – and hopefully would stay here until it was next used after the gale had snapped the branch – all I had to do was figure out the change conundrum. Huh! *All*!

The inside of the boat was exactly as I had seen in my vision, a vision I suddenly realised had been viewed from a high vantage point and not from where I had seen Rambo and me lying in cover. Still, I had no time or inclination to concern myself over such trivialities and I moved around to the bow of the boat with the idea of making a dash to the rhodies and getting a better look at the entire water.

As I moved to the front end of the boat I noticed something I hadn't spotted before, a Fox automatic inflating lifejacket. It was on the ground in some long grass directly alongside the bow and I wondered why it hadn't been left inside the boat like all the other equipment. In a panic I wondered if it had been left on top of the gunwale and my shoulder had dislodged it when I had literally rocked the boat. If I didn't want to make the second meaning of the phrase come to fruition I had better make sure I left everything as I had found it on this purely reconnaissance mission. Feverishly I wracked my brain as to whether I could remember seeing the lifejacket either on the floor or on the gunwale when I had first arrived at the boat. There was no answer either way. Logic said I would have been more likely to have seen it on the gunwale than on the grass – so that pointed to it being originally on the floor. On the other hand where was the most likely place to put a hundred pound lifejacket when you had finished with it? Feeling I was procrastinating and getting bogged down by seemingly unimportant minutiae – who the hell would make a connection between me being here and a lifejacket not being *exactly* where it had been left – I put the lifejacket back on the gunwale and sprinted to the rhododendron bushes.

If I had felt nervous over trespassing before, I now felt even worse as I was markedly more exposed. Out of the coppice and standing on a clear walkway was bad news; the sooner I was back with Rambo the better. I looked up through the gap and out onto Hollywood's estate lake, the one filled with my fish. It looked around eight acres' worth, tree and rhodie-lined with several patches of attractive lily pads. The lake eased in from where I was standing affording me a good view of the two closest swims up to eighty yards away. Promisingly the first one had a large tree in it and double promisingly no angler! My luck was holding good!

Taking a deep breath I ran across the gap between the rhododendrons and up the side of one clump of them. Small trees and bushes lined the margin as I ran up towards the big tree swim. Over the far side I could see two bivvies, presumably with two anglers inside them. The voices I had heard earlier? I didn't know and didn't care. I reached the swim with the big tree and recognised it immediately. Despite all the sweat and heat caused from my exertions a cold chill ran down my back. This was it! The tree, with its big branch still attached, as any self-respecting tree would want it, the swim opening and to the back, the area where future Darren and future Rocky would stack the chainsawed logs. Well to the rear, back in the coppice, was where Rambo and I would lie behind the small bush. Sorted. My vision was correct; the branch had yet to break and my recce was done and dusted. I was out of here.

I ran directly back to the coppice and pushed on a good hundred yards into it, turning right once I was in relative safety. I forged on, passing the boat and hopefully began to retrace the way I had come from the day ticket water. As I walked further and further from danger a feeling of pride and achievement superseded my earlier fear. I had done it. On my own!

Although my dread of being apprehended faded I still kept the balaclava on just in case. My only concern now was finding my way back to the spiked metal fence and climbing back over it. I must have managed to hit a pretty straight trail because the fence duly appeared and, although it wasn't exactly where I had originally climbed over, I was only some twenty yards out of line. I ripped off the balaclava and rang Rambo only to find him engaged. Five minutes later I managed to get through. He told me to hang fire while he wound in and not try to climb the fence until he was present. I did as I was told and waited for him to turn up, which he soon did armed not only with the Glock but a shortish length of sturdy rope. Rambo threw one end of the rope over the fence, wrapped his end around his right forearm and told me to grab my end as tightly as I could and start to climb. Again I did as instructed and what with Rambo heaving and me scrambling with my feet against the substantial metal stakes I was soon able to get up to the spikes, carefully place my feet between them and jump down.

"How'd it go?" he asked.

I told him how I had found the swim, the boat and its contents, that the branch was still intact and I hadn't, despite a close shave with a heart attack, been spotted.

"Excellent! Well done, boy!" Rambo enthused. "Now we wait for the weather to change."

"Yeah, but I've still got to work out what to do to *change* what I saw happen. If I can't do it, everything's been a total waste of time," I reminded Rambo. "The hardest part is still to be done!"

"You can't do anything about it now," Rambo pointed out. "Personally I think we need to be back at the boat shortly after the branch gets blown down. That's our window of opportunity, our chance for you to make the change."

I wasn't too keen on how the collective emphasis had suddenly changed to hang purely around my neck – but it was, in truth, the reality. *I* had to supply the answer.

"Oh, *shit!*" I cried. "I've suddenly remembered! I didn't pull the cover down over the chainsaw. I left it up a bit when I looked underneath it."

Rambo's huge chest expanded in a sigh. "What fucking difference is *that* going to make?" he demanded with exasperation. "Look, boy, switch off for a while. You deserve a bit of fishing. You can fish my swim for the rest of the day if you like. I've had a couple while you've been gone." Rambo gave me a nudge as we started to walk back. "Spodman's had fuck all and is getting more and more agitated every time I get a take," he said gleefully. "We'll have to have a sweepstake on what time he comes round to ask what bait we're on. I mean, even you had one from open water before you had to wander off. I tell you, it's killing him me keep on picking fish up from under the overhanging branch after all the bait he's put in."

I could cope with that, I thought. A few hours' doubles bashing, rubbing Spodman's nose in the dirt with our boilie superiority. It would be good to chill for a while and you never know your luck, the answer to my riddle might simply pop into my head! The way my revenge had panned out so far it was always plausible!

"Who were you on the phone to?" I asked changing the subject. "It was engaged when I first tried."

"Steffi. I gave her a ring to see if she was okay…"

"And?"

"Fine. She's been sorting out getting all of her stuff moved from her rented place in Holland."

"Moving in permanent." It wasn't a question.

"Looks like." Rambo bowed his head as he walked. "Look at the state of them."

"What, the trainers?"

Rambo nodded. "Fucking things."

"She'll want to have kids next," I said before rather disconcertingly imagining

Steffi and Rambo in a lactating porn movie.

Oddly Rambo never thumped me, not for my perverted inner thought – *I'm* the psychic one of the duo and don't forget it – but for the mere suggestion of a family. "After wearing this lot today," he said stopping and holding out his arms so he could peruse the inside of his sleeves, "*anything's* possible!"

It was some admission. Rambo was changing before my very eyes.

Regarding the sweepstake, I said ten minutes after the next take either one of us had, Rambo said half past four. It was one o'clock; I was in Rambo's swim (one under the tree, one up the margin) and Rambo had moved into mine (both open water). The timings on Spodman's little visit were placed and all other bets were off.

As I relaxed in my chair I pondered not only on the carp catching power of Pup's revolutionary, indented, dirty brown bottom bait boilie, but also on its innate ability to fuck with other carp anglers' minds – the ones who didn't have it. It must have been doing Spodman's head in, especially as I had started to catch from under his bait's nose in the overhanging tree spot. I could imagine him sitting over in his swim trying to put on a calm exterior and underneath his brain being addled with angst. What am I doing wrong? Is it the bait? Is it the rig? Is it the tactics? Is it my hooklength material? And all other manner of questions would be running through his mind in order to ascertain why the two blokes over the other side had caught and he hadn't. Of course, as things wore on the questions would get more and more desperate and more and more surreal. By the end of the day, if he had blanked and we had notched up a few he might even be blaming the toothpaste he had used this morning!

Part of me suspected this was the main reason why Rambo had offered to swap swims with me – to drive home our superiority and to blast Spodman into something akin to a bait boat being hit by an Exocet! I couldn't help a smiling wryly to myself. How mean! What delicious fun! Come on you carp! Pull my string! Ruefully I admitted they were the only thing that *had* been pulling my string recently and the thought made me consider phoning Sophie to see how she and Amy were doing. A rash, rapid, raging, rakish, ransacking, ravishing, rollicking, rattling run ripping my right-hand rod right round in its rest put all phone calls on the back burner! The 'one up the margin' bait had been snaffled! I swooped on the take like a falcon diving on its furry lunch and devouring it.

As I played the fish in I couldn't stop myself glancing across at Spodman. He looked seriously pissed off! In time honoured tradition I gloated and revelled in his blanking and basked and preened at my catching. I could be quite a snide little shit when I wanted. No sooner had I returned my mid double mirror (I didn't bother to weigh it. I'm such a carp snob now, I only bother to weigh fish I think are over twenty. Hamworthy! What *have* you turned me into?) when Rambo's open water left-hand rod did the diddley-diddley-diddley song.

As Rambo eased his fish into the landing net Spodman cracked, wound in his open water rod and to my chagrin re-cast it closer to where Rambo had had his take.

"I'm not going to win," I complained to Rambo. "Ten minutes is well past now."

"And half past four marches inexorably nearer." Rambo gave me a wide smile, turned and watched Spodman from beneath his eyebrows. "I wonder how close he'll dare encroach on my water?"

"Who knows?" I said. "Keep hauling and you'll find out. He's becoming a Desperate Dan. Desperate Dan Spodman!"

I left Rambo to deal with his fish and plonked myself back into my chair. Pup's boilie was awesome! No doubt about it! What magic ingredient had he shoehorned into such a dull, uninspiring looking bait to transform it into the undoubted wonder bait it was? If I could shoehorn him into Hamworthy I would find out. It was a curiosity thing as much as anything. I didn't have the time or the inclination to go back to rolling my own again – all the fucking around with powdered ingredients, eggs, flavours, oils and all other manner of potions and additives. No, Pup could have all that – he was more than welcome. It was the nagging feeling of fishing with something I knew nothing about compared to our original red bait, which I knew everything about that piqued my interest. Admittedly for years Pup had rolled the red bait, I wasn't 'hands on' as I had been on the night I had mixed fifty kilos of the stuff with Rambo before embarking on the TWTT – thank God! But it didn't detract from the fact it was a bait of mine – and the revolutionary, indented, dirty brown bottom bait boilie wasn't. (I was firmly in Maddocks/Middleton who-invented-the-hair-rig territory by claiming the red bait was 'mine' because in actuality it had been Rambo's concept.)

My smugness soon evaporated into sheepishness with a single thought. Pup was a commercial bait maker! He was hardly going to sit on a wonder bait and let Rambo and I use it exclusively. The selfish bastard! It could, no, *would* make him a fortune and once it hit the grapevine he and Melloney would be rolling the stuff 24/7 until their bodies collapsed with multiple repetitive strain injuries. Jesus! Worst case scenario, Pup might be forced to sell out to one of the big boys in order to cope, what with his tendon twanged, ligament lacerated and muscle mullered body giving out on him! Market saturation would eventually dull the bait's impact and I would no longer be able to sit in an ivory tower knowing I had the best bait attached to my hook on any venue... *unless*! I resolved to have a quiet word at an opportune moment. I was the owner of Hamworthy Fisheries – within reason I could do what I wanted.

As the afternoon wore on the sun reached my chair and bathed me in warmth and I felt myself starting to doze. It was such a mundane thing yet a few weeks back I couldn't have done it – the videos in my head would have been far too vivid for relaxation. Seemingly they were under some semblance of control and now I had a new one – the vision I had seen in The Eye's mind. As I sat, relaxed, chilled and somewhere betwixt sleep and wakefulness, I groomed it with a nit comb, trying to tease out anything to point me towards my MNC. A half hour later I teased out a twenty from under the branch and the sight of the pair of us weighing an obvious good fish prompted Spodman to wind in – not to come round and visit us – but to pack up and fuck off out of it.

"He couldn't hack it," I told Rambo. "We blew him away!"

"*We?*" asked Rambo pointedly.

"Okay. Pup's *boilie* blew him away!" I picked up one of the revolutionary, indented, dirty brown bottom bait boilies and crumbled it in my fingers and sniffed it. "What the hell do you think is in it?"

Rambo ground a few crumbs I had inadvertently dropped onto the ground into the bank and kicked the dust into the water. I gave him the eyebrow treatment. "Getting a bit paranoid aren't we?"

Rambo laughed. "Best we check the margins before we go, we don't want to go leaving any strays. Even though we can't work out what's in them, some smart arse might!"

"Pup'll be selling this," I held out an open palm of boilie crumb towards Rambo, "to all and sundry, mate. They won't have to work out what's in them."

"I've been thinking about that," Rambo divulged. "I was going to suggest you fast track him into Hamworthy in return for some kind of exclusivity deal on this bait."

"Funny you should say that," I declared. "I was thinking along those sort of lines. I *am* the owner of Hamworthy Fisheries and if I want to fast track someone and increase the membership by one for certain undisclosed reasons I don't see why I shouldn't." I hesitated as I thought things through. "I might have to give him a special rate to persuade him."

Rambo shrugged in an unconcerned manner. "It's the force of the open market, boy," he stated. "He's got something you want, you've got something he wants. It's mutually exclusive, you both become better off and everyone's happy."

"*Everyone?*" I questioned.

"Who else is there?"

"The other members of the syndicate. They might not see it quite in the same light."

Rambo was animated. "'The other members of the syndicate!' Fuck them! What the hell have they got to do with it?"

I made a 'V' with my thumb and four fingers around my mouth and rubbed each jowl with the separate parts. "You're quite keen to keep this bait for us and Pup only, aren't you?"

Rambo coughed. "I was rather hoping you could grind out a deal to stop *him* fucking using it."

"We might have to let The Eye use it, provided he signs a contract of secrecy," I said.

"*If* he lives!" said Rambo obviously having mixed feelings over the whole issue.

"Another aspect is we could ask Pup to make it in a dedicated room, say the twenty-five millimetre plus room, and keep other clientele right away from it…"

"And suggest tightening up security at the house… new alarm, that sort of thing."

"Yeah…" Consternation gripped me. "What about if his relationship with Melloney goes sour?" I said with agitation. "*She'll* know what's in it. She could walk away with *our* exclusive bait and blow the whole gaff to someone like Mainline or Nutrabaits… or set up on her own!"

Rambo lifted up his sweatshirt and patted the Glock. "*She* won't get very far!"

Luckily one of Rambo's open water rods belted off and brought us back to reality – or rather *emphasised* it. We *had* to have an exclusive deal on the revolutionary, indented, dirty brown bottom bait boilie. I didn't want to ever suffer role reversal and be in Spodman's bivvy slippers!

Chapter 17

We had arrived back at Rambo's close to nine in the evening, a rake of fish under our belt and a feeling of elation from our successful reconnaissance mission and day of 'fun' fishing. A text had sent Steffi our ETA and a hot meal awaited both of us once we had unloaded the Scudo. Over the dinner table I told Steffi how I had found the boat and the swim.

"Voz it exactly as you had seen it in ser vision?" she asked. I nodded. "And ser same sing happened vhen you saw ser asylum seeker ready to shoot Rambo?"

I nodded again. So she knew my dark secret – was I bothered? I told myself now she and Rambo appeared so settled it didn't seem such a big deal. "Not quite the same. The vision I saw with The Eye hasn't happened yet, but the components I saw within it, the boat, the swim, the branch, the chainsaw were all as I perceived them... except the branch *hasn't* broken yet, thank God!" Steffi smiled at this. "With Rambo's one," I continued, "I arrived at the instant to match *exactly* what I had seen in my head. I seem to remember thinking time had juggled itself so I had arrived bang on cue. It's a fair drive from my... Sophie's house to the syndicate water and who knows how long a journey like that might take? Not to the split second at any rate," I explained.

"It is remarkable," Steffi enthused. "I vood never haff believed it possible."

"I would never have believed it possible to see him fishing without camo clothes!" I said.

Steffi leaned over and kissed Rambo on the forehead and laughed. It was hard to imagine what she used to do in such a cosy domestic setting; the home, the cooked meal, the partnership – one slightly unbalanced by yours truly playing gooseberry.

"Vhy don't ve all go to ser pub for a quick drink tonight?" Steffi suggested.

"You two go," I said. "You don't want me cramping your style."

"Do not be so stupid," Steffi chastised me. "You saved his life, you do not haff to vorry vhezzer you are in ser vay or a pain in ser arse." Steffi leaned over the table and put a hand on my shoulder. "I vill tell you vhen you are a pain in ser arse." I got the impression she would as well. A British reservation over such social niceties was hardly likely to be wired into her Germanic genes. She lifted her hand off me and turned to walk out of the kitchen. "I vill go and get ready," she said over her shoulder. "You two clear ser dishes and sen get ready for yourselves."

I gave Rambo a glance but he said nothing and we started to clear the dishes like we had been told. "I saved your life," I reminded him. "And *don't* fucking forget it!"

Rambo gave me a smirk. "I don't think she'll let me. You know what, boy, she thinks you're the most fascinating person she's ever met."

I felt my Adam's apple bob – Melina and all that. Rambo cared this time. "Oh?"

"Obviously not in a sexual context, she doesn't fancy you or anything." Thank God for that I thought and then immediately afterwards, with mild disappointment, wondered why not. "It's all this future seeing, mind-melding, ghost chatting malarkey that absorbs her…" Rambo faded out and a picture of circumcision whisked across his face. "I suppose she's got a point really. Perhaps I've become so embroiled in it, being so close, I forget how fantastic a tale it all is. My life would have been a lot less richer if I hadn't met you, boy."

"And shorter," I reminded him – again.

"All right," Rambo said grumpily. "Don't keep fucking on about it."

Rambo and I stood at the bar ordering the drinks while Steffi temporarily sat by herself on a stool at one of the high round wooden tables in the lounge bar. The first drink poured was Steffi's, so I ran hers over to her out of politeness and returned to the bar and Rambo. We had decided to go to the wine bar along from the tackle shop Rambo and I frequented because it wasn't far from Rambo's house and there was ample parking around the back of the pub.

"Does she always dress like that when she goes out?" I asked.

"Looks like it," said Rambo shaking his head. "There'll be fights, I can see it coming. Mind you," he said rubbing his palms together and warming to what he was going to say next, "I reckon the pair of us could take on anyone!"

"And there's always the Glock," I suggested.

"Always the Glocksss!" said Rambo stressing the plural. "They go everywhere with us now."

"Where the hell is she hiding it?" I asked looking over at the woman with the short vibrant blonde hair set off perfectly by the plunging 'V' neck blouse and tight hipster jeans.

"It's in the little black bag," Rambo answered. "Bit risky carting them around with us but I'm never going to get caught out again.

I looked at Steffi once more. The slightly hard features of her Germanic roots gave her an extra hint of something vague and tantalising now she was dressed up. It was hard to put your finger on what exactly it was, but the overriding impression was one of 'interesting' sex. Any man, or woman, if of such inclination, would look at Steffi as she sat perched on the high stool and think the same thing – here was a woman who looked as if she had unusual sexual preferences. It was an amazing transformation because the first time I had set eyes on her and all the time we had been in Holland I hadn't looked at her in that way. But tonight, dressed up, make up on and hair done, she had returned to how she had been in the video – less obvious and classier, true – but the strong undercurrent was there. Once a porn star always a porn star.

I suddenly had a not very strange compunction to watch the DVD Japp had given me – something I hadn't yet done. I wouldn't ever admit to Rambo I had watched it and I wondered if he ever would. It would be almost akin – worse in fact – to me re-running my Sophie/Hollywood mind's-eye liaison. Seeing your partner getting shafted by another bloke – and in Steffi's case another woman, 'strapadicktome' style by Nikki – was tricky viewing for all except those on the extreme fringes of sexual attitudes. I say *almost* akin – the big difference being the relative states of where each pair was in their relationship. The porn DVD was, after all, BR!

God! As soon as I started thinking of sex Hollywood's smiling face kept cropping up! I *had* to wipe that smile away and try and get completely back to normal. I had come a long way but there was still this major obstacle to cross. Could I ever deal with making love to Sophie and not think of Hollywood's handsome face and all the women he had had and was going to have?

I sipped a mouthful of lager and was distracted by the lounge bar's door opening. The mouthful of prime Danish lager nearly came flying back out again. Holy shit! I jabbed Rambo in the ribs and surreptitiously nodded towards the new customers coming into the pub. It was only the two stunning looking, lap dancing, ex-international gymnasts, who were also bisexual nymphomaniacs. Hollywood's girlfriends! Hollywood's *ex*-girlfriends even, given his – grind teeth like a cow in an Olympic grass eating competition – propensity to shag his way through umpteen women a year.

I watched the pair of them sashay over to the bar and vague memories of a previous long distance sighting at Hamworthy flooded back. Two girls, one white, one dark coffee in colour, the feline grace, the silky motion, the supercharged sexual promise, the oozing sex. Wow! These girls were some product. Everyone – even those trying to be *really* cool – gawped at their entrance. Everyone, that is, except Steffi, who only eyed them with casual distraction.

"I *told* you I saw them come out of here!" whispered Rambo.

"I hope to fuck *he* doesn't turn up!" I said starting to get a little excited and worried in equal measures.

"Easy, boy," said Rambo. "This could be another of those wonderful coincidences along the path to your revenge. Listen! We won't go and sit with Steffi. I'll stay here, you go to the bogs and wait for a few minutes, then I'll send Steffi out. Tell her to try and get talking to them to see if she can get any info out of them."

"How will…?" The penny dropped – the Nikki and Steffi scene. "I get it," I said abruptly. I sloped off to the toilets and hung around until Steffi came out of the lounge bar five minutes later.

"Vott is it?" she said. "All sis eyebrow lifting and secret talking stuff."

"Those two girls!" I said. "They're Hollywood's girlfriends!"

"Oh," said Steffi slowly. "Lucky guy. Bozz of sem?"

My head moved in the style of a jealous rear car shelf noddy-dog bulldog with the expression it might have after licking a wet toilet seat. "Rambo wants you to try and get chatting to sem, er, them, and see if you can find out any useful info on him or his syndicate water. Anything really," I blurted. Steffi tilted her head as if she wasn't too sure she could do it. "They're two stunning looking, lap dancing, ex-international gymnasts, who are also *bisexual* nymphomaniacs!" I said.

Steffi pouted. "Sen I am ser perfect bait," she said with authority. She undid another button on her blouse and eased her breasts together. She inched over to me and unexpectedly squeezed my crotch. "I vill try my best to help get him," she nodded at my dick as she let go, "back vitt Sophie. Tell Rambo not to get jealous if he sees me acting like ser old porn star Steffi. Ja?" She went to go back into the bar, but turned back to face me as she put her hand on the door handle. "I vill only do sis again because you saved his life. You understand? Zat part of my life is now over."

"Thanks, Steffi," I mumbled, still a little shocked from her explicit show of concern for my poor underused cock. Still, I consoled myself, if anyone could pull it off she could – *not* my cock – the useful info from the 'Hollywood's girlfriends' scam!

When I thought a safe we-have-no-connection-with-each-other time period had passed, I re-entered the bar to imagine everyone thinking I had either had a horrendous toilet de-commissioning crap or a pull off because I had been gone so long. No one cared a fuck about me or batted an eyelid at my re-emergence – they were all slyly watching Steffi talking to the two stunning looking, lap dancing, ex-international gymnasts, who were also bisexual nymphomaniacs.

I re-engaged Rambo at the bar and for the next hour we stood and watched what can only be described as an Olympic gold medal performance in the art of flirting. Steffi was fantastic, Steffi was tactile, Steffi was sexy, Steffi was vivacious, Steffi was frolicsome, Steffi was provocative, kissable, kinky, slinky, sensual, sensuous and seductive. All the years of faking(?) it for pornographic films had stood her in good stead. She was the master, the pornmeister – or rather the mistress! The two stunning looking, lap dancing, ex-international gymnasts, who were also bisexual nymphomaniacs couldn't get enough of her – for obvious reasons I guess. They touched her whenever they could, they touched her *wherever* they could and the more they touched Steffi the more they started to touch themselves, in lingering, long, clinging caresses. I have to admit to getting a faint stirring I hadn't felt for months. It was slow dance time at fifteen again! I was getting a bit of a boner, which seemed *totally* wrong and out of place for what I knew was really happening in front of my eyes. The trouble was it was so convincing and genuine my male 'switch' couldn't differentiate!

I wasn't too sure what Rambo was thinking and I felt compelled by decency not to ask. Mind you, I eventually reasoned; if he could deal with what she had done in the past, this minor piece of sparring shouldn't bother him unduly. Besides, he had suggested it and taking it on a step further – deep in the darkest recesses of his wilder fantasies – he might even have designs on hitting the sack with all three of them! I mentally grabbed my own throat and gave myself a violent shaking – I needed Steffi to come up trumps with something, some small golden nugget of information to help ascertain my MNC.

When the bar closed and a host of frustrated males – me included – were forced to head for home, Rambo and I caught up with Steffi outside on the pavement. The two stunning looking, lap dancing, ex-international gymnasts, who were also bisexual nymphomaniacs, had already departed.

"I am meeting sem in an hour at sis address," Steffi informed the pair of us holding up a scrap of paper. "Sey are going home to get ready."

"What to charge up their batteries? ...Are *we* invited?" I said before my brain could interface with my mouth and override my automatic first-thing-that-comes-into-my-head facility.

Steffi gave me a withering look. "*No*," she said to me emphatically before quickly checking Rambo's face for tell-tale signs of disappointment. "No one is going. Let us get into ser car and I vill tell you vott I haff found out for you."

We cut back round to the bar's rear car park in silence and got inside the Scudo. "Well?" I asked anxious to find out.

"Sey don't go out vitt him any more. Sey say zat he got fed up vitt sem and dumped sem," Steffi stated.

"*What!*" I said, my incredulity off the scale of all known measuring gauges. "And you believe them? What man in his right mind would ever, ever, *ever* dump them! They're two stunning looking, lap dancing, ex-international gymnasts, who are also bisexual nymphomaniacs *and* one's black and one's white! What more could you ever hope to achieve in a ménage-a-trois? You could walk the Earth until the end of time and not better it!" I rambled.

"Not unless you're Handsome Hollywood, apparently" said Rambo with a hint of admiration that sickened me to my very bones. Fucking Handsome Hollywood! Talk about being a love monkey on my back. He was fucking King Kong's big brother!

"Sey said it voz ser best sex sey had ever had... vitt a *man!*" Steffi said. My expression must have said more than a million words because she apologised straight away. "Sorry, Matt," she said. "I didn't mean to hurt your feelings."

"Don't worry," I said deadpan. "Just get out the Glocks and shoot me now!" I almost meant it. My aspirations of getting over Hollywood's run of revenge had crumbled a little. Even if I could exact my own version to mine and Sophie's satisfaction, how could I ever erase the deep wound I felt because of what he had done to her and *she* to *him*? Just a sentence from Steffi had brought it all crashing back. How would I feel when – if – I ever made love to Sophie again? What *would* wipe the smile off Hollywood's face once and for all?

"Did you find out anything useful?" asked the ever-pragmatic Rambo.

"For ser revenge? Not really. I can tell you how big his..." Steffi stopped herself before she presumably pissed me off even more than I already was and forced me to snatch away her black bag, hook out the Glock and shoot myself in the head splattering my sometimes psychic grey matter all over the inside of Rambo's nice new van! I'd probably miss. "Sey didn't know anysing about ser fishing or ser fish, sey only said zat sey had sex in a fishing tent vonce... Zese girls have no interest in anysing much else ozzer zan sex. Ser only sing sey said vas zat Hollyvood vas a very arrogant man. Very self-assured…"

"What's known as a cocky fucker!" Rambo interjected.

"Ja. Ser only sing he lacked confidence in vas vater. He couldn't svim, sey vood go to ser beach in ser summer, but Hollyvood vood only pose and sunbathe, he vood never go in ser sea… but you already know zat. You saw zat in ser vision, you saw he couldn't svim."

"*Shit!*" said Rambo with feeling. "I was positive this would be the last piece of the jigsaw, boy. You know, what with how everything else has sort of gently drifted into place."

My mind was elsewhere and I hardly heard Rambo at all. "So it really worried him did it, not being able to swim?" I asked Steffi.

She lifted her shoulders. "I don't know if it *vorried* him. Sey never said he vas frightened or bozzered, only zat it vas ser vun sing sey knew he vasn't good at. You said he even looked an expert vitt ser chainsaw. It seems he is vun of zose men who is lucky enough to be handsome and good at everysing… *nearly* everysing. He can't svim, so vott?"

Rambo started up the van and pulled off. "Looks like the ball's back in your court, boy."

"Yeah," I said in distracted enough manner to make Rambo stop and pull up the handbrake.

"I can hear that rambling brain of yours ticking over again! Come on! What is it?"

I gave Rambo and Steffi a confused shake of my head. "I don't know," I admitted. "I was thinking, when I went on the reconnaissance mission I touched two things. I lifted up the canvas cover on the chainsaw to look at it and never pushed it back down properly and I *might* have knocked the lifejacket off the boat and put it back in a slightly different position… *or*, it was already on the ground and I put it back in a completely different position back on the boat. You see, now we know that Hollywood can't swim, would he really chance it and go in the boat without a lifejacket? "

"He *would*," answered Rambo. "You saw him in the vision in the boat without a lifejacket, so by definition he would go in the boat without a lifejacket. He obviously wasn't that arsed about it."

"But he *should* have been, he could have drowned. If it hadn't been for Rocky fishing him out, he might have done," I said.

"Obviously he'd be safer wearing the lifejacket, but he doesn't *know* that does he? He hasn't been on the absinthe!" said Rambo."

"Perhaps you haff said ser answer!" said Steffi excitedly. "If you can somehow stop Rocky saving Hollyvood he might drown!"

"Yeah, you can shoot him, Rambo," I said sarcastically. "And just to make sure, shoot Darren *and* Hollywood!"

Rambo let out a grunt. "A distraction for a few seconds might be enough. It's how much we're prepared to reveal ourselves in making it. Remember, we know what's going to happen, they don't! That might be an edge as big as Pup's revolutionary, indented, dirty brown bottom bait boilie!" Rambo puffed out his cheeks. "It's either that or you think of something to change on the boat if we can get to it just before it's due to be used."

"I'll think it over tonight," I said. I decided to change the subject. "What about the two stunning looking, lap dancing, ex-international gymnasts, who are also bisexual nymphomaniacs? They're going to be disappointed."

"Don't vorry over sem. Sey haff each ozzer and can make up sere own fun," said Steffi.

And you've got Rambo and I've got no one I mused bitterly – all I've got is Hamworthy Fisheries, the finest carp fishery in Britain. For most it would be enough, more than enough. I resolved not to wallow in self-pity. "Thank God for Duracell, eh, Rambo?"

Rambo laughed, while Steffi tut-tutted at my juvenile humour, and began the short drive to take us home.

The next morning after a restless night grappling with my prospective MNC – an *unsuccessfully* restless night grappling with my prospective MNC – the breakfast TV weather forecast ironically applied even more pressure upon me by announcing an impending front of *low* pressure. As the three of us munched our cornflakes – Steffi and Rambo had been at it all night like wild dogs, I could tell – a severe gale warning was issued for the evening across the south-east of the country. How nature abhors anything trying to resemble a vacuum! The big blow rushing to fill the low pressure void was a hoolie of a south-westerly, ripping across the south of the country from the Atlantic. Wind speeds of fifty mph were expected with the odd gust up to sixty making it definitely branch-breaking material.

As the forecast washed over me I realised this – by all recognisable means – was it. Not exactly a ground-breaking or breath-taking thought, I admit, but fuck it up tomorrow – because tomorrow seemed the obvious time a keen Hollywood would be out checking over his beloved syndicate water – and it was game over. My revenge would be dead in the water rather than Hollywood dead *under* it. Ruefully I realised I wouldn't be able to afford my beloved Hamworthy the same treatment. I would be concentrating on trying to get the other big thing in my life back into shape – my family. On the spur of the moment I decided to go and see them to explain what I was going to do and what had happened of late. However, I still wasn't exactly sure what I *was* going to do. Slight drawback there, I felt. The nagging in my head persisted and I still wasn't convinced Steffi's suggestion was the right course of action – although it certainly was the most cogent.

I informed my hosts of my plan of campaign – like the teenager in a family of three telling his mum and dad what he had planned for a day in the school holidays – and buggered off to see Sophie and Amy.

My unannounced arrival took Sophie by surprise, but she welcomed me in all the same. Amy had grown, or seemed to have, and I sat with her snuggling on my lap as Sophie made me the compulsory cuppa. I told her – fully – of all what had happened lately. Sophie asked about Steffi and Rambo and their unlikely ex-porn star meets ex-army, ex-mercenary, ex-arms dealer relationship and – catching me with my pants *right* down – ours.

"Oh, Matt," she said handing me my tea. "Don't you wish you could turn the clock back and go back to how we were?"

I decided not to point out mine would have to be turned back a hell of a lot further than hers – pre-Rebecca in fact.

"Yeah," I said simply.

"We've blown it, haven't we?" she asked. "We had everything. Amy, money, a nice house, then you got Hamworthy and even *more* money… and it still wasn't enough," she said with disappointment.

"That was my fault," I admitted. "I started it all. I gave you a reason to do what you did. I've always had this destructive streak. You should have seen the light during the TWTT and left me for good then." My confession wasn't a ploy, it was heart-felt and genuine and a little surprising, even to myself. I had often told myself she deserved someone better and I still believed it. "I'm sorry... Can you forgive me?"

Sophie glanced into her tea as if looking for an answer. You won't find one in there, I thought, you used a fucking tea bag. "Can you forgive *me*?" Sophie countered.

"Never answer a question with a question," I said.

"Or avoid the question with a statement changing the subject," Sophie replied.

"I *honestly* don't know," I confessed. "I think I want to. No, I *know* I want to… I keep thinking of him and you, though."

Sophie tilted her head. "Likewise, with you and those other… *girls*." The word 'girls' was virtually spat out.

"We've hurt each other big time haven't we?" I said and then looked at Amy nestling in my arms. She had fallen asleep.

Sophie put her hand on my forearm. "Too much so, Matt," and she kissed me. I kissed her back. She kissed me back harder still. "Put Amy into bed," she whispered, "and then come to bed with me!"

Although as ultimately startling as a mid winter run from an iced-over swimming pool, curiosity and a lack of any sexual involvement for nigh on a year persuaded me to have a crack at it. The curiosity was; could I keep Hollywood's handsome smiling face out of my head during sex with Sophie? Ten frustratingly flaccid minutes later I knew I couldn't. It was there, like The Eye's brain tumour, only it wasn't a black smudge it was his handsome smiling face riveted to my cerebral cortex. So much better looking than mine, so much more confident than mine. He was better at sex than me, so much better he had managed to get Sophie to do something to him she had never done to me! He was better at *everything* than me – apart from swimming. Well, big fucking deal!

Hollywood could even afford to dump the two stunning looking, lap dancing, ex-international gymnasts, who were also bisexual nymphomaniacs! I hadn't really realised how apt his nickname was. Hollywood. Handsome Hollywood – the world, and especially its women, falling at his feet, all because of a genetic abnormality making him abnormally handsome. Not because he was a decent person, not because of his intellect, not because of his compassion or his contribution to life, but simply because of his appearance. A handsome, manly, attractive appearance outshining anything else he had to offer and one capable of outshining any defect. In the modern age of image and aesthetic quality riding roughshod over practical ability, with the cult of celebrity triumphing over true worth, with the average man and woman turning to plastic surgery and various 'life-coaches' and 'make-over' consultants screaming the message; 'how you look is the most important thing in the world', Hollywood had it all – without even trying. He had been born beautiful and the world loved him for it. For just as the real Hollywood dealt only in glamour and image so did Gary James. His fuck-fest of a life was testament to what a handsome face could achieve – and I couldn't get it out of my head. The power of Hollywood was his face. So handsome it opened so many doors. I suspected even Michael had been swayed by it in the beginning.

I apologised to Sophie – she had been hot, wet and ready, which made me feel a *bit* better, open thumb and forefinger two millimetres and peer at the spark plug gap – and she started to cry.

"Oh, Matt," she sobbed and not purely from sexual frustration. "You've *got* to get even with him. Make the revenge happen and maybe it will release us from this agony. I *hate* him!" she cried vehemently and whispered. "More than I hate myself."

"I promised," I said trying to console her and convince myself, "and I won't let you down. Not like I have in the past." I held both her hands in mine and looked deep into her watery brown eyes and thought of Pup's revolutionary, indented, dirty brown bottom bait boilie. What *was* it with me?

When I left, walking over the very doorstep on which Hollywood had so smugly detonated my life-shattering bomb, I was more distraught than ever. A stiffening breeze reminded me of the task ahead and the one I hadn't been able to achieve in Sophie's bed earlier – *and* I still had no final game plan. The final link in the chain was as elusive as ever, the last jigsaw piece apparently lost in the attic or down the side of the sofa. I got into my van and cried, for lots of reasons, but mainly because at this precise juncture I was impotent and not even thirty-five. Pathetically I had rounded up to the mid thirties to give me a few more years to put things right!

I recovered some dignity – although not much – by the time I returned to Rambo's house and found him rummaging through a huge trunk filled with old army outfits in the garage.

"Remember this, boy?" he asked with enthusiasm, holding up some army fatigues.

I considered his question and puzzlement turned to amusement. "Not the outfit I wore when we pre-baited the old SS syndicate?"

"The very same, boy," Rambo replied looking admiringly at the army camo jacket and trousers. "The boots are in here somewhere," he informed me peering into the huge trunk. He turned his eyes back to mine and gave me a defensive look, sheepish almost. "I thought if we both wore the same outfits it might bring us luck. One successful operation might lead to another."

"Let's hope so," I said, my words not exactly conveying the sentiment they were supposed to.

"How'd it go with Sophie?" Rambo enquired picking up on my inflection. I told him the brutal reality. My ego was already crushed enough – telling my best mate such a delicate truth could hold no more pain than I felt at present. "Ouch!" commentated Rambo with feeling. "At least *she* was…"

"A *minor* compensation."

Rambo turned away and looked into the trunk. "Yeah," he concurred and moved on to practical matters. "What's your shoe size?"

"Nine."

"We'll have to be up early tomorrow," Rambo told me as he searched the trunk. "We can't be late for the show. As long as we're in the coppice by the branch swim before six in the morning we'll be fine. He won't be out before that time… Ah! Here they are!" Rambo held a pair of black army boots aloft in triumph. "The wind is only going to be strong tonight, by morning it'll have dropped considerably… according to the forecast."

"Let's hope they get it right," I said.

"Catch!" Rambo lobbed the two boots at me. "And I want to be able to see my face in them by the morning, private!"

Chapter 18

I hadn't slept much and not solely because of the wind howling at my window. My duvet had mimicked a tempestuous sea as it had pitched and troughed under my constant tossing and turning. Over and over again I had re-run the vision, straining to pick out something I may have missed before. Nothing came to light – nothing apart from my failed intercourse with Sophie and a picture of Hollywood's handsome face laughing at my useless efforts. Alongside all this, the worry concerning the two items I had touched during the reconnaissance mission kept returning. I had discounted the touching of the chainsaw's canvas cover – it surely could have no relevance – but there was also the matter of the lifejacket. If indeed I was Technician Williams, then I was in desperate need of a Life-Plotter and Computer to work out the ramifications – if any – of what I had touched and altered.

The previously advocated idea of making the MNC before the time of the vision, possibly at the boat as Rambo had suggested, seemed hopelessly optimistic now I had given it extensive thought. What *could* I do? What could I possibly change? It was an unfathomable question; one I had no hope of answering. Realistically in terms of a plan of action, the distraction option still looked the most hopeful. Perhaps if I jumped out of the coppice and flashed my privates at Rocky it could hold his attention long enough for Hollywood to drown. No court in the land would find me guilty of murder, or even the lesser charge of manslaughter! Indecent exposure, maybe, because as Rambo had also pointed out, we knew what was going to happen next! No one could prove the fact; no one would even *believe* it, certainly not unanimously amongst a jury of twelve! Despite all this, whatever the supposedly perceived merits of the distraction option, somehow it didn't *feel* right. I decided to make an inspired decision later – one induced by last minute panic!

It was hardly an edifying situation and in desperation I considered, if push came to shove, I might take the Glock from Rambo and simply riddle the bastard into a seventeen-hole human colander. I had done it before – it was simply a case of working out the mathematical equation. Life term in prison < letting Hollywood live, or; Life term in prison > letting Hollywood live. The most obvious formula was; No revenge = lifetime of purgatory. Time *might* let me get over it to some extent – I would still own Hamworthy – but it was hardly a solution. To summarise I wasn't in the most positive of mindsets when the alarm sounded at four in the morning – I won't say *woke* me at four in the morning.

I got dressed in my camouflage uniform and went down into the kitchen where Rambo was stuffing himself while Steffi was sipping a cup of coffee, her blonde hair tousled, her usually searing blue eyes a little bleary.

Rambo by contrast looked in rude health and full of it. He was back in camo and loving it. "An army marches on its stomach, boy!" Rambo exclaimed on seeing me. "Get some food down your neck and tell me the game plan!"

Steffi looked up from her coffee with expectation. She was soon to be disappointed. "I haven't got one!" I confessed wearily parking my arse onto a chair. "Other than being there at the time, as seen on TEV... The Eye Vision," I explained. I blew out my cheeks. "I'm waiting for last minute panic to induce a form of last minute decision-making inspiration," I explained dryly.

Rambo was unperturbed by my admission and engulfed a large rasher of best back bacon. "Knowing you, it will... The wind's dropping now," he said pointing a fork at the window, "but by Christ it blew in the night. Did you hear it?"

"Every bloody gust," I said pertinently.

Rambo attacked a sausage. "I hope Hollywood's on the case and gets to do the branch today otherwise we'll have to stay over there or shuttle back and forth. I don't fancy getting up at this sort of time and trotting up to his water for days on end." Rambo dunked the last bit of his sausage in a fried egg. "I have put a load of grub and drink in the van in case we have to stay."

"I reckon he'll do it today," I said confidently. "What else would he have planned?"

"To see ser person he dumped ser two girls in ser bar for?" suggested Steffi.

"Hmm! She *must* be something else," I conceded thinking of the sexual magnetism this unknown woman must possess to blow out the two stunning looking, lap dancing, ex-international gymnasts, who were also bisexual nymphomaniacs. "They didn't mention who she was, did they?" I asked.

Steffi indicated they didn't, frowned for a moment and unexpectedly said. "You're sure it's not Sophie?"

"I... I," I was flabbergasted.

Steffi suddenly looked very uncomfortable. "Sorry, Matt, *sorry*! I'm not being horrible, I suddenly sought it. I don't know vhy."

"I *didn't* tell her what happened," Rambo informed me before scoffing his last piece of fried bread.

"Vhy? *Vott* happened?" Steffi enquired.

"Matt met Sophie yesterday..." Rambo began.

"You didn't tell me..." said Steffi.

"I know I didn't tell you! I just *said* that!" said Rambo. "They had a reconciliation..." he started.

Steffi's eyes lit up and she shone a smile at me. "Oh! *Gudt!*"

"Only it wasn't a *full* reconciliation," Rambo told her.

Steffi's eyebrows pitched downwards. "Vott?"

I could see where this was heading and wondered if it was humanly possible to die of embarrassment. Telling Rambo was one thing – but him telling *Steffi* was another! And she was in the trade – or at least she had been!

"His nerve failed him." Rambo gave me a glance. "Didn't it, boy?" He spoke again directly to Steffi as if I wasn't there – which I wished were true. "The boy couldn't get Hollywood's handsome face out of his head and his dick didn't kick in."

I let my forehead slump onto the kitchen table with an audible thump. No one noticed.

Steffi was very understanding. "Oh! Such a shame! I used to get zat vitt some of my leading men! *Zey* couldn't get ser camera out of sere heads. Vott I used to do vas…"

"*Easy*, girl!" exclaimed Rambo holding out a huge flat paw of a hand. "I think we're *all* in territory we'd rather not discuss!"

"Phh! You men are!" said Steffi.

"You had enough to eat, boy?" Rambo demanded.

I lifted my head from the table. "I've *heard* enough!" I groaned.

"Well get your fucking boots on and let's go! There's plenty in the van if you start to keel over from hunger!"

Although I was filled with trepidation at the impending finale of my plan of revenge, I was only too pleased to get out of the kitchen, get my clodhoppers on and get in the van.

"Sorry about all that, boy," Rambo said as he got in the driver's seat and slammed the door. "Here. Have a Mars bar." He handed me the piece of confectionary as if it were a peace offering, started the Scudo, put it into first and we were off! "We'll put on our face camouflage when we get there," he informed me. "I've sussed out where we're going to park. You sit back and relax and see if the last minute panic weaves its magic."

I gave Rambo a sour look. "What sort of comment is that? 'Sit back and relax and see if the last minute panic weaves its magic'!"

Rambo curled up his top lip in sync with a minute shrug. "You know what I mean. Let *me* worry about getting us there and into our hiding position, while *you* concentrate on the final bit of the puzzle."

I gave him a forlorn smile. "Okay, mate… but it's not last minute enough for the last minute panic to set in yet, I'm afraid… I didn't mean to be snappy… it *is* a big day today," I added by way of explanation.

"I know, Matt," Rambo said gravely. "Let's hope we can pull it off like we have in the past... I'm sure we will."

I hoped so too. I hoped it more than anything else – even getting an exclusive deal on Pup's revolutionary, indented, dirty brown bottom bait boilie – and that's saying something. As Rambo drove me to our destination and for the umpteenth time, I asked myself what I needed to do in the next few hours. The nagging thought concerning the lifejacket came around again along with the distraction theory, but I was left bereft of lucidity and utterly bamboozled. It was hopeless, *nothing* was any clearer. I lent back in the car seat, mystified and totally answerless, wondering if I would have the guts to shoot Hollywood seventeen times with the Glock if I had to.

After an hour or so journey, Rambo pulled the Scudo into a parking lay-by he had evidently noticed when we had driven up to the day ticket water before. We scurried from the van to the fishery gate – the walk taking only a brief ten-minute yomp. On arrival and on seeing the gate devoid of people, I gratefully thanked the fishing Gods no super-keen angler had arrived the best part of two hours before opening time to secure a first pick of swims. We climbed the gate with ease and stealth, making our way around the Broomham venue as we had the other day. It was a lot easier as we weren't encumbered by massive amounts of tackle this time!

There were obviously other ways to arrive at where we were going – possibly shorter ways – but there was no point in taking a chance on getting lost or spotted. The way I had sneaked into Hollywood's syndicate had given me plenty of cover and had fortunately come out on the correct side of his estate lake. It was a good way into enemy territory and for the second time I took it, this time with Rambo to accompany me.

Once we had climbed the 'keep the bastards out!' syndicate security fence we put on our face camo. It was twenty to six and a pleasant summer's morning, or at least it would have been pleasant if it hadn't been for the undertaking we were due to embark on. The tension was starting to mount within me now with the realisation I was soon to hit the ultimate, no second chance, this *really* is *it*, you stupid fuck-wit, climax to my meandering, see-what-happens-next plan of revenge. My state of happiness for the rest of my entire life was in the balance. The outcome of whether I would regain my family back into my bosom hung by a thread and the prospect of avoiding love-making courtesy only of Viagra – with a backdrop of Hollywood's laughing handsome face – was a spinning coin yet to be called. It was – by all definitions – a seminal moment. And not unreasonably I was shitting myself.

The last remnants of the blown out gale gently caressed my hair. "This is it, Rambo," I said urgently. "The moment of hideous truth approaches and I haven't got a *fucking* clue what to do!"

Rambo's painted skin creased in a manner that might have been amusing under different circumstances. "Gut feeling?"

My head dropped to face the ground and shook in dismay. "Part of me keeps on harking back to the things I touched… part of me thinks we've got to do something positive."

"What the distract-Rocky-and-then-maybe-Hollywood-will-drown scenario?"

"Either that or I gun the bastard down. I haven't got anything better up my sleeve… besides how we distract him is almightily vague… I'm clueless on that front as well. Ideally it would be without us getting seen… or at a push recognised."

"If we get seen, we'll get recognised," Rambo said bluntly. "This camo's to help stop us getting spotted, not to disguise us, you know."

"Do you know what?" I said earnestly. "I'm dreading this but at the same time I hope it's over soon. I hope to God we don't have to lie down near to the swim for hours and hours waiting… or even worse have to come back tomorrow. I want it over, now... one way or another. The waiting would be worse than the moment of truth."

"It's how I used to feel before going into battle, boy. The thought of what's coming can eat away at you something terrible. I guess it's a little similar, but only a *little*, to a footballer playing in a crucial match. You want the waiting to be over and you just want to get out there and play," Rambo gave me a wild stare. "Of course, in battle if the shit really starts to hit the fan and everything goes totally tits-up with people getting brutally mown down left, right and centre with horrendous casualties and fatalities, you'd be only too pleased to have the chance to go back to the safety of only *worrying* over it!"

"Thanks," I said caustically. "Nothing's so bad it can't get fucking worse! Number one rule of the universe!"

Rambo rolled his right hand over to flash me a palm and immediately rolled it back. "Shit happens," he explained. "That's the reality."

"Let's go and see the reality of my vision," I said flicking my head in the direction of the lake. We took several strides and I stopped. "You've got the Glock with you, haven't you?"

"Always."

"Seventeen bullets up?"

"Seventeen bullets up."

"Seventeen... is a magic number," I sung.

Rambo put his huge mitt on my shoulder. "I don't think you'll get away with *another* seventeen bullet, water side murder, boy."

"Who says I'm worried whether I get away with it or not?" I asked. I raised my eyebrows in time with my answer, but as I think I had thought once before, I wasn't sure if Rambo had noticed due to the dark brown camouflage paint caked on my face as thick as a tart's make-up on a Saturday night. We started to walk on in silence.

For once *I* led Rambo – through the coppice – steering my straight-ahead course as I had on the reconnaissance mission, only this time I kept a keen lookout for the boat. The illusionary vastness of the coppice I had felt on my first visit was gone – experience told me we had a fifteen-minute walk. We pushed on quietly at an unhurried pace, picking our way between the slender and sparsely spread trees – our leisurely speed directly at odds to my pounding heart and mental demeanour. My heart thrashed away (see last excursion for more details!) and my mind floundered with apprehension and distressing disquietude. This was hardly a pleasant walk in the woods.

After what I thought was the allotted time I anxiously looked away to my left scouring the distance for the boat. Where *was* the bastard thing? I was convinced we had covered the approximate distance and it should have been over there. Somewhere.

"We *should* be able to see the boat any time now," I whispered to Rambo. He nodded and we walked on for another hundred yards after which I stopped, feeling something was wrong. "We should have seen it by now!" I said with rising panic starting to inflect itself on my hushed voice. "We'll have to go over that way," I pointed to the left, "and see where we are in relationship to the lake."

Rambo nodded again and I pushed on in the new direction. After a short while I could clearly see what was the edge of the coppice. "We're nearing the edge of the coppice," I told Rambo. "After that it's a short clear area of grass, then trees, rhodies or whatever around the edge and after them the lake."

Carefully, with both of us stooping along in a crouched manner, we came to the edge of the coppice. I saw the lake and didn't recognise the swim in front of me. Wild disorientation flooded my mind. Where were we? Frantically I craned my head out beyond the last sapling of the coppice and looked up and down the grass area, firstly to my right and then to my left. To my left – thankfully – I saw something I recognised. The swim with the large tree and the huge broken branch lying in the water! We had come too far!

I quickly told Rambo and we headed back the way we had come, but not before returning back some distance into the wispy cover of the coppice. When we were level with the broken branch swim we stopped.

"Look!" I said softly and pointing. "There's the bush we're going to hide behind." I turned my attention to the broken branch. It was exactly as I had seen in my vision, which made me feel a bit happier, but there was still the matter of the boat. I motioned to Rambo to keep on backtracking and we made our way down to the gap in the rhodie bushes where the boat had been left previously. To my chagrin it wasn't there!

"It's not here!" I proclaimed. "The fucking boat's not here! It *was* here, you can see where the grass has been flattened, but it's been moved!" I scoured the ground – there was nothing left behind. The boat and everything in it had been moved.

"Well, that's blown one option out of the water. You can't alter anything on the boat if the fucking thing's not here!" Rambo exclaimed. "Let's get back to the bush," he suggested. "Perhaps Hollywood's been fishing overnight and has been up and about very early… We don't want to miss our rendezvous. It's a good job we made the effort to be early too."

It was. It would have been a disaster of all disasters – to miss the boat to coin a phrase. Although we *couldn't* have because I had seen we were going to be there. It was all very confusing this future vision lark, especially when you had to make a decent fist of altering it into the shape you wanted it to go in. I took a final hard look through the rhodie gap and manage to pick out three bivvies over the far side. I wondered if it belonged to my cast of three – the three central roles in my vision. I noted I had better come up with a good part for myself fairly quickly or the act would end as it had before – and I didn't want that!

Within minutes Rambo and I were, for the second time, hidden behind a bush ready to spy on Darren, Rocky and Hollywood. The last time had been behind a bush at Hamworthy's stock pond, in the dark, trying to ascertain who was nicking fish and who had murdered the ghost. We had pulled those particular conundrums out of the fire, hosed them down and solved them. No worries! Hollywood – to re-iterate – on losing Hamworthy, had then proceeded to hit me with *his* run of revenge, right out of the blue, leaving me both flat-footed, off-guard and speechless... oh, and tipping me spinning into a vertigo inducing, spiralling, freefall drop of unimaginable angst and mental disability. In short, as he had said on the doorstep of despair, he had fucked up my life. And now here we were at the end of *my* plan of revenge – one way or another. My revenge would either peter out into a non-existent phut – one so puerile and pathetic Hollywood wouldn't even notice I was employing one – or it would hit him like a raging tsunami, ripping his world away from underneath his feet and wiping the handsome smile off his face once and for all. I *wish*!

Rambo and I, flat on our stomachs, waited to find out which one would prevail.

Seconds passed... into minutes... into tens of minutes... into half an hour... into an hour.

We carried on waiting.

It would be impossible to describe what was going on in my head during this period of physical inactivity as the pair of us lay motionless behind a bush – because it was everything and nothing. Everything was the endless list of images, recollections, thoughts and theories which had happened in my wildly fantastic, unbelievable life – the one I had been living since I had teamed up with Rambo – and nothing was the sum total of what I had sussed out I was going to do when Hollywood turned up... *if* he turned up.

Another hour went by.

Rambo suddenly grabbed my arm and stopped its circulation – and then I heard it. Voices! My heart, lungs, stomach, spleen, kidneys – and any other vital organ I've forgotten – somersaulted, rocketed up into my throat, dived back down again, only not – by the way everything was churning inside – in the anatomical order or location they should have. Rambo reached into his belt and pulled out the Glock. I looked at him. He looked at me. I looked at the Glock. Was it this one or was it the one Steffi had tucked in her G-string with which I had murdered the asylum seeker? Rambo looked at the Glock but hung on to it. I turned away and peered around the bush to see Darren and Rocky walking around to the swim with the broken branch in it. My ears soon picked up another noise – the faint putt-putt-putt of a small outboard engine. The good ship Hollywood was on its way!

My flesh crawled. This was going to be the first time I had clapped eyes on him – in real life rather than the absinthe fuelled/video replay in my head version – since his revelation. My eyes glazed and I re-ran his and Sophie's spunk guzzling get-together through my mind once more for good measure – if it hadn't left a bad taste in her mouth it certainly had in mine. My flesh stopped crawling and started to bristle instead. I had let him get away with my doing nothing once before, but it *wasn't* going to be the same this time! Rambo, ever aware of the body language of men in his charge, gripped my arm tightly once again and gave me an 'easy, boy' stare.

180

The wooden boat pottered into view. My eyes drank in the scene. It was as before – but d*ifferent*! *Hollywood had the lifejacket on*! I whipped my head round to Rambo and tugged demonstratively at my camouflage jacket to indicate what I had seen. He nodded vigorously and I noticed his fingers flex on the handle of the Glock in his grip.

We saw – and I saw for the second time – Hollywood feather down the engine via its twist-grip throttle/steering handle and then stop it. The wooden boat glided alongside the large branch and came to rest as the friction between branch and hull took its toll. Rambo shook my shoulder and shrugged energetically. Last minute panic wasn't doing the stuff in terms of producing inspiration so I mouthed the words 'nothing yet'. As predicted Hollywood retrieved a hidden petrol chainsaw from the bottom of the boat, started it up and proceeded to cut up the large branch. Hollywood wielded the chainsaw with consummate ease but not as consummately as before – the lifejacket made working the tool slightly more cumbersome!

I turned to Rambo and spoke to him – the cacophony of the chainsaw masking any fears of being heard. "He can't wield the chainsaw so well with the jacket on! I *must* have moved the jacket from the grass onto the boat! In The Eye's vision of the future he must have taken the boat and not noticed it lying on the ground! I've altered the future already! I've made the MNC!"

Rambo looked unconvinced. "But will it have the MDR?" he asked flatly. "He's not going to drown *now*, is he? Even if we distract Rocky until next Thursday with a million pound firework display!"

The wind slipped from my sails and I re-focused on Hollywood slicing the branch into more manageable pieces with only a little awkwardness while Rocky and Darren manoeuvred the lumps onto dry ground until gradually, piece by piece, the swim was made snag free. Oh fuck! This wasn't what I had hoped at all – the bastard hadn't cut his own head off!

Mesmerised – *paralysed* – I watched as Hollywood jumped safely onto dry land, cranked up the chainsaw yet again and cut the pieces pulled from the water by Rocky and Darren into foot-long sections. Once completed, and while the two landlubbers piled the logs neatly in an area away from the swim, Hollywood turned his boat around, placed the chainsaw safely in the bottom, climbed in and started up the outboard motor with its rope pull. A little voice in my head said, '*Come on*, son! Time is *slipping* through your fingers! The window of opportunity is closing! If you don't do something soon it's game over. Revenge spurned: revenge *reneged*!' With the outboard engine running – my brain transfixed in neutral – Hollywood sat himself on an integral plank running across the boat's breadth and settled down for his tiny cruise back across the lake.

Out of the corner of my eye I saw Rambo lift up the Glock and take aim at Hollywood's back. What on *Earth* was he doing? And it wasn't an ethical would-he-shoot-someone-in-the-back question I was concerned with. I rolled over and grabbed his arm with both hands and pulled it to the ground with all my upper body weight. Not even Rambo was strong enough to hold me on the end of a straight arm and fire a gun accurately – until he had snatched it violently away from my grip and re-set his sights.

"*No!*" I hissed pushing the Glock aside. "*Please*, no! You *mustn't*! You mustn't risk getting caught! This is *my* war!" I pleaded.

"Then *start* fighting it!" Rambo snarled through gritted teeth. "He's getting away! Look!"

My head jerked back to see the re-run of my vision – exact in every detail apart from the lifejacket Hollywood was wearing. Hollywood twisted the outboard's throttle and pulled away from the bank.

I turned in reckless impetuosity to my camouflaged buddy. "Give *me* the Glock!" I demanded.

"*No!*" said Rambo pulling the Glock away from me as if I was trying to take his favourite toy. "Eighteen months is a different ball game to *life*, Matt!"

My heart sank – plummeted, in fact, to the Earth's core and back out the other side. We were boned! We had *both* stopped each other shooting Hollywood! Reciprocated friendship coupled with the high possibility of getting caught (police forces please take note) had combined to make the ultimate action-stifling device. It was over. My revenge was dashed on the rocks – it was holed, scuppered and sunk.

By the time I cast my eyes back to Hollywood something had already caught his eye in the water, a fish perhaps, and he had already got to his feet to gain a better view only for him to stumble over the chainsaw. I regained my second viewing of the action as he lost his balance and his hand revved the twist-grip throttle to maximum as well as yanking the steering handle to full lock. The boat lurched hard to starboard and the extra movement coupled with a loss of balance caused him to pitch head first into the water.

With utter despair I watched him disappear under the surface and the boat drive itself over the top of him. Interestingly – because this was now a different version of what I had seen in The Eye's head – the back of Hollywood's head popped out of the water a split second after the boat had gone over the top of him. A hideous watery scream filled the air. Darren and Rocky turned to see what the commotion was as the boat continued to run on a long arc before thumping into the bank. Hollywood was *not* underwater. Sure the dork couldn't swim, he didn't have to, the automatically inflating lifejacket had seen to that and had popped him straight up to the surface. What Hollywood *was* doing was bobbing on top of the water, his hands held up to his head, and screaming – a terrible harrowing screaming.

Alerted by the scream we all could hear, Rocky ran into the water, dived in and swam to Hollywood. Transfixed I watched him pull Hollywood back towards the bank until he could get his feet onto the bottom. As Hollywood found his feet, he turned to face us and, guided by Rocky, stumbled up and out of the water. Blood cascaded from between his hands. His screaming, an unworldly feral mewing, never ceased. I flicked a glance at Rambo who was under the spell as much as I was.

Quickly I returned to the Rocky/Hollywood horror show in front of me.

"Phone for a fucking ambulance!" Rocky shouted at Darren over the top of Hollywood's noise. "*Quickly* for God's sake!"

Rocky and Darren were distraught and at their wit's end, or at least probably thought they were, until Rocky pulled away Hollywood's hands to see what he had done to himself. The sight of what he saw made him pull away in terror and thrust *his* hands up to *his* face. Darren simply collapsed in a dead faint. Rambo and I saw it as well – only obviously not as close up. If it was minimally less horrific from a distance then that was all it was – from thirty yards it was still spectacularly repulsive.

Hollywood had no face. From his right cheekbone just below the eye, across his nose and mouth down to the bottom left jawbone hinge was nothing but a gaping crimson mess save for the white of teeth and skull bone showing here and there. Flaps of shredded skin hung around the edges of the wound and Hollywood's teeth, with rivulets of blood running between them, announced themselves in a macabre flashing smile because he had no lips to hide them. Hollywood's face had been ripped off, or rather sliced off, by the propeller of the outboard motor. Whereas in my vision he had sunk under the boat and avoided the flailing blades, now, because of the lifejacket, because of my unwitting MNC, he had floated back up to encounter – face to propeller – his nemesis in the form of spinning, slicing, severing, carving metal. A cruel leering smile spread across my countenance. It was job done. I think it was safe to say I had wiped the smile off Hollywood's face forever.

Rambo and I turned and crawled away from the hideous gore-fest Rocky and Darren were trying to deal with. Hatefully I knew they would be scarred for life by today's incident as well – but nothing like Hollywood. His handsome face was no more. No plastic surgeon would ever repair it, *could* ever repair it – there was fuck all left to repair! They might not even have the chance because there was a strong possibility he might bleed to death. I crawled away fighting back laughter. Things could hardly have turned out better – my MNC had been deft, precise and a masterpiece of spiteful maliciousness. True it was a tad fortunate in as much as I had no conception of what I had been doing at the time but who cared? Not me. I had *won*.

I had wiped away the very essence of Hollywood's entire persona – his looks. Let him see how he would fair in a world where he was facially disfigured, grotesque to look at, where adults and children shunned him and avoided eye contact because of his disconcerting – *frightening* – appearance. What a shock that was going to be for him! Talk about role reversal! Let him see how many women he could pull *now*! Now he had gone from film star to monumental minger in a matter of minutes. Ha ha! He had better start working hard on his personality because he sure as hell wasn't going to haul on his handsome factor!

It's funny how bitter and twisted hate can make you. I searched my soul for a scintilla of remorse or pity for Hollywood. There wasn't an atom's worth. I turned to Rambo as we walked back through the coppice – Hollywood's screams now out of earshot – and patted him on the back.

"Would you have really shot Hollywood in the back for me?"

"Yep. Sure would have, boy."

"Thanks, mate. Appreciate the offer," I said sincerely, "but I couldn't let you risk it and ruin your new life with Steffi." I had another question. "Why did you stop me?"

Rambo threw his muscular arm over my shoulder. "You see, boy, *I* couldn't let *you* risk throwing away *your* life. You can't fish in a prison and although you would have been gutted if your revenged had bombed the alternative was worse." I pulled a face. "Well, I thought it was worse so I made a split second decision."

"Which was the right one," I said approvingly. I moved on to my triumph. "Fucking horrendous injury. Have you ever seen anything as bad as that in battle?"

"Oh, yeah, worse... But from your point of view, never one so apt." Rambo laughed. "You really did wipe the smile off his face, didn't you?"

"That's what I reckon!"

Rambo scrunched my shoulder. "Me and you, boy. We're a world beating team." Rambo stopped walking and turned me round to face him. "Now when the fuck are you going to move out of my house and give me and my lady some space?"

Chapter 19

Sophie hadn't been quite so euphoric as I had been over Hollywood's facial demise. She had, however, laughed at my joke when I had stated, hypothetically speaking, if Hollywood's face had been on Mount Rushmore it would have suffered ten million years' worth of erosion in three seconds flat.

"Was it *really* gruesome?" she had asked with morbid fascination.

"*Really* gruesome," I had assured her. "He had a face like roadkill."

Sophie had shuddered. "Eww!"

"Eww, indeed!" I had concurred. "Of course, the best part, and also the worst part, is he has *no* idea whatsoever my shadowy hand of intervention was to blame. Good because I'm not implicated in any shape or form and bad because a perverse part of me wants him to know I've got my own back." I had held her eyes with a level stare. "Just like I promised you."

"I think we'll settle for us knowing…"

"And Steffi and Rambo," I had reminded her. "And The Eye… if he pulls through. I'd have to tell him," I had reminded myself.

"How are Steffi and Rambo?" Sophie had asked.

"Fine," I had told her. I had to broach the subject and I had. "Rambo's keen for me to give them some space in their new love nest… only I've nowhere to go."

Sophie had walked over to me and took hold of my hand. "Do you want to come back here?"

"If you want me."

"Can you forgive me?" Sophie had asked.

"If *you* can forgive *me*."

"I want to try… try and get back to where we were," she had said, and me being the super revengemeister I was, had agreed.

This had happened a month ago and we were steadily working our way through a period of reconciliation. I would be a liar if I said there hadn't been the odd thought of what she and Hollywood had done, but in my head things had changed mightily. It was as if a priest had performed an exorcism upon me and had expelled my evil spirit – the one embodied by the smiling face of Hollywood. Thanks to the invocation of my holy revenge now I saw a different Hollywood in my mind's eye – a gruesome, horrifically mutilated one. There was no smile now, believe me. His power over me and all other members of society had gone and all I had to do was rationalise my poor adulterous behaviour – twice – with Sophie's singular piece of poor adulterous behaviour. With Hollywood's looks now gone and thus the threat of him gone it seemed so much easier. I don't know why this was so. Hollywood having his chops sliced off by a spinning propeller thanks to my magnificent MNC still didn't alter the fact he and Sophie had done what they had done. But it sure made me feel one hell of a lot more at ease over it! I tried not to analyse it too deeply (fat chance) but the revenge *had* changed everything. Nothing could gloss over our compounded mistakes of the past, nothing could wipe the slate completely clean, but it was clean enough for us both to want to give things another try and that was exactly what we were doing.

The other big plus was the return of my ability to get a hard-on – to put it in layman's terms. With no smiling head to mock me, and the enormous satisfaction of my face-wrecking revenge to bolster my ego, I had performed the first time of asking with Sophie. And it had felt good. It hadn't lasted very long – I admit to that – but so what. I was hard, well hard and would be again and again and again.

Some three weeks after the 'accident' – excuse me while I slope off and choke on my laughter – the fishing press and then the national press discovered Hollywood's tragic story. Hollywood was alive, he hadn't bled to death – on retrospection I suspected he might have wished he had. Gleefully I had read the chilling words of how the poor, ex-handsome Gary James (pictured above left) had become an odiously disfigured freak – don't let the children look at this one (pictured bottom right). The tragic events of Gary's life-shattering misadventure had been written in a sombre 'isn't-it-awful' tone that had gladden my heart and made me positively radiate bonhomie. How I chuckled at his terrible pain, how I had giggled at the operations he had already had and the many he would have to have in the future. I had guffawed at the sickening irony of how a Health and Safety initiative had contributed to his misfortune. In the ensuing days while the story ran – until the editor decided the public would be bored of it and pursued the tale of a cat riding a skateboard – various pressure groups had immediately jumped on the bandwagon to disgrace and attempt to pour ridicule on the whole 'nanny-state syndrome'. 'The state does not know best,' a spokesperson had commented, 'surely it is up to the individual to decide upon risk when it purely relates to himself alone.' Sagely, a Health and Safety Executive had pointed out Gary may have drowned and lost his life had he not been wearing a lifejacket as he was a non-swimmer.

I had slapped the newspaper with the back of my hand on reading this. "I've got news for you, dickhead, he *wouldn't* have fucking drowned! And he already *has* lost his life! The fucker would be better off dead! Go and ask him!" I had shouted at the paper. "You'll see I'm right!"

There's nothing like a chirpy news story to pep you up in the morning and set you up for a good day.

Many of the syndicate members had phoned me to discuss Hollywood's demise and to a man, although they had no time for Hollywood and actively disliked him, none had proffered a 'serves him right' opinion. What did I care? I had enough bile and bitterness to counterbalance *all* their humane viewpoints! The last thing to reach me on the carping grapevine via the members was that Hollywood was going to see the pioneering surgeon who had performed a face transport on a French lady.

"Let's hope it's an ugly fucker's face," I said to Rambo, "or a pig's! Pig organs work don't they, so why not a pig's face?"

Rambo gave me a cool look. "You know, I never thought you'd be *quite* so vindictive, boy. You're actually revelling in it, aren't you?"

I gave it a thought. "I guess so. Whatever happens to the bastard can't be horrible enough," I said philosophically. Rambo went to speak but stopped. I knew what he was going say, even without The Eye's absinthe, which was still unopened. He was going to say the only crime Hollywood had committed was to have sex with another man's partner, an act we had both been guilty of. I soon put him straight. "He deserves it. The shithead! He used Sophie in a horrible way to get back at me. Whatever agonies he goes through can't be enough in my book. Fuck him! I hope he lives until he's eighty and has to get up for thousands of mornings and look at his ugly, scarred face."

"Don't get me wrong, boy, I'm with you... just let go of the anger and get back to living. You did it! *You* won!" Rambo laughed and waggled his head. "Once again I'm at a loss as to *how* you managed to win and how you managed to get there... but you did. You're back on a level keel. Enjoy it. The last few years have been up and down since we came back from Lac Fumant second time... I think it's time to chill out and enjoy Hamworthy and your family."

"Likewise," I commented.

"That's true, boy. I'm on fresh ground for sure."

We lapsed into silence.

"Have you looked at the DVD yet?" Rambo surprisingly asked.

"What, Japp's one?"

"Yeah."

"No," I answered truthfully. "Have you?"

"No. I'm not sure I want to, to be honest."

"No," I said with understanding. "I wonder if Betty watches them?"

"If we meet up with Frans again we'll have to ask. I like Frans," said Rambo. "I think that's part of the reason why I don't want to watch it."

I liked Frans as well. I also liked Steffi – on a couple of different levels – if you know what I mean. I had forgotten about the DVD what with the successful revenge and Sophie and I re-uniting, but Rambo's question had re-ignited my interest. I made a mental note and jotted down the phrase, 'When next alone, watch porno DVD'. You know, when I had a spare hour I could take it out and look at it, only out of curiosity, mind you. I mean it wasn't as if I was falling back into old habits or making old mistakes, nothing like that. I was only going to watch a porno DVD about carp fishing!

"Yeah, I see what you mean," I said glossing over my iffy intentions. I knew they were iffy really!

"When are you going to talk to Pup?" Rambo's voice was charged with urgency at this new subject. "We don't want the revolutionary, indented, dirty brown bottom bait boilie in every Tom, Dick and Harry's catapult pouch."

"Good point! There's no time like the present, I'll give him a ring now," I said getting my mobile out of my pocket. I rang the hotline to the master of all things round and smelly. Melloney answered. "Hi, Melloney," I said. "It's Matt Williams here, is Pup around?"

"Oh, hi, Matt. He's rolling at the mo. I'll go and get him."

"He's rolling," I told Rambo.

"Rollin' rollin', rollin'," said Rambo grinning.

"Hello," said the voice on my phone.

"Pup! All right, mate? It's Matt here."

"Did you see what happened to Gary James?" Pup asked before I could say anything else.

"Terrible wasn't it," I lied.

"Terrible he wasn't still in your syndicate, I could have had his place! I can't see him doing much fishing for a few years. He'll be in hospital for ages!"

"Funnily enough that's the reason I wanted to talk to you. I might be able to swing it to get you into Hamworthy this season!"

"What, has one of the members died?"

"No…"

"One of the members has been *killed*? Matt, you *didn't* have to do that!"

"Very funny! Actually it's neither. It's more of a proposition than anything. A deal if you like," I said while looking at Rambo who was nodding in agreement.

"Does it involve bait by any chance?" Pup was shrewd; you had to hand it to him.

"Yeah! It involves bait," I acknowledged.

"I *thought* it might. Does it involve my revolutionary, indented, dirty brown bottom bait boilie by any other chance?"

"Might do."

"I *told* you didn't I! *Revolutionary!*"

"Well?" We were deep into our game of poker now.

"Come round tomorrow at nine in the morning and we'll discuss it."

"Nine tomorrow round Pup's to discuss it," I relayed to Rambo.

Rambo grimaced. "Shit! I'm taking Steffi shopping tomorrow," he whispered obviously not wanting Pup to hear and damage his reputation forever. I gave Rambo a look I had probably never given him before. "I'll cancel," he said matter-of-factly. "Some deals *have* to be done."

"See you tomorrow at nine," I told Pup.

"I thought you'd agree," came the reply and Pup hung up.

I gave my phone a quizzical look and then gave it to Rambo – the look, not the phone. "Just so I'm straight in my head on this… who's holding the whip hand here? Who's got the running flush? Me and the possibility of securing Pup a place in the finest carp fishing syndicate in Britain, or him," I jolted my head towards the mobile, "and his revolutionary, indented, dirty brown bottom bait boilie?"

Rambo gave this tricky teaser a little consideration. "From *his* viewpoint *you*, from *your* viewpoint *him*. He'll know that, and now you do as well, boy. From a third person viewpoint I reckon he edges it. An exclusive deal on a killer boilie is a big ask, boy, a big ask!"

Steffi didn't have a big arse; it was pert and perfect, like the rest of her body and boy – to coin a phrase – could she take it. Anyway in any hole! Crude but factual! It was gone midnight before I finally, surreptitiously, furtively, conspiratorially put away the world's first pornographic carp fishing DVD into its secret hiding place like a lewd sexually self-abusing teenager. It had achieved its artistic goal, I suppose, and because of it I woke Sophie up and made love to her. My appetite had been caused by the pornography, but at least I was eating at the right dinner table – if not for completely the right reason. Men, eh? Flick the switch… I had thought it all before.

"How is Sophie? Is she okay?" I nodded enthusiastically trying to crowbar the images of the porn star Steffi out of my head. Easing Hollywood's smiling face out of my mind might have been achieved, easing the images of a writhing Steffi at this point in time wasn't! "Gudt! I am glad zat you two are back togezzer…"

"Yeah, because we couldn't stand you living with us *any* longer!" said Rambo with heavy sarcasm.

"Nice trainers, mate, *and* tracksuit bottoms!" I said returning the favour.

"Go on you two. Get on vitt vott you are doing today… Dinner at five, remember, Rambo."

I gave Rambo a sly piss-take of a look. How the mighty have changed!

As we drove to Pup's I didn't tell Rambo I had ogled his lady the previous evening – it was strictly a need-to-not-know decision – and a wise one, I felt. We discussed other matters instead – like which one of us was most likely to catch a new British carp record from Hamworthy. Naturally we wouldn't claim it – publicity was not a requirement of my fishery, quite the opposite in fact. On the subject of a British carp record, seeing as Rambo hadn't even caught an English *sixty*, as I clarified to him, it seemed more likely I, having had the experience of having caught said fish, would be the one to do it first.

"You're getting cheeky in your old age, boy. Did you know that?"

"Not at all! Facts, mate, undeniable facts."

"If I'd have let you shoot Hollywood you mightn't be around to have the chance," Rambo pointed out to me.

"I *could* say the same to you," I retorted doing a bit of re-pointing on my brickwork-like defence.

"To be honest, boy, it wouldn't be the same if you weren't around," Rambo confided. "You add the elusive what-the-fuck-is-going-to-happen-next quality into my life. I used to have it in spades during the old days but my lifestyle has changed radically because of you-know-who and I might need a fix of it again sometime in the future…"

"Your *clothes* have certainly changed!"

Rambo ignored me. "And I'm not ready for my pipe and slippers yet. Long may our vaguely carp fishing orientated adventures continue!"

"I'll go along with that! Although I'd like to suggest to fate the angst and uprooting of my personal life is not necessarily a requirement for any of our future adventures!"

On the other rolling table Pup's revolutionary, indented, dirty brown bottom bait boilie appeared to be very *much* a requirement for our future fishing, particularly if we could stop anyone else having access to it. We were all too aware how selfish we were being, how mercenary, (Rambo knew more about that than me!) how self-interested, self-centred, self-seeking, self-first, self-last and anything else self-again our attitude was and… we didn't care! Not a jot! Exclusive rights in exchange for an exclusive spot – a nice spot – in Britain's premier carp syndicate!

"*Exclusive rights!*" bellowed Pup after he had had to sit down and recover – not from the exclusive rights proposal – from seeing Rambo *sans* camouflage! "Are you trying to *ruin* me?"

"Of course we're not…" I started and definitely didn't finish.

"*Exclusive rights!*" bellowed Pup again – only louder. "Do you know, have you *any* idea how much R & D went in to the making of a bait like the revolutionary, indented, dirty brown bottom bait boilie?"

"Have you any idea how much effort it takes to set up the finest carp fishery in Britain?" I retaliated.

"*None!* For *you!* You had it *given* to you!" screamed Pup. "If I hadn't introduced your names to Michael, God rest his soul, you wouldn't even have got in it in the *first* place!" Rambo gave me a 'nice one, boy!' roll of the eyes but Pup was off again. "I *told* you this bait was revolutionary, bring down the government if you put it on the streets. I had to talk you into using it but *now*, now you know how brilliant it is, you want to keep it all to yourselves! And deprive *me*, a poor old baitmaker, the chance of making a few quid and clawing back my R & D costs!"

I was a bit dubious of how much Pup's R & D costs were likely to have been, but as we were on the subject of money I played one of my trump cards.

"You won't *ever* have to pay to be in Hamworthy," I said slowly.

Pup went quiet. "I'm listening," he eventually answered.

"Ever," I reiterated.

"Ever?"

"Ever."

"How much is it?" Pup enquired. He had stopped bellowing and was now talking normally.

"£1250 *a year*, at the moment. I *will* be putting it up next year," I said gravely. "*Plus* you *have* to pay the '1st deposit'. It's a £2500 deposit I keep in the syndicate's account and only give back if and when you leave… *But*! *If* you transgress a major rule you can get chucked out and then you lose all the money! The 1st deposit *and* the annual fee!"

"What sort of transgressions?"

"Catching more fish than me, not having LED to hanger colour co-ordinated bite indication, irritating Rambo by clocking his non-camo clothing, wearing Realtree underwear, taking photographs of fish with white bait buckets in the background, stripping off and going in after snagged fish with a poorly exercised, pallid flabby body, listening to test cricket on a DAB radio, drinking more than ten cups of tea in a day, drinking *less* than ten cups of tea in a day, reading carp magazine articles on the latest killer rig and then having the temerity to actually tie one up and *use* it… all the normal sort of stuff."

"I see," said Pup playing along with the charade. "I don't get out much to exercise or get a suntan."

"Well, there you go! Remember, *I* decide on whether to chuck somebody out or not, so it always pays to be on the right side of me! I'm not saying giving Rambo and me an exclusive deal on the revolutionary, indented, dirty brown bottom bait boilie will make you *fully* immune to my violent mood swings and unreasonable membership decisions… but it'll be the best vaccination you could hope for!"

Pup pursed his lips. "Free membership for life?"

"Effectively."

"Of Britain's finest carp fishery?"

"Undisputedly."

"Can *I* use the revolutionary, indented, dirty brown bottom bait boilie?"

I looked over Pup's shoulder to see Rambo shaking his head as violently as a pike trying to throw a lure. "Not for an initial four grand waiver and a fifteen hundred yearly one!"

"If I give you exclusive rights you'll still have to pay for it and any bait you might want to give to anybody else," said Pup.

"We won't be giving it to anyone else, don't worry on that score!" I said laughing. "I guess The Eye can use the revolutionary, indented, dirty brown bottom bait boilie if he wants it. I gave him your number, if he phones you can make it for him, but *only* for him… I'm afraid he's seriously ill so don't expect you'll hear from him for a while."

Pup shrugged, the news of The Eye and his non-use of the revolutionary, indented, dirty brown bottom bait boilie left him unperturbed. "I've got other baits… there'll be new baits, maybe an even better one… it's not a major problem."

I sensed Pup was cracking. "You did *really* enjoy it at the fish-in, didn't you? Getting back into fishing… there's *nowhere* better to fish, mate. You *know* that don't you?"

Pup stood up straight and eased his shoulders back and thrust out a hand. "Deal!" he said. Provided…" he pulled his hand back.

"What?"

"You buy me a completely brand new set-up, with all the latest must-have bits and bobs… one placing me firmly in the fashionable, without being overtly ostentatious, tackle tart stakes! I wouldn't know what to buy so you'll have to buy it for me!"

"What!" I spluttered.

"No worries," said Rambo whisking his huge body alongside mine and forcing my hand into the one Pup had re-presented to me. "We've got a bit of loose change kicking around the syndicate's cash draw!

I shook hands with Pup and kissed the FAC slush fund cash-for-carp money goodbye.

"Excellent!" said Pup adding smugly. "I *did* have a lever! I told you last time, a dirty brown coloured one!"

I looked at the hand on the end of a disproportionately muscular forearm, one showing due to a rolled up sleeve. All the years of rolling baits had given Pup tennis player's forearms. I released my grip on the hand that had touched a thousand different mixes knowing full well Pup had been correct – I had wanted the bait real bad. "Great! I'll sort out the paper work and forward all the details. Rambo and I'll sort you out a top notch load of kit… rest assured you won't be getting a camo bivvy and all your kit will have tasteful style and élan!"

Rambo gave me a clenched fist behind Pup's back and a huge smile. He was happy, in spite of wearing jogging bottoms and losing some of his cut from flogging the fish in the stock pond.

"There's one thing I want to know, two actually," I continued. "How could you be so sure the revolutionary, indented, dirty brown bottom bait boilie was going to be a killer bait… and what's in it?"

Pup gave me a glare from beneath his eyebrows. "Some things are sacred as well as secret," he begun. "You haven't negotiated the right to all of those things, but if you promise on your *lives* not tell anyone, I'll show you both something."

"Okay!" I said quickly.

"Me too!" said Rambo.

"Follow me," Pup instructed.

We left the fourteen millimetre room where we had been standing and ascended Pup's House of Bait staircase. A new burgeoning bouquet attacked my olfactory senses from the first riser and an avalanche of aroma cascaded down the stairs as we climbed higher to embrace pungent perfumes, forceful fragrances and an omnipresent odour of all things round and stinky. Pup led us to what turned out to be a box bedroom. Surprisingly there was no bait making paraphernalia within this room, although there was shelving racked out around the entire room storing many different bags of boilies. In the corner was a basket and in the basket was a tabby cat doing what cats like to do best – it was sleeping.

"There he is," said Pup in a hushed reverent voice.

I gave Rambo a glance – as I'm prone to do in such circumstances – and wondered just how unhinged Pup had become over the years. Dedicating a lifetime to making rounded balls of bait had perhaps had the reverse effect on his personality. Even the late introduction of women into his world of boilies in the unlikely form of Melissa and latterly Melloney couldn't possibly hope to undo the years of solitary dedication and anorak obsession with bait.

"It's a cat," I pointed out.

Pup nodded. "But no *ordinary* cat."

"Mixes your bait with its tail does it?" I asked with a dash of acerbity. "Or is it purely involved in the monitoring, marshalling and mutilating of rodent infestation?"

"Nope! Try again."

"Is it Melloney's moggy?" Rambo asked.

Pup frowned. "No. Wilton is *my* cat and has been instrumental in my bait development over the years."

"*Wilton?*" I said.

"*Instrumental?*" said Rambo.

"Wilton! Wilton! *Wilton*! I can scarcely believe your ignorance!" said Pup admonishing me in ham actor style. "Fred Wilton was one of the leading original exponents of the HNV bait theory. A man years ahead of his time, a colossus in the chain of modern thinking and creativity within the world of carp fishing baits!" To finish off Pup gave me a look as if I was a sub-human form of close-knit community interbreeding – with all the associated learning difficulties and speech impediments. I sniffed. My time would come, I thought, let me catch you with a blue LED combined with a red hanger and I would bust his poorly exercised, pallid flabby arse from here to eternity. It goes without saying, but in time honoured tradition I will say it, the other proviso being I had a lifetime's supply of revolutionary, indented, dirty brown bottom bait boilie in an industrial-sized freezer somewhere.

"Instrumental?" Rambo repeated.

Pup turned to my non-camouflaged buddy. "Yes. Wilton is my bait tester."

I let out a guffaw. "Fuck me! He must have trouble casting out and winding in. Do you fit him with prosthetic opposable thumbs!"

"Not in the *field*! In *here*! Bait tester stroke bait taster!"

"*Bait taster?*" Rambo and I were virtually ten out of ten on synchronicity.

"Yeah. When I develop a new mix I feed it to him. Over the years I've come to trust his inclination towards the mix as a direct correlation to how carp will respond to it. If he bolts it like a gannet I'm onto a winner. If he turns his nose up at it I know it's not a good bait!"

"You're having a laugh aren't you?" I sneered.

"On the contrary. Look at this." Pup rolled up the sleeve on his left arm, the right one had been rolled up but not the left and I hadn't really noticed because Pup's appearance was typically dishevelled. All the way up Pup's left arm were thin white scars where he had been cut many times. They ran from below his elbow down to a few inches above his wrists, they were parallel and closely spaced. "Wilton done that. Fucking mauled me! I was *well* happy!"

I looked at the sleeping cat and then back at Pup's arm. It was unusual to hear him swear and his words seemed contradictory.

"What do you mean you were *happy*?"

"When I first made up the revolutionary, indented, dirty brown bottom bait boilie I gave him a bowl of the mix and he went mental. I'd never seen such a positive response. When I took the bowl away he went berserk and attacked my arm, scratched it to bits! He didn't want to let it go! It was all gone, apart from minute bits stuck to the bowl, but he wanted to lick it clean! That's how I *knew* it would be a killer boilie! And you've subsequently proved it in the field. If he doesn't eat it, I don't even bother!"

"Jesus!" I said with genuine amazement.

"*Don't* tell anyone!" warned Pup poking his finger at me. "He could be cat kidnapped..."

"As opposed to just cat napping!" Rambo said.

Pup was undeterred. "The big bait companies would do *anything* to have a taster of his experience. Imagine being able to know how your bait was going to perform before you fished it in a lake! That's the edge I've got with Wilton!"

"What happens when he dies?" I asked. "A cat's life expectancy is way shorter than a human's?"

Pup pulled both his sleeves down. "I'm hoping to have enough new baits to see me out before he's not around. I'm testing all the time... I've got five other crackers I'm sitting on... I let you guys have the revolutionary, indented, dirty brown bottom bait boilie because I trusted you and I knew it was *the* one!" Pup's face morphed into a sly smile. "Plus I thought something like this might happen. A good bait always opens a few doors... in this instance a door opening into Hamworthy!"

"You cunning whelp!" I exclaimed laughing and walking over to Wilton. I squatted down and stroked the cat gently on its head. It stretched out all fours in the luxuriated manner of felines. "Come on, Wilton," I said in a voice a good deal higher than normal, "tell Uncle Mattie what's in the revolutionary, indented, dirty brown bottom bait boilie!" I put my ear close to the cat's mouth to catch its imaginary words and in a flash it lashed out at me and clawed my ear. "Shit!" I said jerking my head out of the way while rubbing my ear. A palm of smeared blood revealed itself on inspection.

Pup speedily rushed between Wilton and me, bent down and petted the cat back into relaxation. Pup turned and gave me an evil look before resting his loving gaze upon the cat. "Good boy, Wilton! *Good* boy! You keep Daddy's secret safe from the nasty inquisitive carp angler!" Pup stood back up and jerked a thumb towards the bedroom door. "Right you two. *Out!* Let me know when you want some more bait made up... and I'll be seeing you on the banks of Hamworthy as soon as you've got me my gear! Say by next Thursday?" Pup's voice went hard and mean. "Exclusive rights on a bait *aren't* the same as the right to know what goes in it!" Pup explained.

"Any more nonsense and I'll set *him* on you!" he said directly to me.

"Who, Rambo?" I said facetiously.

"Wilton," said Pup levelly, then cocking a head towards Rambo. "*He's* not so scary without his army fatigues on."

As we walked back to the van – with me checking to see if my ear had stopped bleeding as we did – Rambo asked me a question. "Do *you* think I look less menacing in jogging bottoms and a sweatshirt?"

"You're still scary enough, mate" I reassured him. "But not as scary as that bloody cat! It ripped the piss out of me!"

"Forget it," advised Rambo. "Think of how many fish you're going to catch!"